PONDER THE PATH

BY

Gary H. Wiles, B.A., J.D.
and Delores M. Brown

PHOTOSENSITIVE™
LAGUNA NIGUEL, CALIFORNIA

PONDER THE PATH
Revised Second Edition

This is Book One* of our Talking History Series. It is an authoritative historical work based upon the extensive research in its Bibliography, the authors' interviews of historians and photographs of artifacts and natural sites.

For Information write to:
PHOTOSENSITIVE™
P.O. Box 7408
Laguna Niguel, CA 92607
or
☎ or FAX (714) 495-8897

PRINTING HISTORY
First Printing 1994
Revised Second Printing 1996

ISBN: 1-889252-02-6

PRINTED IN THE UNITED STATES OF AMERICA.

Library of Congress Catalog Card Number 96-71065

Other Books by these Authors

*BEHOLD THE SHINING MOUNTAINS, Book Two of our Talking History Series
HOW TO STOP SMOKING WHILE SMOKING

Please See Order Form on Page 279 To Order These Other Exceptional Books

TABLE OF CONTENTS

	Chapter or Data	Chronology	Page
	Map of Fur Country of West		
	Foreword	1808 - 1830	A
	Acknowledgment		i
	Prologue		iii
1	The Attack	Spring 1808	1
2	War In the Wind	Spring 1808	10
3	Ponder The Path	Spring 1808	19
4	Colter's Hell	Spring 1810	28
5	War Upon The Land	Summer 1812	36
6	Jackson's Thunder	February 1815	45
7	On To St. Charles	Summer - Fall 1817	53
8	Constable One Punch	Fall 1817 - Spring 1823	62
9	Around The Beaver Pond	Early 1823	71
10	Up The Missouri	February - March 1823	76
11	A Pair Of Fugitives	March 1823	85
12	Fort Atkinson	Spring 1823	93
13	Arikara Dawn	May - June 1823	100
14	Arikaras Revisited	June - August 1823	107
15	Fight for Life	August 1823	119
16	Mountain Surgery	August - September 1823	127
17	Bridger's Ocean	Winter 1823 - Fall 1824	135
18	South Pass And Back	Winter 1823 - Fall 1824	144
19	A Horse Thief By 40	Fall 1824	155
20	Henry's Fork Rendezvous	Fall 1824 - Fall 1825	163
21	Milton And Achilles	Spring - Fall 1826	175
22	Three Aces	July 1826	181
23	Beware The First Of March	Fall 1826 - March 1827	188
24	Under Arrest	Summer 1826 - Spring 1827	196
25	Pinckney's Savior	March - July 1827	200
26	Blackfeet At Bear Lake	July 1827	205
27	The Trappers' Fandango	Spring - Summer 1827	209
28	California Calabozo	Summer 1827 - Spring 1828	215
29	Peg-Leg Smith	Summer - Winter 1827	221
30	Safe In St. Louie	Summer 1827	225
31	The North Edge of Forever	Summer 1828 - Spring 1829	229
32	Blackfoot Country	Summer 1828	237
33	Brothers Again	Summer - Winter 1828	243
34	Time To Try Wagons	March 1829 - February 1830	248
35	Opening the Way West	February - October 1830	256
	Epilogue		267
	Bibliography [159 Volumes]		269
	Index with Identifying Data		271
	[Your] Notes [on This Book]		277
	Book Order Form		279

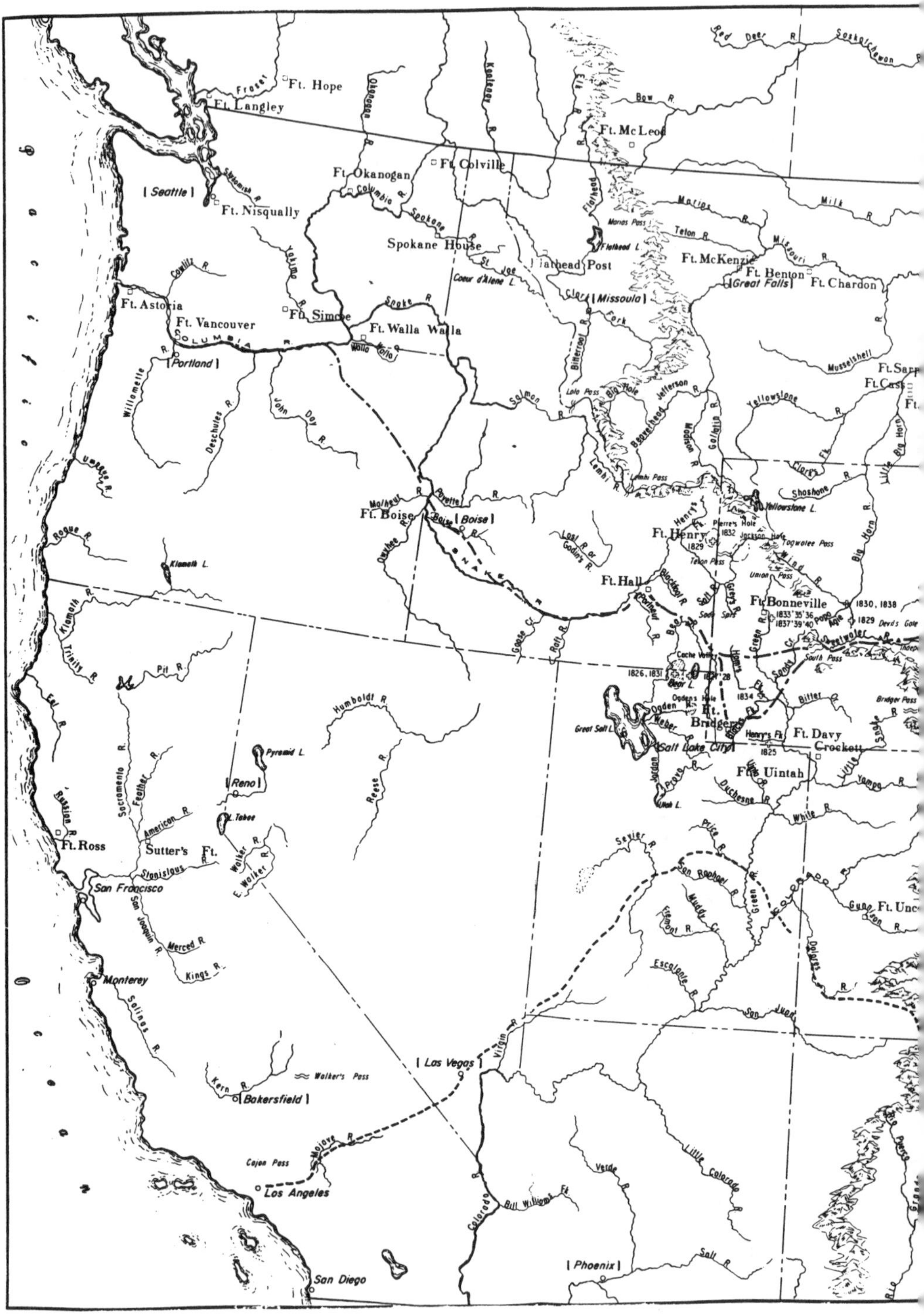

Ft. Hope
Ft. Langley
Fraser
Ft. McLeod
Bow R.
Red Deer R.
Saskatchewan
Ft. Colville
Ft. Okanogan
Columbia R.
Kootenay R.
Okanogan R.
[Seattle]
Ft. Nisqually
Spokane House
Spokane R.
Flathead Post
Flathead L.
Marias Pass
Marias
Teton R.
Milk R.
Missouri R.
Ft. McKenzie
Ft. Benton
[Great Falls]
Ft. Chardon
Coeur d'Alene L.
St. Joe
Clark [Missoula]
Fork
Cowlitz R.
Yakima R.
Ft. Astoria
Ft. Vancouver
Ft. Simcoe
Snake R.
Ft. Walla Walla
Walla Walla
COLUMBIA R.
[Portland]
Willamette R.
Deschutes R.
John Day R.
Bitterroot R.
Lolo Pass
Big Hole
Beaverhead
Jefferson R.
Madison R.
Gallatin R.
Yellowstone R.
Musselshell
Ft. Sarpy
Ft. Cass
Salmon R.
Umpqua R.
Rogue R.
Klamath L.
Lemhi R.
Lemhi Pass
Clarks Fk.
Shoshone R.
Yellowstone L.
Big Horn R.
Little Big Horn
Malheur R.
Payette R.
Ft. Boise
Boise
[Boise]
Owyhee R.
Lost R. or Godin's R.
Ft. Henry
Henry's Fk.
Pierre's Hole
1832
1829
Jackson Hole
Togwotee Pass
Teton Pass
Wind R.
Union Pass
Ft. Hall
Blackfoot R.
Portneuf R.
Salt R.
Grays R.
Soda Spgs.
Ft. Bonneville
1833'35'36
1837'39'40
1830, 1838
1829
Popo Agie
Devil's Gate
Sweetwater R.
South Pass
Klamath R.
Trinity R.
Pit R.
Goose Cr.
Raft R.
Bear R.
Cache Valley
1826, 1831
1824'28
Bear L.
Green R.
Hams Fk.
Sandy Cr.
Ogdens Hole
1834
Ogden R.
Weber R.
Ft. Bridger
Blacks Fk.
Bitter Cr.
Bridger Pass
Great Salt L.
Salt Lake City
Henry's Fk.
1825
Ft. Davy Crockett
Little Snake R.
Yampa R.
Eel R.
Humboldt R.
Pyramid L.
[Reno]
Reese R.
Sacramento R.
Feather R.
American R.
L. Tahoe
Jordan R.
Provo R.
Utah L.
Ft. Uintah
Uinta R.
Duchesne R.
White R.
Russian R.
Ft. Ross
Sutter's Ft.
Stanislaus R.
Walker R.
E. Walker R.
Sevier R.
Price R.
San Rafael R.
San Francisco
San Joaquin R.
Merced R.
Kings R.
Muddy Cr.
Fremont R.
COLORADO R.
Gunnison R.
Ft. Uncompahgre
Dolores R.
Monterey
Salinas R.
Escalante R.
San Juan R.
Virgin R.
[Las Vegas]
Kern R.
Walker's Pass
[Bakersfield]
Mojave R.
Cajon Pass
Los Angeles
Colorado R.
Bill Williams Fk.
Verde R.
Little Colorado R.
Pecos R.
Salt R.
[Phoenix]
San Diego

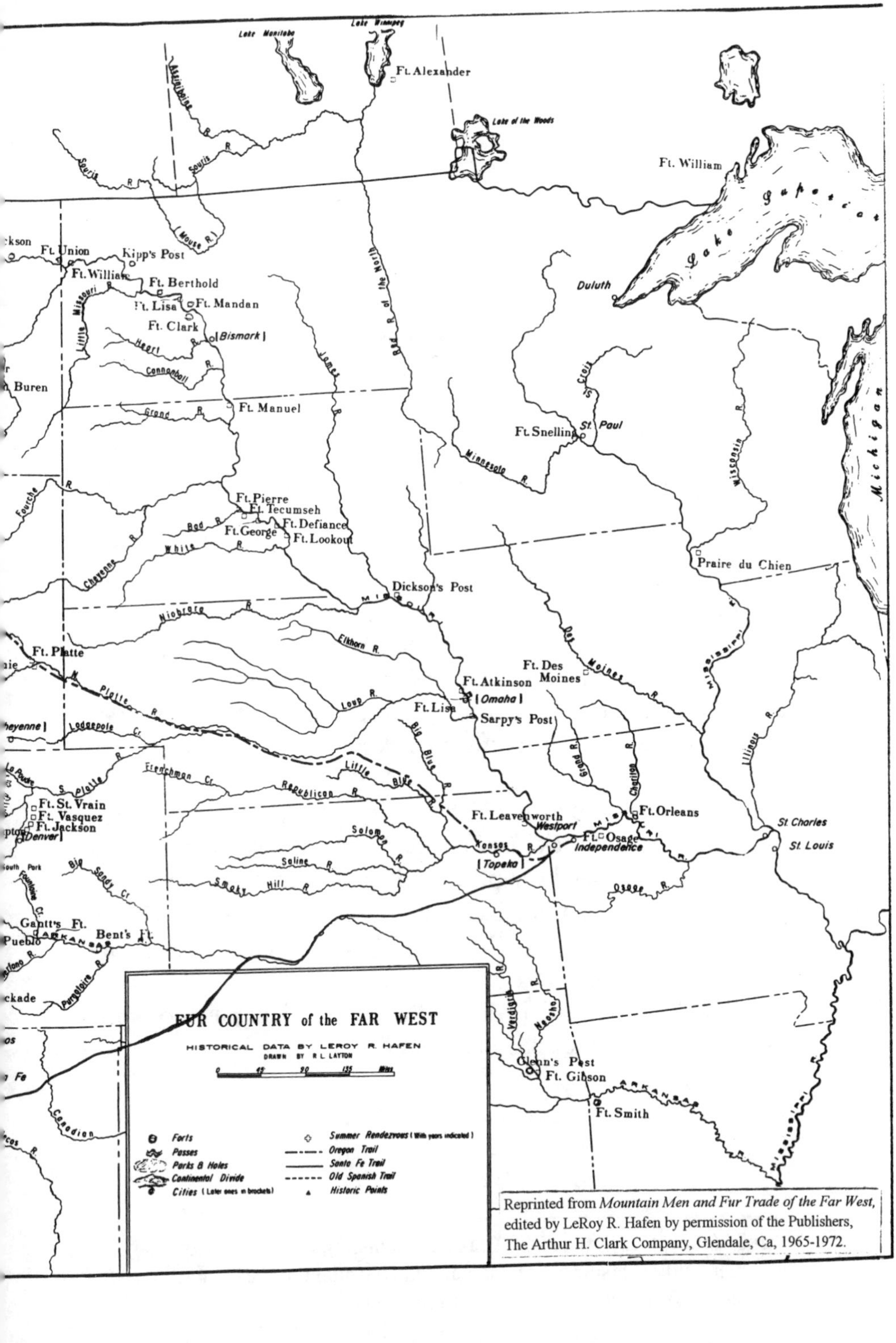

Reprinted from *Mountain Men and Fur Trade of the Far West*, edited by LeRoy R. Hafen by permission of the Publishers, The Arthur H. Clark Company, Glendale, Ca, 1965-1972.

FOREWORD

by Ray Glazner[1]

PONDER THE PATH is a stirring narrative of the westward expansion of the United States between 1808 and 1830.

The authors Wiles & Brown have combined history and excitement to bring one of America's most important but least understood eras to life.

Told through the real life Sublettes and other legendary men of this inspiring age, this book is as well written and factual as anything one can find on this subject. Page after page, real history unfolds as you follow men destined to lead America to greatness.

Rich in fascinating detail of its real people, this book embroils them in crucial national and international conflicts that start fist fights around campfires and pistol duels in Congress.

Sketches of the Absaroka, Apache, Arikara, Blackfeet, Commanche, Mandans, Mojave, Pawnee and Sioux are insightful and intriguing.

PONDER THE PATH is the kind of living history book most people wish they had in school!

---

[1] Simi Valley, California's Ray Glazner is a distinguished educator, historian, author, historical re-enactor and consultant to local, state and national museums as well as the entertainment industry.

ACKNOWLEDGMENT

Our initial salute goes to the legions of librarians in public and private libraries, colleges and universities across this great nation, who unearthed priceless books, diaries and journals with yellowed pages and pressed spiders.

We especially thank busy historian, museum and entertainment industry advisor, Ray Glazner who took time from his whirlwind schedule to read *PONDER THE PATH* and write its FOREWORD!

We bow to museums who gave us access to their public, and not-so-public, collections to photograph and study. In random order, we thank the Museum of the Mountain Man at Pinedale in Wyoming's Sublette County, repository of hundreds of precious artifacts.

Our sincerest gratitude to Director Dr. Charles Hanson Jr. and his wonderful wife Marie of the Museum of the Fur Trade at Chadron, Nebraska for the interview and for allowing us to photograph the hundreds of artifacts in this temple of history. Every writer who has ever put pen to the fur trade owes these fine people a boundless debt of gratitude for expending $200,000 of their own funds and maintaining this magnificent collection for over three decades without remuneration!

Our appreciation to David Hansen, Park Curator and Historian of Washington's Ft. Vancouver National Historical Site. David granted us interviews with himself and staff and guided us through the restored residence of Chief Factor, Dr. John McLoughlin, complete with Hudson's Bay Company menus of lavish meals, one of which appears on page 234 this book.

We thank David Hunsaker, Center Director of the resplendent Flagstaff Hill National Historic Oregon Trail Interpretive Center near Baker City, Oregon for his insights on every exhibit in the massive complex, inside and out.

Our gratitude to the National Park Service at Louisiana's Chalmette Battlefield Visitor Center where we reviewed films, archives, uniforms and weapons of the Battle of New Orleans in which General Andrew Jackson and his American Dirty Shirts routed the prestigious veteran force of Major General Sir Edward Pakenham. [See Chapter 6.]

Our hats off to the patient Park Rangers who guided us through scenic and historical sites and located wild animal populations in Glacier, Grand Teton and Yellowstone National Parks, which we photographed to authenticate our descriptions.

We thank the ranchers who got on their phones or horses to pinpoint ancient trapper rendezvous sites for our cameras and notepads.

Our appreciation to the Tribal Councils and Indian school staffs who shared their rich Native American heritages, albeit the attitudes in this literary work represent the early 1800s rather than their enlightened counterparts of today.

We gratefully acknowledge the source works of fine historians whose scholarly tomes make up our 159 volume Bibliography beginning at page 269 of this text. Reading and annotating these books, letters and journals in public and private collections to reconstruct the dialogue of these historical figures with their own words, driving over 10,000 miles up and down the Oregon Trail and taking 1,600 research photographs of artifacts and original sites rounded out our research, for which we can only thank each other.

We also thank each other for the many bleak nights that evolved into dawn at the computer -- the tedious editing -- the drudgery necessary to revisit this thrilling era of national pride, so that our readers may relive **history as it happens** with the magnificent men and women who made it. Now please join us in our stirring American beginnings!

PROLOGUE

This Revised Second Edition of *PONDER THE PATH* is a streamlined version of the first edition with even more exciting historical clout. The innovative Chronology built into our Table of Contents provides the reader with another valuable tool, which is amplified by a historical time frame heading for every page. Thus, we've accelerated the action without losing our place in time. Now you can truly *read history as it happens*!

This revised Book One of our Talking History[2] Series, features the true and painstakingly researched exploits of the real life Sublette family and their legendary Mountain Man cohorts between 1808 and 1830. This is the very human story of how eight year old William Sublette's grandfather Whitley inspired him to become the explorer who would one day stun the nation with an impossible journey.

PONDER comes to life in the Kentucky of 1808, one of only 17 states of the United States. The smell of another war with Britain taints the wind. Kentuckians itch to penetrate the rich, mystical lands of the recent Louisiana Purchase, but frontier life is a full time struggle to stay alive.

Join Judge Phillip Sublette, his indomitable wife Isabella and their wagon load of youngsters bumping through the misty hills of Pulaski County where they are just about to be attacked!

Gary H. Wiles, B.A., J.D. and Delores M. Brown

---

[2] In Talking History, the real people are alive instead of being moved about like dead butterflies pinned and repinned to the tapestry of history.

CHAPTER 1

THE ATTACK SPRING 1808

Spring painted Pulaski County Kentucky's wooded hills with the brilliant hues of new growth. 1808's mild winter had staked green-up time to a head start. Fuzzy blue anemones and violets beneath budding dogwood and bloodroot spread a shimmering bright patchwork quilt over waving green grasses.

Dawn's chill lingered in the forest shadows. Dewy buds speared by the sun's yellow lances spread languidly into blossoms of crimson, mauve and gold. Their delicate scents sugared the breeze. Anxious pollen-dusted bees worshipped at one petalled altar after another.

Golden mists from Pitman Creek rose from its glinting swirls. A silvery bass skied to gulp a mosquito, then slapped the water into wavering target ripples.

A spotted fawn suckled sweet moisture from the loins of a wary doe. The doe waited for her own turn to suckle the stream, turning one ear then the other at the creek's muddy edge. At the jangling gobble of a turkey cock, the startled doe wrenched her teat from her adoring fawn. The fawn crouched, licking precious drops of milk from his glossy black nose, then bolted to follow his high bounding mother.

Wild hogs blundered through the underbrush like a rock slide, their collisions jarring grunts from them. A sour stench cloaked them. Their leader, a hulking black monster with three-inch sabre tusks and squinty white-lashed eyes, wheeled and bowled over two of his squealing mob. The lesser pigs scattered, for only yesterday the tusker had devoured a runty sow, bones and all. At 320 pounds, this lop-eared killer put bears to flight. Having established his sovereignty, the king hog slurped vulgarly at the creek's edge. Without warning, he charged the humbler hogs, driving them northward along Pitman Creek's bank toward Buck Creek.

Just east of Pitman Creek, wagon tracks stretched from the hamlet of Somerset toward the village of Stanford some 33 miles north. A team of high stepping cinnamon Mulassier mares with taffy manes clip-clopped north on the wagon road hauling a whitewashed wagon with its dry-hubbed rear wheel screeching.

Lanky Judge Phillip Sublette hunched forward on the spring seat beside his wife Isabella. Being unselfish with his family, he wore reddish moth-eaten velvet dress pants and a coarse brown homespun tunic. Naturally cold blooded, he'd draped a threadbare orange and white trade blanket over his shoulders. He wanted to wear his new stovepipe beaver hat, but it kept blowing off because it wouldn't snug down over his flowing mane. His wavy raven hair glistened in the sunlight, its bear grease dressing resisting the wind admirably. His delicate white hands were abraded with red stripes by the long reins of the horses, and he clenched an unlit clay pipe in the notch it'd worn in his teeth.

Having been pregnant all but a few of their married days, plump brunette Isabella Sublette cradled another still-red new infant in her pudgy arms. Her frilly blue gingham bonnet sat askew on her head, its long ties fluttering behind her like tired banners. Her puffy body jiggled with each jolt of the wagon. She tried to cushion baby Andrew's ride so he wouldn't fuss again. Her milk was up. It blotched the bosom of her dress. Soon, she'd wake Andrew and feed him.

Isabella's pale oval face was too delicate for the rest of her. Her sunken eyes aged her nearly a decade beyond her 32 years. Since girlhood, she'd patterned herself after her mother. Even sliding toward the abyss of middle age, she was still doing it, birthing one oversized baby after another. Now she felt smothered, trapped by the offspring of her own body and the surfeit desires of husband Phillip.

Isabella Sublette claimed she chewed a cinnamon stick, but spit a might too often for spice. Some said she was surely dipping snuff. If she did use the smelly stuff, it was in self defense to Phillip's perennial pipe.

With two baby girls at home and another two young sons in the back of the wagon, Isabella seldom got a night's sleep. She nodded, then dozed fitfully, lolling against husband Phillip on the wagon seat. The three inch brown stick fluttered loosely in her lips as she snored ever so ladylike.

Their wagon flaunted navy blue spoked wheels and flaking red words flourished on its white side boards that read "Sublette's Ordinary." The red, white and blue colors were no accident. Phillip had spruced up their wagon for Thomas Jefferson's 1804 campaign for a second term. Besides, patriotism befitted a Justice of the Peace and federal Postmaster of Pulaski County, to say nothing of the owner of the finest tavern in Somerset, Kentucky. At 35, Phillip had already been Keeper of the County Jail and Registrar of Stray Animals and deemed himself an accomplished politician.

For all it's patriotism, the Sublettes' springless wagon pitched like a ship in heavy seas each time a wheel thumped over a grass clump or dipped into a trough in the dark earth. One rear wheel squeaked twice in every full turn. These screeches bansheed above the crashes of the wagon bed with every bump.

Bouncin' in the back of the family wagon always turned eight year old William Lewis Sublette queasy. His past middlin' sick stomach wasn't helped by the damp air's raw smells tormenting his sensitive nose. The road smelled sour like a fall orchard before the hogs ate the fallen fruit.

Like the other poor boys in Somerset, William wore no shoes in warm weather. Some boarder twice William's size had left his old clothes at Sublette's tavern. William's arms twigged from the cavernous cut off sleeves of his faded green shirt. His bulging blue pants were big enough around the middle for Papa Phillip, and only the leather galluses over his thin shoulders kept them from dropping off without even touching his legs.

His prize possession was a fold-up knife with a bone handle he'd won by out-jumpin' the preacher's son. William won plenty of things by jumpin' over fences and outrunnin' other boys. He could still beat his brother Milton at jumpin', but it weren't smart to race agin Milton. Milton was only six, but the fox hound could barely keep up with this fastest of the Sublettes.

Nausea sweat beaded young William's nose that was already showing a hawkish curve. William's wavy saffron hair hung to his shoulders. His mouth was redder than usual. His wide set blue eyes were flecked with hazel. But for the hint of a beak and a smattering of bran-sized freckles, William was more comely than any of the young girls in Somerset, Kentucky.

William didn't feel comely. He felt gut-sick and all the stinks made it worse. Mama Isabella smelled of lye soap. Baby Andrew reeked of sour milk, or maybe it was Mama's dress. Milton, hangin' out over the tailboard of the wagon, stunk like their hound Seneca. William swallowed hard. His stomach flailed like a bull grouse wing-beatin' its ruff.

And Papa Phillip was talkin'. Mama was asleep and Papa was too busy talkin' to notice. Papa never stopped talkin' around the stinkin' pipe clenched between his teeth. Papa's voice had a screech in it, almost like the back wheel's. William guessed that was from Papa talkin' so much in Court. Besides bein' a Judge, Papa was always suin' folks and getting sued.

Young William seldom spoke. Grandpa Whitley said the reason a man had two ears and only one mouth was so he could listen twice as much as he talked. William wanted to hide his wagon-sickness from brother Milton, who would tease and tell everybody about it. Milton oughta learn silence.

Tousled Milton had a penny sized scab on his left cheek from a fist fight. The elbow of his coarse homespun shirt was ripped. The only time Milton held still was when he was asleep. Milton didn't talk as much as Papa, but he sneaked in a lot of words under his breath.

Just turned six, Milton Sublette was missin' his right front baby tooth. It had been knocked out in one of Milton's fights or he'd pulled it out with a string like he said. Milton got into more trouble in a week than William had in his whole life. Milton stretched the corners of his mouth with his fingers to make faces at Seneca, loping behind their wagon.

Seneca, a brown and white American Foxhound, loped along, ears flappin' with his tongue hangin' out the side of his mouth. Seneca stopped to sniff now and again, then lurched to catch up, his loose coat slippin' and slidin' over his body.

Seneca was supposed to be Papa Phillip's, but the whole family knew Seneca was Milton's dog. Milton and Seneca was never apart. They smelled exactly alike, except when Milton had chewed peppermint leaves or Seneca'd rolled in some dead animal.

William was a good listener -- especially when the wagon hadn't made him sick to his stomach. He recalled Papa Phillip carryin' on about Seneca in their tavern in Somerset, his eyes too bright from rum. Papa Phillip bragged that Seneca was worth more than the best saddle horse of any man there.

"Brought this American Fox Hound from Virginia, I did! Offspring of a sire hound give by Lafayette to George Washington! Seneca's a fox dog, but his smeller is dang near good as young William's. Seneca is a nose -- followed by a dog!"

That always made the men laugh. They knew if they laughed loud enough, Papa Phillip would buy ale for the house.

Papa Phillip would go on, "Of yore, these American Foxhounds like Seneca hunted hostile Indians -- which has got to be why all them *Shawnee* and *Cherokee* up and left eastern Kentucky."

It smelled to William like baby Andrew had just done something to make the Indians clear out of *western* Kentucky too. Crinkling his nose, William crawled over the bundles of spare clothes and bedding to get to the wagon's tail board.

William wondered what'd happened up there in Stanford that was so dang important it couldn't wait. That was what Grandpa's note said. "*Come now. Too Important Too Wate!*" Grandpa Whitley wasn't to be trifled with. If he said it was important, it was *important*!

Milton hung over the tail board dangling a slimy strip of raw bacon in front of Seneca. As William drew nigh, Milton whacked his arm with the limp bacon, "Stay to yer side o' the wagon sicky Bill!"

William knew Milton should be hit back, but William was too sick. As ever, William would wait until the time for hittin' suited him. As Grandpa William Whitley said, "All good things come to him who waits."

Maybe William was the thinker in the family the way

Papa Phillip always said. Papa was fond of tellin' people in the tavern that William was born in 1799, the year George Washington died, like that somehow meant William had got President Washington's brains.

But the Sublettes' tavern slave, Artemis, had taken William aside and told him sternly that General Washington had freed his slaves by Will at his death. William had looked away from her big dark eyes. He didn't like it when she told him slavery stuff. William didn't know about slavery. Artemis told him he needed to think about slavery.

Now, thinkin' might rescue William from a stomach ready to retch up his breakfast. He tipped back his head and pretended to look for *Shawnees* under the shadowed branches of the great oaks overhead. There wasn't supposed to be no Indians left around here, but if they was, Artemis was one slave that could shoot them dead!

Artemis's shoulders were so big, she could pass for a buck. She had a moon shaped scar in her eyebrow and a space between her front teeth. Once William saw a "R" branded into her shoulder. She'd yanked her shawl over it. And Artemis never wanted nobody to know she could shoot. "Slaves cain't be shootin' no guns, Little Bill." He wondered why Artemis was allowed to call him *Bill.* Nobody called Grandpa William Whitley *Bill.* Some called Grandpa *Colonel.*

Right now, Artemis was back in Somerset watchin' over William's baby sisters Sophronia and Polly and waitin' tables in the tavern. Papa often bragged in the tavern that he would not take two thoroughbred saddle horses for Artemis.

After making William cross his heart and hope to die three times, Artemis whispered to William she *would* take two saddle horses for Papa Phillip. But he didn't laugh and that hurt her feelin's. He didn't see her alone for a long time after that.

William heard many times how Artemis had held him as a babe all the way on the wagon ride south on this very road in the spring of 1801, when Papa and Mama moved from Grandpa Whitley's big house in Stanford down to Somerset. That must have been before Milton was borned.

Artemis sure could shoot that brace of pistols in the brown wooden box under the wagon seat. When Artemis didn't have to carry sacks to the tavern or tend the babies, she would sneak off with William down past the duck pond. Artemis would charge the pistols with powder, patches and shot. She said Master Whitley always put two bullets and extra powder in the barrel, so she did too.

Artemis'd wrap the fingers of William's wee white hand about the pistol butt, then steady William's aim with her big black hand that knew just where to send the pistol balls. He'd squeeze the trigger into an orange blast that would nigh tear the pistol from his grasp.

With the powder smoke searin' his nose and his ears ringin' like the church bells at Grandpa Whitley's house, they'd run to what was left of the punkin on the fence. William would stick three fingers through the little hole in the front of the punkin. Then they'd laugh about the whole back of the punkin bein' blowed off. Artemis would whisper what a fine shot Little Bill was. Her breath always smelled of rum, and her licorice and horehound didn't hide it. One day William would tell her to try chewin' peppermint like Milton did.

But William knew who'd shot the punkin and would shake his head. Artemis would grin. Then they'd move off fast, snaggin' themselves on the blackberry bushes before somebody turned up to see who was doin' all that shootin'. Artemis always charged the pistols again before she sneaked 'em back inna box under the wagon seat. She said, "Masta Phillip never check for no powder and shot. He think he can jist mail them bullets later!"

The horse pistol game with Artemis never changed and together, they *never* missed the punkin! William wondered if *he* could hit the punkin without Artemis. It always bothered William that Artemis got mad when he asked her why she learned to shoot.

William thought maybe he really should watch for Indians and not just pretend. Nobody else in the wagon was much for shootin'. Milton was daft. Mama had her hands full with baby Andrew. Papa Phillip was always talkin' and talkin'. Papa wouldn't know if ten Indians jumped inna wagon. Besides Papa would just tell them Indians he was Judge and Postmaster and they better git!

Much as he hated to, William groaned, "Stop the

wagon." He climbed down, easing his bare feet into the wet grass. He wanted to run but forced himself to walk slowly toward the big trees.

"Sicky Bill's gonna puke!" Milton squealed.

After Milton tattled, William had no reason to choke back his vomit. He ran for the trees, his great pants flapping and the sour vomit spewing from his lips. He put his hands on his knees and lost the rest of the hot slime. He did this every time he rode inna wagon. He hated the burnin' up behind his nose and the chunks of hot sour food caught up there. Worse, he hated the shame of facin' his family afterward. He wiped his mouth on his sleeve, then daubed at his tears with his knuckles.

William thought Milton was yellin' at him agin as he trudged back toward the wagon, but it was Mama Isabella. "Run, William! Run and get up here quick!" she cried. Then she hollered, "Milton, you *stay* in this wagon or I'll *tan* you bloody!"

William lunged into a run but stubbed his toe on a rock, flinging him face down in the wet grass. He tried to see through the tall grass and between the wagon wheels. His tears made everything blurry, but it looked like a black bear had Seneca down! The hound's yelps suddenly stopped.

The whinnying mares reared. Papa Phillip yanked their reins and their giant hooves slammed into the ground like thunder.

William bolted out of the grass like a stepped-on cat. He thought he was just standin' there watchin' his mother cover baby Andrew with her body on the wagon seat, but realized he was runnin' toward the snarlin', screamin', yelpin', rearin' mess. He knew Milton would be crazy enough to jump down any second to keep Seneca from being kilt.

Papa Phillip toppled backward off the seat into the wagon bed, his boots thrashing the air, giving William room to jump up and whip the pistol box open. Suddenly he was *Little Bill* again! He had to hug the pistol to his chest to cock it as he ran around the wagon. He hoped the powder was still in the pan. He came out behind Seneca. Seneca was up, bloody and snarlin', with his teeth bared. Before Little Bill could focus on the black brute a few feet away, it snorted and charged!

Grasping the pistol in both hands just like Artemis was

there, Little Bill fired point blank. The monster blasted Seneca on top of him. Little Bill tasted blood. All three went down in a heap. His chin felt broken. Little Bill was too dizzy to think.

CHAPTER 2

WAR IN THE WIND   SPRING 1808

Bleeding from a rip in his neck's loose skin, Seneca wiggled from under the heaped bodies and shook himself, spattering young Milton Sublette with congealing blood.

"Seneca!" Milton yelled, oblivious to the dog blood running down his face and the fact that brother Bill was still under the sprawled monster.

"Here, boy!" Milton said, thrusting raw bacon toward Seneca. But the gory hound rolled in the dirt. Milton flopped down and hugged Seneca, as Papa Phillip clambered awkwardly from the wagon to rescue William.

Clutching baby Andrew, Isabella Sublette strained to see if Phillip could drag that thing off William. She'd even lost her "cinnamon" stick in the commotion. She leaned drastically each time Phillip yanked, as if she could somehow help Phillip pull the great beast off William.

Phillip pulled till his neck veins strutted into ropes. He couldn't free William. But that didn't stop him from talking. "Shot through the head! Must be worth $10, dressed out!"

Isabella lost her temper -- something she seldom did. "God all mighty, Phillip! Our boy's under there!" She laid squalling baby Andrew on a rumpled quilt in the wagon bed, caught up her skirt and jumped from the wagon, losing her bonnet. Desperately shouldering Phillip aside, she seized the monster's back leg and hauled it off her William like a harness mule pulling out a tree stump.

The dazed boy's only visible injury was an inch long gash

up the left side of his chin. Isabella staunched the blood with her skirt hem, kissing William's dirt-caked saffron hair as she muttered, "Oh thank God. Thank God. Thank God."

She plucked her droopy bonnet from the wet grass, then rushed to baby Andrew sucking his thumb in the wagon.

William cupped his bleeding chin in his hand. "I kilt a bear. I kilt a bear!"

"No, sicky Bill," Milton jeered. "You kilt a *pig*! A big stinkin' pig!"

Joyously Phillip hollered, "You have just kilt the biggest boar hog in the history of Kentucky! He'll make a passel o' meals at the Ordinary!"

Still trembling, Isabella returned to daub the crimson trickling from William's gashed face. "What if this boar belonged to somebody, Phillip?"

Prowling the grass for his lost pipe, Phillip Sublette pronounced his Judicial sentence, "Everybody knows these woods is fulla hogs gone wild. But if this boar has a owner, then we'll settle for the *corpus dilecti* for the hurt this hog done William and Seneca!" He finished by scooping up his pipe and wiping the stem on his pants. It felt odd talking without it.

"That's what we need, Phillip! Another lawsuit. What do you have going now, 25?" Fuming, Isabella turned her back on Phillip and hauled herself aboard their wagon like a harvest hand. She nuzzled baby Andrew. With the touch of her cheek on the baby's, calm flowed over her like cool honey. She was ready to make amends, but Phillip was busy pawing through his scarred leather satchel.

He squinted at William's wound. "This gash gits a snorter. If you was older, William, you'd get one too." With that, Phillip uncorked a dented pewter flask of sour mash whiskey and gave William a terrible start by dribbling the fiery stuff into his open cut. "Hog tusk gotcher chin. Rest o' this blood's not yours. Seneca and the hog bled a-plenty. You feel like anything's broke?"

William hurt all over, but he wasn't one to caterwaul. He shook his head. "How we gonna git this hog inna wagon?"

Papa Phillip grinned at his boy's practicality. "We'll shove the hog onto this tarp and drag it behind us." He flicked a flat gray bug off his wrist, realizing that the hog's lice were looking for a new host. "William, check fer bugs. This hog had a batch! Leave your clothes in the wagon when we get to Whitley House. We pack *one* o' these bugs into her place, Grandma Esther will burn everything we got."

Isabella chided, "That does it, Phillip! That pig stays right here!" Since Phillip still couldn't budge the hog, he nodded reluctantly and motioned to William to help roll up the tarp.

To atone for her sass, Isabella agreed for once to let Seneca ride in the wagon. After closing the slash on William's chin with a gum patch, she even daubed goose grease on the hound's neck.

Milton knew this was hard for Mama Isabella. She hated dogs. Said they gave her babies fleas and worms, and you never knew when one of the stupid things would bite. Seneca cowered, expecting to get his ears boxed. When he got his head patted instead, the hound wagged his tail and licked the goose grease off his neck.

Papa Phillip unraveled the reins and talked soothingly to the mares.

William found a louse on his arm and popped it between his finger nails. He looked hisself over good, but couldn't find no more bugs.

The Sublette's Ordinary wagon rolled again. William hated leavin' his $10 kilt pig behind. He felt sad for it. He'd never kilt anything but a punkin before. He eyed the buzzards circlin' overhead. Then looked back at the pig with its head half blowed off and flies already swarmin'. One front leg pointed up at the ugly birds waitin' to rip the meat off him. There weren't no fun in killin' a critter, even when it needed killin'. But he had to get used to it, cause men had to kill all the time.

Bad as he ached, William was glad no one asked him how he learned to shoot. Artemis's secret was safe. Maybe that's why nobody'd thanked him. They knew about him and Artemis shootin' the pistols and didn't wanta bring it up. Right then William knew there was more to Artemis and the pistols than anyone would let on.

When Milton was sure William could hear, but Mama and Papa couldn't, Milton sneered, "Sicky Bill kilt a pig. Sicky

Bill thinks he's big!"

William fingered the gum patch on his chin and tried to think of a good reason for not punchin' Milton. He thought of one. Milton was Milton. William decided noddin' off would annoy Milton the most, so he closed his eyes.

The next thing William saw was a cloud-curdled sunset framing Whitley House and its big dark trees. The empty wagon was parked a respectful distance from Whitley House with William alone in it under a patch quilt. The mares munched the oats in their feed bags.

William's ribs ached. His chin throbbed under the gum patch. A couple of his lower teeth felt loose. He moved the loose teeth with his tongue, but decided to let them be.

A night hawk darted across the red sky making its lonesome "Squee" noises. William shivered. Even in the poor light, William could see the two large Ws for William Whitley in light colored bricks over the front door of the towering three story house. He remembered that there was a big "EW" for Esther Whitley above the back door.

He'd heard people in their tavern talk about the Whitley House sittin' on its hundreds of acres. A woman with bad teeth cackled that the Whitleys, Logans and the Shelbys were Lincoln County's aristocracy. The woman said Whitley House was the social center of the Transylvania region. A man with spectacles said something about *cosmopolitan* but William didn't know what that was.

Cosmopolitan might be the Whitley Racetrack on Sportsman's Hill. Up there, trumpets sounded before every race, and the best Kentucky horses from four counties came to thunder around the dusty track in the summer. It seemed long ago, but it'd only been last summer when the Sublettes celebrated the Fourth of July with Grandpa William, Grandma Esther and hundreds of people at their racetrack.

At nightfall Whitley House looked cold from the outside. Inside, it was drafty, but it got warm when it was full of Grandma and Grandpa Whitley's friends. William remembered Christmas before last when women filled the third floor ballroom for the quiltin' bee. That night the men, dressed like dandies, danced their women to fiddles and a piccolo with the greatest smells ever was. People in their tavern never smelled like that! Whitley house held its smells like they was its walls.

Grandpa built Whitley house to be a fort with little windows way up high. He'd shown William the secret hideout on the third floor for women and children if there was an attack. The basement had food stored on shelves and a root cellar. When Grandpa opened the cellar door, smells of carrots, parsnips, turnips and potatoes were so strong William could see them with their little root hairs.

There was a dungeon down there in the basement that could be a hideout if nobody was locked up in it.

Next to the dungeon was a big oak door. Grandpa said it could be locked with secret locks. The door opened onto a long escape tunnel that came out by a spring, so they could get water under siege or get away if they had to.

The dungeon was mostly what scared William about Whitley House. It was damp and dark with nothin' to sit on. It made a funny echo when you clapped your hands. He always expected to see real big rats in there, but they never came.

Several years back, Grandma Esther Whitley had shown William the bedroom with the high bed on the second floor where he'd been born. She told him he was a part of the house, but he never felt that way.

Grandma Esther always had so much to do, and so many children of her own that she had trouble recollectin' young William Sublette's first name. Since William's first name was in honor of Grandma Esther's own husband, it shoulda been easy for her. Maybe if William had nine children, and some of them had six or seven children, he'd forget their names too. Maybe he did anyway.

Grandpa William called Grandma Esther his "Little Cyclone," because of the way she always swirled around the house. It could have been because the hairs on her head stood out and waved around like tree limbs in a storm.

Grandma's head hairs was almost orange, but her eyebrows was black. William knew some folks wore wigs. And Grandma Esther wasn't little either! She was about as wide as she was tall. Sometimes she would fall into a chair, lean back and let her breath whoosh out, like it was her last. That scared

William too. He knew old people died, but he was scared to see one do it right in front of him.

William wondered why Grandpa had to have the Sublettes all the way up here from Somerset now. What was so dang important? He gathered the cozy quilt around his shoulders, climbed stiffly down from the wagon and headed for the house.

He was surprised at the mess of mosquitoes swarmin' outa the grass, all singin' the same high song. Seemed like they shouldn't come around a place so grand as Whitley House. He pulled the quilt over his head and ran for the front door.

Before he could grab the door handle, the door squeaked open. William looked into the gaping hallway. Nobody there. He lowered the quilt and peered into the solemn face of the biggest, blackest man at Whitley House. It was Benjamin with a face longer'n a mule's. Now Benjamin had long curled up white hair. William pointed at his own tangled hair. "What's this?" he asked, hoping that Benjamin knew he meant the long white hair.

Benjamin's face said white hair wasn't his favorite subject. "Well," he said, sounding like he was talking out of one, "It's a wig."

William hoped Benjamin would never talk to him in that low-low voice in the dungeon. That would just kill anybody. "Where is everybody?"

"May I take your quilt, William? Your mother is discussing the evening fare with Mistress Whitley in the kitchen. Your father's upstairs with Master Whitley in the study."

Benjamin's voice made William tremble. "Naw. I'll keep the quilt." He sidled past Benjamin, and headed for the stairs.

"I wouldn't go up to the study just now, young William. Something big is going on up there."

"I'll jist wait outside the study and listen till I find out what it is."

"You'll get in serious trouble eavesdropping up there. Master Whitley's not the same now -- not the same at all. You can listen down the hall by the bell cord hole in the ceiling, but you can't hear much there."

William didn't understand. Maybe Benjamin was jokin', but he *never* did that! Curiosity overwhelming his fears, William started up the long staircase. The house was scary, and the murmurs from the study sounded mean.

Tallow lamps with white pictures on the glass flickered in gleaming brass holders on the wall. Each of the 23 step facings was carved with the head of an eagle with a branch in its mouth. A wall hung sabre sheathed in a dented silver scabbard reflected the dancing lamps.

William knew from his chill this sabre had cut men. He'd never seen a war, but he sensed the scream of horses, the roar of cannon and the stink of burnt powder. The only time he ever felt these things was in Whitley House. Maybe he'd heard somebody in their tavern talk about war. Old men talked on and on about bein' in battle when they had too much to drink.

He pulled the quilt tighter and eased his ear against the study's polished oak door, but the voices was muffled. He slid down to the crack at the bottom.

It was Grandpa Whitley, but the harsh voice didn't sound like the kind man he knew. "...get the dispatches because I'm still a field grade officer in the Sixth Militia Regiment. I know you're a Jeffersonian, but Jefferson has no head for war. Instead of ordering American ships to fire on British blockade vessels, devil take the weakest, he's embargoed our own ships from exporting to other countries -- a fool plan. A fool plan that'll soon explode in his face. He'll be attacked by the British on the high seas and his countrymen on his own shores. War is now inevitable."

"What can I do about it?" William could tell from the words that Papa Phillip was clenching the pipe even harder in his teeth as he talked.

"You can help me -- but likely to no avail."

"Then your note plain baffles me. What's happenin' here that cain't wait?"

"Phillip, we're quite a pair. You can't speak English, and I can't write it."

Papa Phillip snapped, "Hold on there! If there's one thing I can do, it's talk!"

"That you can, and you talk just like I write. I can't spell. You can't conjugate. Together, we're the essence of illiteracy. But on paper, your eloquence is matchless. Sir, you were educated in Virginia, while I was amassing my fortune. But I must complete my memoirs before it's too late. So I'll recount them and you record them legibly."

Papa Phillip's angry voice suddenly shifted to strange sounding words, "*Monsieur*, would not a boy with French Huguenot parentage be wiser to adopt the vernacular, than to fight all the young bullies in Virginia? Would not a tavern proprietor catering to the provincial backwoodsmen of Kentucky earn more than a foreign sounding lout who might drive them off with his native speech?"

Silence. Young William's head whirled with amazement over his father's words. Now he'd always wonder if anybody was who they was supposed to be.

Finally, Grandpa Whitley spoke, "Phillip, I had no idea you were so complicated. My apologies for the denigration, but I still need your help."

Phillip'd never featured himself a clerk or a mere scribe. He was a Justice of the Peace! Reverting to his long practiced bumpkin dialect, he asked, "Say I do this forced writin'. What do we write?"

William could hear the decanter clink on the glasses and the liquid trickle near the back of the study.

"We begin with crucial dispatches I must send to my high command. We unleash letters with teeth like bayonets instead of bleeding gum holes to others in power in our effete government."

"Who'll sign these seditious missives?" Phillip inquired, letting his gentlemanly French accent shine through again.

"I shall, Phillip. They will bear my words of warning that America must stand strong for herself now or become a vagabond forever searching the wilderness for her self respect. Weakness now will beckon war on the winds of winter."

"And after your letters?"

"After my letters, Phillip -- I must complete my memoirs before I go back to battle. Of course you and Isabella will have to move back up here with your family."

"Memoirs'll take time. We might wait forever for the war that never was. What's to become of my Ordinary?"

"Phillip, I may not be a speller. I'm certainly not a punctuator. Based on your successful masquerade over all these years, I'm not even a sound judge of men. But I am no skinflint! Whatever needs to be done for you and my precious girl, Isabella, shall indeed be done profoundly."

The sound of *one* glass being drained put Grandpa Whitley's final seal on their talk.

Heavy footsteps! William leaped to his feet, dropping his quilt. The door burst open. Papa Phillip nearly trampled him, storming down the stairs without a word. William'd never seen Papa Phillip so upset. He was never rude to anybody.

William blinked at the sunburst of bright candles in the chandelier inside the study.

"Young William! Come here, boy! I've something to take up with you!"

William felt himself cringe. Now it was his turn. Maybe he'd find out who *he* was too.

CHAPTER 3

PONDER THE PATH SPRING 1808

Young William Sublette shuffled barefoot into the study of his namesake. With his split chin patched and his oversized country clothes blotched with dried blood, William felt ashamed and anxious. His face was hot. A lone drop of sweat inched down his temple. He wished Grandpa would say somethin'.

But the old man kept writin' at his desk with a scratchy quill. He seemed real thin. His long sandy hair was streaked with gray and tied behind his head. His fierce light blue eyes looked like an eagle's. The slender nose seemed higher in the middle and sharper than ever -- the once smilin' mouth hardened into a thin line.

Grandpa's blue coat showed lace at the neck. His brown hand was big and thick like a blacksmith's. Without lookin' up, he dipped his quill in the ink right in William's face, turned a page and kept writin'. The ink smelled like boot polish.

Keeping his head still so all his sweat wouldn't run down his face at once, eight year old William let his eyes roam the room. It wasn't the same. Still fancy, but now two big American flags on crossed poles with gold eagles at the top was agin the wall by the window. A blue-black jacket with gold all over the collar and upside-down gold cups on the shoulders hung by the flags. Medals danglin' from bright ribbons buried one side of the jacket's chest. The gun oil smell was heavy, but William didn't see any guns.

The lid on the brass inkwell in front of William was tipped open. The brass eagle, with flared wings that stood up when the lid was closed, was layin' out into the air on his back. The angel face on the inkwell's side had its eyes closed, smilin' like it knew somethin' nobody else did. As William watched, the angel's face changed to a leerin' devil.

He shifted his weight from one bare foot to the other. When was Grandpa gonna talk? William's tongue pushed at the two loose lower teeth inside the cut on his chin. He prayed they wouldn't fall out in here. He picked three stiff flakes of blood off his shirt and stashed them in his pocket. The lump in his throat was growin'. What was goin' on here? He wanted to go home. An ember in the fireplace popped and busted agin the screen, showerin' the brick hearth with sparks.

Colonel Whitley flashed William a cold glance, "I see you're bloody but unbowed!"

"I don't know where my good clothes got to. They was in the wagon."

Glancing at himself in the gilt framed wall mirror, the elegant gentleman rounded the desk. William stiffened without knowing why, but Grandpa just inspected him. "You're backside's clean. Sit down and we'll talk," he said, spearing one big bony finger at the chair beside William.

Always before, Grandpa'd given William a hug and let him sit on his knee behind the desk. William decided to stand as tall as he could.

Standing taller himself, Colonel Whitley peered down his nose at William, then gave a slight shake of his head. He marched back to his high-backed chair and settled in it, making a horsehair-smelling whoosh of air.

William's loose teeth ached. His chin throbbed. He was tired and tremblin'. He had never seen this cold man who'd taken over his friendly Grandpa. "Can I go?"

"Not yet. We must talk."

"What about?"

The eagle eyes seized William, and he felt like a rabbit hanging in their talons.

"The *most* important thing to us all -- our country."

"Kentucky?"

"No. No! The United States of America. Kentucky's but one of seventeen states, and it's not even on the western frontier since the Louisiana Purchase."

William shifted his feet again. His fingernails dug into his palms in his pockets. " I don't know about no *Purchase.*"

Colonel Whitley was openly peeved. He pointed with the frightening forefinger, "Sit down there, boy. Sit down."

William wilted into the chair.

"They should teach you less about how to fill a tankard and more about how to fill a continent! The Louisiana Purchase was an opportunistic triumph by President Jefferson that *doubled* the size of the United States." Colonel Whitley glared to be sure young William got that then continued, "Jefferson first offered France $10 million for New Orleans to open the Mississippi to our trading ships. Then he discovered how desperate Napoleon was for money to support the war in Europe. Jefferson refused to discuss the $10 million offer. Napoleon began to chase the bait. Jefferson offered $15 million for all North American land owned by France. Napoleon swallowed everything but the fishing pole and the Louisiana Purchase was done! It ranges from New Orleans west to Santa Fe, then north to the Rocky Mountains and north again all the way to Canada."

"Is this purchase what you wanted us to come up here from Somerset for?"

"No, William, I've just received a treasure few men have ever seen." With sharp pops, he unrolled a map across the great desk, resting the brass inkwell on one border, and a dagger with a rust pitted blade on the other. "What's it say there in the corner?"

William squinted at the curly letters like in Mama's Bible. He wanted to read it, but it blurred as his eyes filled with tears. A teardrop splatted on the map.

In angry disbelief Colonel Whitley whisked the boy's tear off the map with his frilled handkerchief. He stifled a gruff word with the lacy thing, then read aloud, "A Map of **LEWIS** AND **CLARK'S TRACK,** Across the Western Portion of North America from the MISSISSIPPI to the PACIFIC OCEAN; By Order of the Executive of the UNITED STATES, in 1804,5 &6. Copied by Samuel *somebody* from the Original Drawing of W E Clark." He cleared his throat. His fierce eyes tore into William.

"Now do you know what this is?"

William nodded, swiping at his eyes with his knuckles. "It's a map of some place out past western Kentucky where all them *Shawnees* went."

William looked up to see his Grandpa suddenly beaming with skin all bunched up around those eagle eyes. The old man brushed a long straying hair from his face, then rose quickly from his great leather chair.

"You're not much for grit, but you're not stupid, William. It's a precious map. They've released scant few to the military. Civilians can't buy them with all the gold in all their banks. It'll be years before they can. Sit up there now. I'll tell you how this came about."

Stealing another look at himself in the mirror, Colonel Whitley relaxed into his chair and laid his calf encased in a knee-high black boot across the corner of his desk. Now William knew the gun oil smell came from the pistol showing in that boot.

"Four years ago, President Jefferson sent his private secretary, Meriwether Lewis, and another former Army officer, William Clark, right through Kentucky to Saint Louis, Missouri. Some thought they were going out to explore the Louisiana Purchase we just talked about. But Lewis and Clark were really looking for a water way -- like the Mississippi -- flowing west as a passage to the great Pacific Ocean as well as some way to involve Americans in the great western fur trade. Others thought their trip was also a thinly disguised military mission to reconnoiter British ability to defend Oregon."

Suddenly, William found himself excited. He got up and leaned on the desk, so he could see the map, which the older man tapped with that big brown finger.

Pleasure veiling his fierce eyes, the elder William fanned the spark. "Lewis and Clark took their 43 man Corps of Discovery up the Missouri River right here to *Mandan* Indian Country where they got snowed in for the winter. In April of 1805, they set out anew guided by a *Shoshone* woman named *Sacagawea*, who could talk for them to other Indian Tribes. By mid-summer, they'd left the Missouri River and crossed this high point in the Rocky Mountains. But it was fall before they reached the Columbia River, then followed it to the Pacific Ocean. Just think how they felt looking at that vast ocean!"

"Did they have to fight all them Indians?"

"No, being intelligent men, they knew how to meet the Indians and trade things with them -- all except the Blackfeet. They got into a scrap with those scoundrels!"

"Are Lewis and Clark still out at this big ocean?"

"No, they worked their way back to the Rocky Mountains and split into two exploration groups that rejoined on the Missouri River. They arrived back in Saint Louis in September two years ago to cheering crowds, even though they never found that water passage all the way to the western sea."

"How'd them cheerin' crowds know they was comin'?"

"Newspapers got wind of their return when the expedition was still up on the Missouri River. Newspapers are obsessed with exploration. I journeyed to Saint Louis to witness Lewis and Clark's triumphant return -- most splendid thing I ever saw! Bands. People yelling their names. Never gotten over it. If I was young again -- like you, William -- I'd be going out to this great Western expanse to see what I could see."

"Didn't Lewis and Clark see it all?"

"William, nobody will ever see it all, but the thrill's in the looking. Somebody has to show other people the way out there so the United States can grow. Why some day, William, we might even have *thirty* states! It could be you, boy who shows people the way. It could be you! Read the Bible, don't you?"

"Mama makes me and Milton cipher and read the Bible every day."

Colonel Whitley laid a Bible with its worn leather cover on top of the map. He opened it to a pressed ribbon separating the pages of *PROVERBS* and placed it before William. He fingered Chapter 4: Verse 26. What's that say?"

William studied the words that smelled of musty flowers. He read slowly and clearly, "*Ponder the Path of thy feet, and let all thy ways be established.*" He eyed the old man. "What's that mean?"

"Means something different to everyone who reads it. To me it says *Decide where you're going, then make a path for others to follow.*"

"Should I ask Mama if I can go?"

"William, there's no room among those great mountains for little boys or little men. You must be the strongest of the strong to have a hope of survival. If the time comes when you're *really* ready to go, neither your Mama, nor the Lord God Himself will stop you!"

With that, Colonel Whitley tugged on a velvet cord hanging from the ceiling down through a hole in the floor, tinkling a bell below.

Moments later, Benjamin entered to stand looking at the study's floor.

"Take this boy to Isabella for a bath and send Phillip back up here."

"I'll ask him, Master. Mars' Phillip -- he none too pleased right now."

"Benjamin, tell Phillip I want to see him NOW."

"Come, boy." Benjamin took William's arm and they departed the study like flitting shadows. "Here's your blanket," Benjamin muttered, thrusting the folded quilt into William's hands as they descended the stairs.

Phillip paced the living room like a man awaiting his own hanging. He'd bitten the stem off his clay pipe and stuffed it in his shirt pocket. "Spose I'm summoned up there agin."

Benjamin nodded as he pointed to the floor between William's feet. "Stay here till I bring your Mamma."

Papa Phillip still wouldn't meet little William's eyes, but said, "Vittles'll be ready right quick," as he stalked up the stairs. "Best wash and gitcher clean shirt on. Grandma Esther'll not take kindly to blood stains at her table."

Still wondering how Papa Phillip could change his talk like he was two different men, William was being arm-dragged by Mama Isabella to the washroom off the hallway by the kitchen. He wished big people remembered what bein' little was like, so they wouldn't yank him at a run every time they got mad at each other.

The rich salty scent of roasting meat drifted from the kitchen -- mingling with the yeasty aroma of baking bread and the rooty smell of boiling beets.

William's stomach growled like a dog in a pickle barrel.

He wanted to git after that food. He realized how sore his ribs was when Mama Isabella tugged his shirt off. She lathered up a cloth and jammed it in his hand. He'd expected it to be warm, but its cold sent a chill through him.

"Wash yourself good. I'll bring you another shirt." Her skirts doused him with more cold air as she dashed from the room.

In moments she was back with his newest shirt and draped it over a peg above the bowl. If the water was hot when they poured it in this white bowl, it was a long time ago. William even welcomed the soap because rubbin' the cloth on it warmed it up.

While William washed, he heard the muffled voice of Mama Isabella from the kitchen. "Why's Daddy badgering Phillip like this?"

Grandma Esther answered, "The upcoming war's got the Colonel half out of his mind. He has the same dream again and again where he's killed in a cavalry charge. He thinks everything's got to be done right now. He's putting his personal affairs in order."

"But there is no war. The British're far too stuffy to come back over here for another thrashing."

"There is for him, Issie. When he reads of American sailors being pressed into service by the British on the high seas, he paces the floor and curses. Rants that we don't have the French backing us this time. Feels like he must defeat the lobster-backs all by himself!"

Rankled, Isabella shrilled, "Well Daddy has no right to uproot us from everything we've worked so hard for on some outlandish whim of a war!"

"You're not yourself, Issie -- not yourself at all," Grandma Esther replied, a sharp edge in her own voice.

"Phillip is a Judge and the Postmaster in Pulaski County. Up here in Lincoln, he's nobody!"

"Issie. Issie! Who do you think got Phillip those positions? The Colonel has every right to ask for Phillip's help."

"Are you trying to tell me that Daddy got every one of those political jobs for Phillip?"

Esther cleared her throat and glared at her irate daughter.

"Not *every* one, Issie. Not *every* one. Phillip got the Registrar of Stray Animals -- the *dog catcher* job all by himself!"

Isabella shook her head vehemently, "I'm the last person to find out about anything -- except when *I* am pregnant again!"

Esther choked back an ill-timed chuckle and eyed her big perspiring girl sternly. "Understand this, Issie. It's Phillip's turn! He must do this for the Colonel and his country! We are going to war! It's merely a matter of time."

Young William didn't know much about war. People in Somerset talked about how much it cost to grow corn or what girl they was sweet on. Tired and hungry, he decided to find out plenty about war. He wondered where Milton was. Milton was probably out with Seneca. Milton oughta know more about war. He was wastin' time with that hound when he oughta be learnin' about war.

William eased down the hallway, keepin' an eye out for Mama Isabella. Midway of the hall, he spied the bent silver bell danglin' on its thick velvet cord near the wall. It came through the hole in the study floor above. Stoppin' to look up at the bell, he heard voices through the hole just like Benjamin said.

"Young William's wishy washy. He needs discipline. You've got to bear down on him and bear down *hard*!"

He couldn't believe what Grandpa was saying about him. He thought everything had got all better when they shared the map. But this wasn't *Grandpa* Whitley any more. This was *Colonel* William Whitley!

Papa Phillip made excuses. "We had to start at three this mornin' to make it in one day with the wagon. Ridin' in the wagon gits William's goat. He gits sick. Besides, we're all tuckered. Had a turble time with a 300 pound wild hog bout the size o' your desk. Hog got after my hunderd dollar hound. Hog woulda kilt him, but the hog got hisself kilt. William got his face tore up."

It scalded William that Papa Phillip wasn't tellin' *who* kilt the pig. Barefooted, William moved so silently he couldn't even hear himself. Like a jumpin' contest, he took the stairs three at a time. His ear was suddenly at the crack under the door. His heart hammered. He didn't know what to do. He sure couldn't jist bust in on them!

Colonel Whitley sneered, "Young William looks like a girl. He talks like a girl. He cries like a girl. I can't stand a sniveling..."

William threw the door open, his eyes blazing at the men's shocked faces. "I ain't no girl. I didn't cry for me. I cried for my Grandpa, who don't live here no more. *Colonel*, I shot the pig dead! It charged me, and I blowed its head off like a busted punkin! I got my own war out west, and I'll need that map o' yers when I go."

Benjamin, who *never* laughed, choked back howls downstairs under the stairway. Then he shook his head. His smile died. He muttered softly, "A boy went up those stairs, but a man will be coming back down."

CHAPTER 4

COLTER'S HELL SPRING 1810

In stubborn silence, Isabella refused to go near Whitley House for two whole years. Phillip and Isabella Sublette kept the lid on their simmering feud over Colonel Whitley, but in the spring of 1810 it boiled over. William heard angry voices in Sublette's Ordinary after the last of Somerset, Kentucky's tipplers'd gone home. Mama screamed, "All right, Phillip! So we're only puppets to be dragged back to Whitley's fort, but I'll *never* speak to my father again!"

In less than a week the Sublettes had leased out their tavern and packed their wagon to head north to the Whitley domain of Stanford. Artemis rode along, helping Isabella with toddler Andrew and little girls, Sophronia, and Polly. Barefooted, William and Milton ran behind, waving last good-byes to the neighbors finishing morning chores at their log houses along Spring Street. Seneca loped from tree to tree saying good-byes in his own way.

Phillip tapped the Mulassiers with the whip to get them into a steady pull of the overloaded wagon. He hadn't realized the size of his mistake in leaving Somerset to help Colonel Whitley with his memoirs until now. He watched the bustling street drifting by like a disturbing dream.

Even though Phillip had sued both the tanner and the wagon maker over one thing and another, the lump in his throat said he'd miss them. Litigation was really just Phillip's way of staying in touch with folks. He'd never understood why they took it so personal.

Phillip wondered who'd become Judge and Postmaster. It was too late to turn back now even if there wasn't a decent man to fill either job. He sucked noisily on his empty pipe. He hated being on the outs with Isabella. Without looking at her on the seat beside him, he knew she was sobbing silently with her jaw set like somebody getting a tooth pulled.

But Isabella wasn't one to complain. She'd said her piece agin going back, then helped load the wagon like it was her idea. She was strong as the Colonel in her own way. Phillip had to put his arm around her. Isabella's shoulders tensed at his touch, but before long she untied the strings of her bonnet and relaxed.

Isabella wanted Phillip to feel her anger, but laid her head on his shoulder instead. His shoulder was bony, but there was something solid about Phillip. And for all of his talking, there was a quiet strength in the way he lived his life. She knew that to most people Phillip was merely dependable, but not to her. To Isabella, the man under these threadbare clothes was a cavalier -- a man of passion and purpose. She'd follow him straight through the gates of Hell if she had to -- no matter how furious he made her on the way!

This spring seemed warmer to ten year old William than when they'd gone to Stanford two years ago. He felt good keepin' a steady trot. He wasn't gonna ride in the wagon till he was plumb tuckered. New flowers filled the air with sweet smells. Milton and Seneca flew from one place to another like butterflies. Milton didn't have the good sense to save himself for the long trip. He'd be snorin' in the wagon before William even got tired. Milton oughta learn to slow down.

Sure enough, even before they watered the mares, eight year old Milton squeezed in between Sophronia who was five and Polly, who was only four, all asleep. Having outlasted Milton, William surrendered to the wagon's joltin' ride, glad it didn't buck so hard with a heavy load. If he got sick, he'd git out and walk. At least the back wheel didn't squeal like last time they come through here. William greased the hub himself, and hung the grease pot from the back axle in case it went to squawkin' again.

William watched the way Milton's dark hair blew back and forth from Sophronia's blonde braids to Polly's lace cap.

With three sets of pink cheeks and little red mouths, Milton looked like the girls when they was all asleep. But Milton didn't really look much like anybody but Milton. William was surprised to hear Mama and Papa arguin' about exactly where he'd shot the pig. William wasn't sure himself.

Artemis grated, "Little Bill shot dat devil-hog right dere."

Papa Phillip chuckled, "Artemis, you warn't even here when Bill kilt the pig!"

But Artemis, her eyes glassy, pointed at the same place.

William vaulted out of the wagon and ran to where Artemis aimed her black finger. Milton woke and sputtered, "Sicky Bill's gonna puke."

Moments later, William returned with a three inch tusk between his shaking fingers. He climbed up the wheel and handed the tusk to Papa Phillip, who shook his head and repeated, "Artemis warn't even here."

William pulled Artemis to sit down as the wagon rolled again. Losing her balance, she crashed beside William. He wanted to hug her, but she wouldn't cotton to no huggin'. "How'dja know, Artemis?"

She whispered in a rum-tinged breath, "I helped you shoot dat hog, Little Bill."

None of the God fearing Sublettes ever again discussed Artemis's slave-devil ways of divining where the hog bones were to be found. The rest of the trip to Lincoln County was as quiet as the serene Kentucky countryside.

The Sublettes settled in a drafty, run-down cabin near the rocky bottoms of the Dix River in Lincoln County a few miles from Whitley House.

Since Colonel Whitley was a Presbyterian, Presbyterian services were held of a Sunday morning for the elite of Lincoln County on the third floor of Whitley House -- even though Grandma Esther was a Baptist. Dutifully, Phillip brought Sophronia and both boys to soak up the sermon, but true to her vow, Isabella remained incommunicado at home with little ailing Polly and toddler Andrew who bellered too much for the Presbyterians.

Promises of eternal salvation and threats of Hellfire's damnation still rung the rafters of Whitley House's third floor when the Colonel approached Phillip's long-suffering group. The Colonel thought Sophronia looked like her mother, especially around the eyes. But today, the angelic little face wore dark circles above pale cheeks. "Phillip, I see you'll be getting right home because Sophronia's so peaked, but I hope you'll permit William and Milton to stay for catechism."

Exulted that his own escape was assured, Phillip nodded, then steered sleepy Sophronia into the departing stragglers. Their hair still moist from Mama's morning combing, William and Milton slouched back to their bench like two damp young rats surrendering to the trap.

To their surprise Colonel Whitley showed the gap between his front teeth in a wide grin. "Get a few crab apple tarts from Grandma Esther and meet me in the dungeon! We've had enough talk of Heaven. Now it's time to tell of *Hell*!" They darted down the stairs, seeking tarts and the freedom of *Hell*.

Tart crumbs on their faces, William and Milton sidled into the dark basement. Stored food smells swarmed them, but William barely noticed. His wide eyes explored the torch light flickerin' through the bars of the spooky dungeon. Milton's small fingers dug into William's arm. They edged closer to the iron strapped door standing ajar and peered in.

Solemn Colonel Whitley sat cross-legged on the dungeon's dirt floor in a white shirt and dark knee pants. His rust pitted dagger stabbed through some papers, and a fiery torch on the stone wall behind him streamed smoke. He pointed where the boys were to sit.

William scanned for the rats he always expected down here. Couldn't see none, so he joined Milton on the cold dungeon floor. Maybe they wasn't gonna like Hell as much as they thought.

Colonel Whitley's fierce eyes gleamed in the flickering torch light. His voice boomed, "Hell is many things besides the inferno of the antichrist!" The dungeon's jerky echo roared each word. The boys gaped at each other, their darting eyes spilling their fears.

Colonel Whitley stared at them till they nearly wilted. "I don't know if you boys will ever go west. If you do, you'll discover it's the devil's maelstrom of intrigues. Everybody's spying for somebody. British and Canadians are trying to bluff us out of Oregon. Spaniards'd barricade Texas if they could. Russians are wrestling the Spaniards for a toehold on California. All these foreigners have tricked the Tribes into doing their hatchetry on us. Our country's preparing to fight them all in one way or another. In short, it's Hell, boys--pure Hell."

Mystified, William mumbled, "Then why you want us to go to Hell?"

It annoyed Colonel Whitley to hear this boy say *Hell,* but he enjoyed William's riposte. Before the Colonel could retort, Milton said, "I was borned for the place. Papa says I'm fulla Hell. He's tried to beat it outa my pants, but there's plenty left in between my ears."

Nonplused, Colonel Whitley ignored Milton and said, "Recognizing there's a Hell doesn't mean Heaven's forsaken. It means you may look upward expecting God's infinite goodness, but you better watch where you're walking!"

William added, "I guess you gotta watch who else's walkin' around ya and why."

Colonel Whitley nodded, marveling at this ten year old's ability to harvest the wheat from the chaff. The boy'd proved he had sand in his craw by slaying the wild boar two years ago. He saw so much of himself in young William. That heritage must have reached the boy through Isabella. There was no doubt of her fire. If only Isabella could match her eldest son's ability to reason, she'd come back to the Whitley ways. He missed her so. Colonel Whitley ushered Isabella from his thoughts. "Boys, sometimes Hell is Heaven and Heaven is Hell. John Colter'd know this better than most."

Milton grabbed William's arm so he could talk first. "Who's John Colter?"

"Colter enlisted as a private with the Lewis and Clark Corps of Discovery in 1804. Stepped off on the wrong foot in March of his first year when he and three others got confined 10 days for patronizing a whiskey shop.... Milton, that's not funny!"

William seldom whacked Milton, but a whack on the arm now were a must. "I wanta hear this, Milton!"

Colonel Whitley nodded approval of the summary punishment and continued, "Colter did so well after that, Captain

Clark named Colter's Creek in October of 1805. Colter served as hunter and scout all the way to the Pacific. On the way home in 1806, Colter asked to join up with two Illinois trappers at the *Mandan* towns. Colter'd served with such distinction, Captain Clark agreed and outfitted him for two years from remaining supplies."

"Colter'd learned to travel light in buckskin shirt and leggings with only a buffalo robe, salt, trinkets for trading with Indians and his rifle, powder and shot. He severed ties with those two trappers in spring 1807, but ran into Manuel Lisa's fur expedition on the way home. Lisa'd recruited several Lewis and Clark men and convinced Colter to go back north with them."

"Lisa tasked Colter to search for beaver and friendly Indians for fur trading. It was then Colter embarked upon the most extraordinary solo exploration in the history of the West. Colter trekked through the mountains to the Yellowstone River where he discovered water boiling from the ground between jets of steam -- fiery mud exploding -- grand waterfalls cascading down a great colored canyon -- brimestone [sic] bubbling straight up from Hell. In spite of Captain Clark's recent vouching for Colter's honesty, newspapers have mocked Colter, calling him a lunatic and his magic lands *Colter's Hell.*"

Colonel Whitley raised his hand to forestall interruptions. "I believe John Colter found exactly what he said he found. In the fall of 1808, Colter was trapping beaver with John Potts in Blackfoot country. Hiding out during the day, they set their traps at dusk and collected them at dawn. They'd just retrieved their traps from the Jefferson River, when they were surprised in their canoes by a huge shore party of Blackfeet."

The Colonel paused to savor their scared faces, then continued, "The Blackfeet motioned the trappers to beach their canoes. Colter thought he'd be robbed and released, so he hid his beaver traps in shallow water and paddled ashore. Potts remained midstream. The howling Blackfeet seized Colter and stripped him naked."

"The Blackfeet waved Potts ashore. When Potts refused, a Blackfoot shot him in the hip. Potts fired back, head-shooting the Blackfoot who'd wounded him. The tribe cut Potts to pieces with a fusillade of bullets and shot arrows until Potts and his canoe bristled with feathered shafts and sank."

William blurted, "How'd ya hear about Colter?"

"Well, wait now. Colter wasn't killed right away. The Blackfoot Chief hand-signed a deer to find out how fast Colter could run. Although Colter was tall, lean as whang leather and could run like Milton, he made the turtle hand-sign to show how slow he was. The Chief hand-signed the chase to Colter and gave him a moment's head start."

Milton scratched about in his long black hair. "Why're they makin' all them hand-signs? Cain't Indians talk?"

"Indian tribes can talk, but they all use different words, so they can't talk to us or even to other tribes. Lewis and Clark said Indians use hand signs in place of words, except when speaking among their own people."

The Colonel cleared his throat. "Now, where was I? Oh yes, Colter knew the Madison River was about five miles away across an open plain of sagebrush and prickly pear cactus. By the time Colter was half way to the river, his feet were pin cushions, but he had a good lead on the Blackfeet. About a hundred yards behind, one Blackfoot with a red blanket on his shoulder and a spear was striding easily and gaining on Colter. Colter sprinted harder, but that brought blood spurting from his nose all over his body. Pounding footsteps said the Blackfoot was nearly upon him within a mile of the river....and that'll be all for today, boys"

Both Sublette boys sprang on the Colonel, pulling at his arms and messing up his hair. Milton even pulled the dagger out of the news clippings. "Quarter, quarter," the Colonel begged. "Just what is it you boys want?" Never knowing what Milton would do, the Colonel quickly disarmed him.

Milton growled like a bobcat. "You know what we want!"

The Colonel pushed them back to the ground and smoothed his hair. "Colter increased his speed, then suddenly wheeled. The exhausted Blackfoot lunged. Colter deflected the spearhead downward, and the Indian's weight broke the shaft. Colter seized the shortened spear and pinned the Blackfoot's body to the ground. Too weak to go on, he paused over the dying Indian, his own blood dripping into the Blackfoot's gore.

He seized the blanket from the Blackfoot's body and pulled out the stubby spear. He gave a sigh of relief, then turned to see a horde of Indians closing in on him."

"Staggering onward, he collapsed into the Madison River. Taking cover in the willows, he waited till several Blackfeet were nearly upon him. Then he sank and swam under several driftwood logs lodged against an island. The Blackfeet searched through the day. They made a show of departing, leaving warriors secreted among the cottonwoods through the night. Colter drifted downstream for a mile or so in the dark, then slept among the willows in his wet blanket, clutching his broken spear to his breast."

"Living on roots and inner tree bark, Colter covered the 250 miles to Lisa's Fort in about 11 days, with only the blanket and broken spear. He arrived, footsore, bearded and emaciated."

"And never went back to the mountains!" Milton yelled.

"Oh, but he did!" the Colonel contradicted. "Early the following winter, John Colter returned alone to the Jefferson River and recovered the beaver traps he'd jettisoned from his canoe. He trotted with the traps most of the day, making camp on the Gallatin River. He was cooking buffalo meat when he heard rifles being cocked beyond the firelight. Reacting instantly, he saved only his rifle and darted away into the darkness, the bullets slashing the night and the ashes of his fire. Again Colter fled eastward, praying in the darkness, 'Dear God, if you'll only let me off this time, I'll never come back here again!' "

"And then the Blackfeet caught him!" Milton shouted.

"No, they didn't. He got in his canoe and paddled to St. Louis. I think he's still there!" the Colonel added triumphantly. "Now have you boys learned anything from Colter's adventures?"

William stood up and stretched. "Mr. Colter's mighty fast on his feet, maybe even fast as Milton, but he sure cain't be trusted with no beaver traps."

CHAPTER 5

WAR UPON THE LAND SUMMER 1812

By the summer of 1812, the Sublettes had shed their shabby Dix River cabin for spacious quarters in the Crab Orchard, a vast wild apple tree forest near Whitley House. Their new Sublette Tavern provided toothsome food and lodging to travelers with pasture for their horses. But the United States of America had not fared as well. Its shipping throttled by British and French piracy, the fledgling country had been starved to its knees and humiliated before the world.

The instant Colonel William Whitley discovered President Madison's June 1st declaration of war against England had barely been upheld by a 79 to 49 vote in the House of Representatives and a narrower margin of 19 to 13 in the Senate, he vowed to turn Kentucky's shirkers into patriots.

The Colonel circulated handbills inviting all Lincoln County inhabitants to celebrate Fourth of July around his Liberty Pole on Sportsman's Hill. His posters promised genuine Kentucky horse races at dawn with fireworks following the picnic. He even tried to lure eloquent Henry Clay to Kentucky to inspire hundreds of his home state voters on the Fourth. Clay's reply read that he feared leaving Washington with his opposition searching frantically for parliamentary devices to overturn the declaration of war he and John C. Calhoun had fought so hard to pass in Congress.

On the eve of the festivities, Colonel Whitley sat disheveled in his study, awaiting Phillip Sublette to put the final touches on the Whitley memoirs. His chandelier candles had melted to drooling stubs. He'd refused food all day, telling Esther time to arrange his memoir notes was too precious. But he was actually mulling over clippings and military dispatches for his speech on the morrow.

Someone faintly tapping his study door aroused him. Rubbing his red eyes, he growled, "Come in!" Nothing happened. He yanked the velvet cord to alert Benjamin. Still nothing. "Come in, I said!" Silence. He stormed across the room and jerked the heavy door ajar, blurting "Phillip!" Then his voice fell to a whisper. "My God, *Isabella*, please do come in."

Isabella rested a silver tray of steaming food on her pregnant abdomen, then placed the tray atop her father's papers. "Please eat this before it chills," she asked quietly. She so wanted to embrace this brave, wonderful man who'd endured her petulant silence over *four years* without reprisal.

William Whitley rested against the door jam, overcome at this first sight of his most beloved daughter in a painful eternity. He smoothed his tousled hair, tucked his shirt in and blotted his eyes on his sleeve.

Groping his way to the desk, he sat down, staring at the steaming beef and potatoes bordered by a whole roasted carrot laid on either side of the plate. A pair of biscuits had chunks of butter melting over them. So choked by emotion he couldn't speak, he just sat with his head bowed.

Isabella rested her cool hand on his. "You were right, you know. So very right and I..."

"I don't care about that, Issie. I only feared I'd never see you again."

"You don't have to go to war, Daddy. At your age -- you've done your part!" She rushed around the desk and put her arms around his slender shoulders. "Don't go," she sobbed.

He kissed her hair, then asked quietly, "Want a biscuit, Issie?"

She rose and put her hand out, accepting the biscuit with its runny butter starting to scum over. "I'm sorry I threw four precious years with you away. I never thought it would come to war! I never ..."

He poured gravy on his mashed potatoes. "You will come tomorrow, won't you?"

Isabella nodded, pressed her face into her handkerchief and fled her father's study. He laid his fork on the tray and looked up at the pathetic candle remnants. "None of us have much left, now do we?"

* * *

Before dawn, riders, carriages, and wagons groped up Sportsman's Hill. In his finest civilian top hat, frock coat, white breeches and gleaming black boots, Colonel William Whitley greeted them all in the chill air.

Stable boys led high-stepping, hot-blooded bays to clean stalls to groom for the races. Women and children huddled about the grounds of Whitley House where Mistress Esther Whitley received them, talking of everything but the war. Benjamin and other servants tended their army of babies.

The races minutes away, flasks of strong spirits appeared among the gentry. Whitley servants made hot breakfasts to order, carefully serving the important men first.

Phillip Sublette rolled up in his freshly painted red, white and blue wagon bulging with beer barrels, bread, cheese and cold cuts. He assured Colonel Whitley his memoirs were done except for the final page the elder man wished to add. The Colonel watched with interest as Phillip showed 12 year old William how to bung-start a beer barrel and bleed off the foam.

William Sublette, better groomed than Colonel Whitley had ever seen him, filled beer mugs and tallied beers drawn. Phillip urged his son to become the second honest barkeep in Kentucky, then muttered, "I know ya wanta watch the horses run, but you're the eldest. Come September, you'll turn thirteen. If I gotta go into the Militia, you'll be runnin' the tavern with Artemis. Country's at war, boy. War!" The ugly word let Phillip's precious pipe plummet into the beer foam fizzing on the ground. He snatched it up and wiped it clean on his pants.

Still but ten and not pressed into man's work, Milton crouched in the chilly shadows beside the racetrack. He trotted about, warming up to race agin the horses. Milton couldn't wait to beat those nags. William and the other boys would have fits when they saw what a thunderbolt Milton Sublette was!

The trumpet sounded. Six of Kentucky's fastest steeds lined up between the white starting poles on either side of the track. Milton saw that most jockeys were darkies barely older than him in bright colored shirts. All had billed caps on backwards with their stirrups up way too short.

BLAM! The gun surprised Milton. The horses thundered off leaving Milton choking on their dust. Milton headed for the seats down the way. He spit again. "Boy you dummies don't know how lucky you was I didn't git a honest start. I'da made ya look like you's ridin' broom sticks!"

Horses ran, wagers were paid and the sun rose. Townspeople drifted in. Only Colonel Whitley's refusal to remove himself from between two down-state horse owners thwarted a pistol duel. He settled their dead-heat dispute with two foaming mugs of beer and a coin flip. Reasonably sure Throckton and Bales wouldn't fire on each other, the Colonel ascended the new-wood platform with its shiny nailheads by the Liberty Pole. He surveyed Sportsman's Hill. Upwards of a thousand folks assembled here for Independence Day and more were climbing up the road. Many were unfamiliar faces.

The Colonel longed for his clippings to crutch him through his speech. He hoped he wouldn't forget everything. His hands trembled, so he shoved them in the pockets of his sleek white breeches. He mused to himself that the brain begins to work at birth and does not stop for a second --- until you get up to give a speech to a thousand people.

Colonel Whitley waved his arms to quiet the crowd. "Welcome to our Fourth of July celebration on Sportsman's Hill!" His voice sounded so puny out here. This opening blast would've knocked his sabre off the wall inside Whitley House.

Somebody screamed, "Louder, Colonel!"

Whitley called to the racing steward for the stiff coned-hide used to announce win, place and show horses to the crowd. The cone came bobbing across the sea of faces. Putting the steward's cone to his mouth, he yelled, "How's this?" Several men in the back doffed their hats, so he knew they could hear. The upturned faces appeared tense, squinting into the bright sun.

Colonel Whitley gestured toward the Stars and Stripes fluttering from the Liberty Pole. "The sun is bright today, but that great flag flies under the black cloud of war."

A baritone yelled, "A war we can't win!"

"That's what the Lobster-backs told us during the Revolution!" Perspiration from his hat band dribbled into his eyes. He dropped his hat upside down beside his boot and handkerchiefed his sweaty eyes as the crowd grumbled.

"France's glutton Emperor has devoured Europe. England, having drunk the oceans, has a bloated King with a catastrophic case of indigestion. In their frenzy to dismember each other, this earth's two most powerful, blood-soaked nations are butchering America!"

Colonel Whitley thirsted for water, but had none. He commandeered a warm beer someone had set on the platform, swigged it, wiped his lip and resumed. "In 1806 England and France traded decrees blockading each others' ports. By 1807 both were seizing American ships, deaf to our pleas as a non-combatant. Our ocean commerce dwindled to sneaky sailing along our own coasts. Even in our very harbors, the British plundered our ships, seizing American sailors as 'British deserters.' Sailors they didn't hang outright were pressed into service beaten daily in brigs by the lash of British brutes."

"Since this travesty began, 3,000 American's have been Shanghaied or hanged by the British! *Three times* the people here today!" His audience eyed each other.

Thirsty again, Whitley couldn't afford to stop. "In June of 1807, the British frigate *H.M.S. Leopard*, blockading Annapolis, demanded that our frigate *Chesapeake* muster its crew and hand over deserters. Our Commodore Barron refused. *Leopard* ravaged *Chesapeake* with a broadside, leaving our U.S. ship a burning shambles with crewman, broken and bloodied on deck. Because U.S. Ship *Chesapeake's* guns had not been primed, not a cannon answered. *Chesapeake* was boarded and several crewman hanged. Our Commodore Barron was tried by Courts Martial for neglect and suspended for five years without pay. Now this country abounds with Commodore Barrons who won't prime their guns or pay their taxes."

Whitley'd expected crowd uproar but its mutterings were feeble. "In 1807 these finger-snapping British commanded that all countries trading with France first pay tribute to Britain. Not satisfied just enslaving us, the British ordered our ships to take out British licenses *and* pay tribute, putting the British in the same despicable class with the Dey's pirates of Algiers. American shipping is annihilated."

Somebody yelled, "I ain't never seen no American ships in Lincoln County."

"Well, nobody else has seen 'em on the seas of the world lately! They're not free to bring us the steel we need to make rifles or the rum you've been drinking here today. The men who once sailed our ships are either languishing in foreign jails, dead or furling British sail on pain of the cat-o-nine-tails. No beaver trapped around here is going to the people who make hats overseas. After we've been cut off from the world a while longer, we'll be glad, because we'll all be eating our beaver pelts!" Colonel Whitley observed several men threading through the crowd to get closer to him.

"Jefferson cowed Congress into passing the Terrapin Law embargoing all of our own ships from trading across the seas. Americans pulled in their head and flippers and sank to the slimy mud to snap at each other while their supplies dwindle."

He cleared his raw throat, "Lincoln County people aren't the only ones who disagree how to handle the British dilemma. House debates got so heated Gardinier of New York was shot in a duel -- like we nearly had here today -- by Campbell from Tennessee. But then a New Yorker oughta know better than to get in a shoot-out with a man from Tennessee!" He was relieved to hear a few laughs.

Taking a deep breath he yelled, "When Madison assumed the Presidency, he was able, through William Pinckney's diplomacy to negotiate an agreement with British Minister Erskine repealing all Britain's shipping decrees against the U.S. So we put our boats back in the water loaded to the gunnels with our goods. The British promptly reneged, tricking our ships into seizure by this Satanic agreement. Americans scurried like terrified cockroaches back to the world's gutters."

Whitley ducked for another swig from the warm beer and nearly choked on the foam. He coughed, but hollered, "Last year Britain corked our ports with more men o' war. The sloop o' war *Little Belt* braced the American frigate *President*, but Captain Ludlow commenced fire. After half a score of British seamen were killed and a score wounded, *Little Belt* limped for

Halifax."

A florid man peeking through an unruly orange beard bellered, "America has 12 war vessels against over 900 floated by the British. That leaves each American ship only 75 British ships to sink! Colonel, you better belay the beer and get outa the hot sun!" That was followed by groans of agreement.

"Well, sir, it's clear you care not a whittle for ships, but what of tomahawks? You long to see a tomahawk buried in the brain of every man, woman and child on Sportsman's Hill today?" Audible groans from the crowd.

"If you read the papers, you know that the British have plied the Indians with more than trade whiskey. They've convinced the *Delawares, Shawnees, Wyandots, Miamis* and the *Chippewas* that every evil ever befalling an Indian originated with you Americans."

"Those same papers told us last year, that the *Shawnee* Chief *Tecumseh* and his evil twin, *Tenskwatawa,* The Prophet, called a council of the tribes for the lone purpose of killing you. That includes you, sir -- your beard will be red from more than your Scottish ancestry if these British inspired Indians get their way."

Red beard retaliated, "Irish ancestry sir! We was fightin' the British for centuries -- aye and losin' like you're goin' to."

"The difference between us and the Irish is, we thrashed the Limeys last time. Now we'll show 'em how far Kentucky long rifles shoot. That goes for their murdering Indian henchmen too! General William Henry Harrison defeated them up there in Indiana Territory! And he used your neighbors from right here in Kentucky to do it! If he hadn't vanquished those scalp-rippers, you think we'd be getting ready to eat all that sumptuous food coming up here today? Dead men don't eat, sir. Not even dead *Irish* men with a *Scottish* accent!"

Colonel Whitley suddenly felt the crowd's support shifting to him. "Those Indians'll be back here to butcher us. We better have *our* guns primed when they come ascalping!"

A young dissenter in linsey-woolsey with a chicken scratch beard hollered, "Is this here another case of old men sendin' young men out to die fer old men's principles?"

Colonel Whitley delivered the *Coup de Gras.* "Hardly my

young friend. If you scan the battlefield, I'll be out in *front* of you! I leave on the morrow to rejoin Colonel Richard Johnson's Mounted Regiment as his Executive Officer." The crowd broke into battle yells. Hats sailed skyward. Applause drowned the shouting.

Colonel Whitley decided some of the éclat was for the food wagons which arrived with his battle announcement. He knew it was time to end his address.

"Those previously in charge of America's affairs sought to avoid armed conflict at all cost, creating our distrust of each other at home and contempt for us abroad. Now the freeborn sons of America must fight to preserve this land their fathers won with their blood! In this war Americans will prove to the world that we have not only inherited that liberty which our fathers gave us, but also the power and the will to maintain it!" Cheers rang long after Colonel Whitley left the platform to look for Isabella.

Colonel Whitley found Isabella and the youngest of her brood in the seats. She was dressed in a dark blue fabric with reddish-green highlights. She looked into his face, rivers flowing down her cheeks. "Don't say anything, Daddy. Just hold me for a moment, then go!"

He hugged Isabella to him, feeling her hard pregnant belly. "If your baby's a boy, will you name him Harrison for the General who saved us from the Indians?"

"No, Daddy, I'll name him Pinckney for the diplomat who tried to absolve us of this awful war!" He shook his head, hugged Isabella again, then merged into the crowd to find young William.

As expected, Colonel Whitley found William Sublette staving off the onslaught of thirsty patriots on the beer wagon. He paused long enough to shout to William to meet him at the Whitley House stable at dawn.

* * *

A rooster's shrill crow startled William as he groped through the gray dawn at the stable. He hadn't slept all night for fear of missin' this farewell.

Though it was July, William could see his breath. His bare feet were cold enough to crack like thin ice. The crowd's cheers still rang in his head. William hadn't cheered. He didn't want *Grandpa* Whitley to go off to war. The warm, musky scent of a horse hung heavy in the air.

The Colonel's stallion, Ebony, stood saddled. The sabre in its dented silver scabbard from the stairway in Whitley House hung from the pommel. Colonel Whitley brushed his stallion's neck glinting in first light. Without turning, he smiled, "I know you're here, because you *said* you'd be here, William, so I don't have to look."

William was about to bawl. He grated, "Yes sir, I'm here. Milton's comin' too, but he's gotta find Seneca first."

Colonel Whitley's smile broadened. Yesterday he'd been a hero cheered by a thousand. Today -- upstaged by a hound. "William, I can't wait for Milton. I must join my regiment. I'll tell you my philosophy of life. You can pass it on to Milton after he finds his hound."

"What's a philosophy, sir?" William queried, his breath whisked away by what a figure Grandpa cut in his blue uniform with all the gold braid.

"My recipe for living. William, be true to your country and yourself. Be courageous even when you have nothing left to give to the fight. Be honest in all things. Keep honest accounts and pay your debts even if it costs you your supper."

"Yes sir."

"Here take this Lewis and Clark map for your trip out west someday." Then he added with a wink, "But the two most important things to remember are *never hit a man without your bullet pouch inside your fist* and *always carry a pistol in each boot!*" Colonel Whitley mounted and thundered out of the stable, his fiery stallion's shod hooves clanging sparks from the cobblestone floor.

CHAPTER 6

JACKSON'S THUNDER   FEBRUARY 1815

Lightning outlined the gigantic man against the darkness outside the Sublette Tavern doorway. "C'mon in," 14 year old Milton Sublette yelled over the cloudburst's roar. "Most folks don't knock."

Tumbling thunder followed the black bearded giant inside. Wet air hung about him like his own cloud. He clawed his cape off and draped it over a wall peg. Puddles fanned from sodden leather boots rising above his knees. He stood his rifle, barrel-down, in the corner to drain. His sopping buckskin shirt had rents showing the hair on his bear-sized chest. "Stalled my mount in yer stable," he grunted.

The giant looped his rain-beaded sabre's handguard over a wall peg. It wasn't a dress sword. Its oily blade was notched and battered. He dumped his soaked saddle bags under the sabre and plopped his hat on them.

"You're *somebody*, ain't you, Mister?" Milton asked.

"Everybody's *somebody*, lad." the man grated.

Milton paraded him like a prize stallion between the tables of gawking patrons. Most quit eating to watch his ponderous strides. The man dwarfed the empty chairs, so Milton sat him on the oak bench beside the hearth. It creaked but held.

Tavern slave Artemis helped Milton slide up a table that barely fit over the man's tree-stump legs. "Hot buttered rum, Mistah?" She yelled over the rain's noise.

"Got coffee that ain't fulla chicory?"

"We gonna fix you some right pure," Artemis replied

flashing white teeth with a space between the front two.

"Bring me the pot. I got a deep cold place."

She disappeared in a flurry of skirts.

Milton knew Artemis had been into the rum agin so he'd steer the pot onto the table when it came. Pitchin' hay and diggin' post holes had filled him out. Milton looked good flexin' his muscles inna mirror, but he was a robin beside this feller.

"Git my wet Muskogee tunic too hot, lad, you'll be cuttin' it offa me when the buckskin shrinks."

"Wanta sit someplace else, Mister?" Milton asked, for once actually wanting to please somebody.

"Naw. Good to let my bones know we's not in the grave yet. This's February. Don't it know when to snow in Kentucky?"

"Does most years. Where ya from, Mister?"

"Tennessee. Got a room left?"

"Jist the loft," Milton nodded at the stout ladder beside the fireplace.

"Good fer me, if it is fer the ladder. Bring your register."

Milton wasn't one for caterin' to patrons, but he trotted for this one. Couldn't read the name the feller scribbled in their book but sealed the loft deal with wet coin. "Roast's nigh done," Milton said, going to get the order of a hunter waving a tankard.

The massive man mused, "Guess I'll smoke out my appetite with a good pipeful." He groped his soggy pockets, then leaned toward the bald weasel of a man with wire-rimmed spectacles at the next table. "Would ya have dry tobacco, sir?"

With barely a nod, the skinny man stopped eating, fished out a limp leather bag and tossed it to the burly stranger.

"Mighty decent, sir. Thank you." He packed his cracked ivory pipe and lit it with the stubby candle on the table. White smoke wreathed the big man's head.

The bespectacled man sucked his teeth, then went after them with his silver tooth pick as he tucked his tobacco pouch back in his worn vest pocket. He proffered a tiny white hand. "Editor of the weekly paper just across the Crab Orchard in Stanford. Avery's my name. Always looking for story."

The giant's clasping hand had the heft of an anvil. Its chairleg-sized fingers, latticed with white scars, were missing the first joint of the finger he'd used to pack his pipe. He let the time to say his own name pass through the four smoke rings he blew.

"Been any place of interest?" the editor asked.

"Probably."

"Like where?"

"Emuckfa -- Tallashatchee -- New Orleans."

The room quieted. Heads turned toward the huge man as thunder bombed the rain hammering the tavern's roof.

"Musta served under Andrew Jackson."

The giant's nod coincided with thunderclaps tumbling like epic dominoes into the darkness.

"Hafta tell you, our editorial policy didn't favor entry into the war -- or Andrew Jackson."

"My own editorial policy toward Andy Jackson's had its ups and downs."

"Why's that?"

"Servin' Andrew Jackson is like ridin' sky-thunder one minute and gropin' through a coal mine the next." The giant leaned back and fashioned four more smoke rings, the last ring firing through the third. Patrons tip-toed to set their chairs down around the big man's hearth side. He had an eye men trusted and the voice of a spellbinder.

Milton Sublette set the dented coffee pot on the giant's table, then sprinted through the rain to get his 15 year old brother Bill from the garret in the barn where he lollygagged over cipherin' books. Maybe the big feller knew how Grandpa Whitley was killed at some place called Thames. Papa Phillip was abed with ague, so they'd tell him about this later.

Milton and William splatted back through sheeting rain to the tavern with Milton winning handily. After toweling off, they eased through their patrons to the hearth.

William hadn't believed anybody'd be big as Milton said. Now William wondered if this ox outweighed the jenny-mule he used to plow Dix River farm's rocky bottom land. William ached to ask the ox about Grandpa Whitley, but there was no way to bust in on the big man's voice. William slicked his long hair back and squatted too near the hearth's shimmering coals for comfort.

"Andy Jackson come by his hatred of the British honestly -- and young. He's told of servin' as a boy of 13 with the Revolution's Continental Infantry in the spring of 1780 at the

Waxhaw under Colonel Abraham Buford. Their outfit got surrounded by Lt. Colonel Banastre Tarleton's 700 British cavalry. American surrender flags was hoisted."

"But agin rules o' war, Tarleton's men of horse rode through American ranks, bloody blades aflashin'. Americans yelled for quarter. None was given. Infantry's not a match for cavalry at close quarters -- 113 Americans perished. Over 50 Americans, too maimed to move outa the swamp o' their own body parts, was left to die -- while Tarleton's butchers hazed 50 others through the awed streets of Camden. That massacre spawned our rebel vengeance cry of *Tarleton's Quarter* -- meanin' none given!"

"Hardly enough to make a boy despise an entire race for life," editor Avery observed.

"Seen many men put to the sword, have ya, Mr. Avery?" The unanswered question hung surrounded by four more smoke rings. "But the massacre's not the nub. In Camden, one of Tarleton's officers ordered Andy to clean the mud off his boots. Andy spit on him. The officer sabre-slashed the boy, layin' his jaw open, missin' his throat by the length of a forefinger. If that sabre-slash was three inches lower, how ya spose the Battle of New Orleans woulda come out, gentlemen?"

Answering voices were crushed under a rolling barrage of thunder. William Sublette's finger traced the deep scar in his chin. He wondered how it matched up agin Jackson's scar. He wished his was cut by a sabre too stead o' bein' bit by a pig -- like Milton was always tellin' folks. Several people said William was Jackson "faced." Maybe the scar's what they meant.

"Is Andrew Jackson myth, bully or bandit?" the editor asked, sipping his ale tankard.

"Andy might be all that. Might be none of it. Andrew Jackson's not like any man you ever dreamt of. He can be a ragin' lion then go kind as a kitten in one beat of his heart."

"Explain," Avery asked.

"At the end of August 1813, Andy got a report that 1,000 Red Stick *Creeks* under Red Eagle swarmed Ft. Mims, killin' 250 people. Children seized by the legs was brained agin the stockade. In Nashville, Andy was too weak from his wounds to git outa bed, but he vowed to avenge Ft. Mims.

Ordered himself tied to his horse and led us south to Alabama."

"At Ft. Strother, Andy roused us a couple hours fore first light o' November 3rd. Ordered us to remember Ft. Mims. Andy loves the pincer tactic. We closed on the Red Stick village of Tallashatchee. Our cavalry leveled it, killin' all 186 men. We captured 84 women and children. One baby of a dead mother was bout 10 months old. None o' them women would feed him. General Jackson give 'em a direct order with *shoot* in his eyes. I never seen nobody refuse a direct order from Andrew Jackson before."

"I suppose he had the women shot," Avery surmised.

"No siree! General Andrew Jackson took that baby boy into his own tent, mixed brown sugar with water and cooed at him till he tuck it. Andy sent baby *Lyncoya* by a captive squaw to Andy's very own home in Tennessee. *Lyncoya* still lives there. That squaw went free fer keepin' her bond to General Jackson."

"Just how do you explain that?"

"Two words. Andrew -- Jackson."

Artemis brought the big man a cutting board bearing a steaming bread loaf, a butter ball and a dish of blackeyed peas. Slipping a dirk from his boot, he sliced the bread in deft strokes.

"Old Hickory's a lunatic -- kills Indians because he loves to coddle 'em," the editor hollered through a thunderclap.

The expression in the big man's eyes left no doubt he'd tired of the newspaper man's anti-Jackson remarks. "You gotta develop a sense o' humor, Mr. Avery."

"Nothing funny to me about Andrew Jackson!"

"That's what the British said at New Orleans last month. But Andy does have a streak o' fun. He ordered every man jack of us, if captured, to confess under torture that our side had 20,000 men. O' course we only mustered bout 5,000 -- mixture o' U.S. Army and Navy regulars, cavalry, conscript pirates, free blacks, backwoodsmen and a passel o' *Choctaws*. Andy was death-sick with dysentery. Had wife Rachel down from Tennessee to nurse him so's he didn't die fore the British could finish the job they'd started when he was 13. Ammo was low and morale was lower."

"Our spies learned 60 British ships o' the line was haulin' 14,000 troops that'd just slaughtered the most powerful land army in the world -- takin' their midget Emperor prisoner. Officers' wives aboard was dancin' cotillions with their tinklin' music afloatin' through the fog. Single officers lusted for New Orleans' booty and beauty!"

"New Orleans was a dreamy city of divided factions lyin' helpless above the mouth of the Mississippi -- awaitin' under trees hung with Spanish moss."

The giant mopped up the last of his blackeyed peas with a fat hunk of bread. "Andy stationed five American gunboats on Lake Borgne. On December 13th Redcoats lowered 45 barges into Lake Borgne and manned them with a thousand sailors and marines. Next mornin', as the British always do, they made a spectacle o' their attack. It was a chillin' sight, even from the hills where I set my horse -- a unbroken front o' barges, red-shirted sailors bristlin' shiny muskets, dippin' their six oars to a side in perfect time, and sportin' a cannon in each bow. Our gunboats put up a fierce fight, but before tea time, all five was at the bottom of Lake Borgne. We's sweatin' if we's all gonna die."

"Swamp skirmishes follered, but the genuine battle stepped off in endless ranks of British regulars at 4:00 a.m. of a Sunday at Chalmette Plantation on the 8th of January -- last month -- though it seems a century ago. Andy dug our cannon in on a levee behind a canal and positioned his long rifles to fire from behind cotton bales sunk in the mud. Nothin' eats bullets like a bail o' cotton."

"British 44th Regiment led the advance through the mist marchin' to their pipes and drums. They was to carry bundles o' sugar cane called facsines to fill the canal and ladders to scale the levee, but they plumb forgot 'em, then scrambled back through their own advancin' troops to git 'em."

"Congreve rockets screamed red rainbows at us through the fog. Thousands o' Redcoats steppin' to their drum cadence come straight at us American *Dirty Shirts.* Before British troops got in musket range, Andy's boomin' long rifles felled rank after rank -- like the scythe o' the Grim Reaper. When they reached the canal, Andy's cannon fired canister shot and chain point blank in their faces. British was blowed backards in bloody giblets. We raked their retreat with cavalry attacks. Kept on till the British left the field -- save a wounded drummer boy that kept playin' till Andy's boys come out to tend the wounded."

"Battles is numbers. Over 2,000 British was killed includin' most o' their field grade officers -- 1262 wounded -- 500 captured er missin'. We lost 13 killed, 39 wounded and 20 missin'. European domination of the western hemisphere got its back broke at Chalmette, and Andy shipped the body o' British Commandant, Major General Sir Edward Pakenham, home *butt-up* in a keg o' rum. Treaty o' Ghent was ratified by Congress this month. Can you bleeve that Ghent Treaty was actually signed by all emissaries on Christmas Eve 1814, a fortnight *before* the greatest battle ever fought on this continent."

All but the newspaper editor bellered for a drink to toast the victory, sending William, Milton and Artemis scurrying.

"I notice your tale never gets around to the treason conspiracy with Jackson's long time crony and house guest, Aaron Burr," the editor needled.

"What of it? That treason ruckus was near *ten years* before the Battle o' New Orleans!"

"Well, there's never been a clear resolution of who all was guilty of treason."

"Far's I'm concerned there has. Grand jury right here in Kentucky indicted Aaron Burr fer treason and conspiracy, and attorney Henry Clay beat all them charges."

"Wasn't Henry Clay Andrew Jackson's own personal lawyer?"

"No, Clay represented a tradin' firm that Jackson and I owned. Andy himself was a lawyer and a Judge for many years -- handled all his own legal matters."

"I reported on that federal trial in 1807! It was based on President Jefferson's proclamation of a conspiracy in progress and called for the conspirators' apprehension. Some high American officer was peddling military secrets to the Spanish and planning the destruction of New Orleans as a preliminary to destroying the Union. It wasn't the district's other ranking officer, General Wilkinson! Instead of embracing Aaron Burr, Wilkinson turned Burr over for prosecution. Wilkinson didn't sell those boats to Burr to attack New Orleans. Jackson sold Burr those boats. Maybe you did too."

The giant's jaw muscles writhed under his black beard as

Artemis stepped between the men with a platter of steaming roast beef. Mindful of the dirk in the mammoth storyteller's boot, the circle of patrons began to ease their chairs back.

The giant's eyes flamed, but his voice was steady. "Because of your civilian ignorance of military affairs, you sir, are in the position of takin' a knife to a gunfight. When James Wilkinson got cozy with Benedict Arnold, he was forced to resign in the Conway Cabal. Took a bribe from the Spanish in 1791, then sold Burr out after conspirin' with the Spaniards again. But Wilkinson wasn't any better General than he was a traitor, and his career ended with his despicable Montreal campaign in 1813. By contrast, Andrew Jackson is the most fiercely patriotic American I've ever known. You'd be neck deep in British Infantry right now if Andy hadn't been the savior of the very city you're claimin' he betrayed."

Basking in the unaccustomed attention, the editor retorted, "I don't believe I got your name. The many engagements you've placed yourself in and the events you describe don't fit any single man I'm aware of. Are you some writer who's injected himself into the life and times of Andrew Jackson?"

The editor having challenged the giant as an impostor besides branding him and Andrew Jackson as traitors, Sublette Tavern bystanders edged away from what was certain to be a gory killing.

The giant leaped to his feet. His crouch said any moment he'd lunge forward.

Artemis gripped a pistol under her shawl. William's bullet pouch was clenched sweatily in his fist. Milton grabbed a wrought iron poker from the hearth. Tension hushed all but the peals of thunder.

The behemoth said quietly, "Name's John Coffee -- Brigadier General John Coffee. He bent over the cringing editor's table, "Mr. Avery, if it wasn't for the unwaverin' bravery of General Andrew Jackson, your newspaper would now be Stanford, Kentucky's town crier for King George the Third! Try that fer yer editorial policy, sir! Now, could I trouble you for a pinch er two of that salt for my roast beef?"

CHAPTER 7

ON TO ST. CHARLES SUMMER-FALL 1817

With the 30 acres Mama Isabella inherited from Colonel Whitley and Papa Phillip's Dix River land, 17 year old William Sublette's farm work was eternal. But William's heavy shoulders and brawny arms kept the plow deep and straight, scrolling the rocky sod behind his favorite jenny-mule, Sarah.

The sun'd blackened his face. He'd let his short sandy beard with its blond highlights cover the scar on his chin. His hooked nose made his face hawkish. He'd tied his long wavy hair behind his head with a thong so he could see to plow. He loved the sweet-sour smell of fresh plowed ground. Sarah stopped to drop her water and used hay and ruined the aroma.

Squintin' upward, William decided the sun wasn't high enough to noon no matter what time his stomach thought it was. He peeled the red kerchief off his neck and swabbed sweat from his blue eyes.

William didn't like plowin' this Dix River parcel. It was way too rocky to make a crop like the Colonel's rich black dirt over the hill. But he wouldn't give up on Dix River. Where the plow couldn't bust through the ornery bedrock, he'd let it go to pasture to graze the stock. Wherever he could plow a furrow, William planted corn because it'd stand the limestone run off.

Rein-flickin' Sarah's hip, he rammed the plow through the scraping stones again. Sometimes William talked to Sarah but seldom spoke to men and never said anything to girls. When he wasn't too wore out, he read books on cipherin' and keepin' accounts. But he did a lot o' thinkin' all the time.

Brother Milton was a mystery to William. For weeks, Milton worked the farm like a harness mule. Helped Artemis evenin's at their Tavern when her shoulder got too stove up to hoist them heavy trays. Only 16, Milton was husky enough to manhandle drunks that wouldn't go home at closin' time. But ever so often Milton disappeared for days and wouldn't say where he'd been when he come home. He was gone agin.

William needed a hand with both farms, so he'd asked Andrew. Andrew Sublette was only nine, but like a man he'd quit fishin' and playin' in the swimmin' hole at Crab Orchard Lake to hoe weeds out of the new corn over the hill. Andrew was graveyard-quiet most o' the time. But if anything, Andrew was wilder'n Milton. A wiry boy with wavy hair black as a Indian's, Andrew would fling himself off a 30 foot oak limb to explode in the water. Even Milton wasn't that crazy. Andrew kept fish on the table at home and never got whupped.

The Sublette girls couldn't help William with the farm work. Sophronia jist turned 12 and Polly was almost 11. Both was growin' things that made 'em quit swimmin' in the raw with Andrew. Them girls had their hands full carin' fer little Pinckney and baby Solomon -- what with Mama Isabella ready to birth another baby any minute.

Between tendin' babies, Sophronia and Polly peeled crab apples for jelly, sewed rags together fer braidin' rugs and washed dishes in their Tavern. Sophronia giggled even when she was jist shellin' peas, but Polly seemed like somebody had jist died.

"Bill, I got vittles here that'll stick to your ribs!" Papa Phillip yelled from under the apple trees.

"Give some to Andrew over the hill in the new corn," William yelled back, then *whoa'd* Sarah, took the bit outa her mouth and fitted on her feed bag. Her eyes thanked him. He patted her sweaty neck and checked under her collar with his finger. Her hide was sound. He headed for Papa Phillip across the plowed ground with a two furrow stride.

"Ain't you the big brawny feller, Bill?" Phillip asked looking up at his 6' 2" son.

It made William nervous when his father flattered him

like that. He wondered if Papa'd bought more land for him to mine rocks on.

They sat together under a crab apple tree. Phillip opened a flour sack with faded printin' and removed an embroidered dish towel. While Phillip was spreadin' the towel on the ground, William lurched to his feet. William grabbed the food sack and dangled it in front of the coiled Cottonmouth Moccasin by the tree trunk.

The poisonous viper struck the sack. William's free hand pounced behind the snake's head, then bashed it bloody on the tree trunk. He dropped the writhing snake and ground its battered head under his boot heel till it quit twitchin'.

"I hope this's the over-growed maggot what kilt Seneca!" William gritted through clenched white teeth.

The bulge left Phillip's eyes. He spread their bread, meat, fixin's and cookies on the towel. Blood letting left him shaky. He admired the way William manhandled emergencies like they bored him.

Finally Phillip answered, "I hope it is too. I surely do. Milton's never been the same since Seneca come home with his head all swole up and died of the tremors in Milton's lap. I didn't think nothin' in this cruel world'd make Milton Sublette cry. Nothin'! He didn't even cry the time the Miller boy's rifle went off half cocked and shot his tampin' rod through Milton's thigh! But God Above, did Milt sob over that dead hound! Seen Milton today?"

"Prob'ly around here, Papa," William mumbled. He'd haul the cottonmouth up by the Liberty Pole and bury it on Seneca's grave tonight. He'd take food in case Milton was keepin' vigil. He'd tell Milton Artemis swore this snake kilt Seneca. Artemis was never wrong. She'd know right away it was good and back him up with Milton.

Papa Phillip charged through William's thoughts. "Gotta letchu know what's goin' on, Bill. Eight Million acres of bounty lands is under survey in Missouri and Illinois. Them grants in Missouri is comin' any day now. Editor of that Lexington paper I'm always a writin' to says..." Phillip fished his glasses out and read from a wrinkled letter," '*The prospects for unparalleled prosperity in Missouri are legion.*' "

William gaped in disbelief. He'd slaved for *two years* to make the Dix River land worth keepin'. Now they was jist gonna walk off and leave it! "You gotta wait till Mama has the baby."

Phillip grinned -- Bill Sublette always thought of others first. "No sir! Baby Sally come fer breakfast!"

"What's Mama say bout Missouri?

"Says she's got no more room behind the Tavern. Makes her chafe when customers complains bout baby Solomon hollerin'. She's fixin' to sell that 30 acres you got in corn to her brother Andrew. I tried to peddle this rock quarry to her brother Solomon. But danged if your Uncle Solomon don't wanta go to Missouri with us! Isabella's brother Andrew's gotta partner to buy this parcel too."

William felt helpless. His hard work'd been sold off quicker'n a squirrel could scratch a flea. "Think I'll put up the mule. Me and Andrew'll give that swimmin' hole a try. When're the Sublettes leavin' for Missouri?"

"Soon as I kin draw up the deeds on these two parcels and settle my court cases in Pulaski and Lincoln County."

William intended to frolic inna water with Andrew till dark, but wore out before sundown so they headed home. They tickled their new sister Sally's toes, but didn't wake Mama Isabella, who snored in a deep sleep after two days in labor.

William had to find Milton. He put on dry clothes and headed for Sportsman's Hill with the dead snake in a grain sack. Milton wasn't at Seneca's grave by the Liberty Pole. William was fixin' to bury the snake, when he swung the sack round and round his head and let it go.

A full moon balanced on the horizon like one o' them punkins him and Artemis used to shoot years ago. William scooped a handful of soil from Seneca's grave and let it trickle out on the earth. He waved at the moon and yelled, "The Sublettes do not love the land."

The deed of Isabella's land to her brother Andrew was dated August 4, 1817. The ink was still wet on it when the wagons of the Sublettes and Solomon Whitley rolled west for Missouri with 42 other families.

William took the miserable job, ridin' drag behind their stock on Sarah. It was better'n gettin' sick drivin' one o' them wagons. The wagons were hooped with white tarps over them to protect the furniture and beddin'. William was amazed at the many other columns of wagons goin' west along their same road.

Isabella didn't complain about the caravan's dirty air. Missouri spelled freedom to her. At 43, Isabella Sublette had birthed eight children, one for nearly every two years of her 20 year marriage. She was nursing her last baby ever -- no matter what! She'd be 60 by the time baby Sally got married. She had her own money from the 30 acre land sale. She was prepared to do whatever necessary to protect her exhausted body.

Their wagons rolled through Danville, a big town of 200 homes, half a dozen stores, three factories and a printing office. Isabella remembered her father serving in the Kentucky Legislature at Danville. Tears welled and she kissed baby Sally.

After Danville, the towns began to look like the same pigpen over and over again -- dirty and overcrowded with drunken Indians skulking their outskirts.

An Indian sold them Black Spring Water to ward off swarming mosquitoes. Sarah nearly went crazy from the bites till William wet her hide with the smelly Black Spring Water. Uncle Solomon bought Black Spring Water for starting fires. After that William suffered his fat Uncle's jokes about what would git burnt if somebody decided to light the mule.

Solomon Whitley was different from his father as a gambler from a preacher. Rail-thin Colonel Whitley never cursed, chased loose women, got arrested for fighting or made bad jokes. Fat Uncle Solomon did, bragged about it, and was a glutton for new gambles. Solomon had a knack for making money without working that made him the envy of everybody. Friends called him *Nuggets,* claiming if people threw rocks at him, they'd turn out to be gold.

Solomon's ribald ribbing of William produced an unexpected effect. Milton confided to William and Uncle Solomon that he'd been getting a lot of romantic experience back in Lincoln County -- the reason for his disappearances. It sounded like Milton'd spared no one in his escapades. Solomon exploded in racking laughter that always ended in coughing fits.

Nobody laughed when an irate Welshman from a wagon ahead of the Sublettes braced Papa Phillip with a blued-steel English shotgun, demanding to shoot Milton for trifling with *both* his daughters. Milton, smirking at the Welshman's wrath, made the rest of the trip lying low in Uncle Solomon's wagon.

By mid November, the Sublette's several hundred mile journey ended as it had begun -- in clouds of suffocating dust -- as they rolled into St. Charles, Missouri with their caravan's other trail-weary families. William climbed off his smelly mule, swearin' he'd never make another wagon trip till this mule ran for President.

Turning 18 on the trip, William was a growed man in every sense of the word -- but one. Milton goaded William mercilessly about gittin' him a cell in a convent or enrollin' him in a ladies finishin' school.

The Sublettes were glad to see St.Charles, but it was *not* glad to see them or the hordes of transients flooding this once tranquil French town of 1200.

Papa Phillip bought a newspaper to locate temporary quarters for the eight weeks it'd take the St. Charles bank to verify their new deposit, so they could buy a place. The only rental ad for "ample quarters" was in French, seeking a genteel family to share premises with an old line family of impeccable lineage and manners. He translated the lone rental ad to English for Isabella.

Phillip also read her the newspaper's page one article, "*St. Charles is now crowded with the refuse of Kentucky. Fighting, maiming, blaspheming, thieving, & every specie of riot & outrage are now the order of the day & night.*"

Isabella was furious. "Who do these pompous Frenchies think they are?"

Phillip bowed deeply, "*C'est moi, mon petite chou.*"

He hated divulging his fluency in French or his Huguenot heritage, but he was no longer in Kentucky where provincials would be prejudiced against him as a foreigner. The Sublettes could not hibernate in their wagons for two months through the coming snows while their bank drafts cleared.

Phillipe Sublette had himself outfitted at Godoine's Haberdashery by a French tailor sporting a thin moustache. During the fitting, *Phillipe* practiced his Virginia French on the small dark man with the flying pins. The tailor collected his bill in cash, promising to have *Phillipe's* clothes ready by close of business -- then added in English, "Phillip, if you can get the cotton bowls out of your vowels, I think you will pull it off!"

Next day, *Phillipe* met Monsieur Pierre Perrault, advertiser of the "ample quarters" at his ramshackle home. This French aristocrat, and proud father of three adorable daughters, pressed *Phillipe* relentlessly for any ties to Bonaparte's revolutionists until at last absolving him of that taint.

Phillipe grudgingly admitted to having *seven* children and a portly brother-in-law who smoked cigars. Only then did Perrault permit *Phillipe* to see the lease specifying a monthly rental four times its reasonable value with three months rent payable in advance and no stable privileges. *Phillipe* handed the lease back to the irritable Perrault and stumbled to the veranda to overcome his shock.

Phillipe calculated they'd have to sell one of their wagons and who knows what else to come up with Perrault's ransom money. *Phillipe* was about to tell his would-be landlord to do something anatomically impossible with the Perrault *chateau* when a carriage drew up. Several well dressed gentry alighted. Perrault had raised and called. *Phillipe* folded and executed the exorbitant lease.

Phillip Sublette paced his rented stallion glacially, rehearsing his explanation to Isabella how he'd omitted mention of one child, namely Milton, and signed a lease for some back rooms costing as much in advance rent for three months as they expected to pay to buy a whole house in St. Charles, Missouri.

The answer came to Phillip riding past the court house. The Sublettes would stay at Perrault's long as they had to, then move out and file a lawsuit charging fraud to get their money back. He spurred the strange stallion, was nearly thrown and barely regained his composure before reaching the wagons.

Phillip decided to practice his presentation on Isabella's brother Solomon Whitley, who would soon reside at Perrault's.

He was nearly through the painful yarn, when Solomon, seated like the Great Buddha, grunted, "It's enough to buy that run down dump twice, Phillip, but here's my half."

"Solomon, could you possibly loan Isabella and myself the other half for a brace of months? And I do believe we should spend a few *francs* to put Milton up in a hotel until we're fully settled in. Fathers of nubile daughters sweat uncontrollably at the mere sight of Milton."

"Yes I know."

"You do?"

"C'mon, Phillip I was there when the irate Welshman was gonna pepper you with quail shot! From what you say, not only should we use Milton for a hole-card for a few days, but I might set this Perrault off -- not exactly being the soul of propriety myself. Let's send good old *dull* William over there to unload our wagons. We'll all be in there with the rent paid by the time Perrault loses his self control. It's the only house we can get."

"No wonder, they call you *Solomon*! Your plan's nothing if not wise."

"Here's the money, Phillip but why are you talking like a clam digger on stilts?"

William Sublette was allowed to begin unloading the Sublette and Whitley wagons only after Pierre Perrault had taken the Sublette rental coin to the bank, verified its value and learned in confidence of the deposits awaiting confirmation from Lexington, Kentucky.

Overheated by the noonday sun, William pulled off his heavy shirt. His shiny muscles rippled as he lugged a trunk in from Solomon's wagon.

Flashing-eyed, 20 year old Monique Perrault, watching William from her bedroom window, gasped and pinched her sister Annette's cheek in maidenly delight. Rubbing her cheek, Annette dashed out the side door to get their youngest sister, Fifi, from her job at Godoine's so Fifi could also see this Adonis bearing great burdens into the Perrault home.

The moment she'd dispatched her filial competition, Monique let out her small yipping dog, then rushed pellmell to retrieve it.

"I do hope my guard animal did not terrify you all over," Monique said in her best finishing school English.

Normally, William would have been tongue-tied at sight of this beauty with dark bouncy curls and a smile that could kill, but her English made him chuckle.

"Well, not *all* over," he grinned showing her the whitest teeth she'd ever seen in a man's mouth."

The radiant French girl stared at his gleaming teeth.

"What's the matter?" William asked, lifting a lead-heavy, rolled up carpet. Without waiting for the answer, he shouldered the rug and staggered for the door. The rug seemed to get lighter as he went. When he dropped it in their largest room, Monique barely let go of her end of the rug in time.

She adored his naive surprise. She brushed the dirt from his shoulder and chest, then kissed him full on the mouth. She backed away. "Not like a boy so little. Open you mouth." He did and she put another kiss into it with warm, searching extras he'd never even heard of. This must be what it was like when a feller lost his mind. William watched her swirl through the doorway down the dark hall and wondered if he dared follow with them two wagons out there still needin' to be unloaded 'fore sundown.

CHAPTER 8

CONSTABLE ONE PUNCH   FALL 1817-SPRING 1823

Strangely, the "piratical" lease ran its course with nothing more chaotic than Pierre Perrault screaming insults in French at Solomon Whitley for drunkenly fumbling at the wrong door. But Solomon and the Sublettes were sent packing at lease's end. Even stranger, no litigation ensued, because Phillip and Pierre learned to hate each other with a grain of admiration.

Though 1817's winter was mild by Missouri standards, it froze the tide of emigrants long enough for the Sublettes to buy a town house with lot and stable on reasonable terms.

The halted flow of hated emigrants had an odd effect on the irate inhabitants of St. Charles. It made them *more* irate, because the flow of "rabble" money these noble Frenchmen had come to know and love was constricted to a trickle. The saving grace was that they got to curse the "rabble" for choking off prosperity without having to endure their impertinence.

But French Monique Perrault had no such ill feelings for emigrant William Sublette, whose father spoke the crippled French. Her own father had spent years convincing her she was Galatea incarnate -- the legendary statue carved by Pygmalion and given life by Aphrodite in response to the sculptor's prayer.

Monique's clandestine meetings with young William meant more to her than the food she ate or the air she breathed. Besides being a statuesque beauty with flawless complexion and naturally curly hair, Monique was an accomplished astronomer and shared her knowledge of the stars with him. He was as captivated by the idea of celestial navigation as he was by her.

While most St. Charles girls were deliberately deprived of education, Pierre Perrault told Monique of the 15th century's Nicholaus Copernicus, and 16th century contemporaries Galileo and Kepler. In turn she introduced these visionaries who'd conceived the geocentric notions of the Solar System to William.

Just before 1817's Christmas Pierre listened in appalled silence to his half-brother's rumors that "a Perrault girl" was trysting with "one of the Sublette boys." After mulling over the possibilities, Pierre guessed Monique must be the daughter and the Sublette boy, witless William. Perrault must save Monique before she even thought of marrying this Anglo Protestant ox.

Always compensating for his delicate size with finesse, Pierre's youth was spent as a matador in Spain. He'd salvaged enough from bull fighting purses to emigrate to St. Charles while it was still under Spanish rule. With half-brother Godoine, Perrault opened their garment store. On the few occasions he'd done a fitting on a patron, he'd stifled the urge to use the pins like a picador. All the same, his earlier calling had fostered his sense of exactly when to belay the cape and thrust the sword.

Perrault's plan would have been stillborn if he'd tried exiling Monique alone to Paris. Monique's vulnerability lay in her instinctive protection of her younger sisters. Deftly, he convinced Monique to rescue sister Annette from the baleful ignorance of Missouri and become her guardian against the depredations of the gentry in Paris, where she and Annette would attend university together.

William Sublette spirited Monique out for a secret night sleigh ride. They kissed and whispered while the frosty air sparkled about them, clear as the jingles of the harness bells. They halted atop a hummock overlooking the winking lights of St. Charles. Monique pushed the buffalo robe aside and stood up. Raising her arms to the sky, she murmured, "I give you the stars for our memoirs. Remember Polaris -- the North Star -- right there? It will guide you when I cannot." He didn't understand then why Monique cried all the way home.

Monique suddenly vanished, but not before giving him a grand sense of being a man. Their moments could never be shared with anybody, no matter how he needed to overcome her loss.

Monique and Annette were Parisians by the time Pierre Perrault saw William Sublette working at the Sublette's ferry landing on the Mississippi during 1818's spring thaw. Perrault felt he should have taken two ears and a tail from this big ox of the backwoods. How easily he had bested this ignorant bull!

Phillip Sublette never got his shoulder into his sporadic ferry business. Traffic across the Mississippi could swell to 50 wagons and 500 folks a day, bringing a cash flow like the river -- then dwindle to a wet spot in the road. Phillip felt him and the boys coulda done better herdin' quail, another flighty business.

News in 1818 was like the ferry business, all good or all bad. Passengers rejoiced when Andrew Jackson conquered Florida in a few weeks. Milton and William asked people if General Coffee's cavalry fought agin the *Seminoles* and "hated Dons," in the swamps, but nobody knew.

People despised Congress when it spent more time trying Jackson's actions in commencing the *Seminole* War on his own, than the Florida war itself had taken. Congress finally approved all Andy's conduct, and he was mobbed by adoring Americans wherever he went.

When Phillip heard Britain and the U.S. had signed the Joint Oregon Occupation Agreement of 1818, he was sure there'd be a rush of American emigrants across the Mississippi. Then he read in the *Missouri Gazette* it was absolutely impossible for wagons to reach Oregon. There were no roads, no bridges, no usable maps, and a grand excess of hostiles. The Great American Desert was impenetrable to wagons. W.J. Snelling, who'd wintered with the *Sioux*, wrote that even Indians perished from famine in between burning off the prairies twice a year. More ferry business lost before it was found! Phillip knew things would get better. They always did.

Spain sold Florida to the U.S. in 1819 for a third of what the U.S. paid France for the Louisiana Purchase. But the Second National Bank's tightened monetary policy strangled the nation, bringing panic and depression. The 1819 Panic sank Sublettes' ferry. Milton was glad because it got "me and Bill outa the Navy!"

Phillip was forced to run to the arms of his real love -- operating a tavern in his home after Morgan Swope put up the seed money in 1819. No sooner opened, Sublette's tavern was the community meeting place.

With most tavern arguments, there'd be a flail, then everybody'd lose interest. Not so with Missouri's claim that it was entitled to admission to the Union as a slave state -- which would tip the Senate majority to slave states. Whenever that argument went past the first minute, fist fights were certain to follow as colored leaves in the fall. Phillip was being considered for Justice of the Peace again, so he ducked Missouri statehood discussions by stepping into the storeroom with Artemis.

As a father, Phillip never showed favoritism between his eldest sons. But when it came to keeping order in the tavern, he liked 19 year old Bill ten to one over Milton. At 6' 4" 18 year old Milton was two inches taller and a more savage fighter, but he didn't know people like Bill did. Milton would pick a man out of a bar brawl and beat him bloody, like it was real personal.

Bill calmed brawlers by bein' quiet and impersonal -- kinda like herdin' sheep. But if anybody hit Bill too hard, he'd drop 'em like a hammer-hit steer, and the nickname *One Punch* came to mean *Bill Sublette* in St. Charles, Missouri.

Mama Isabella Sublette deplored their tavern violence. She feared some vicious fool would cripple her boys. She smiled for the first time in months when Phillip was appointed Justice of the Peace *on his own* in 1819, even though he couldn't start serving until settlement of personal litigation. As she wrote of Phillip's judgeship to Mother Esther, she dearly wished her father had lived to see it. She also told of her brother Solomon's good fortune in St. Charles and that he'd soon be home to get his wife and six children for return to this land of opportunity.

It seemed to Judge Phillip Sublette that tavern donnybrooks over statehood would soon be bad memories. Maine's application for statehood enabled Congress to pass the Missouri Compromise on March 6, 1820, admitting Maine to the union as a free state and Missouri a slave state. But Missouri foiled Henry Clay's solution by passing a state constitution excluding free blacks from the state.

St. Charles got rowdier. William's reputation as a peacemaker prompted Constable Osborn Knott to appoint him as deputy, soon serving his father's court process. On his first arrest, he missed the knife in a half-breed's boot. The jailer spied it and bellered for William's firing. Constable Knott made William carry the blade between his teeth for a week. After that a Sublette pat-down was like a cipherin' audit. He even unearthed a stubby Hawken pistol tied in a prisoner's topknot.

Ever since the Sublettes yanked their farmland out from under him in Kentucky, William'd wanted his own land. In the summer of 1820, he leased 200 arpents of timberland and got even brawnier turning trees into fence rails when he wasn't on court business.

However burly his body, William was crushed by Papa Phillip Sublette's death three days after Christmas 1820. William was amazed that Papa, three times a sitting Judge, left no Will.

Phillip's funeral during a heavy freeze was attended only by family. As Phillip's icy coffin was lowered into a frosty grave in the tiny Protestant cemetery, Mama Isabella leaned against William and sobbed, "Why Phillip -- when we still have all the children to bring up in this desolate place? What's going to happen to us?" With dry snowflakes clinging to her face, Mama Isabella looked a hundred years old to William, though he knew she was barely 46.

"Mama, what do you hear?" William asked, his voice quavering.

"Nothing."

"That's right, Mama. Papa's silent. He's finally at peace," William whispered.

She brought her clenched hands to her lips that were blue with cold. She tried to speak but could only weep.

William guided her unsteady walk through the blowin' snow toward their home full o' little children. It killed him to hear this brave woman cry. He clamped his cold hands over his ears, but he could still hear her.

Milton crunched through the snow to catch up and put his arm around her. They walked together into the soft whiteness moundin' the stones and fences of the graveyard. Milton glanced back at the black hole in the snow that had swallered Papa and asked himself if it was hungry fer Mama Isabella too.

Phillip's net estate was valued at only $153.25, so William and Milton worked all the harder to feed and clothe the other six children. Both had grown into large, powerful, fine looking men, but they could only hold down so many jobs. No one ordered fence rails while the ground was frozen too hard for digging post holes.

Morgan Swope struggled to run the tavern with Artemis. Her shoulder was stiffer in the winter and so was her drinking. Without Phillip Sublette, it was a tomb. There was no tavern party when Missouri achieved statehood August 10, 1821 after amending its constitution to allow free blacks in the state.

Mama Sublette choked down calomel, sulfur, elixir and bitters, but nothing helped. She made son Bill kneel and promise to take care of his brothers and sisters as long as they lived. The doctor increased her dosages and bleedings, but on the gray morning of January 22, 1822, Isabella Sublette did not stir. She'd lived barely a year after Phillip's death. Sophronia dressed her for burial because William couldn't. During a lull in the blizzard, the sobbing Sublettes buried Mama Isabella beside her beloved Phillip, uniting them in death for eternity with neither meager grave stone paid for.

The day after losing Mama Isabella, William waited by their old Mississippi ferry dock, watching the river bubble under the lacy ice at the edge. He'd had the papers inside his coat drawn at the courthouse. He turned sensing Artemis would be there in the snow. She said, "Little Sally died bout 20 minutes ago. Like yo Mama an' yo Papa, Sally got somethin' bad wrong in the chest. Maybe you got it too, Little Bill."

"I don't have nothin' wrong with my chest, Artemis. You're the one with the bad shoulder, but I got somethin' here that's gonna make you better."

"I know what you got an' I don't want it, Little Bill. You got to sell me to pay fer all them grave stones."

"They said in their Wills, just like George Washington did, you're to go free, Artemis, and you're gonna go free. Even Missouri's ready for free blacks."

"Little Bill, Phillip Sublette didn't leave no Will. They aint nothin' in Isabella's bout me neither."

"You callin' me a liar, Artemis?" he glared fiercely as he could at this graying black woman who'd raised him from a pup.

"I sho, am, Little Bill. Now you gonna hit me with that

bullet pouch in dat big right hand?"

"No, Artemis. I'm gonna hit you with that freedom all around where you're standin'. Take this paper to Morgan Swope at the tavern. Tell him whatever was Phillip's is now yours by order of this other paper right here. You take what Morgan gives you. Set up your own place, and Artemis, lay off the grog -- just lay off and git a new start."

"Where my gonna do dat, Little Bill?"

"Any place you want Artemis! Gimme a hug and go."

"I'm goin' and I aint givin' you no hug."

"You gimmee a hug every time you look at me, Artemis. You cain't help it. Now git on outa here! If there's one thing I can't stand, it's a uppity nigger."

"If you cain't stand no uppity nigger, how come you cryin', Little Bill?"

He couldn't answer her because his throat was fulla howl. He pointed for her to go. When he turned, Artemis was gone, so he just sat and cried for a while. Her loss was the last straw.

* * *

William was still a Deputy Constable, but his pay wouldn't feed a barge rat. Neither would his rail business. Having become a penniless orphan in charge of a family of penniless orphans, William begged Uncle Solomon Whitley to take Andrew, Pinckney and Solomon. For all his ribald ways, Solomon Whitley was a warm hearted man. He'd loved Isabella to the end. Now he loved what remained of her in these three boys. They cried and he hugged them as his sleigh left young Bill forlornly standing in the ice-ridged road.

William had it worse with the Girls. With little Sally dyin' almost on Mama's grave, they was scairt to death. They clung to him, moanin' and beggin' him to remember his promise to Mama. Holdin' back his tears, he said he was carin' for them by gettin' Mama's married sister, Levisa McKinney and her husband James to take Sophronia and Polly.

But Milton went haywire, losin' one job after another, usually for toyin' with somebody's woman or knockin' slobber outa the man who found out about it. By April 1822, Milton Sublette was desperate. After readin' the newspaper ad of some fur outfit that'd pay $200 a year for hunters, he eased into the courthouse. William heard Milton out as he sorted papers at his desk. "I guess you don't wanta try cuttin' logs into rails now that the ground's thawed."

"Naw Bill. I had about all this St. Charles merriment I kin take for a while." Milton sat so he could see his reflection in the window. Milton had pulled his hair tight behind his head the way Bill wore his hair when he plowed.

Milton confessed, "I had eyes for that little Fifi Perrault after we moved in with those Frenchie Gumbos. Tried to coax Fifi to the loft a dozen times. Thought it'd be easier'n droppin' a hot rock once her sisters tuck off fer France. But I never got no place with that little gal! Tell ya what though. Ole man Perrault was *so* nasty, I'm gonna give him a little goin' away present fore I go up the Missouri with Ashley and Henry."

"Milt, don't rile Perrault. Last time I seen eyes like his was on that cottonmouth that kilt Seneca."

True to his word, the last thing Milton did before he boarded Major Henry's keelboat was to stop by Godoine's around noon and give Fifi Perrault a long and very public kiss on her angry rosebud mouth.

Less than a month after Milton went up the Missouri, William Sublette was appointed Chief Constable. The pay was still a pittance. For a short time William thought he might get his father's old job of Justice of the Peace, but he was only 22 and the appointment went to a man twice his age.

William got re-elected Chief Constable August 5, 1822, then come to the realization he was riskin' his life daily in St. Charles for next to nothin'. He kept watchin' boat loads of fur worth thousands floatin' down the Missouri for storage in warehouses along the levee over in St. Louis. He read about the hefty prices them furs brought. A right smart fur trapper'd make a hunnert times more'n a Constable er even a lawyer. But William wasn't one to back away from a job. He vowed to stick out his elected term as Chief Constable.

By the spring of '23 he was as sick of starvin' in St. Charles as Milton was last year when he'd lit out for the mountains. Then William spied an ad in the *Missouri Gazette* for 100 men to ascend the Missouri to the Rocky Mountains as hunters for $200 a year for Ashley and Henry. William hadn't heard from Milton but was sure that was his brother's outfit.

William got that floaty feelin' Papa Phillip always talked about fore he started the family on one o' his grand moves -- a feelin' everything was gonna git better. Before the feelin' wore off, William handed his resignation to the clerk of the township. It made the newspaper, and the editor wanted St. Charles to offer *Constable One Punch* more money. By now, more money wouldn't do it.

Constable One Punch sold his only asset, a bed, at auction for one dollar, then returned to the courthouse and turned in his badge.

Having read that William Sublette was resigning to join the fur trade, Pierre Perrault steeled himself to do the unthinkable. He managed to catch William Sublette leaving the courtroom for the last time.

"Constable Sublette..."

"Ex-Constable, Mr. Perrault," he corrected, pointing to the empty place on his shirt. William watched Perrault's hands in case he pulled a gun to get even for the situation with Monique.

"As you wish. I have done a grave injustice at you."

William was astounded. "What's that, Mr. Perrault?"

"I have send Monique away to Paris because I think you was being the -- the husband to her. Since then, I have seen with my own several eyes that it was your *brother* putting himself to Monique's *sister* Fifi! It was wrong also upon Monique, for in Paris, she marry to a worthless student. I'm bad sorry, Mr. Sublette! I did not know you brother's evil reputation prior to what I do. You a good dog of the law. I salute you!"

Before William could digest Monique's marriage, Perrault saluted him and dashed out the courtroom door.

William leaped the railing in front of the Bench, bulled out the courtoom door into the sunlight, sprinted past the startled Perrault and never looked back.

CHAPTER 9

AROUND THE BEAVER POND EARLY 1823

The sickliest snowstorm of 1823 began as a puny thing that kept losing its way among the Black Hills. It's weak winds were barely able to rustle the cedar branches. The storm nearly broke up in a box canyon, but a quick temperature drop energized it. It bansheed through Hell's Canyon into the Powder River Basin, driving animals to cover. It snowed respectably, then played into the hands of a pale sun in the late afternoon.

The storm had been too frail to freeze the sparkling creek darting through the willow thickets to feed the beaver pond. Once inside the pond, the creek fanned out and drifted into deep water. The crystal waters harbored trout, frogs and a family of beavers packing their snow capped lodge near the pond's heart with tasty twigs. The beavers' sentry watched for otters and weasels that devoured their kits. The pond's surface reflected snow-crested mountains where glaciers relived the Ice Age.

Dislodged by an enormous creature crashing through the willows, starry snowflakes fell as halos in the orange sunset to melt instantly on the pond. The sentry tail-slapped her warning, then darted through the beaver lodge's submerged entrance.

Two yearling beavers fled the massive beast cracking the willows like dry bones. The female escaped into the maze of red rocks bulging through the light snow. The skinny male dropped the gnawed branch he dragged in long yellow teeth. Scanning the ground between himself and the pond, he saw no reason for the pond alarm. He scampered through the snow toward a stand of scrub pines, leaving small front tracks scratch connected to large web-footed ones with a center-dragging tail track.

A sleek female puma, kicking snow, glided from the shadows of the scrub pine to head off the scurrying youngster. In a graceful, floating leap, she straddled the scrawny male beaver and clamped her jaws behind his head. She crushed his neck, then devoured his thin body except for one hind leg and his tail, which jerked about in the bloody snow.

The puma's lustrous head rose. Her terra-cotta nostrils flared as she tested the chill air, jutting occasional plumes of warm fog. Most of her information came from smells. But the wind blew from her toward the pond, so she learned nothing of what its scents might offer.

Crystal snow jewels settled into the velvet fur of her face, melting at once to dew drops. From her nose to the tip of her tail she was six feet long and weighed nearly a hundred pounds. Miniature zephyrs wiggled the long whiskers sprouting from dark patches on both sides of her white muzzle.

Her luminous golden eyes inspected the scrub pines behind her. She flicked the collecting dew from the flared hairs inside her small black ears. An icy wind teased tan guard hairs along her tawny back and swirled in the white fur adorning her under body. Her distended breasts said she had young. Her slender tan tail with its black tip undulated thoughtfully, as if it were making the decision to call her mewing cub out of the brush to join her for its tiny part of the beaver kill.

The regal lady puma was a prime specimen of *Felis concolor hippolestes*. She'd never seen man. She knew herself as Keesigh, a love call she'd taken down when she and her own body spring had the go away so long before now.

Except for biannual stints with her cubs, she was a solitary animal. Her only contacts with the sire of her cub occurred during a delicious, passionate, burning fortnight when she was in estrus. That was her doing. She'd started the hot love time by leaving her scent on scrapes -- piles of debris she'd made with her paw, then scented with urine and her propagation glands -- irresistible to a lone ranging male.

Her memories of her lover faded each day. She harbored but a hazy vision of his beautiful broad face and strong fangs --

the power of his body -- the dreamy joy of not caring about dangers. He was gone. In fact, if she saw him now, she'd attack him to protect her cub.

Keesigh's life centered around her young. She'd purr and nurse each cub pleasurably at her warm belly and gradually teach them to eat meat. Then she'd teach them to hunt for a couple of years until her own instincts forced her to disown them, so she could begin the birth cycle over again.

Like most large cats, Keesigh was crepuscular, using her exquisite night vision to hunt at dawn or twilight when her prey was also hunting or seeking water. And like all flesh eating predators, Keesigh's life was hunger driven. This skinny beaver had barely taken the edge off her ravenous appetite. She'd trotted most of the rocky, broken terrain in her 30 square mile range in the past 10 days. Deer were climbing into the high country. The only buck she'd seen was nearly ten times her size and wanted to fight. She'd skirted that by leaping up a pine tree.

A herd of spry antelope had outrun her. An antelope had to be old or hurt for her to catch it. It was going to be a spring of rabbits, squirrels, skunks and porcupines for the high country cougar and her cub.

Eating porcupines was dangerous. She could flip them onto their back and gut their quill-free bellies. Her digestive system could even soften and pass the quills. But if the quills blinded her eyes, she could not hunt. Likewise if they pierced her face or neck and festered, she could be impeded enough to fail on other kills and die of starvation. Grizzly bears, wolves, coyotes, full grown lynx and even other pumas, would be eager to kill her or her cub to satisfy their own frenetic appetites. If she wasn't injured or killed, she'd live up to 15 summers.

She wasn't always sure which plants and berries to eat between prey kills. A wrong choice could leave her too sick to function or end her life. She ate vegetation only when hunger drove her insane.

Keesigh was a creature of the present with vague recollections of the past and little concept of the future. Her mind dealt in images and sensory impressions, basically without language except for a few calls she exchanged with her young.

Before now, as her two cubs suckled her milk in the

warm darkness, Keesigh purred the body spring call, Lamal, for her girl cub. She purred Pantuk for the male urine smell cub, but she saw a flashing image of Pantuk's ear part wet with coyote stinks. Keesigh felt more warm to Pantuk than warm to cub Lamal, but Pantuk came to her no more. Only Lamal remained.

Cub Lamal, left hungry under a scrub pine, waited for her body spring's call to share hot smelling meat. Lamal's hungry belly rebelled against more waiting. The cub headed for where her body spring crouched over the food.

Windblown snow flurried across the stiffening grasses. Cub Lamal blinked as the snow tickled her blue eyes and flecked her dark rosette spots and ringed tail. A dried leaf stuck to Lamal's tail and dragged noisily along the ground as she neared her body spring.

Sounds from the dragging leaf pinned Keesigh's ears flat to her head. She wheeled and cuffed cub Lamal. Lamal squealed, submissively dropping her belly to the ground. Keesigh boxed Lamal again. Lamal cried. Keesigh nosed the last of the scrawny beaver parts to her cub. Lamal chewed the leg with its webbed foot, but ignored the large flat tail which Keesigh relished as a delicacy. Keesigh licked Lamal's back fur as the cub gnawed the beaver leg.

Remnants of the errant snowstorm merged into the eternal clouds that swathed the mountains in their cold glory. The sun caught on the tip of a snowy peak and spewed brilliant gold streaks across the carmine and mauve firmament.

Keesigh led her cub toward the beaver pond, circling to the side bordered by willows for better cover. Keesigh tested the wind again as it blew past her toward the pond. The dark hunt time would come soon. She'd hide in the willows beside the water and wait for thirsty prey.

A huge owl hooted. The fur between the shoulders of the fiercely maternal puma was rankled. She crouched over her cub, ears back and fangs parted until the great owl swooped into the adjoining canyon. Cautiously, she forded the creek with Lamal, who paddled, when the cold water got too deep for her short legs with their broad pads. Keesigh led her playful cub toward the willows growing out into the shallows at the edge of the beaver pond.

Keesigh surveyed the pond for signs of more easy beaver kills. The beavers' musky body smells mixed with the welcome smell of the pond water. But the beaver lodge was too far out in the water for Keesigh to attack. Besides, with the mud hardened over the lodge's sticks, she knew she couldn't rip into the lodge. At first Keesigh made out the dark hump of another beaver lodge in the shallow water just offshore from the willow thickets, but then her light-dazzled eyes told her it was only a big rock.

The beaver pond melted into molten glass as it gave the sky back to itself in flaming colors. The surface was motionless except for rivulets of skyfire trickling over the spillways in the beaver dam. The snow storm had silenced the hordes of mosquitoes that would ordinarily be swarming near the water. Keesigh lowered her trim muzzle to the water, then crouched low enough to lap its wetness into her mouth. The reflecting sun blinded her overly sensitive eyes for a moment.

The nine foot grizzly exploded from his long-practiced big rock simulation, drenching Keesigh and Lamal with icy water. Keesigh screamed, instinctively throwing her body, claws out and fangs bared, between the grizzly and her cub.

Keesigh's spine snapped under the smash of the grizzly's forepaw, and she went under. The grizzly, towering over the sunken bones of his many prior victims, crushed Keesigh's neck in his massive jaws.

Goaded by centuries of inbred ferocity, the cub charged into the bloody water to fight for her kind.

The grizzly stopped dismembering Keesigh long enough to rip Lamal's upper lip half off with a swipe of its five clawed forepaw. The monstrous blow catapulted the bloody cub into a pile of dead branches left at lakeside by the beavers. She whimpered, then rolled on her side, but made no more sound.

Roaring its mountain thunder, the scar-covered grizzly fell upon Keesigh's body, ripping away mouthfuls of fur and flesh.

CHAPTER 10

UP THE MISSOURI   FEBRUARY- MARCH 1823

Surveying paid well, but after two years of laying out townships isolated in Illinois's wilderness, James Clyman relished the wild scrapping St. Louis waterfront. With all the commotion on the levee, the slender six footer couldn't believe shipping was stalled till the river pilots could steer through the ice break-up of the 1822-23 winter.

Though he was 31, it was Clyman's first glimpse of shipping facilities that were cities in themselves. Clyman yelled, "William Ashley?" at a man in a visored blue cap reading wind whipped papers tacked to a big swaying board.

The icy wind snatched Clyman's words, but the man jerked a thumb toward a counting room. Inside, a sallow clerk scribbled directions. He looked enviously at Clyman's ornate rifle, then grunted, "These'll gitcha to Ashley's house."

Clyman's blackened buckskins and blanket capote marked him a backwoodsman to all he met. But that wasn't why the townspeople gawked. During the War of 1812 a *Shawnee's* rifle barrel bashed out four upper teeth on the right side, giving Clyman a perpetual leer, though he seldom actually smiled. Most figured he was sneering at them. Their overlong stares irked him, but he learned to stare back impassively. High cheek bones and craggy forehead heightened his rough look.

As Clyman wended between mudholes in the St. Louis streets, his wilderness instincts evaluated every place he intended to step, injecting a pause in the midst of each stride.

Lamps yellowed one window after another as Clyman penetrated St. Louis civilization. Their warm glow heightened his loneliness. At Ashley's stately home, a carriage horse stomped its shod hooves at the hitchrack in the sideyard. Clyman padded silently onto the porch and knocked. A black servant admitted him and left him in the entry way.

James Clyman could hear a fireplace, but couldn't feel its warmth. The nattily dressed man striding so militarily toward him with his bold chin stuck out was 3 inches shorter and ten years older than Clyman, but weighed his 140 pounds.

"I'm General William Ashley." Ashley's steel gray eyes gave his lean guest a brutally thorough search.

Clyman didn't flinch. "James Clyman. Surveyor by training, but here on the hunter job you advertised, Mr. Ashley."

"*General* Ashley. Can you come back?"

"Mebee."

Ashley felt Clyman disappearing. "Being Lieutenant Governor of Missouri means signing bales of papers. My morbid curiosity prompts me to read a few now and again. Can you hold still a minute till we can talk?"

"Where?" James Clyman wasn't intentionally rude with his curt replies. He was always cool on a first meeting.

Ashley jutted his prominent chin at the sitting room, and Clyman eased inside. Leaning his rifle in the corner where he could watch it, he pulled off his capote, and got a whiff of himself. He was gamy enough to make a dog dash to an outhouse for a breath of fresh air.

Poised over the fancy red mohair couch, Clyman eyed his black-blacks. His buckskins didn't start off filthy. Three year ago they were new grainy-gold deerhides. But greasy hands wiped after eating, bloody hands wiped after skinning and living in them 24 hours a day, befouled them to greasy, bloody, shiny black. He dropped his capote on the couch and sat on it.

As General Ashley signed each official document, a clerk in a high collared white-shirt sanded the ink to dry it. Ashley contrasted the clerk's sterile starched shirt with Clyman's reeking buckskins and considered asking them to swap clothes, generating a bemused smile that wilted to a frown.

Ashley needed 200 men like Clyman by next month or

the Ashley & Henry keelboats, *Rocky Mountains* and *Yellow Stone Packet,* would be frozen at the levee long after the ice melted. Delays might mean missing the trapping season. Coupled with capsizing that boatload of supplies last spring, a delay could sink their partnership into bankruptcy. "That's all for today, gentlemen." He showed them the front door with a thrust of his chin, then marched toward the sitting room.

Before entering, General Ashley straightened his coat and smoothed down the hair he combed across his bald spot. He knew just the mien he wanted and assumed it. He strolled into the sitting room looking bored, but mildly inquisitive.

Clyman asked, "When's your outfit launching up river?"

"Early March to get in a trapping season before fall freezes."

"Thanks," Clyman said resignedly, rising to his feet.

"What's your hurry? Beaver's bringing $5 the pound. Might offer you a sweetener."

"Too soon. Been two years surveying Illinois's backwoods. Down here to get my pay and have a fling." Balancing his treasured rifle in one palm, he padded for the door.

Ashley stifled his desperation. "Look me up when you've tamed the tiger." This surveyor had to be vulnerable, if he could get him talking. "Look like you served in the Indian campaigns."

Ashley's brilliant shot in the dark hit Clyman dead center. "Served under Colonel Hamilton in Illinois!" Clyman smelled a stratagem but didn't mind. The bond between men daring death together in war was harder cleaved than the Gordian Knot.

"Major Henry and I fought the Indian campaigns in Illinois."

"General, you'll do to ride the river with!"

"I'll need 200 men for that voyage, Mr. Clyman."

"And have them you shall! Where's a man look?"

"Grog shops -- brothels -- graves if the body's still warm." Popping his gold watch open, Ashley saw William Sublette was due. He recalled appointing Sublette's father Justice of the Peace in St. Charles. "What's your price, Mr. Clyman?"

"Dollar a day if I recruit your 200 men."

"One down when you sign this Sublette boy! His brother Milton's trapping with Major Henry on the Yellowstone. Dollar a day's yours if you sign 200 by March first. That's nigh four weeks. Do it, and you'll clerk for the season at $1 per day. That's double hunters' pay. As a surveyor, you must have a degree."

"I do."

"What college?"

"University of the Wilderness."

"Have a diploma?"

"I *am* the diploma. Fact I'm here's proof of graduation."

Clyman's wit tickled him. "You're quick enough to clerk for me. I like a Virginia accent. Lost mine after all these years in Missouri."

"Well, General, since you've tasked me like Falstaff, I'll enlist ten score of ribald rascals ere the month is out!"

"Falstaff -- wasn't he the clever knight from Shakespeare's *Merry Wives of Windsor* -- or was he in *Henry IV*?"

"Both, General!" James Clyman chortled.

Watching Clyman's wry face twist all the more in mirth, General Ashley broke the ropes on his booming laugh. He hadn't been this giddy since his beloved wife Mary died two years ago. Jousting with this spindly knight in buckskins impersonating Shakespeare's fat Falstaff was hilarious fare!

"Worst part o' having me for clerk is my spelling's sweet as a grizzly's breath."

The General groaned, "Long as your numbers add up!"

William Sublette knew he'd picked the wrong house when roars of laughter busted through its walls. Leaning into the window's light, he verified the address on his recommendation letter from St. Charles. His booming knock brought teary-eyed General Ashley to the door.

"C'mon in. I'm General Ashley. You'd be William Sublette, and this sad fellow is James Clyman."

Sublette crushed their hands in turn. Both took stock of the 6' 2" Sublette. Ashley saw a statuesque man with icy blue eyes -- Jackson-faced -- long sandy hair in waves to his neck. A chin scar peeked through a curly, straw-hued beard. Sublette was an overbright oil painting with the carriage of a man who knew what to do. Only time would tell if he did.

Skinny James Clyman envied the young fellow's bulging muscle. Sublette's big square hands'd fit plow handles. Bullock like him'd be slow and clumsy. Too handsome to be dependable. No telling what he'd do under fire -- but Clyman was now one man closer to signing his 200 -- if this sleek ox could write.

Clyman gasped, "He's big enough to pull a plow. He should haul in the men you need. You're hired!"

The General chuckled. Clyman had no inkling he'd just met *Constable One Punch.*

To Sublette, the string bean's attitude was as irritatin' as his odor, but he took it in stride, realizin' it was some kinda joke. Sublette tucked his recommendation in his pocket. Only showed your hole card if they called.

Clyman grinned, "General, we'll be recruiting at dawn, but tonight we'll catch some catfish on the levee -- "

Knowing he was too broke fer a night on the levee, Sublette shook his head.

"On me!" Clyman added.

"No, on Ashley and Henry, gentlemen."

"Will the General be joining us?" Clyman inquired.

Ashley couldn't afford being seen in a grog shop with 1824's run for governor before him. "Another time, gentlemen."

* * *

February 2nd's dawn found James Clyman waiting in a levee back alley for Sublette. He had enough trouble watching out for himself in a Frenchie Gumbo sewer like this.

"Brought the band wagon," Sublette grated inches behind Clyman, shooting lightning through the spindle-shanked fellow.

Regaining his composure, Clyman muttered, "Let's try that dive an' see if anybody wants to jump out of a warm bed to go keelboatin' into a frozen wilderness full o' unfrozen Indians."

"Be easier if you don't dwell on them details."

Entering stealthily, they stared down a gun barrel. "Never sneak up onna sleepy woman gotta shotgun!" the droopy woman cautioned. "You the law?"

"We're fur trappers trappin' fur trappers," Sublette explained.

"Wha's innit fer me?"

"We haul your ashes for a change," Clyman interjected.

Her shotgun drooped, and she scratched herself in an

unladylike way. "Take 'em. Not sposed to be in here now."

In the first dingy room, a snoring woman's arm lay across a pair of bony feet sticking out of the blanket beside her.

Clyman whispered, "Strictly speaking, these feet have strayed from the path of righteousness."

Sublette nodded pensively.

"But you wouldn't deprive 'em of the chance to get rich over a little gin, now wouldja?"

Sublette shook his head, "Never."

Clyman signaled Sublette to toss the feet in the wagon.

* * *

Clyman leaned over the tavern table, waving the smoke away to reveal five goatish faces. "$200 the year to anybody who'll keelboat up the Missouri in March."

Several were too sullen to speak, but one husky boatman rose. "Who you leerin' at, shikepoke?"

William Sublette stepped on the boatman's foot and shifted his weight onto it. "Have a seat, Mister. It's jist a friendly smile. That's all."

The grimacing boatman sized Sublette up and sat down. Clyman and Sublette backed out the door.

Once outside, Clyman said, "I saw you palm that shot pouch and clear the top of your boot to pull your hideout gun. Who are you, anyway?"

"Jist like you thought, Mr. Clyman. I'm nothin' but a plowboy from Kentucky."

* * *

By mid-February, the men remaining aboard the *Yellow Stone Packet* gradually outnumbered those who woke up and jumped ship while the keelboat lay hausered to the levee dock.

Hugh Glass had answered Ashley & Henry's January 16, 1823 hunter ad in the *Missouri Republican* on his 40th birthday. Having just stowed his seabag aboard, Glass watched a defector slide over the *Yellow Stone Packet's* side into the freezing water. The fool could o' walked down the gangplank to the levee dry.

A former tall ship seaman, stocky, thick-bearded Irish Hugh Glass remembered himself and Tommy Pine slippin' from a pirate ship off the Texas coast two and a half years ago. Unlike these pub crawlin' drunks bein' let to escape at will, theirs was done on pain o' death.

Hugh Glass and Tommy Pine was deck hands on a British merchantman, when the pirate Jean La Fitte's cannon toppled her mizzenmast into the Gulf o' Mexico. La Fitte's Number Two gave Glass and Pine the choice o' kissin' the cutlass or joinin' La Fitte's buccaneers.

Since a man'd rather live as scum than die anonymous, Glass and Pine embraced La Fitte's Articles. But they had no stomach for puttin' other seamen to death. So they jumped ship under cover o' darkness.

Wanderin' inland they were captured by the *Pawnee*. The followin' day Tommy Pine was burned to death, but Glass escaped bein' roasted by paintin' the Chief with vermilion and okra. The Chief adopted Glass into the *Pawnee* tribe. A tribal visit to St. Louis allowed his escape. Glass longed to be with his dark-eyed angel, Dawn's Wing, but could not abide the rest o' the *Pawnee's* heathen life.

Hugh Glass yearned for a normal, God Fearin' Life more than anythin' -- except the adventure of a fur expedition up the Missouri.

Only one other new Ashley and Henry man, slender, sharp-featured 23 year old Thomas Fitzpatrick, had come to America as a boy from County Cavan on the Erin Isle. Fitzpatrick and Glass'd tossed about a bit o' Gaelic. Fitzpatrick spoke like he'd had a sound Catholic education as a boy.

Glass's job was to train the keelboat crew to handle sail, it bein' the expedition's plan to sail this pathetic excuse for a vessel with its pitiful riggin' upstream against the current. Hugh knew these keelboats'd spend little time under sail and would surely be hauled on cordelle by gaspin' men on the muddy banks.

* * *

From the *Yellow Stone Packet's* deck, William Sublette watched James Clyman guide five men onto the levee and aboard the *Rocky Mountains.* The keelboat's rocking motion reminded Sublette of a wagon's. Any excuse to git ashore was a good one. He waved to Clyman, then joined him on the levee.

"Where'd ya git them five fellers?" Sublette asked.

"Try this. Ashley tells me exactly where these five'll be in the White Heron. They're all in the same new civilian clothes, talking barracks lingo. I'd say the Army has landed."

"Why?"

"Not sure."

"Clyman, there ain't nothin' you're not sure of."

"Guess one. The Army wants General Ashley to succeed with American fur trappers because it will cut the number of guns being traded into Indian hands for furs. Guess two. The Army wants all the free intelligence it can get on the Indians, the British, the Russians and the Mexicans and Ashley's going to furnish it."

"What's Guess Three?"

"You mean what does Ashley get besides being a patriotic General serving his country?" Clyman mused.

"Right."

"Ashley gets Army manpower, supplies and dispatches."

"Sounds like three good guesses to this plowboy."

"All right, *Constable One Punch,* half the men I signed stayed outa St. Charles cause of you. I won't tell 'em about the shot pouch in your fist or your boot pistols, if you'll forget that plowboy story."

William extended his hand, "Deal."

Clyman slipped his rifle butt into Sublette's vice-grip. "Here, crush this, Sublette!"

Bad omens cursed the March 10th sailings of the keelboats through the broken ice floes of the Missouri River with 90 men aboard each of them. One voyager drowned and three others died in the explosion of a cask of gunpowder.

St. Charles looked different to William from the water, but it held too many Sublette graves and orphans fer him to look kindly on it. He wondered where Artemis went and if her shoulder still hurt her now she was free. Was Monique still in Paris? These memories o' the past were like maggots in his mind. He made himself look up river -- beyond the barges with their bells and the flat boats with their sloshin' oars -- and into the future. His life was changin' before him. Behind him the pain -- before him the adventure.

* * *

The keelboats inched up river, making some headway under sail, but most by the trappers' brute strength. Early cordelle parties towing the boats from the slippery banks lost men daily to desertion.

Sublette hunted often just to stay on firm ground, usually with James Clyman. Sublette came from the birthplace of the long rifle in Kentucky, but he'd never seen anybody that could outshoot Clyman at 200 yards. Then the game ran out. Settlers complained of random shots hitting livestock. Boat crews and hunters went hungry.

Both keelboats tied up at Franklin, Missouri. As they were casting off the next morning, a mob of outraged townspeople demanded to search the boats for stolen livestock and food.

General Ashley never made subordinates handle miserable situations. He stood ramrod straight atop the deck-house of the *Yellow Stone Packet*. The shifting morning breeze blew his hair every which way. "I'm General William H. Ashley, Lieutenant Governor of the state of Missouri. Gentlemen, I welcome you aboard. Search my vessels to your hearts' content!"

Both boats swarmed with angry farmers and merchants. In half an hour their fury flagged. The townspeople slunk off the keelboats. Several apologized for impugning the *honor* of the crews and their right *honorable* General. Satisfied that his *honor* had been vindicated, the General retired below to finish the cold breakfast growing colder in his quarters.

After the last of the citizens cleared the landing, the sails were unfurled. Pigs, poultry and vegetables in abundance plummeted to the decks of both keelboats. Somebody yelled, "Clear the decks!"

One of the "civilians" from the White Heron yelled, "To our *honor*!" Raising his bugle, he blew *Taps*.

CHAPTER 11

A PAIR OF FUGITIVES   MARCH 1823

It was an impossible trek from Terra Haute, Indiana to the Powder River Basin southwest of the Black Hills. X wanted it that way. His life depended on it. Rain splashed in under the rocky overhang where he'd been dozing since a little before midnight. X pulled his buffalo robe up over his flowing red hair and beard. He seized his warclub as a snarling wolf pack crashed through the underbrush.

X's hand brushed a small wet gasping animal. He trapped it in his buffalo robe and prepared to leap up onto the rainy rocks to escape the wolves. But the pack blundered on into the night. Fate was a perverse hand maiden. The wolves chasing their dinner in the dark had just served it up to X!

The sounds of the wolf pack died, leaving only the dripping rain. No. There was another noise. A weird noise. X probed the darkness with wild eyes. In the wilderness, your first chance to survive was your *only* chance.

When his senses stopped jangling, X realized the sound was vibrating his buffalo robe. It wasn't a growl. The thing in the robe wasn't shaking from fright. The animal had to know it was about to die. It wasn't nearly big enough to kill X.

X waited for the bobcat or lynx or whatever it was to try to escape. He'd brain it with his warclub. He might even risk a fire to cook something this big. Could go 15 -- 20 pounds. What a feast! But the freezing rain seeped through the buckskins X had taken from a rotting Indian corpse on a burial platform.

These buckskins were too new. That's why they leaked. When they got dirty enough to shine, they'd turn water.

Cautiously, X eased the robe open. A pretty little head with a mauled face looked back at him with luminous eyes. It purred like a barn cat. It closed its eyes and snuggled back into the robe. Now how was he supposed to kill it with it purring like that?

Might be better to club the thing while it was still inside the robe. That way, it couldn't run if the first lick didn't kill it. X mulled that over. The buffalo robe was powerful thick. Scrawny as X was, he wasn't all that strong. But he was that cold. The thing in the robe had purred itself to sleep while X sat shivering with his starving gut growling.

Choking it was out. It'd have four clawed feet free to rip him. Might even gut him. But if he choked it inside the robe -- that was it! Choke it inside the buffalo robe, then look for some dry wood. Hadn't cooked in years. Fire was against X's personal laws. Only certain laws were made to be broken. X wasn't going to think about that day -- memories of that afternoon were killing him -- the afternoon when he'd broken the biggest law of them all.

X groped for its neck through the stiff buffalo robe. He had to get this over with. Rain'd stopped. Freeze was coming. Might snow. Wind screamed in the trees. X clamped his jaw to stop his chattering teeth. He found the neck! But as he squeezed, the miserable thing started purring again.

The purring confused him. More hungers lurked in him than just in his belly. Hadn't talked to anybody but himself in five years -- more like seven or eight years. Didn't keep a calendar cause it would drive him mad.

Perhaps he was mad -- a lunatic hermit. The one thing X was sure of was that he was COLD! He got into the robe and hugged the warm wet thing that he'd soon have to kill. The young creature got the collar of X's buckskin in its mouth and began to suckle it, kneading his chest with its front paws. It purred while X cried, warm inside as well as out for the first time in nearly a decade.

He knew the cat would be gone when he woke up. Didn't care. He'd have this night between himself and all the loneliness -- the God awful longings to touch another being -- to say words and be heard. He didn't want to spook the cat, but hugged it gently, resting his cheek on its damp head that had a rich spicy smell. X's sleep was deep and peaceful for the first time in so long.

But when dawn came, the cat was still somewhere under the robe. X could feel its cozy warmth. Last night, the cat was tuckered out from the wolf chase. Now it'd want to run wild and free. And what of X's starving? Was he going to let his food jist run off?

Yes. Yes he was -- idiotic as that was out here in Hell where a mouthful of food could mean living another day stead o' dying. Maybe it should run to save itself from his maddening hunger. He wondered if he'd kill it by reflex before his mind made the decision.

X yanked the robe off them. The wide eyed panther cub leapt to its feet, bared the little fangs in its torn face, hissed with its tongue arched and bounded away through the scrub pines like a cork bobbing on a mill race.

The bony hermit in his undersized buckskins dropped his scraggly orange beard to his chest and wept. This emptiness -- this plunge back into total loneliness hurt far worse than the hunger pangs that haunted him. Hadn't said a word to the little thing. Now it was gone! He was *alone again* in this great silence.

X felt empty and useless, but couldn't hide in the robe and let the day slip away. The air was brisk with traces of frost in the shadows. The sun was weak, and the wind was rising. He must find food before the storm.

Startled Finch calls filtered through the pines. Bird calls made X nervous -- especially when they were too perfect. Could be from some Indian's mouth. It was like when he'd worked for the jeweler before the war.

When a gem looked too perfect on the surface, it wasn't all that sound through the loupe. X studied his bony, freckled hands with their filthy twisted nails. Could these hands ever be those of a chemist and a jeweler -- a man so shamed he'd taken the designation for the unknown as his name?

Why did he cling to this miserable life? Why didn't he

throw himself on the panther before he pulled the robe off? Then it might still be here. That was wrong!

Couldn't make something stay by jailing it. If he'd offered it food -- that would have done it! Might still do it! How far could a little gash-faced thing like that run anyway?

Maybe the panther was what was riling the birds. Birds! He'd snare some birds with berry bait and eat a few berries -- even if they pained his innards.

But as X set his gourd snare, he knew the panther was gone. X had carved the gourd so the bird entered through the remnant of the neck pecking away at seeds or berries. Its weight would tip the gourd and cover the entrance, leaving the bird on the ground unable to budge the gourd.

After the trap was baited, X waited to chase off squirrels that might spring it. The squirrels did not come. Several times X killed a meddling squirrel with his bow -- once with his crude spear.

He'd had at least four chances to thieve a rifle from the Indians. They were careless with their things. Most of their guns looked neglected and rusty. X stole plenty other things from the Indians, but never a rifle. If he had a rifle, he'd shoot it. Then it'd be a whipstitch before the Indians found him, got their gun back and fed him in little pieces to their dogs.

He remembered how soldiers in his outfit during the war complained about "them thieving Indians." Now X realized how right stealing was when you'd die if you didn't.

Sounds in the trees behind him wheeled X, his heart hammering. He crouched to fend off attack.

Nothing. X scurried noiselessly to the safety of his rocks, stepping only on the hard ground. Seizing his bow, he notched an arrow onto the string, but still had nothing to shoot at. He lowered the bow, the bright feathers tied at either end flitting in the wind.

X checked his lair to see if anything was gone. At first he missed his spear, but it had only been moved. Something -- probably a wood rat -- had chewed off part of the leather wrapping the rusty steel tip onto the shaft. He'd fix that when he got his hands on some leather. His life depended on the spear.

Movement below the rocks grabbed X's eye. A large doe

grazed within range of his bow. But there were pine branches in between that might deflect the arrow. X settled to his haunches to wait. The deer's huge ears rotated, testing every noise. He remembered a friendly Indian scout telling him that when a pine needle falls to the forest floor, the eagle sees it, the grizzly smells it, but the deer hears it.

The doe tasted a small fern, her dainty tongue moving the greens into position to be chewed. Her eyes cast about, but X knew she hadn't seen him. If she moved four feet east, she was his, but if she retreated into the trees, X would just go back to starving.

His stomach growled. The deer heard it and started backing into the trees! X released his arrow. It threaded the branches and sank deep in her chest.

Instead of bucking off through the scrub pines like most deer would, her front legs buckled, she coughed and sank to the pine needles. Her head flopped to the side and her shiny red tongue lolled out.

X dropped beside the doe and slashed her throat with his knife. Many a hunter'd been ripped apart by a dying deer's razor hooves for failing to make this cut. As he skinned the doe, X had the same argument with himself he had every time he made a kill. He hated raw meat. He was going to break his rule agin fires if the wind stayed low, so the smoke wouldn't carry.

He'd burn only tinder or old dry branches -- nothing wet -- nothing full of sap -- maybe a few pitch knots he'd soaked in the oil spring to make them burn white hot when the ice was so bad. He longed for his own fire. Watching the Indians sitting around theirs made his yearning unbearable. But a fire would bring his death so quickly. The argument was over. He'd lost again.

X was stunned, dropped his knife and gaped! The panther cub crouched ten feet away licking the torn side of its face. It tilted its head and switched its tail. X cut a chunk of bloody meat from the deer's flank and tossed it toward the panther.

The cub dodged and disappeared!

"Stupid fool!" X griped, breaking his own law against talking. He'd also broken his law against being addlebrained.

Staying with this kill in the open was more idiotic than the talking. A grizzly could smell deer blood for miles. So could an Indian.

X dragged the deer up into his rocks. He was child-weak from lack of food, and the carcass felt heavy as a horse. He lay panting. He realized he had to go back down and cover all tracks and sign, but he couldn't move. He hadn't eaten anything but roots for nearly a week.

He sliced some deer brisket and ate it ravenously, the blood oozing into his orange beard. He couldn't let himself gorge. He'd get sick and founder like a dumb colt in the alfalfa. He wiped the blood from his beard with his forearm. When X lowered his arm, the panther cub was tugging at the hock of the doe's hind leg. "I'd like to help you with that, Slash, but if I move, you'll bolt again."

The young panther growled at X and moved its bites up the deer leg until it reached the haunch. She blinked at X and kept chewing, growing bolder as she ate. X was sure the panther would fight him for the deer carcass. The idea that this little thing would fight him made him grin through his wild beard. The only sign of sharing X could think of was to cut more meat and eat, so he did. It calmed the cub.

Her fur was punctuated with dark spots like the "clubs" in a deck of cards. She might have been something besides a panther except for her long tail. Even with the odd rings around her tail, she couldn't be lynx or bobcat Her eyes were blue like a child's, and she shut them to chew.

Emitting tiny growls, the cub kept gnawing at the deer leg, as X clambered down from his rocks and took a pine branch to the ground. He smoothed away the drag marks and pinched up all the bloody pine needles. The piece of meat he'd thrown to the panther was gone. X walked backwards from the spot of the kill and scattered some of the bloody needles four times until he had fanning trails that went in every direction -- and nowhere.

Thunder shook the sky. Rain would wash the ground clean of the deer kill. Large drops splatted on X's buckskins, driving him back to his lair.

Dreading finding the panther gone, he crawled in cautiously. The doe'd lost most of her hindquarter. X had lost a panther. He soon lost the rain as the thunderhead moved higher up into the mountains, but that didn't keep the hot rain off his cheeks.

X finished skinning the deer. He used the back of the stiffening hide to wrap the best cuts of meat for storing in the trees. He'd soon cut the meat in strips and dry it to jerky in the tree tops. He gouged the doe's throat ragged like an animal's kill, then carried the head, bones and entrails in the remaining hide half a mile to the edge of a clearing. He roughed up the ground around the deer's remains with her severed hooves, then disappeared into the trees, certain he was being watched. He prayed it wasn't a grizzly, cause he could outrun most anything else.

X strode swiftly through the gnarly pines, eyeing his backtrail. He made a quarter mile circle around his rock lair, then stopped and listened. Only the sounds of a light wind and distant thunder. If anything was stalking him, it wasn't a grizzly. Fearing nothing, grizzlies crashed through the brush like an avalanche.

Scanning the tree line, X spied the panther cub, peeking from behind a twisted cedar trunk. He stifled his yell of joy, then climbed for home, hoping the panther would follow. It did.

That first day back, Slash would only perch in the rocks and watch him. But when night came with its numbing cold, she crawled under the robe with him, purring herself to sleep. The red raked scars on her face were too straight, too even and too deep to have been put there by anything but grizzly claws. Her fur was like goose down. He'd expected it to be coarse as a deer's.

Even though he knew the cub was asleep, X found himself mumbling words he'd been aching to say for eight years, "I can't remember a thing about the day I left for the war. But I can't forget nothing about the day I come back. There she was -- my wife Colleen -- in another man's arms! I hog tied their necks together with a rope and left. Now there's a rope with thirteen knots waitin' for me in Terre Haute."

The cub was nursing his buckskins again when X fell asleep.

At dawn, X checked his bird trap. It was still empty.

The birds wouldn't come until he put something in the trap they couldn't find all around it.

X picked more berries. He crushed them with bits of meat into pemmican, then put some down for the panther. She sniffed the stuff, pulled the good side of her lip back disdainfully and eyed him till he put down real deer meat. He ate the pemmican himself, while he told her his laws. "The kill must be silent. We trade with no one. Never sleep where you cannot see the stars. Make no fires. Walk the rocky ground. Lie low in daylight. That's your way anyway. You'll like it here! We're a country of fugitives."

X adored touching her. He stroked her silky fur till she purred. "Slash, you'll most likely grow into one powerful hunter. Are you gonna be my salvation and feed me -- or am I just saving Indiana a hanging by hand raising my own executioner?"

CHAPTER 12

FORT ATKINSON   SPRING 1823

Posted as a sentry in the keelboat *Yellow Stone Packet's* bow, William Sublette searched the Missouri River's murky shorelines in the hazy light of false dawn. March's icy mists swirled around him. Hoarfrost whitened his Hawken rifle barrel. He wrestled the leaden buffalo robe off the deck rail and draped it over his shoulders. Swollen with run off from meltin' ice and snow, the Missouri let her floatin' ice floes ram the hull. He'd watched this river half his life but never got this intimate with her before. She was a fickle wench that could make him seasick anytime she felt like it!

William took a deep breath, but the frigid air numbed the river's smells. William wished he'd gone Up the Mountain with Milton last spring. Now the older brother was a Pilgrim and Milton was the Mountain Man. William knew Milton'd lord it over him. Even if Milton did, it'd be good to see blood kin. With Milton there wasn't no *sort of.* He'd either be Major Henry's top trapper with plews piled high as a tall pine or a mutineer chained to one.

Sun-up was special to William. Everything got a new chance. The sun's young rays chased the mists off the middle of the river and made 'em glow gold along its banks where noisy ducks led strings of fuzzy swimmers through the reeds. Squeakin' bats darted through the dawn toward a cave someplace. Unseen birds sang from their hideouts.

The deck lurched under William's boots. Hugh Glass had the French crew layin' on more sail to catch the risin' breeze. Dawn was dead. So was his bow watch. William shucked the buffalo robe and went to the galley for some of the sizzlin' sausage that'd been teasin' his nose since the one-handed Indian cook fired up the stove before first light.

* * *

Hugh Glass got transferred to the *Rocky Mountains* to sail-train its crew. Even though *Yellow Stone* lagged behind in the afternoon doldrums, William Sublette was glad to have Glass off the boat. William sized Hugh Glass up as a man wound so tight he could have no peace, nor could any man around him.

Moses "Black" Harris paused beside Sublette at the rail to eye the shore uneasily. Sublette took stock of him. Dressed like most of the Mountain Men, Harris was carefree as any man aboard either boat. Just under six feet, he was broad across the back, thick arms, but lean legs. Mahogany skin made his teeth flash extra white, except the gap where his upper left dog tooth used to be. His badger skin cap had a sea captain's bill. A bullet pouch dangled from a thong around his neck, and a scarred powder horn peeked under his right arm, its strap holding his bullet mold, ballscrew, wiper and awl.

Beaded fringe decorated Harris's knee-length buckskin shirt, but the beads had come off his leggin's from long hours of wadin'. A wide belt slimmed his shirt tight with a Green River butcher knife in one side and a cheap pistol in the other. Harris's right little toe peeked through a triangular tear in his worn moccasin. His oily rifle looked sound.

Sublette figured Moses Harris for a run-away slave, but that didn't mean squat to anybody out here. William hoped Artemis was half as happy as this strappin' Negro seemed to be.

Moses Harris, a veteran of Ashley's 1822 trapping expedition, left the rail and padded down the ladder well. But moments later Harris returned to the deck, ordered by General Ashley to teach the green men on the *Yellow Stone* to trap beaver. His ever present smile had become a puzzled scowl.

This black man had never taught nobody to do nothin'. The grat big blond man at the rail had a kindly face. Moses picked him [Sublette] and three others in settler clothes.

Moses herded them to the stern. As Moses was ready to put his rifle down, a dozen low flying ducks soared over, their wings slapping the air. Moses raised his rifle and fired. *All* of the ducks veered east, and flapped right on up the river.

From his cloud of black powder smoke, Moses muttered, "Men, you has seed yo fust mountain miracle --argh -- a *dead* duck what kept flyin'!" Sublette and the other men eyed each other, then the holy look of Moses's upturned face. They exploded in laughter.

Moses leaned the rifle he secretly called *Judas* against the bulkhead. He gave each man a rust-pitted beaver trap about a foot and a half long and sank to the deck with his own trap.

Moses crooned, "Dis trap weigh 'bout tree pound -- argh -- unless dey's a beavah in it. Den it gonna weigh from foty to ninety pound."

Moses laid his trap on the deck and forced its jaws open. He set it by pulling the trigger pan down and hooking it into a notch. Moses lowered his forefinger between the trap's gaping jaws to barely an inch above the trigger pan.

While the novices waited tensely for the trap to snap his finger off, Moses said in his sing-song baritone, "What you wants to ketch in here's a grat big crazy rat --argh -- wit yaller teeth so big -- so shop -- he kin bite through seben inch aspen tree in fibe minute. Beavah looks like a rat on dis boat but -- argh -- big as a dog wit a big flat tail. Sumpthin strange make him chew off trees and drag 'em cross da cricks. Makes grat big ponds wit his lodge o' sticks inna middle -- argh -- where he holes up inna winter. And don't none o' you *nebbah* do dis!"

With a lightning thrust, Moses jabbed the trap's trigger pan with his finger, yanking it clear as the trap jaws bit thin air. "Men, you has jist seen yo secunt mountain miracle --argh -- a man do sumpthin stupid and still got *all* o' his fingahs." Moses turned his face upward while Sublette and the others chuckled.

"Beavah can take you fingahs off fasta dan dis trap, so you gotta kill 'em if they aint -- argh --drowned by da time you comes fo dem. You skins 'em out and string da hide on a willow stick tied into a circle -- makin' a plew dat gonna weigh bout a pound an' a half. Betta learn to like beavah cause you gonna be eatin' a lot o' dem -- argh -- flat tail cook up real good if you da kind dat make a fire. Dis niggah don't make many fire. Fire's wuss dan springin' dis trap wit yo face if you got Blackfeet joinin' you fo dinnah." Moses looked askance at them with his eyebrows raised above deliberately widened brown eyes.

Moses's students eyed each other, but nobody laughed.

* * *

General Ashley's long boat rowed toward the whitewashed buildings of Fort Atkinson on the Missouri's west bank near Council Bluffs. Ashley stood in the long boat's bow. With the practiced eye of a military commander, he inspected the fort. The stockade was 200 yards square with three gates. Two log houses stood on either side. A stone powder house sat the interior grass parade ground. On the south side a squatty grist mill stood ready to grind corn and wheat from the fields along the river. It wasn't laid out the way he liked it, but it would do.

William Ashley relished the idea of greeting his old friend Colonel Henry Leavenworth at the Commandant's house. The intelligent, but indecisive, Leavenworth was to be Ashley's contact for whatever he needed from the Army.

As the longboat broached the shore, Ashley spied the crude lettered sign, *IndIAn AgEnT*, above the Indian council house near the artillery sheds. Ashley'd like to avoid a confrontation with Major Benjamin O'Fallon, the powerful Indian Agent for the area, if at all possible.

Last summer, Major Benjamin O'Fallon had written to the Secretary of War "... *the harmony so happily existing between us and the Indians in the vicinity of Council Bluffs is likely to be alarmed and disturbed by the intrusion of Ashley's trappers.*"

Although young O'Fallon had never served a day in the military, he'd received the title of Major when his uncle William Clark, current Governor of Missouri -- and Lt. Governor Ashley's boss -- procured O'Fallon's temporary appointment as Indian Agent for this region. Both O'Fallon and nepotistic Governor Clark had ownership interests in the Missouri Fur Company headquartered here at Council Bluffs. Neither wrote letters of outrage to Secretary of War Calhoun about where Missouri Fur Company trappers went.

For Ashley, it was a frustrating -- even maddening

situation. You couldn't break your riding crop over the nose of your boss's stallion no matter how hard it kicked you! Young O'Fallon was dangerous as the nastiest stallion. He'd proven that with savage attacks on other fur companies.

Ashley's anger goaded him to kick a dirt clod to powder as he neared the fort. Published in the *Missouri Republican,* O'Fallon's letter damning Ashley & Henry'd inspired a rabid essay by St. Louis Judge J.B.C. Lucas. Lucas opined that the Ashley-Henry venture had no legal right whatsoever to take a large body of trappers into Indian Country. Lucas's article concluded that Ashley was clearly *a wrong doer* who disturbed frontier peace. Ashley could but wonder if Lucas would be his opposition in the upcoming Missouri Governor's race of 1824. His opponent could even be young O'Fallon setting his cap for the job of the uncle who'd raised him!

The militia General's knock on U.S. Army regular Colonel Leavenworth's door reeked of imperative. A pallid junior officer with paper thin lips answered the door. "The Colonel awaits you, General. Come with me."

Colonel Leavenworth's greased-down hair was especially shiny above his full graying mutton chop whiskers. He rose from his desk and offered his soft hand to Ashley.

Ashley was too agitated to mince words. "Is the War Department still backing Major Henry and myself with men and supplies?"

"Within reason, of course. But there's been serious trouble," Colonel Leavenworth added querulously, brushing downward at his substantial paunch as if to make it disappear.

"Fill me in, Colonel."

"Several fur groups have had recent skirmishes with the tribes. The *Arikaras* were allegedly fired upon by the Missouri Fur Company Garrison 80 miles south of the *Arikara* villages on the Missouri River. We don't have confirmation on that."

"How about the others?"

"Blackfeet murdered several men in another Missouri Fur Company group under Jones and Immell on Pryors Fork of the Yellowstone. Attacked a small band of your trappers near the mouth of the Smith River, but far as we know, nobody was killed."

"Major Henry all right?"

"Our report is sketchy -- third hand. We know Major Henry wants you to buy 20 horses, so the Indians may've just run his stock off."

"Can I get 20 horses from the Army?"

"Not now. Army'll supply you with food and a few more men in case of trouble, but we can't provide trained horses with this Indian trouble festering. General, I'd consider it a *personal favor* if you'd garrison your people here till we get better intelligence. You could be charging headlong into a hornet's nest of hostiles."

Ashley wondered who was behind this stall request -- O'Fallon -- Lucas -- the Missouri Fur Company -- the War Department? Leavenworth could easily make his request into an order -- even an arrest! Ashley's stand had to be a dramatic frontal assault. He'd start by lobbing in some artillery. "Colonel, I know that Major O'Fallon arrested trader Robert Dickson to weaken his effectiveness on the St. Croix River. I'm also well aware that O'Fallon was behind Colonel Chambers' arrest of the two American Fur Company agents at Prairie du Chien on the thinnest of charges. That's going to end up in Court. Will I be clapped in irons if I don't agree to your delay, Colonel?"

"What's the matter with you? A gentleman's request for a harmless delay shouldn't unhinge your mind!"

"Well no delay of these keelboats is harmless! It'll mean bankruptcy, Colonel! You're asking a General Officer to suffer the humiliation of bankruptcy. If we tarry now, the entire 1823 fur trapping season will vanish! Major Henry will join my shame. Our resources are already faltering. We must either advance north to trap to pay our debts or slink south and surrender our life's possessions to our creditors. It's your decision, Colonel. Yours alone."

Leavenworth turned his back to Ashley. His voice was hoarse with anger, "Call off your cavalry. I had no intention of ordering your expedition to remain at Fort Atkinson or arresting you. My orders from the War Department are to provide reasonable aid to your western exploration, not to hasten your commercial castration."

"If you can issue us enough ball and powder, we can

trade it to the Indians for the horses Major Henry needs."

Aghast at Ashley's arrogance, Leavenworth grated, "General -- more ball and powder are the *last* things the U.S. Army wants to deliver to these insurrectional Indians!"

"I can't count on conjuring up 20 horses for Major Henry with squaw trinkets and vermilion sticks. It's too late in the year to wait for horses from St. Louis. They'll have to come from the Indians. I'll try trading trinkets for horses. If that doesn't work, I'll be forced to resort to the powder and shot!"

Leavenworth's face blushed crimson. "All right, General! Against my considered military judgment, you shall have the powder and shot! But you get them on French requisition -- no telltale records. I don't want expulsion papers from this man's Army when the War Department wants a scapegoat after this powder and shot blows up in our faces! We'll deliver *the vegetables* to river's edge this afternoon. Your people will have to put them aboard your keelboats."

"You won't regret this, Colonel. You have my *personal* assurance on that!"

Henry Leavenworth was too furious to reply. He shut his eyes and bowed his head, leaving no doubt the meeting was over.

Around noon, Sublette and Clyman hobbled their pack horses laden with deer at the edge of the Missouri by the fort. They watched unfamiliar men in new linsey-woolsey struggling to hoist boxes labeled *VEGETABLES* into the long boat. The boat sank dramatically deeper in the water with each box.

Sublette spit out the flayed willow stick he'd been chewing on. "Musta packed the ground that grew around them vegetables. Looks like you cut dead center with all three o' them Guesses on General Ashley's quiet deal with the Army."

Clyman squinted and shook his head slowly. "Maybe so. But right now I'm real worried about Guess Four. I wanta be dead wrong about what I think Ashley's got in mind for those *VEGETABLES*!"

CHAPTER 13

ARIKARA DAWN   MAY-JUNE 1823

By the last week of May, General Ashley's keelboats were 400 miles up the Missouri past Council Bluffs. Ashley still had no word from Major Henry, and they'd found no Indians with horses to trade. He paced the *Yellow Stone Packet's* deck like a balding panther. Just north of the Rampart River's mouth, a lookout yelled, "Canoe ahead!" Ashley strode to the railing.

A square-shouldered man in buckskins paddled his bark canoe, riding gunnel deep, along side the *Yellow Stone Packet.* Gazing upward, he said, "General, you really should learn to relax." Ashley just shook his head.

William Sublette and other men crowded the railing. Somebody lowered The *Yellow Stone Packet's* rope ladder. The man in the canoe handed up his rifle, his oar and a couple of buckskin sacks, then stepped onto the ladder. He stomped his moccasin through the bottom of his sinking canoe, watching with pleasure as the swirling brown waters sucked it under. Climbing the ladder, the bronzed, clean-shaven man announced in a New York accent, "Never buy a canoe from a Crow."

General Ashley addressed all hands. "This Crow canoe kicker is Captain Jedediah Strong Smith, second in command of my Yellowstone expedition under Major Henry. He doesn't smoke or drink, but he does conduct gospel services on Sunday -- I know you'll all want to attend because he recites all the important passages of the Good Book by heart -- every time!"

Sublette judged Jedediah around his own age of 23, six feet tall, ramrod slender with long black hair like Papa Phillip's.

Jedediah's sky blue eyes never rested. He'd tied a red bandanna around his Bible so he could carry his rifle in the same hand.

Ashley steered Jedediah to his cabin, where the General blurted, "What's going on up on the Yellowstone?"

"Major Henry sent me after replacement horses."

"What happened up there?"

"*Assiniboines* fired on us stampeding our horses. Cut our travels to a crawl. Blackfeet raided in April, butchering three of our trappers outright. The squat gent from Pennsylvania got his windpipe tomahawked and wheezed for half the night before the Lord took him home. We dug potato holes and took shelter in 'em, but the Blackfeet skulked away in the dark. Ice's kept the trapping light, but Major Henry's working the thawed streams around there till we return with fresh horses."

"Heard you needed the 20 horses. Have goods to trade for at least that many, but can't locate Indians with horses to trade. You'll have to write that dead Dutchman's family."

Jedediah Smith nodded, then continued, "I paddled by two *Arikara* villages a couple of hundred yards apart along the east bank of the Missouri six miles north of here. Brought that leaky Crow canoe ashore below the second one and reconnoitered both. The *Arikara* have a host of horses -- and a host of warriors."

"How many horses make up a *host*?"

"Too scattered for even a rough count, but I wouldn't get struck dead for lying if I said a thousand."

"Is a host still a thousand for Indians?"

Jedediah shook his head thoughtfully, "More like six hundred -- but well armed -- mostly trade rifles with a dash of British military pieces."

"Sounds like the *Arikara* could trade some horses if they wanted to."

"General, look elsewhere for the horses. You've never seen Indians fortified like these. Must fight all the time."

The General appeared skeptical. "Army says the *Arikara* and the *Sioux* have been at war long as anybody can remember, but we're not involved."

Jedediah Smith shook his head. Finally he said, "Could be. Judge for yourself. The *Arikara* have dug between 50 and

100 potato holes about 15 feet across. Each is fortified by willow brush layered with dirt, grass and mud. Be lucky to penetrate one with a cannon."

"Couldn't the *Arikara* be living in these potato holes?"

"Logically they could, but the way they're spaced with gun ports all around says they're for war. It's what they're for, General -- war," Jedediah replied.

When General William Ashley didn't hear what he wanted to, sometimes he didn't hear. "See any other Indians we could trade with for horses?"

"Plains nomads. None we could count on by the time we get these boats up there."

"I can't fritter the summer away scouting for horses because I'm too timid to trade with Indians I've already found!"

Jedediah's unwavering eyes froze to blue ice. He generated a knife-thin smile, "Major Henry sent Edward Rose, a mulatto Crow War Chief down here with me."

"Rose -- I've heard the name. Major's talked of him like he's some kind of legend. Can't remember exactly what he said. Where is Rose?"

"I dunno, but if you ever spent five minutes with Edward Rose, you'd never forget him!"

"Why's that?" Ashley yawned.

"Rose lives in the devil's body with the tongue of an angel that speaks 20 languages. Got his nose slashed as a boy in a brawl on a New Orleans keelboat. Crows he lived with called him *Nez Coupe'* -- Cut Nose -- till he slew five *Minnetarees* in a battle where he took on their whole tribe -- by himself. Now the Crows call him *Chee-ho-carte* -- Five Scalps -- and worship him as a demon. When Manuel Lisa fired Rose, Major Henry says it took 15 men to hold Rose down long enough for Lisa to get away to St. Louis. And Rose was sober -- he's worse if he's drunk."

Now starkly awake, Ashley snapped, "Where is Rose? Gotta keep track of a man who acts like that."

"Can't. Rose comes and goes like the vapors."

"What good's Rose to us?"

"First time Major Henry ran into Rose was in 1809 -- living in an *Arikara* village. Speaks their language better than they do, but if he shows up here, don't say anything about that leaking canoe that I sank."

"Why?"

"I bought the canoe from Rose. He's fiendish, but makes up for it with an evil temper."

"Send Rose to me when he gets here, then set up our shore camp -- to make a show of force -- along the river right under the noses of these *Arikara* villages."

"What'll we offer them for their horses, General?"

"I'll open with squaw trinkets, trade blankets, mirrors and vermilion sticks. If those fail, I'll trade powder and shot for horses."

Jedediah Smith's jaw dropped in disbelief. "As you say, General. As you say."

General Ashley timed his short voyage to arrive at the lower *Arikara* village under cover of darkness. He ordered the French crewmen to set the anchors of both keelboats midstream.

General Ashley wanted the awakening *Arikaras* to see two great boats rising from the mist, but got his own grim surprise when Edward Rose materialized aboard the *Yellow Stone Packet* in the midst of its night arrival.

Ashley'd expected Rose to be big as Sublette, but he wasn't. His skin was dark; his eyes were obsidian arrowheads. His new buckskins flashed the finery of the Crow nation -- or *Absaroka* as they called themselves -- complete with plumes, beads and embroidery. Rose glowered till they brought him two blankets, then secreted himself on the keelboat. General Ashley slept with a candle burning and a loaded pistol beside it.

On dawn watch again, William Sublette cradled his rifle in the crook of his arm. He knew the *Arikara* village sprawled on the prairie along the Missouri's east bank, but the fog muffled starlight left the river banks pitch black. He was too excited to feel the cold. William never heard of an *Arikara* before last week. In St. Charles people swapped tales about Blackfeet massacres, friendly *Sioux* and horse-thievin' Crows.

Dark as it was, William Sublette already knew plenty about the *Arikara*. There was hundreds of 'em and they didn't bury their dung. They kept too many horses. Didn't fish much fer people livin' by a river. Gutted their buffalo kill just to the south, keepin' their curs quiet fer now. To the north they was dryin' meat into jerky. They cut willows an' put peppers in their food. One snored worse'n Uncle Solomon.

At first light, William made out a horseshoe bend in the river that'd dropped a sand bar along the east bank. Still no *Arikaras*. His jaws ached from clenchin' them under his blond beard. Towers of willow sticks like overgrown corn shocks loomed above the river bank. Two men came to relieve him on guard, but William told them to go eat and they did. He wanted to see a real live *Arikara* before breakfast!

William was less than impressed when the *Arikaras* swarmed the river bank. They were skinny fellers in buckskins with stringy black hair wrapped in dirty blankets. Some carried rusty rifles -- by the barrel. He got a man to take the bow watch so he could eat breakfast.

General Ashley sent Jedediah Smith and Edward Rose ashore to open the horse talks in one of their stuffy potato holes with a toothless Chief, obviously long out of power. Unable to understand the lingo, Jedediah bowed out to set up the beach camp Ashley'd ordered.

Minutes later Rose told Jedediah, "The *Arikara* are still mad as a bag-bit bull because Missouri Fur Company shot at them over a *Sioux* squaw -- a miserable slave. Two younger Chiefs came, but won't see the difference between us and the Missouri Fur Company. They demand tribute for that shooting before they talk of trading horses."

Jedediah Smith grumbled, "Go back to the boat. Let them wonder if the talks are over."

Besides the 12 "civilians" Ashley directed Smith to deploy on the sand spit, he furnished a list of 28 more, including Jedediah, William Sublette, James Clyman, Moses "Black" Harris, Thomas Fitzpatrick and Hugh Glass.

Jedediah selected surly Edward Rose for the beach to keep a knowing ear on the *Arikara*. It was torture for Jedediah to league himself with Rose. The man was Satan incarnate. Major Henry'd hired Rose, so the question was whether to use Rose to serve Christian ends. Smith relayed General's orders to the beach party to make a show of cleaning and aiming weapons.

After Smith reported to Ashley on the keelboat, Sublette

asked Clyman, "Whatta you think o' bein' down here on the bare sand lookin' up at all them willow forts sproutin' rifles?"

"Now you know what it's like for the turkey at a turkey shoot," Clyman grimaced.

Next day Rose agreed to tribute of ten pounds of powder and two bars of lead to meet the main *Arikara* chief, a powerful fellow with fierce eyes and the front half of his head shaved.

But when Ashley made Rose ask the Chief's name, the chief acted insulted. He could have talked with Rose, but hand-signed that the tribute must be put on the dirt floor between them. Even after it was, the chief folded his burly arms and refused to talk, ignoring the mosquitoes sucking blood from his face. The General returned to the keelboat in disgust.

Bartering between Ashley and "the half wit," as he'd dubbed the Chief, began the third day midst clouds of mosquitoes. Ashley matched the Chief's indifference to the vampire insects, demanding that his trappers select the horses. He aborted that demand when "half wit" tipped his head back emitting animal howls. Ashley doubled the ante of powder and shot. When "half wit" bared ragged teeth in a brown smile, Ashley knew the dickering for the 20 horses was done. Ashley and "half wit" exchanged hand-to-heart signs of friendship.

Rose growled, "You know this Chief cannot be trusted."

On General Ashley's way back to the *Yellow Stone Packet*, rain deluged his long boat in a fittingly dismal end to this June first, birthday of his dead wife Mary, whom he missed so desperately. Old Ezekiel Able's prize daughter would have been proud of him, sticking to his guns to get these horses when everybody'd damned his trying.

Rain lashed the sand spit as the *Arikara* delivered wild, unbroken paints and scarred renegades piecemeal. Men and horses welcomed the downpour because it banished the feasting mosquitoes. Hugh Glass chided, "I'm only a sea farin' man, but these divel steeds don't look worth usin' for ballast." Cursing men wrestled halters and hobbles onto the unruly horses.

Tired of parsing out powder to match sporadic horse deliveries, Ashley ordered the last hundredweight of powder delivered, half to each *Arikara* Village. A German trapper staggering in the dark asked, "Vonder vot dese rotten Rees gonna do mit all dis powder and chot?"

At dawn on June 2nd, 300 *Arikaras* raked Ashley's horses and 40 man beach detachment in their blankets with fusillades of man-made thunder, lightning and death.

Blasted awake, Sublette grabbed his rifle as Clyman disappeared among the stampedin' trappers. From the horses's screams and sharp whacks of bullets strikin' heavy bodies, Sublette figured the horses were the *Arikara* targets. But after every horse sprawled in the sand, the Indians kept firin'. He saw Hugh Glass flop across the bodies of two other men. This couldn't be happenin'! Men dropped everywhere!

Sublette dived behind a downed horse and thrust his rifle across its ribs. The horse's blood drained warmly onto William's thigh, seethin' with gorgin' mosquitoes. Instead of shootin' blindly, he waited to fire at muzzle flashes. Bullets kicked sand on him, but he loaded and fired. Loaded and fired. It dawned on him the men were all firin' together and heard himself yellin', "Stagger your firin'. They'll charge when we're all loadin'."

From the *Yellow Stone Packet* midstream, General Ashley angrily ordered men to save his brave sand spit fighters in the skiffs, but only Reed Gibson obeyed his suicidal orders.

Agonizing that his command was suffering the worst disaster in the history of the western fur trade, General Ashley grabbed his long rifle and looked for "half wit." The wily *Arikara* had traded him worthless horses, massacred them and Ashley's men -- with Ashley's own powder and shot. Ashley realized the real "half wit" was holding his rifle.

Clyman saw his chance to be rescued in a skiff by his friend Reed Gibson, but bullets ripping the air forced him to sprint up the beach with several warriors on his heels.

Glancing over his shoulder, Clyman saw Sublette's blond head buck from the kick of his rifle. With typical Clyman detachment, he recalled concluding at Ashley's house, that Sublette would break and run under fire. Now Sublette was back there battling to the death while Clyman broke and ran. Clyman's twisted grin barely showed in the half light. He doubted either of them'd live long enough for him to apologize to Sublette.

CHAPTER 14

ARIKARAS REVISITED JUNE-AUGUST 1823

Infuriated that these cowards were hiding from their brave bullets behind dead horses, the *Arikaras* launched feathered shafts screaming from the sky, to thunk into downed horses and men.

When an arrow tore Sublette's boot heel off, he realized death had come for him. His pulse pounded in his throat. He'd never been so excited -- nor so calm. He saw Jedediah Smith wavin' toward the river.

Fallen Hugh Glass's bloody hand clawed the air. Sublette shifted his rifle and grabbed Glass's arm, dragging the Irishman. Somebody hoisted Glass from the other side. It was Moses Harris. Sublette heard a bullet smack one o' the men with him. Moses lurched, dragging one leg, but didn't quit.

Arikara bullets ripped the bloody Missouri, spronging ricochets. Ashley's trappers, some shouldering wounded comrades, splashed toward the keelboats. The *Arikara* ceased firing, but not out of mercy.

While the General's men hoisted their wounded aboard the keelboats, about 50 squaws in bright colors danced among the dead trappers littering the gory beach. Some waved rock-headed war clubs. Others brandished butcher knives. The youngest squaws stripped the dead of their clothes.

Badly winded, William Sublette hung over the bow railing where he'd stood watch on the *Yellow Stone Packet.* Too stunned to scrape gorgin' mosquitoes off his face, Sublette gaped as chantin' squaws smashed the skulls of his fallen friends. Others butchered scalps off and flapped them at the keelboats before drapin' them over their own stringy hair. Sublette wished Clyman would flatten these hags with his long rifle. Where was Clyman anyway?

Amid wailing squaws, skinny nude Jack Larrison leaped up and scampered for the river. Flailing his arms and legs like an albino water-skipper, Larrison dodged the clawing squaws and floundered to safety while keelboaters cheered.

Ashley ordered both crews to weigh anchor, and the two keelboats slunk southward in disgrace before the current.

Sublette found dazed Hugh Glass with his head bandaged and his left arm trussed up in a bloody rag. Sublette knew if anybody survived, it'd be Hugh -- too badger mean to die. He searched for Clyman and Harris. No luck. He hollered at the other boat, but they couldn't hear over the Missouri's roar.

About 25 miles below the *Arikara* villages, the keelboats hove to at a small island near the center of the river, affording modest protection from both shores.

A bedraggled General Ashley braced himself against the wind on the *Yellow Stone Packet's* deck, his hair flailing his bald spot. His powerful voice echoed, "Without provocation, these treacherous devils murdered a dozen of Missouri's finest men -- and wounded as many more -- then had their vicious harpies befoul their bodies!"

The General shook his fist. "My valiant friend Reed Gibson just choked to death on his own blood. Other brave wounded will follow him to an unmarked grave on this Godless prairie -- through with life as we know it. But I'm *not through* with the *Arikaras*!"

Ashley paused, scanning his men's upturned faces. "Some might be ready to slink away. If you are, you can join the wounded headed for Fort Atkinson on this keelboat."

"Well General, I'm nicked up a bit, but I'll not be tuckin' my tail from those divel heathens!" Hugh Glass roared, joined by the shouting men around him.

Ashley yelled, "Sharpen your butcher knives, men! We're going back -- this time with the United States Army and heavy artillery!" Ashley bowed his head, his hair flapping all the more wildly, "Let us pray!"

While his men uttered prayers for dead comrades, Ashley prayed fervently that *after* Colonel Leavenworth got over his rage at the disaster he'd predicted -- and *after* the unpredictable Major O'Fallon got past the idea of hauling Ashley to jail in chains -- they'd send troops and cannon to avenge his dead.

Aborting his prayers, Ashley retired below to pen the most impassioned plea of his career to Colonel H. Leavenworth. He asked Moses Harris, aboard the *Yellow Stone* with a broken leg, to deliver the dispatch to Fort Atkinson.

Ashley knew his partner, Drew Henry, called the *Arikaras* "Rees." He wrote the Major a terse note, describing how the Rees had sold him the horses Drew wanted, then butchered them and a score of men. He called upon Drew to muster every man and head for the Cheyenne River's junction with the Missouri. Ashley handed the express to Jedediah Smith, whispering, "God Speed." Jedediah Smith soon trotted northward up the Missouri's west bank.

After watching the squaws defile men he'd broken bread with, William Sublette never gave a thought to leavin'. He moved his gear to the *Rocky Mountains*. He'd never felt the hot thirst for vengeance before. He didn't like it -- or maybe he did. The other men shared his fury, for *only* the gravely wounded set sail for Fort Atkinson.

At sunset of the second day after the *Yellow Stone Packet* left, James Clyman, barebacked, sunburnt, scratched and gaunt, climbed the *Rocky Mountains'* ladder. Sublette, boarding with several sacks of small game, braced Clyman, "Glad to see them lunatic squaws didn't dump your brains in the sand."

Crow Chief Edward Rose laid his game on deck, slitted his ebony eyes and growled, "The squaws were *not* crazy. *Arikara* halt an enemy's voyage to the spirit world by crippling his body. They knew when you saw your warriors lose their afterlife, you'd flee from their land."

Sublette's eyes hardened along with his voice, "If they was right, this keelboat'd be empty. We go back -- I'm gonna geld me a few o' them skinny *Arikaras* and see how that sets with their plans fer the spirit world."

Clyman intervened, "Who's your new hunting partner?"

"Jim Clyman, this's Ed Rose. We been huntin' with bow, snare and knife to keep from stirrin' up them *Arikaras*. Rose is a Crow by choice and hunts quieter'n a snake."

"Ah," said Clyman, "*A rose by any other name would smell as sweet.*"

Sublette added, "Clyman amuses himself with them fancy book-sayin's."

Edward Rose was not amused. He thumped his thick chest with his fist. "Gentlemen, I'm a cross breed between a white trapper, a *Cherokee* squaw with hair too kinky for an Indian an' a mountain donkey, but I'm not so mule minded I never heard o' Shakespeare!"

* * *

The *Yellow Stone Packet* debarked its 14 wounded men, at Fort Atkinson midday of June 18th. Before Moses Harris and the other wounded men set foot ashore, news of Ashley's defeat engulfed the fort, scorching every corner like a prairie fire.

But the massacre wasn't hot news to the pallid, 30 year old Indian Agent Benjamin O'Fallon, lying sick abed with his chronic liver ailment. Several days before, an *Otoe* medicine man'd chanted it as the fulfillment of a divine prophecy.

At first, O'Fallon had been perturbed at Ashley's abuse of the Indians, vowing to take official action against him. Then a *Pawnee* gloated over the *Arikara* scourge of many whites, divulging that it really started when the Missouri Fur Company fought over a *Sioux* slave. The event's complexion changed. O'Fallon wasn't a man to be humbled by a *Pawnee* who couldn't even count the bear claws on the thong around his own wrist.

When a friendly *Teton Sioux* horse trader pitied O'Fallon over the ambush, the punitive expedition order started to write itself in his head! Benjamin O'Fallon wasn't a man to be pitied by a pock-marked horse trader with two teeth! He'd only awaited official verification. Now the *Arikara* would get theirs!

O'Fallon sent his orderly to summon Joshua Pilcher, his partner in the Missouri Fur Company headquartered at Council Bluffs. Pilcher was field leader and president of the firm.

Never married, Ben O'Fallon tried to outlive his illness without help of wife or servants. Wrapping himself in a knubby blue blanket, he bent over his desk writing instructions with his wispy blond baby-hair waving gently in the airless log building.

Square-jawed, 33 year old Joshua Pilcher was one of those perfectly proportioned men. Standing five-ten at 160 pounds, Pilcher's ornate clothes made him more impressive. His buckskin coat was neatly trimmed with red wool cloth and embroidered with red and blue porcupine quills. His matching red cloth shirt set off his golden buckskin pants and new blue-beaded moccasins. A former medical student, Pilcher seemed reluctant to approach O'Fallon mired in his mysterious illness.

"Come in. I'm not contagious. Just my liver crucifying me again," O'Fallon gritted, wiping sweat beads from his lip. "Joshua, you've seethed since the Blackfeet murdered Bob Jones, Mike Immel and our other trappers on the Yellowstone in May. You'da been up there in a whipstitch, if I hadn't nailed your feet to the floor till just the right time."

"This the right time?" Pilcher asked, his gray eyes bright.

"O'Fallon nodded. "Will be after Henry Leavenworth comes down out of the rafters. The good Colonel did everything but jail Ashley to hold him here -- then as usual, Leavenworth folded -- even giving Ashley disguised powder and shot to trade the *Arikara* for horses! When Leavenworth is rational, tell him I've appointed you Indian Sub-Agent to head a punitive expedition against the *Arikara.*"

"And have you?"

O'Fallon wrote out Pilcher's orders as he talked. "Yes. Recruit a sizable force of *Sioux*. Take all the Missouri Fur men you need, expense to be borne by the Indian Factory System. Your only limitations are One -- Take no whiskey into Indian Country and Two -- Do not fire on the Blackfeet less you think you can get away with it."

"Missouri Fur traders'll go to a man! Murdering Blackfeet near bankrupted us when they stole our $30,000 in peltry and all our horses. Our men know a trapper's life on the upper Missouri's not worth a moldy plew till all these massacres are avenged! When we going after the Blackfeet?"

"Don't know, Joshua. Blackfeet stay well west of the *Arikara*. Leavenworth won't be spoiling for a second fight -- particularly after he loses the first one. Take that old Claymore o' yours and lead him against the *Arikara*!"

As O'Fallon predicted, Colonel Henry Leavenworth, his rage burnt down, closed the day writing to General Atkinson, Commander Western Department, announcing his expedition against the *Arikara*. Leavenworth's letter ended with a flourish, "*We go to secure the lives and property of our citizens.*"

At dawn on June 22nd, six full companies of the Sixth Regiment, comprising 220 troops, stowed their howitzers and six pounder artillery pieces aboard Army boats, then marched through the mud for the Upper Missouri.

Dashing Joshua Pilcher, leading 60 stone-eyed trappers, soon overtook Leavenworth's force, adding two more boats and helping to crew the *Yellow Stone Packet.*

Ten miles above the White River, several small parties of *Yanktonai* and *Teton Sioux* received trade blankets from Joshua Pilcher for telling their brothers of their grand chance to fight the *Arikara* -- all to avenge the death of a *Sioux* slave.

* * *

Nearly 50 years old, Major Andrew Henry had no idea why he was still in the trappin' business. The slender, gray-haired six footer'd had an independent income from his Potosi, Missouri lead mine for the entire 15 years he'd spent hidin' from Indians while he waited for some overgrown rat to smell the sex extract on his beaver traps.

Major Henry eyed Jedediah Smith's strained face in the firelight. "Jed, only way things changes in the fur business is they git worse. Bad nuff, I lose four trappers an' a passel o' horses. General's gonna fix it, so he loses 20 horses, three dozen more men and starts a Indian war. One o' these days I'm goin' home. Waugh! Gonna play my fiddle on the front porch while listenin' to these war stories with mild to middlin' interest."

Jedediah Smith ignored the despairing words and asked, "David Jackson in camp?"

Major Henry shook his head. "Davie's due back soon's he finds that loco Milt Sublette."

"Where's David looking for Sublette?"

"Dunno, but if I's lookin' fer Milt, I'd start in the lodge of the fanciest Crow squaw ever wore white leggin's to a horse-thief picnic. Waugh! If he's not there, Milt might be taggin' after some *Hidatsa* lady -- provided her husband's the ugliest, man-mauler ever drew breath north o' the Black Hills. Milt cherishes a bit o' risk now an' agin."

"Be serious, Major. General Ashley needs every man headed south *yesterday*," Jedediah pleaded.

"Waugh! You think it ain't serious lookin' fer Milt Sublette, then you look fer him! Ain't none of us ever found him 'cept when he wanders in with all them plews now and agin."

"Can we leave at daylight?"

"Can if Davie's back. Gotta teach them Rees not to jump on old Bill's tail. Besides, Davie's brother George is down there with Bill's bunch. Waugh! Davie'll sure pine fer any fight George got hisself into."

"Well, Milt's brother William is with General Ashley, so Milt'll likely want some of this fight. William Sublette's a big fine man with his head nailed on straight -- nothing like Milton."

Jedediah sent four men to find Field Manager, David Jackson, then wrapped himself in a blanket by the red coal fire.

At daybreak David Jackson gently shook Jedediah awake. Jedediah found it hard to believe David Jackson was only 35. Lines in his kind face were like deep cracks in brittle rock. He knew David was married with four boys and had fought in the Battle of New Orleans. Whatever aged Jackson so hadn't tamed his spirit. David's smile was constant. "My brother George all right?"

"Last I saw George, he was fine," Jedediah yawned. "Ready to head south now?"

"Can't find Milt Sublette, but he'll never miss us. Here's a strip o' jerky. Eat it slow. Got one to a man," David cautioned. "If we hurry, the 50 of us might catch the Major by noon. Major Henry's headed for the bull boats at our fur cache."

In the last week of July, Major Henry's buffalo hide bull boats drifted past the two *Arikara* villages in the heat of the day. *Arikaras* gestured to entice the trappers ashore. The Major laid into his paddle. "Injuns gitchu once, shame on them! Waugh! Gitchu twice -- well shame on you!"

On July 30th, the largest military force ever to reach the Upper Missouri camped near General Ashley's keelboat *Rocky Mountains*. With 220 soldiers, 200 trappers and 600 *Sioux*, the expedition exceeded 1,000 men -- but no Milton Sublette.

William tracked down Jedediah Smith, who was holding a prayer meeting for about 40 trappers in a grove of baby cottonwood trees. After Jedediah's last "Amen," William asked, "Seen my brother, Milton?"

Incensed by mere mention of Milton's name on grounds of a prayer meeting, Jedediah snapped, "Nobody can ever find Milton Sublette when they need him -- a chronic condition."

"Don't even hint he's a coward! Milt Sublette's the best fightin' man you'll ever see!" William surprised himself with the fire of his anger.

Jedediah Smith laid a worn silk ribbon in his Bible as a bookmark, "I've never struck a man with a Bible in my hand."

"Then drop it, er quit slanderin' my brother!"

Jedediah knew one of them would be dead in seconds if he forgot the Word. "Any man perishing over an insult will surely descend into Hell, for God shall not abide such a fool waste of life. Tell Rose and Clyman to form hunting parties. Form another yourself, Mr. Sublette and send your senseless wrath down your gun barrel!"

No longer worried about the *Arikaras*, foraging parties under Sublette, Rose and Clyman took rich harvests of game. After two days of feasting and brave talk, the *Sioux* war-danced. *Sioux* warriors were given muslin head bandages -- blessed to ward off evil *Arikara* bullets -- and to make them stand apart from the *Arikara*, day or night.

To William Sublette, the *Sioux* stood apart from anybody else on earth. The *Sioux* were a tall, handsome people with chiseled coppery faces and beads braided into their hair, but that wasn't all that made them unusual. Sublette asked Edward Rose, "How do them *Sioux* git to smellin' like that?"

"Come with me," Rose answered. As the sun rose, many *Sioux* lay down and rubbed themselves with smoked entrails of polecat or raccoon.

"They rubbin' them guts on nere to keep mosquitoes off?" Sublette inquired, wrinkling his tortured nose.

"For some, it's their way of bathing. Others do it to keep their enemy from counting *coup* on them." Rose rarely laughed, but he couldn't help himself. "Pilcher's whites riding with the

Sioux are in for a surprise. *Sioux* think differently from whites. Plains Indians believe counting *coup* on their enemy's more important than killing him."

"What *is* counting *coup*?" Sublette asked in exasperation.

Rose only shook his head and grinned.

* * *

As time for battle drew nigh, General Ashley wanted to make another inspirational speech, but refrained because of "chaotic indigestion." Instead, he asked Colonel Leavenworth to speak at twilight when the mosquitoes were most catastrophic.

"As of today, Ashley and Henry men'll be called the *Missouri Legion*. General Ashley, myself and Major Andrew Henry'll man command headquarters. Captain Jedediah Smith'll take half of you and Lieutenant George Jackson'll take the rest. Ensign Joshua Pilcher'll command the *Missouri Legion* force from the Missouri Fur Company. Field commanders'll pass out non-com ranks to trusted men among you. I wish every man here God speed on the battlefield."

After their near brawl over Milton, William Sublette was surprised to git a warm handshake and Sergeant Major's rank from Captain Jedediah Smith. "What'll I do now?"

Smith replied, "Fight like you did on the sand bar. Men will follow you." Smacking Sublette's shoulder, he left, the sting of the blow telling William their differences were dead.

The armada advanced up the Missouri. Leaving their boats with token crews, the *Missouri Legion* made a forced march to within rifle shot of the fortified *Arikara* villages on the sultry afternoon of August 9th.

Joshua Pilcher's mounted trappers and head-banded *Sioux* warriors rallied on the prairie just south of the villages. Pilcher planned an orderly charge, but when he saw the *Sioux* slam their heels into their ponies, he spurred ahead of them wielding his Claymore like a great scythe cleaving one *Arikara* after another of the hundred that charged to meet his cavalry.

The trappers were astounded to see Indians of both sides *slap* their opponent or his horse and ride on. Still outraged by the deaths of their comrades, the trappers did not play "Indian patty cake." They shot or knifed every *Arikara* they could.

Half a dozen dead *Arikara* and several *Sioux* sprawled in

the hoof-torn grasses. Many *Sioux* dismounted to cut off hands or feet from fallen *Arikara*, though Pilcher pointed his sword futilely at enemy horsemen fleeing back to their villages. The cavalry battle disintegrated. Pilcher withdrew his men in disgust.

The *Sioux* decided the war was over. They loped their ponies toward an unguarded cornfield with their *passé* white head kerchiefs flapping, one man's war being another's mystery. Joshua Pilcher begged them to open fire on the village with their rifles, but the *Sioux* refused. They wanted an open fight where "*coup* could be counted" or nothing, so nothing is what they got. Loading their blankets with *Arikara* corn, they trotted for home.

William Sublette knelt by the river with the other Ashley men on the right flank, the Army regulars to their left. As sunlight failed, the whole line was ordered to fire two rounds at *Arikara* fortifications "for effect," but Sublette couldn't see any effect. *Arikara* returned scattered fire from their potato holes.

The following dawn Army riflemen fired volley after volley into *Arikara* potato holes from a hill about 100 yards away. Sublette shot at gun ports in the willow-bush strongholds as the trapper infantry advanced, firing into both villages.

Fed up with useless tactics, James Clyman stood behind the young officer commanding the artillery. Six pounders and howitzers lobbed visible rounds that roared through the air to explode harmlessly around the potato holes. The bombastic cannon reports were thrilling though accomplishing little. Clyman called out, "*Your cannon, their bowels full of wrath, spit forth their iron indignation against the walls in preparation for a bloody siege*! *King John, Act II, Scene I.*"

The artillery officer fanned his hand behind his ear shouting, "Kenneth Morris, Lieutenant, Lexington, Kentucky!"

Throughout the hot, sticky, mosquito-festered day, the *Arikaras* stubbornly returned fire, though seldom coming near anybody. Major Henry opined, "Them Rees is lyin' down toe-pullin' them triggers. Waugh! More likely to shoot some trapper's horse in the butt than make any St. Louie woman a widder."

By noon, Colonel Leavenworth ordered his cannoneers to cease fire to preserve nearly exhausted ammunition. All riflemen were ordered off-line to forage for food.

Sublette and Clyman shot a pair of wary does, sharing them with Edward Rose and several others drawn by the tantalizing aroma of roasting venison. Sublette wiped his mouth on his forearm. "This ain't what I come back up here fer. Why don't we drag 'em out o' them potato holes? Next thing you know we'll be buyin' more horses from 'em."

Rose stared into the fire. "The *Arikara* have wisely remained hidden, but they are ready to surrender."

Ashley, Leavenworth, Pilcher and Jedediah Smith were conferring aboard the *Rocky Mountains* keelboat near the venison roast when a delegation of four *Arikara* Chiefs straggled into camp with tears streaking their faces.

Rose held his hands out accepting the unexpressed credit for his prediction. "They'll want me to translate." Rose walked toward the *Arikaras*, his hand on his butcher knife.

"Lookie them Rees, amarchin' in here like sorry orphans. Waugh! We should be aroastin' their treacherous butts stead o' these deer," Major Henry howled.

Edward Rose translated the *Arikara* Chiefs' pleas on the deck of the *Rocky Mountains,* still pocked by Ree bullets from their June encounter. "Chief Little Soldier says their homes are bitten by bullets and torn by thunder from the sky. The Chiefs beg mercy for their families. Say they will give back all things taken from the men of this great boat. They will attack no more whites. They will smoke the calumet upon these things they have said." Rose concluded, "They are four terrible liars."

Leavenworth, having suffered virtually no Army casualties, eagerly smoked with the Chiefs and urged Ashley and Pilcher to do the same. Ashley took one puff. Pilcher flatly refused and warned the Chiefs to beware of his men.

Next morning Colonel Leavenworth scribbled a rambling "treaty," which the chiefs all "X'd." Pilcher refused to sign. Ashley signed, then smeared his signature illegible.

Chief Little Soldier returned three rifles, a horse and 18 robes to Ashley, saying this was all he had, and the rest must come from other Chiefs. When the upper village Chiefs refused to return anything, Lieutenant Morris asked permission to resume the attack at once.

Colonel Leavenworth replied, "U.S. Army's soldiers are

not bill collectors!"

"Bill collectors!" Ashley yelled. "Colonel, you wrote the treaty that says they give back all they took. The ink's not dry on it, and they've already broken the treaty!"

"That seems to be the way of things on the frontier, sir. The interests of my nation are opposed to renewed warfare at this time," Colonel Leavenworth announced.

When Joshua Pilcher learned of the Colonel's decision, he had to be restrained by three of his stoutest trappers.

Having silenced U.S. Army guns with mere words, the *Arikara* fled in the night, leaving both villages deserted on the morning of August 14th -- except for one crazy old crone.

Colonel Leavenworth ordered his men and artillery aboard the Army vessels and disembarked down the Missouri. The military unit had barely reached the speed of the current when both empty *Arikara* villages went up in flames.

As his own boat sailed toward civilized venues, outraged Joshua Pilcher wrote letters decrying Leavenworth's pathetic campaign of retribution as "ladylike" and "senile." If Indian Agent O'Fallon agreed, Pilcher's diatribes would land at newspapers capable of creating repercussions far greater than Colonel Henry Leavenworth's effeminate artillery.

Aboard the Army's lead boat, Colonel Leavenworth anticipated Pilcher's rash denunciations by launching accusations that Pilcher was an arsonist in two of his own letters.

As they broke camp and prepared to head into beaver country, William Sublette asked, "Major Henry, whatta you think of this *Arikara* shindig?"

"Bill, by hisself your brother Milt has give a Crow horse trader more *what fer* in five minutes than we give them Rees in five days with the U.S. Army and the *Sioux* nation -- and we still ain't got no horses to show for it."

CHAPTER 15

FIGHT FOR LIFE AUGUST 1823

General William Ashley leaned his elbows on the *Rocky Mountains'* starboard rail, peering through deepening twilight at the ember-popping rubble that'd been an *Arikara* village till yesterday. He hated this smoldering monument to his greatest failure. The fate of the rest of his life would be decided any minute. Major Henry and Captain Smith were due at dark.

This obscure bend in the upper Missouri had Ashley's destiny by the throat. He'd suffered 34 men killed and wounded here in the June 2nd ambush. Three more'd died since. Though his forces had taken but a wound or two in the August 9th fiasco, all but 30 of his men had deserted. Ashley and Henry's fur partnership was in its death throes on this leaky tub.

"Waugh. Battlefields is special sad, Bill -- black and dead -- spindly colyums o' smoke risin' agin the red sky -- like a piece o' the earth died right along with them people that died on it," Major Andrew Henry mused from the deck behind Ashley.

Ashley turned to his lifelong friend. Another defeat lurked in Drew's words. Maybe it was all over. "We've seen a lot of battlefields back during the war, Drew. They have absolutely nothing to recommend them. Battlefields are memorials to man's inability to live peacefully -- the curse of our kind. But a battlefield's like a mystery. It's the end of everything for the dead or the beginning of something new for the living."

"Men's the mystery, Bill. Our men tuck their June butcherin' in stride. Waugh. Not one turned tail. Then Leavenworth come up here and done his barn dance -- wouldn't let nothin' happen -- and pert near all our men th'owed up their hands an' lit out! There's yer mystery."

Andrew Henry joined Ashley at the rail. "They's one crazy squaw awanderin' around them smolderin' villages with mosquitoes achawin' her sumpthin fierce. Waugh. Maybe she knows the answer to the mystery, cause I cain't figger it."

Ashley pointed. "That's her, lying dead by the river."

Jedediah Smith climbed the ladder and crossed the deck, his usual confident stride weakened to an ordinary walk. Obviously troubled, he just nodded. "Shall we go below and starve these bloodsuckers?"

The three filed down the ladder into the man-smelly cabin and squawked their stools up to a tilted table where two tallow candles flickered among a litter of burnt mosquitoes.

"Gentlemen -- what must we do to save this fur venture?" Ashley queried. No reply. Ashley peered into their poker faces in the flickering yellow light. "Is this a wake?"

Finally, Jedediah Smith grated, "Flee this foul place. I christened it Devil's Bend on the map I'm making. I don't have a say in how you decide the future of your venture -- if it has any."

"Bill, we're busted with a few men and fewer horses. Hate to jine them quitters, but I think our goose's done been cremated. Waugh. I been at this fur game too long. Tell ya, Bill, I'll resign an' give ya my share o' the leavin's. Jist go home to Potosi an' play my fiddle on my front porch."

"Drew, you resign every year, whether we're mining lead, making gun powder or chasing beaver."

Major Henry's callused thumb snuffed a candle. "Bill, if you had a plan, I might roll the dice agin, but we're asittin' here dead waitin' fer them Rees to bury us -- an' they done run off."

Ashley pulled out a slip of paper, laid it on the table and tapped it with his forefinger. "Far as I can see, our fortune's laid out right here."

"What's your plan say, Bill."

"Says Drew takes the *Rocky Mountains* and crew with an overland party of a dozen to the Yellowstone post and traps out the rich streams. Says Jedediah leads the other dozen men into new beaver country south of the Yellowstone and finds a pass through the Rocky Mountains to open up the west for our people. Says I take the *Yellow Stone Packet* to St. Louis, sell the few plews in your bull boats to raise money for more men. Guess it's no secret I'm running for Governor next year."

Wondering how Ashley'd got all that on one paper scrap, Major Henry grabbed it, then grinned. "Bill -- you're a borned politician!" Henry folded the blank scrap and jammed it in his pocket. "Waugh. Sumpthin' to remember you by."

Since learning of his new missions, Jedediah'd been mentally choosing the very best men to accomplish them. Major Henry tapped Smith's shoulder with a horny finger. "When you git through with yer roster Jed, I'll take them what's left. Waugh. We'll trap enough beaver to fill my fiddle case."

At dawn on August 16th, both keelboats sailed south on the Missouri to Fort Kiowa where Ashley recouped the supplies and horses he'd left there. But there was barely enough to outfit Smith's group. Ashley felt sure his partner'd raise enough cash to outfit the others by selling the *Rocky Mountains*. While Henry's men spruced the boat up, Jedediah Smith headed overland due west from Fort Kiowa with his hunting party of William Sublette, James Clyman, Thomas Fitzpatrick, Thomas Eddy, Edward Rose and five of Ashley's "civilians" that palavered in barracks lingo.

Major Henry expected to cover the 350 miles from Fort Kiowa to their Yellowstone camp in 25 days. Henry and his field manager David Jackson parsed their meager supplies to Hugh Glass, Jim Bridger, John S. Fitzgerald, Johnson Gardener, Daniel S.D. Moore and five other trappers.

But they were short three rifles, 200 pounds of powder, 50 traps and a ton of supplies. Major Henry confided to Davie Jackson, "Foolhardy ta take good men to the Yellowstone when ya cain't supply 'em right where they stand."

Fort Kiowa tradesmen had staked busted trappers before, but none so snake bit as Ashley and Henry. Their credit'd vanished like the *Arikaras*. Tradesmen wouldn't touch their keelboat with a deep water pole.

Then Major Henry spied a powerful feller striding toward them from Fort Kiowa. "Davie, remember last June when you was searchin' everywhere from the North Pole south fer Milt Sublette?"

"Yeah," David Jackson muttered absently, reconfirming there weren't half the lead bars their party'd need for bullets.

"Waugh! Davie, if you owl yer neck around in about two seconds, you're a cinch to find him."

Bronzed, 6'4" Milton Sublette, his black hair down his broad back like an Indian, his buckskins shiny enough to see yourself in, casually towered over them like he'd just finished a five minute errand. "Heard at the fort my brother's joined this outfit. Bill here?"

"Waugh no, Milt. Bill's with Jedediah Smith explorin' parts unknown fer beaver uncaught," the Major answered as nonchalantly as Milton.

"I stored two bales o' beaver plews fer you at Fort Kiowa, Major. Since yer still here, ya wanta do sumpthin' with 'em?"

Major Andrew Henry knew why Milt Sublette never got caught by any of the husbands he hoodwinked. The man was a master of timing. "Why Milt, I think we'll cash 'em in so's we don't have ta graze with the horses this trip. Milt, you goin' up the Yellowstone, er you gonna stay here an' romance the commandant's wife till he gits his new firin' squad shaped up?"

David Jackson lost control and fell across his lead bars in paroxysms of laughter.

"What?" Milton Sublette asked.

"Comin' er goin', Milt?" the Major asked.

"My brother Bill gonna join up with your party later?"

"Waugh! With luck Milt, you might be able to put sumpthin' in Bill Sublette's Christmas sock -- besides your foot."

"Then I'm comin', Major. Lieutenant Parsons says you kin moor yer keelboat at their dock if you wanna. David, where's your brother?"

"George caught a bullet in the armpit in the second *Arikara* skirmish and had to go to the settlements," David Jackson answered, wondering how George was by now.

"Make up another kit fer me. Major, if you'll leggo my cut o' the plew money, I gotta buy a trinket er two at the fort. They's romance in my future up river!"

* * *

Major Henry's newly supplied trappers were barely out

of gunshot of Fort Kiowa when a war party of 26 *Mandans* made a play for their pack horses.

The Major immediately turned to Milton Sublette, "Waugh! You do sumpthin' to them *Mandan* women, Milt?"

"No, but I'm gonna do sumpthin' to their men!" With that, warhooping Milton Sublette stormed into the *Mandan* horse charge, busting it apart around him. Milton fired, unseating a warrior wearing a buffalo head over his own, then splintered his rifle stock on their leader's face. The feathered Chief was dead of a broken neck before he hit the ground.

As Milt Sublette chased the Chief's paint horse, Major Henry howled, "Now there's a man knows how to count *coup*!"

Before Major Henry could set his men defensively, their emotions, stifled by their disgusting set-to with the *Arikara*, exploded. Screaming madmen, the trappers attacked the milling *Mandans*, dragging seven off their ponies and gutting them with butcher knives.

The 18 *Mandans* who could still ride, did, realizing they had attacked a ghost caravan of evil demons from the spirit world. Those escaping vowed never to speak of this in darkness for fear the demon spirits would return.

At Henry's direction, the trappers used four captured Indian ponies to tote all eight *Mandan* corpses. By the end of the second frying pan August day, the corpses were too ripe to travel with, so the trappers set them in a council circle with their buckskin shirts pulled up over their faces.

Hugh Glass let three pack horses graze while the dead *Mandans* were set up. Unaware of exactly where the other trappers were, Hugh strayed from Major Henry's party.

Barely able to hear the other men, Glass paused under a shady scrub pine tree to wait. Suddenly his three pack horses were shrieking, bolting and gone!

Bold a man as he was, Hugh Glass's Irish heart froze in his chest. Before him reared a snarling grizzly over three feet taller and 600 pounds heavier than himself.

The grizzly's head was big as peach basket. It's snout, square on top, showed a mean little eye at each corner. The mouth was bigger than a horses -- and full of spiked yellow teeth the size of a man's fingers. The roars from the grizzly's drooling mouth were louder than any gale winds Hugh'd ever heard. The bear's torso was thick as a pregnant horse with tree stump arms and legs sprouting three inch claws.

When Hugh's frozen heart thawed, it leaped free of his ribs, thumping in his throat, hammering in his eyes, hissing in his ears. "Blessed Virgin, save me!" he gasped

Hugh's Hawken rifle fell when the pack horses went berserk. The rifle lay there glinting in the sun, nearly aiming itself at the sow grizzly's mammoth foot.

As though he was watching himself, Hugh Glass snatched his Hawken, cocked the hammer and fired it's lone .60 caliber bullet into the grizzly's chest -- with no effect -- except to make her smash Hugh flat with a ripping ham-sized forepaw. Hugh spit dirt and blood, his own blood blinding his left eye.

Hugh screamed, "HELP!" with more lung than he'd ever put into a "Land ho" from the highest crow's nest in the British fleet. The memory of a high mast sent Hugh scrambling up the scrub pine. But the stocky pine groaningly supported the grizzly as she clawed him from the tree and smashed him to the ground, shattering several of his ribs.

Her rotten breath suffocated him as she bit the flesh off his cheek and ate it.

He slammed his fist into her great black nostrils, startling her enough to stop her from eating his head.

Hugh heard welcome gunshots and felt the bullets slam into the grizzly, but she didn't drop this time either. Instead, she seized Hugh in flesh-ripping forepaws and bit through his left shoulder, smothering him with her putrid breath.

His urine was suddenly hot wetness in his buckskins. He pulled his butcher knife and stabbed the grizzly's neck again and again till she dropped him in their pooling blood.

Tottering, she fell to all fours, turning as if to leave him. He drew back to stab her leg and thought better of it.

More gunshots. She fanged Hugh's stomach muscles, yanking him off the ground. He stabbed her throat till she collapsed, sprawled on him with the weight of a dead horse, and crushed out what little breath he had left.

Hugh drifted in and out of consciousness, mindful the sow's crushing body was gone, and that he was Mister numb.

Then his nightmare misted up around him. Hugh heard Major Henry say no man mauled that bad could live out the day. Hugh wanted to say that he could, but he couldn't utter the words. In Hugh's dream the whole hunting party could not just sit and wait till one man died. They had to go on ahead so's they could get into somebody else's dream.

Hugh Glass heard young Jim Bridger and the old carpenter, John Fitzgerald, volunteer to stay with him till he died and give him a Christian burial before they caught up with the hunting party. After that, they lingered for what seemed several days, lamenting his failure to die so they could leave.

But when Hugh's agony awakened him, he was alone being sniffed by three skinny coyotes. He bellered in their faces, sending them yipping into the hot morning.

Able to open one eye, he searched for Bridger and Fitzgerald. Where were those scoundrels? They'd taken everything. Here he lay, a pile of bloody buckskins with no rifle, no food and no chance to live. Anger seared every blood vessel in Hugh's mutilated body. He'd live by the Grace of the Blessed Virgin till he choked the life outa both those faithless divels, even if he died in the doing of their deaths!

Hugh's new dream began. In this dream, he couldn't lie still. In spite of the hurt, he had to drag himself through bushes, over rocks, down hills, into dreams of dead *Mandans*, dreaming of dead trappers, and back up into the hot sky where the Virgin pointed him onward without easing his pain.

When he sensed something near him in the dream, he'd strike at it and gurgle because he had no voice.

The Missouri River teased Hugh from afar in the dream. When he could not drag himself with both arms, he used his butcher knife. With each stab in the ground, Hugh dreamt of plunging the knife into the cowards who'd deserted him. He climbed the torturous rigging of jagged rocks when he could only thrust from his toes and strike sparks with his butcher knife.

Hugh awoke amid snorting buffalo that ignored his whispers for help. He spread their cooling dung over his torn face, soothing away the white fire. Then the buffalo drifted into the sun and dream rains beat his fever down.

Rolling painfully onto his back, Hugh open-mouthed

water that was so hard to swallow he finally quit trying. Storm clouds grew into *Sioux* faces that took his knife. But instead of killing him, these beloved *Sioux* liked to carry him. They had very big knees, no feet and no bodies, but they knew of Fort Kiowa, because he heard the bugle after they faded. A bugle sounded just like it had after all the contraband food fell out of their furled sails at Franklin, Missouri so many centuries ago.

Hugh Glass lost the blurry comfort of his "dream world" when it turned into a cot in the Fort Kiowa Infirmary, where Hugh and a dead black man were the only patients. The greenish bottle flies clustered on the dead man's nose and mouth. Two orderlies with their suspenders hanging down for burial detail dumped the black man on a stretcher.

One of orderlies dropped his end of the stretcher, yelling, "The bear man's alive! His eye's open. Gonna fetch the O.D. so's he can see what a live dead man looks like!"

Hugh didn't want to know what he looked like. There were two other men who wouldn't want to know either!

Hugh Glass gasped, "My solemn oath to the Blessed Virgin on me mother's grave in County Cavan, I'll be takin' the lives o' them two filthy divels that left me to die though I must crawl through the flamin' fires o' Hell to do the deeds!"

CHAPTER 16

MOUNTAIN SURGERY   AUGUST-SEPTEMBER 1823

Jedediah Smith's trappers expected it to be powerful hot and dry west of Fort Kiowa on the way to the Black Hills. Mountain Men called it the Great American Desert. Water levels in their bags and gourds shriveled. The only running "water" they saw the last week of August was the White River. As they followed the White west, its milky water curdled to wet plaster.

Jedediah Smith ladled a handful out of the White that clung to his hand like porridge. "Keep the horses back. Good water hole shows on this trapper's sketch, so it lies in this basin."

Smith's party trudged west two more days through the White River valley's treeless gulches lined with spiny cactus. Men sucked rocks to wet parched throats with their spit, walking their horses in the shimmering heat. The second pack horse in line stumbled, then toppled. They stripped the kicking bay's load to save it, but it died chewing its tongue bloody in the rocky alkaline dirt.

The skinny Greek emigrant called Coon Dog collapsed beside the crinkling waterhole scrawled on the map. The fall snapped off one of his upper front teeth. His faltering breath whistled through the gap. Coon Dog lay clutching his mouth, sweating away what little water he had left.

Slender young Scotsman, Thomas Eddy, knelt and ran his sunburnt hands over the mud broken into cupped fragments. His orange beard stuck to his face in ringlets of dried sweat. "Mah horse kin go no more. Ah cannot walk another step. Best ah stay here to the end with Coon Dog."

"Captain, if we bury them up to their necks here where the ghost of the water lies, they may live till we bring water," ventured half-breed Edward Rose.

"What makes you think so, Rose?" Jedediah Smith croaked, suspicious of anything this evil man wanted to do.

"*Dakota Sioux* legend."

"Expect me to gamble two men's lives on some heathen legend?"

"Captain, *Dakota Sioux* are a noble people, but they do not make marks others read like the whites. Legends are told by *living Sioux* to other *live Sioux*. The dead pass no legends."

Jedediah mused, "Sand may harbor some moisture. Bury them. We'll follow this wash till we find water."

Edward Rose squatted and pawed sand.

Sublette saw punishment in the chore. It wasn't right. Rose wanted to help. Sublette let the other men stagger past him, most clingin' to their saddles tryin' to keep step with their horses. Clyman, his twisted face a skull, pulled out of line. Without a word, they untied shovels from their pack saddles and helped Rose bury Thomas Eddy and Coon Dog. Rose finished by pulling up sage bushes to shade their faces from the sun.

Clyman grasped Thomas Eddy's chin. Eddy's eyes opened. "*Alas, poor Yorick, I knew him well,*" Clyman muttered through split lips.

Eddy grinned bloodily, "Ye got to find water. Tomorrow's mah birthday. Wanta live to see it. Mah heartfelt thanks, laddies!"

Sublette looked from Rose to Clyman, "By God, we're gonna git these boys some drinkin' water."

Just before sunset, Jedediah whooped, "I hear geese!" Soon he dived from his horse headlong into four feet of murky water under a ledge in the basin of a gorge. Noisy Canadian honkers, who'd paused in their southward flight flapped into the air, made their winged "V" and disappeared in the dusk.

All the other men splashed in, flailing with school boy shouts of joy. Sublette sat in the water till he'd swilled enough to douse the fire in his throat. Horses crowded around him, sucking roiled water into their muzzles. He patted their heads, then sank under among them.

Though William Sublette's body ached too much to move, he filled gourd canteens strewn along the waterhole's bank with tremblin' hands he barely knew.

Still dripping, Jedediah Smith tied four filled vessels to his trapper's saddle. "I'm going back to get those men, Sublette."

"We'll both go, Captain," Sublette gasped.

"No. Camp needs meat. Take two men and shoot some." Jedediah rode the strongest pinto back down the trail, leading a pair of dun horses that still trickled water in the dust.

"If we hadn't made that ruckus, we'd have game!" Edward Rose fumed. "In dry lands, the hunter does not hunt game -- he hunts water -- then waits."

"Rose, by the time you an' Clyman git sitiated in them rocks fer a clear shot at this water hole, I'll git ever'body outa here," Sublette rasped.

"Sublette, just put dry charges and double loads in them Hawkens in your boots. No need to miss a dark shot because we can't see both rifle sights." Rose stabbed his butcher knife into the bank and rolled under the water hole's ledge.

Sublette reloaded the boot pistols Grandpa Whitley'd left him and reached them under the ledge to Rose, then moved horses and packs up the draw. Sublette and the other bone-weary Mountain Men dozed amid pack saddles and hobbled horses as a new moon cast its silvery haze across the jagged shadows in the gorge. Stars were radiant in the indigo sky.

None of the snoring trappers heard the first pistol blast, but all seven heard the second. Gun shot echoes bounced through the rocky gorge while the thunder of stampeding critters dashed the starving men's hopes.

They lumbered stiffly down the gorge to find Edward Rose slitting a downed buffalo's throat amid pungent smells that smother a hot kill. "Start them fires boys. Time to gorge," Rose grated.

Brittle desert woods crackled like little lightning around charring cuts of buffalo meat smoking on sticks in the fires. Rich drippings flared orange in the ashes. The night air tasted good enough to eat.

Jedediah Smith rode into the firelight followed by two slumping figures roped on the duns behind his pinto. Whooping men ganged the horses to help their feeble friends off. Jedediah slid from his horse. "If I'd been blind, I'd have found this camp by the smell. That meat ready yet?"

Sublette muttered as he chewed, "Tis if you eat it blood rare. Eat mine soon's it stops bellerin'."

Men wolfed smoking chunks of juicy buffalo meat that had never tasted so good before.

Clyman squatted beside Thomas Eddy, "You said it was your birthday. When were you born?"

"August 30, 1799," Eddy answered in a Scottish brogue thick as cold syrup. Campfire exchanges between the feasting trappers revealed that Jedediah Smith, Thomas Fitzpatrick and William Sublette were *all* born in 1799.

Edward Rose grated glumly, "I'm oldest of all. Think I'm 36, but don't know my birthday."

Clyman waited for a lull, then letting his Virginia accent loose, he said, "I wasn't born in 1799, but I was seven years old that year, when I met President George Washington. My folks were tenant farmers with a life-lease on land President owned in the Blue Ridge country of Virginia."

Jedediah Smith asked, "What'd President Washington say to you?"

"Told me not to chew tobacco because that's what ruined his teeth. Washington died that year. His Will left our family a tattered set of books called the *Plays of William Shakespeare*. Many's the night we read them to each other."

William Sublette recollected Artemis tellin' him when he was eight that Washington freed his slaves by that Will. *Little Bill* felt warm recallin' the day he'd freed Artemis to be her own woman. Artemis had always been her own woman. He'd just made her legal. He wondered how Artemis was.

* * *

Jedediah Smith's horses'd quit dying, but were too weak to ride. Smith talked with the man-devil Rose about trading the jaded animals to the *Sioux* for fresh horses. As they conversed, they rode along the timber lined banks of a clear stream that rippled over the rocks.

Edward Rose said, "We're in the land of the *Bois Brulie Sioux*. If we don't find them, they will find us. When we meet --

you must let me talk even if I use the hand signs of the plains for words I don't know."

"Why?" Jedediah asked caustically.

"The *Sioux* are a polite people with ancient ways. If you don't know their ways, they will not trade. *Sioux* take being shot at, but will not stand for rudeness."

"You talk. I'll listen," Jedediah snapped.

"Listen well now. Do not ask for the horse of a warrior. Warriors are so warm to their horse they call it the *God Dog.* They sing to their horse as they sing to a woman. Warriors carve small totems of a horse killed in battle. They choose horses they will trade. Their choice has little to do with how sound the horse is. The generous *Sioux* will give you extra horses if you are not rude."

Jedediah Smith glowered at Rose. He knew Rose's renown as a cheat. The extra horse talk was a ruse. When a cheat promises more, you will get less!

A handsome, bare-chested *Sioux* in buckskin leggings, riding a paint with a war bridle and carrying a fringed leather bag full of lacrosse sticks fell in beside Edward Rose. With a closer look at Rose's face, the *Sioux* said softly, "*Chee-ho-carte*" and made the hand sign for *welcome.* Rose murmured and made other signs back.

"What was that about?" Jedediah asked.

"This *Sioux* lacrosse player knows me by my second Crow name --five scalps -- for a battle I made upon the *Minnetarees*. He takes us to his home. I told him we have fresh buffalo presents, and that we want to see the lacrosse game."

"What about the horses?"

"I will bring them up in disappointment when we cannot watch their lacrosse game. All trappers but you and me must wait here at the edge of their village."

The *Sioux* led Jedediah and Rose past tipi lodges of tanned buffalo hides bearing bright paintings. Behind a lodge a young warrior repeated a tune like a bird call on his flute, making Rose laugh.

"Why's he keep whistling like that?" Jedediah asked.

"He's playing a magic flute the medicine man has promised will win the heart of his woman."

"What's funny about that?"

"If you looked inside the tipi, you would see the woman loves another!"

To Jedediah's delight, the *Sioux* traded them 27 fresh horses for the frail 22 they had, took the buffalo presents and gave back venison in return. Smoking the calumet made Jedediah dizzy, but Rose said he had no choice.

The *Sioux* herded the horses to the camping trappers. To Jedediah's surprise, all but one of the horses proved well-broken and sound. In charge of the expedition's horses, "Shamrock" Thomas Fitzpatrick was going to leave the spavin-legged old horse behind.

But Edward Rose said, "Refusing the gift of this worthless horse will cause trouble. They gave us the ancient horse because its owner loves it too much to kill it. They hope we'll kill it for them, but far from here. We cannot let it wander back and break the owner's heart."

Jedediah Smith was puzzled. "The *Arikara* sell us 20 horses and slaughter them. But some *Sioux* cannot bear to kill one horse. How can this be?"

"As we've talked of these *Sioux* horses, the Crow have stolen a hundred horses. Other tribes beyond the mountains keep horses to eat as whites do cattle. Indian peoples are not all alike. Captain, you and I are trappers in the same group, but even *we* are not exactly alike."

"Let me think on that, Mister Rose. There must be some difference between us."

* * *

By the time Jedediah Smith's men learned the rockstrewn Black Hills were not rich in beaver, their fine *Sioux* horses, too long without the rich grasses of their homeland, were faltering.

Jedediah Smith dispatched Edward Rose into Crow country, to trade horses with his adopted tribe. Smith's men back-packed their own supplies, staggering through Hell's Canyon into the Powder River Basin.

Walking his horse, Smith threaded willow thickets as the sun sank into the mountains to the west. He expected Jim Clyman before dark with fresh meat from his buffalo kill. But Jedediah did not expect to be watched from the rocks by a red-headed fugitive with his twitching-tailed puma. Sublette, Fitzpatrick and several other men followed close behind Jedediah without spotting the wild-haired man above them.

Two miles further, Captain Smith was elated to find a beaver dam ponding the stream with their lodge near the middle and another lodge -- or large rock -- a few feet out into this crystalline water. Lazily, he contemplated spending a day or two trapping the pond while Rose traded horses with the Crows.

The nine foot male grizzly exploded from his long-practiced big rock simulation, drenching Smith with icy water and seizing his head in its teeth.

Smith felt his skull flexing in the bear's jaws as his feet flailed empty air. Deafening growls rung his ears as the smell of rotten meat stunned his nose.

Sublette raised his rifle.

"Don't shoot! You'll hit the Captain!" Thomas Eddy yelled, grabbing at Sublette's rifle. Sublette tried to dodge past Eddy, but Eddy stepped in his path.

Sublette kicked Eddy in the belly, clearin' his shot at the bear's chest beside Jedediah's floppin' body, and fired. The heavy bullet struck the scarred bear near the heart, but it kept chewin' Jedediah's head. Sublette pulled a stubby Hawken pistol from each boot and charged the bear.

Jedediah's weight bent the bear's head low. The Grizzly's head was big as the punkins he used to shoot with Artemis as a boy. Sublette fired one pistol point blank into its left eye!

Its eye blasted out, the grizzly dropped Jedediah and lurched toward Sublette. Sublette jammed his other Hawken into the bear's bloody maw and fired the double load into its brain. The grizzly reeled backward, crashin' into the shallows across the sunken bones of a puma and a host of its prior victims.

Congealing blood splotched Sublette's face, arms and chest. While trappers pulled Jedediah Smith from the gory water, Sublette moved down shore and rinsed off the blood in the cold water. The smooth scar on the left side of his chin was sticky with blood but didn't feel like he was cut. He heard himself whisper, "Thanks Artemis!" but couldn't believe he'd said that.

Jim Clyman examined Jedediah's lacerated head. The bear'd sunk a fang close to the Captain's left eye and bit in another by his right ear. The giant teeth'd laid Jedediah's chalky skull bare to the crown of his head. His left ear dangled from the jagged edge of his scalp. "What can I do, Captain?"

Jedediah dammed the blood pouring into his face with his buckskin sleeve. "Get your needle and thread from your possibles bag. Sew my scalp on as best you can. My chest hurts, but all I find there is my bullet pouch is gone."

Clyman located his scissors and cut away Jedediah's thick hair. He stitched the torn scalp, like sewing the sole on a moccasin. After nearly an hour, Clyman grunted, "Finished except the ear. Can't sew your ear on. I just don't know how all these shreds go together."

"Jim, you must sew my ear on too. I must be able to hear the Lord from either side."

Clyman sewed as others held pitch knot torches so Clyman could see to finish. "I've sewed your ear on the best I can, Jedediah."

"Well then make camp, so I can sleep. I'm weak --very weak."

Sublette squinted at Jedediah's stitched ear in the torch light. "Not so fast Clyman. That ear looks catty-wampus. Captain, I think Clyman's gotta start over. We cain't have the Lord talkin' into no crooked ear."

Irish Tom Fitzpatrick's voice boomed from the darkness, "Now see here, Sublette -- a man has to leave well enough alone. If Jim sews that ear on back'ards, the Captain'll be jumpin' right onto rattlesnakes, stead o' backin' away from 'em!"

CHAPTER 17

BRIDGER'S OCEAN WINTER 1823-FALL 1824

Two French Canadian trappers loaded winter supplies on pack horses in the coppery late afternoon light outside new Fort Henry on the Big Horn and Yellowstone rivers.

Jim Bridger peered through the gun slit in the trading post's front wall, his gray eyes darting back and forth. Treetops whispered in the wind, but the trail beyond the clearing was empty. He dearly wished these two Frenchies'd never found this place. Bridger sleeved the sweat from his lip. He had to find Old John quick!

Young Bridger dashed out the back door where John Fitzgerald sharpened the blade from his jack plane with a whetstone. "John -- he's alive! He's after us!"

Chubby old John ran his thumb along the edge of the plane blade. "Who's alive?"

"Hugh Glass!"

"Glass alive? Cain't be, Jim. Man bled five days till he run outa blood. Somebody's playin' a joke on you, boy."

"Them two Frenchies jist now said it's a joke -- but I know it ain't!"

"The Frenchies that tole you about Glass say it's a joke -- but you know it ain't. Jim, that's 'cause you're 19. When I was 19, I knowed more'n everbody inna whole world."

"John, willya jist listen? Them Frenchies was at Fort Kiowa. Some Irish Army Cap'n went on bout a bear-mauled Irishman with his face half tore off boltin' their Infirmary to hunt down a old man an' boy what tuck his gun an' left him to die. Them Frenchies seen it was a Irish joke. Cain't understand how anybody kin take one o' them Irish gargoyle stories serious."

But John Fitzgerald understood. His face went gray as his beard. "Jim, any man livin' through what that grizzly done ain't human!"

Fitzgerald kicked his horse in the flanks. "I'll Join the Army at Fort Atkinson. I aint waitin' here fer that *thing*!"

Bridger yelled, "John, you ain't even gotcher tools! You gotta tell Glass it was *you* made us leave him!"

Jim stood with his hands out till the hoof beats died away. Major Henry'd be back to the fort in a day or two. Jim'd have to tell him they lied bout buryin' Hugh Glass.

Jim had been trying to save wood, but he went back inside and built a blistering fire in the rock fireplace. He sat cross legged, muttering "Never shoulda watched him when we's awaitin' fer him to die, but a feller cain't take his eyes off'n sumpthin' that ugly. His face made a man sicker'n eatin' a maggoty polecat -- three claw marks through his left eye to his nose. Grizzly'd bit his cheek off leavin' red meat swole open. That face's in my head every night!"

* * *

Nobody knew better than Hugh Glass that he'd never been a handsome lad to set a colleen's heart beatin' faster. But folk had never shunned sight o' him the way they did at Fort Kiowa. Some thought Hugh couldn't see from his left eye under its weals and pointed at him from that side, but he could.

Fort Kiowa's aging Executive Officer, a Captain with an Irish brogue thick as Hugh's, scrounged a used trapper's outfit of buckskins, powder, shot and a possibles bag. The trade rifle was tired, but the post gunsmith put it shipshape. It hurt Hugh that nobody wanted to be owed for his kit. Made him feel guilty for hatin' 'em all.

In Fort Kiowa's barren chapel Hugh prayed, "Holy Mother of God, guide me to them faithless cowards that robbed my goods and left me for dead." Hugh couldn't hear the Virgin answer his prayers but he felt in his heart she had.

Before the cursed bear attack, Hugh knew Major Henry was leading them 350 miles back to the mouth of the

Yellowstone. That meant Fort Henry. He had but to follow the Missouri north to the Yellowstone. He'd navigate by the stars, if the Indians made him steer shy of the river.

Hugh cast about Fort Kiowa till he found six men headed up the Missouri. They'd heard of the *Arikara* uprising, but thought they could skirt the hostiles in their boat. Somehow they knew who Hugh was and what'd happened to him. He was glad to see Fort Kiowa in the boat's wake.

The oldest *voyageur*, Toussaint Charbonneau, was friendly and talked of his life. Like Hugh he'd taken an Indian wife -- a *Shoshone* named *Sacagawea*. Charbonneau'd bought her as a slave from the *Hidatsa* before she'd accompanied him on Lewis and Clark's expedition. Hugh enjoyed traveling with Charbonneau, who knew many native tongues.

When they were well north of *Arikara* country into the land of the *Mandans*, the men landed their boat to rest and hunt. Hugh Glass was first ashore with his rifle and most of his kit. Charbonneau bid them *au revoire,* and packed overland into the dense brush. Seconds later, the *Arikara* fell upon them, tomahawking the five men on the boat to death.

Hugh thanked the Blessed Virgin for sparing him. But when Hugh thought it was safe to leave his thicket, it wasn't. An *Arikara* scout slammed his butcher knife deep under Hugh's shoulder blade. Hugh wheeled.

While his attacker froze in shock at Hugh's hideous face, he slashed the man's throat before collapsing into the cattails. Bent reeds held Hugh's face above water, but were not so kind to his rifle and kit.

Hugh sensed something close to his face and opened his good eye. Unable to believe what it saw, he tried his lame eye. A green turtle the size of Hugh's chest with a feather dangling from each leg hovered over his face. When the turtle flew away, he realized it was painted on a leather shield. The face where the shield had been was *Mandan*.

Horrified, Hugh recalled waiting for Henry's trappers to arrange eight *Mandan* corpses into a mock council when the grizzly'd struck. Had this *Mandan* seen Hugh Glass during the fight with Major Henry's men?

Nonatuo, the *Mandan* behind the magical Turtle Shield,

saw the dream face rising from the river. He knew it was a spirit from the waters that had flooded the earth to whom the *Mandan* danced the *o-kee-pa*. Some fool had wounded it. This water spirit must be taken to the village and made well.

A husky, middle-aged *Mandan* squaw beached her round buffalo hide bull boat of firewood near *Nonatuo*. Behind her a young squaw ran her overladen bull boat aground in a foot of river water. The younger woman waved to her husband's mother, who turned her back. The angry young squaw wrestled her bulging boat to the marshy shore alone.

Nonatuo ordered the squaws to fetch the fallen spirit up the bluff to the Shaman. They lugged the ugly spirit up the hill without looking at its head. Looking at devils was man's work.

Even hot with fever, Hugh Glass knew one thing for sure about Indians. A white man never knew what they'd do next.

The squaws dumped Hugh at the feet of *Tomayo*, a chanting gray-haired Shaman wrapped in a precious white buffalo robe. *Tomayo* stood before two poles several times his height, a short pole bridging between them half way up. The tallest pole flashed a died grass sun at its top and a twig moon rose atop the other. Furious at being interrupted by infidels, *Tomayo* stabbed his finger toward the lodges as he muttered incantations to his Gods.

The angry squaws grabbed Hugh's wrists and ankles and toted him to the cluster of huge domed lodges, each with a tinier dome centered on top. The younger squaw asked *Nonatuo* who would bear her firewood while she dragged this spirit about. *Nonatuo* rasped that she would, then ordered the insolent women to take Hugh inside the lodge of *Tomayo*, the Shaman.

Hugh feared the vast building was a place of sacrifice. The lodge was like a huge European cathedral dome with blue sky showing through the fire hole in the middle. Four tree sized-timbers supported the center. A spar ran from the top of each timber to the next. These timbers braced a framework of bent poles covered with stretched skins.

A dozen horses and several dogs loitered about inside the lodge. Big enough to hold a hundred people, sour odors wafted about its dim interior from drying animal carcasses on the altar.

For four days, Hugh was chanted over and fed cooked

dog by *Tomayo*. The fifth day it snowed, sending his host to perform some special rite. Hugh wrapped himself in a supple buffalo robe, selected the sturdiest snow shoes and merged into the feathery snowfall.

Finding his rifle and kit strewn under the skim ice where the divel *Arikara* stabbed him, Hugh set out on foot for the old Fort Henry -- a good 250 miles northwest along the Missouri.

Fueled by hatred of the dirty divels who'd abandoned him and the carcass of a tan buffalo calf he wrested from three spindly wolves, Hugh snow-shoed north along the icing river.

Hugh didn't know how the *Mandan* medicine man healed the stab wound in his back. He apologized to the Blessed Virgin for even thinking of heathen cures. Surely, she'd done it her Beloved Self!

A scarred bull elk wintering among the junipers stepped into Hugh's sights and died instantly. Hugh kept piling on more animal skins agin the cold. Each night, he burrowed deeper in the snow to sleep under his welter of skins.

But when Hugh broke into the old Fort Henry, it was deserted. He cursed himself to sleep inside the fort, in spite of the Blessed Virgin, with wood rats scampering on him like witless leprechauns. At dawn Hugh scraped crusted snow from a board someone had burnt with a running iron on the front of the old fort. It crudely showed the junction of the Yellowstone and the Big Horn rivers and said "Ft. Hnry."

Hugh would've wintered in the old Fort Henry if he knew it was another 200 miles up the Yellowstone to the new one. But like everything else Hugh Glass had ever done, he learned the hard way. Game grew scarce along the way. Fortunately, Hugh had a bag full of frozen leprechauns to munch on.

Snow blindness forced Hugh to make a snow mask with eye slits in a hunk of buffalo hide with the hair on it. But his right eye hurt so, he halted often to pray to the Virgin. Shivering mightily, he shot at a huge-footed rabbit left handed. The Virgin had guided his bullet. But he had to devour the rabbit raw -- fur and all -- because his frost bitten hands couldn't skin it or strike sparks with flint and steel.

Suddenly, there it was -- a trading post with its smoke rising up through the trees into a white sky. Hugh wasn't sure either o' them desertin' divels was inside the new Fort Henry, but he was sure what they looked like.

Hugh Glass removed his mittens, then checked his rifle's load and prime. He stuck his butcher knife under the front of his belt. After knocking feebly on the heavy door, he nearly yelled a curse when young Jim Bridger pulled the door ajar. Astounding Hugh with his calm, Bridger said, "Watch that stair. Come in an' git warm."

Glass'd forgotten the snow mask covering his upper face. This lout had no idea he'd just opened his door to the angel of death. Bridger took Hugh's arm and led him to the fireplace. He lowered Hugh gently to the hearth and leaned his rifle in the corner. "If'n ya ain't too weak, you kin pull them hides off while I gitcher food. You'll warm up a site faster without 'em."

Tears welled in Hugh's eyes. This divel was a youngster -- a thoughtful lad tryin' to comfort him. Hugh prayed to the Virgin. Would he burn in Hell for it if he wreaked the full measure of his vengeance on this boy? Hugh gripped his butcher knife and waited for Jim Bridger to return.

Jim took the butcher knife from Glass's hand. "Ya won't need this. I seen how bad yer hands was froze an' cut up yer elk meat. It's plenny hot there on the table."

Hugh knew the Blessed Virgin had answered him. He turned his back and gestured to Bridger to untie his snow mask.

Bridger loosened the mask and laid it beside Hugh, then looked into Hugh's torn face and reeled against the fireplace. "Oh God! It's you." Bridger stood up straight. "I know what you gotta do. If I's you, I'd feel jist like you do."

Hugh Glass looked into the terrified face, "I'm near starved, I am for sure. Gotta eat this elk you fixed me." He raised his bleeding, frost-bitten hand. "Boy, I come to kill you, but I can do you no harm. It's over with us. Where's Fitzgerald?"

Realizing his livin' nightmare was over at last, Jim Bridger put his arms around Glass's shoulders and shook with relief. Finally he muttered, "Ole Fitzgerald lit out last fall. Said he's a jinin' the Army at Fort Atkinson. I cain't lie about that. I guess I ain't never gonna lie to nobody about nothin' fer the resta my life!"

"Sit and eat with me boy, it's been a long winter."

* * *

By autumn of 1824 Major Andrew Henry'd led his men over 400 miles into the Rocky Mountains southwest of Fort Henry. They'd taken a rich haul of beaver and had to find the best way to move their plews before the rivers froze over. Several freezes had already dressed the aspens in carmine and gold. Poorly marked rivers on their doeskin trapper's map clouded their choices.

Andrew Henry was drawn by the clashing of antlers to a pair of brawling bull elk in rut. Admiring the winner's pluck, he shot the gored loser, a huge-racked elk, heavy bodied enough to feed all Henry's men. After a night feast, Henry gathered his best men around the embers to git their notions where the rivers ran.

"Them elk in rut eats tough, but they ain't half as tough as this map I got. Follerin' the Bear River on here's more confusin' than a new preacher's sermon on how to git to heaven. They got the Bear a'flowin' north -- then they got the Bear a'goin' south a few miles apart. An' the way they show it here, the Bear must run down a gopher hole right after Cache Valley 'cause it's jist gone."

Young Jim Bridger pitched more limbs on the fire so the older trappers could study the weathered doeskin map as it passed among them.

Thick-necked ex-sea Captain John Weber spit a hissing stream of tobacco into the fire and passed the map on. He shifted his chaw to say, "Based on this pitiful excuse for a chart, I'd say we're now lost on both sides o' the Bear River at once!"

Daniel Potts, the skinny 28 year old son of a Pennsylvania miller, raised the vague map to the firelight. "I ain't been brought to ground this bad by anything since Mike Fink shot his ram rod through both my knees!"

Several men passed the map along shaking their heads.

Major Henry rose and took the map back. "Maybe the Bear River *begins* jist south of Cache Valley and that's why it don't show none past there. I'll bet a gallon o' trade whiskey, a dozen fish hooks and a pound o' black powder that's it!"

"Major, izzat trade whisky cut with pepper water an' tobacky juice?" Jim Bridger asked.

"Bought that gallon o' whiskey from Army stores at Fort

Kiowa -- guaranteed pure as the Vicar's maiden aunt fer two dollars -- which o' course is zactly what the Vicar's maiden aunt charged!" Major Henry hooted.

Bridger rose, grinning with the wisdom of youth, "I'm a'bettin' you two prime plews, five feet o' used string and a pair o' stepped-on spectacules that the Bear River don't begin south o' Cache Valley. Cap'n Weber can hold our stakes! I'll be takin' one o' yer bull boats an' leavin' in the mornin'!"

"Take this miserable map with ya and draw what's really there," the Major hollered over the whoops of the trappers.

At dawn Jim Bridger broke down a bull boat to fit on his pack horse and headed for what appeared on the doeskin map as the western leg of the Bear River leading to Cache Valley.

Jim'd secretly had Dan Potts explain everythin' on the map, cause Jim Bridger couldn't sign his own name -- let alone read. Dan promised to help him mark the map if Jim ever returned.

Captain Weber told Jim to steer with the paddle behind the boat for a rudder if he hit white water, then added, "Glad to see you taking it upon yourself to solve this mystery, Jim. Getting your bearings is important on the river -- and in your life. Sometimes they amount to the same."

Reaching the Bear River, Jim whang-leathered the willow limbs back together, then stretched and tallowed the buffalo hides on them to remake the bull boat. He launched the bull boat with a strange excitement, paddling over foaming waters into the churning current.

The Bear River seized Bridger's bull boat in its frothing white teeth and veered southward. Bridger tried to get the hang of steering with his paddle for a rudder. His heart pounded. Rapids doused him with spray, then soared between towering rock walls like the north wind -- faster than any horse could run. "EEEHaaa!" he yelled as his boat blasted a rock but sped on. "WhooEEE!" This was the most thrillin' day of his life. He hoped he'd live through it -- but stayin' alive weren't nearly as important as jist livin' like this!

Jim struggled to remember what he saw. That got easier after the river went glassy enough to make him paddle. When the current raced, he turned backwards to rest and found himself shaking all over. That's when the bull boat suddenly raised in the water. Jim swung the bull boat around with his paddle, so he could see where it was headed.

"What's this??" he gasped. The bull boat bobbed on the waters of a great lake he couldn't even see across! He'd gone at least 50 miles south of Cache Valley, and this ocean was fer sure no gopher hole!! He'd won the bet! He pushed the snout of his water bottle under the water and was startled by the "Squee -- eeh" of a large gray and white bird with yellow feet skimming the water.

A flock o' them birds, some all brown, all noisy, paid Bridger no mind. He lifted the water bottle to drink a swig before he corked it.

"Aacckk, salty!" He spat, then swigged another gulp rolling the brackish water around in his mouth before spitting it over the side. He tipped the bottle and let the water *glop -- glop -- glop* down the outside of the boat. Jim wiped his mouth. "Must be the ocean. Ever'body knows they ain't no such thing as a salty lake."

CHAPTER 18

SOUTH PASS AND BACK   WINTER 1823 -FALL 1824

None of Jedediah Smith's trappers would ever forget wintering with the Crow nation in the Wind River Valley into the spring of 1824.

At first James Clyman regarded the Crows as elegant enemies. Most were tall, powerful, handsome people. Warrior and squaw showed infinite care in the braiding of colorful ornaments into their long hair. Their buckskins were often white with embroidered quills as comely as any art Clyman had ever seen. He envied their physical perfection and ornamental clothes. They walked erect and looked directly into his eyes like no others ever had.

But Clyman despised guarding his belongings every second to keep them from being thieved by the Crows, or *Absaroka,* as they styled themselves. Clyman wore his Green River butcher knife in the back of his belt to keep it clear of his rifle loading. One foggy December morning, he walked between the lodges, straining to see if visibility was good enough up on the crags to hunt mountain sheep. A subtle tug at the back of his belt brought his nimble hand clamping about a small wrist.

Clyman turned, expecting to see terror in the handsome Crow face that went with the wrist, but saw resignation instead. He stripped his butcher knife from the squaw's mitten. He wanted her told never to steal from him again. Since Edward Rose was a Chief and virtual god to the *Absaroka,* he hauled her by the arm to Rose's lodge. Rose bade them enter and Clyman explained why they were there.

Edward Rose commanded the Crow woman to remove her fur robe and sit. Clyman had never seen a more beautiful person. *Chee-ho-carte* growled at her, freezing her smile to shame. She peeped a few words then stared at Rose's floor embellished by elaborate white mountain sheep skins. Rose barked at her again, and she squeaked her replies.

Rose turned to Clyman, "She is Bright Elk. You have your knife, so what is it you want of me?"

"Tell her not to steal again."

Rose sneered, "Tell the wind not to blow. Tell the moon not to rise. Tell a Crow not to steal! Are you mad? Robbery is their life. Their most ancient *Absaroka* motto is 'Rob, but never kill, for if you kill a man, he cannot return to be robbed again'."

"She should be punished for stealing," Clyman argued.

"Should I beat her -- what?"

The lodge was hot. Clyman shed his buffalo coat. Bright Elk pressed her hand over her nose, then jabbered to Rose.

Edward Rose seldom laughed for it was not kinglike, but he could not choke back his squeals of glee. "She says you stink and your clothes died long before you were born."

"Good, she can make me some new clothes. That'll be her punishment!"

Rose relayed the punishment and Bright Elk hissed a flurry of Crow curses.

"Bright Elk says she should have stolen something far more important to you than a knife for such a bad-tempered punishment."

"She did. Tell her she's stolen my heart."

"She stole what?

"Just tell her."

Rose shook his head, then uttered Clyman's message.

Bright Elk's glowering faded to puzzlement then bloomed into a beauty Clyman had never imagined -- not even in one of these handsome people. She dropped her eyes and spoke quietly to Rose while Clyman cursed for ever exposing himself to such embarrassing rejection.

Rose peered at the floor. "She does not like your idea. Making all your clothes cannot be justified for stealing a mere knife. As to theft of your heart -- she says if she can wash you -- she has a way of making you want her to keep it -- so there will be no punishment at all."

* * *

Cut Face Sublette was not used to Jedediah Smith losing control of himself. Jedediah's hands shook as he grated, "I know the weather's too bad to leave, but if I stay here one more day, I'll kill Ed Rose!"

"Why?" Sublette asked, amazed at this death sentence from a man who read the Bible mornin' and night.

"Life's not easy for a man like me, Sublette. When you shoot another man, it's because you had to. You make peace with yourself and go on. I'm smothered by *Exodus*, Chapter 20, Verse 13 or *Deuteronomy*, Chapter 5, Verse 17."

"I ain't quick ta shoot nobody. Bothers me plenty, and I ain't that good at scriptures."

"I'm too good at them! Both verses say *Thou shalt not kill.*"

"Why you wanna kill Ed Rose?"

"Major Henry warned me Rose'd swindle us. None of us speak Crow. We're Rose's prisoners! Rose is their graven idol! When I talk with Rose, he lords it over me that he must be consulted on all things and that his word is law. Price for his approval goes higher each time. He's robbing us of trade goods and supplies. Next he'll take the plews. What happens when we have *nothing* left?"

"Take the word of St. Charles' ex-Constable. You kill Ed Rose now an' the Crows solve that crime -- they'll be *nothin'* left o' us but our tracks!"

Jedediah's fist smashed his palm in an unbiblical manner.

"I ain't sayin' we oughta stay, Jedediah. I jist say we use our heads 'stead o' leavin' our scalps on a Crow lodge pole."

Jedediah laid his hand on William's shoulder. "Sublette, just do whatever it takes. Let me add one more burden. General Ashley's orders were to find a pass through the Rockies -- a pass that will open the way west -- the way the Cumberland Gap opened the Appalachians. When we leave here, we should head in the right direction to find that."

Sublette chuckled, "You want me to jump Rose fer

stealin', then quiz him bout some empire-openin' mountain pass fore we sneak off? You forgettin' it tuck 15 men to hold Rose down when Manuel Lisa fired him fer this same thing?"

"You'll find a way, Sublette. You're a man who sees what needs to be done -- then does it -- like you shot the Grizzly!"

"All right, Jedediah. You ain't gonna shoot Rose. If it comes to that, *I'll* shoot Rose. They ain't no verse numbers on my boot pistols."

Next morning Sublette met Clyman in a snowy pine grove. They watched their breaths collide as they whispered in the chill mountain air.

"I can't go, Sublette. I've spent my life alone as a solitary farmer, a backwoods soldier and a lonesome surveyor. I read about love in Shakespeare, but till now, I was never spiritually intimate with another soul. To me love was a myth -- a single night's snow sculpture that melted at sight of the sun. Bright Elk's mine every day. I can't leave her."

"We don't git outa here, Jedediah's gonna kill Ed Rose. He does zat, them Crow're gonna kill you an' Bright Elk if she squawks while they're takin' yer ha'r. Ask her about a pass through the Rockies."

Tear-shine brightened Clyman's eyes. "I knew we'd have to leave here someday. You know we'll freeze. Too early to grope for some pass in 20 foot snow drifts. Don't speak enough Crow to ask where this mountain pass is or understand if she tells me."

"You know Bright Elk's lingo er ya wouldn't be standin' inna best lookin' white buckskins ever wore by a unemployed surveyor. We leave friendly-like, nothin' says you cain't come back, Jim."

"You just put me in mind how I got topographical information out of Indians when I was surveying! Took 'em to the sand pile!"

As Sublette and Clyman plotted, Bright Elk waded snow with 20 bullets from the pouch of her man to Keeps-the-Pipe-of-the-Thunder-Spirit. She'd asked him to cast a spell on Always Smiles, so he could never leave her. The seer said Always Smiles must soon go to the mountains with the beaver-killers but would come back to her lodge for the birth of their son -- if she did not tell him the boy was on the way now. She cried for joy.

Bright Elk knew the prophet had spoken truly when she arrived at her lodge. Always Smiles had made many mountains on a buffalo robe with the white sand from the quiet waters.

After bringing both her cousins to move the mountains for Always Smiles, she knew he would be back as the prophet promised. Her cousins showed Always Smiles how to circle the south end of the mountains and cross to the *Seeds-kee-dee-Agie* River. When they left, Bright Elk cast her own sensual spell over Always Smiles. Their son would be called Mountains of Sand.

William Sublette asked Edward Rose to meet him at Mountain Sheep Point at noon the following day to discuss a way to make both their lives better. When Edward Rose arrived at the snowy precipice, he discovered a worn possibles bag under a rock ledge and opened it, finding a handwritten note:

"*Dear Ed -- Enjoyed riding & hunting with you this year. If you take yer sweet time gitting back to yer lodge, we will all be gone & you & me will be hunting together next year. You come back to quick, one of us is going to be real lonsome on the hunt next year.*

Cut Face"

*   *   *

After carefully following Clyman's directions, Jedediah Smith, William Sublette, Thomas Fitzpatrick and James Clyman gathered on the wind whipped hills of the 8,000 foot South Pass.

Jedediah Smith yelled a prayer into the gale winds, "Thank you, Lord for helping us find the place for wagons of our brethren to pass west over these grand mountains of Yours in days to come. Amen."

And in almost the same breath Jedediah added to Clyman, "I'll need your help with the map of this pass to include with my letter about South Pass to General Ashley."

Jedediah Smith led them through the pass where the wind driven snow howled in swirling fury. Treeless South Pass afforded them no shelter amid snow drifted higher than their horses. Their puny sage brush fires blew away in sweeping red arcs that quickly went black in the arctic blasts.

As they shivered around their empty fire pits, Clyman

longed for the warm glow of Bright Elk's lodge. Icy as he was outside, he was far colder inside. Love's insidious flaw was the greater your joy together, the worse your pain apart.

Sublette loaded and fired faster than the others with fine accuracy up to 100 yards. Clyman was their master marksman at 200 yards with his long rifle. Jedediah sent them hunting, but winds howling off the mountain glaciers drove the game animals to ground before them. Even when they shot a snow-stranded buffalo the men couldn't keep their fires from blowing away.

They devoured the meat raw before it froze too hard to chew. They ate snow for water and so did their horses, but it didn't slake their thirst. Clyman discovered that if he tomahawked a shallow depression in creek ice to channel his bullet's force, he could bring up fresh water for man and horse.

They reached the Big Sandy River, then followed it to the Green River where they cut dead willows and feasted on cooked buffalo for the first time in a month. Jedediah licked his fingers and checked his small force over. Most appeared gaunt but fit. "It's mid April. If we split up here, we can scout twice as much territory and still trap plenty of beaver when the streams flow again. I'll take Sublette and five men. Fitz, you take Clyman and the other three. We'll trap out these streams then all rendezvous on the Sweetwater at the end of June."

As the snow receded, Clyman's group trapped many fat beaver and shared their carcasses with a family of *Digger Shoshone*. But when the *Shoshone* left one night, the trappers' horses left with them. Undaunted, they trapped through the first week of June, dug a hole, cached furs and traps, hung their saddles in dense trees and left to rendezvous with Smith's men.

About noon the hiking trappers came face to face with six mounted *Shoshone* on a gentle ridge. "Fitz, those thieving Diggers are riding *our* horses!" Clyman yelled.

"And what would ye be doin' about it?" Fitzpatrick asked, his own anger rising.

"Aim your rifles, charged or not," Clyman replied, watching four rifles come to bear on the startled *Shoshones*. "Fitz, sign to 'em to get off our horses or die on top of them." Reading four rifle muzzles, the *Shoshones* slid off the horses even before Fitz signed Clyman's message to them.

Once remounted, the trappers found it easy to control their horses with *Shoshone* war bridles, amounting to a long rein with the middle tie-looped around the horse's lower jaw. They herded the Diggers to their nearby camp and repatriated the rest of their horses from 18 surprised horse thieves.

Driving their horses, Fitzpatrick's men returned to their cache, unearthed their furs and rescued their saddles and bridles from the trees. But some kept using the *Shoshone* war bridles. By mid June they rode east along the Sweetwater River toward the Platte with no sign of Smith's party.

They stopped for a meal of jerked buffalo meat. Fitzpatrick grumbled, "Never seen so much shallow water in me life! Jim, head east till you reach water deep enough to float these furs in bull boats, but don't stray past the North Platte. Stop soon's ya find deep water and we'll catch up. Jedediah'll be with us by then. We'll shoot buffalo to make the boats."

Jim cautioned, "Fitz, watch out for grizzlies flushing moose calves from willow thickets. I'm plenty low on thread!"

Clyman shadowed the shallow Sweetwater for three days till it flowed into the Platte. Picking a dense willow thicket, Clyman cut a lodge space, then gathered driftwood for a fire.

But before Clyman could strike flint, he heard voices. He struggled to the edge of the willows, then froze. A war party of 22 Indians milled about across the Sweetwater. He hoped they'd water their horses and ride on, but they started four fires.

In the twilight, Clyman couldn't be sure if the war party was *Arapaho* or *Cheyenne*, but with all their feathers, lances and paint, they were too riled to let them see him.

Around midnight two horses crashed through the puny Sweetwater. Many horses followed. In minutes all were back and the angry braves began to torture the fugitives with fiery embers. Clyman wanted to know if the martyrs were trappers, but couldn't see them among the yowling warriors.

Clyman palmed his ears, but the victims' screams forbade sleep. Suddenly he recalled how soft the moon-lit ground was around his thicket. It'd hold his tracks like snow. Taking only his rifle, bullet pouch and powder horn, Clyman backed out of the thicket till he reached rocky ground, then waded the Sweetwater and listened in horror to the shrieking till it ceased at false dawn.

Clyman laid low under a ledge for over a week, eating roots, a frog and nearly a dozen small bird eggs. Each time he tried to leave, he cut fresh Indian sign and went back to ground.

While Clyman hid, Jedediah Smith prowled the willow thicket and found Clyman's things. Jedediah prayed fervently, for he had no doubt Jim was dead at the hands of the *Pawnee* who'd camped there, leaving human finger bones strewn in two of their fire pits. Jedediah trotted into the sun along the Sweetwater to float the bull boats in waters swelling from melting snows.

After 12 days, Clyman figured his friends'd been butchered by what he now knew to be *Pawnees*. He'd wait no longer. Civilization lay to the east, but he didn't know how far.

Having lost his horse while in hiding, Clyman took only the gear he could carry. He had plenty of powder, but only 11 bullets in the pouch that swung from his neck when there should have been 20 more. He couldn't fathom what'd made 20 bullets vanish from a pouch drawn so tight.

Clyman trekked along the North Platte. To his surprise, Clyman found a slashed bull boat on a sand bar by a grove of trees. From the boat's construction and the tracks about it, he knew it'd been built and beached by trappers. But the sandy beach was also gouged by deep *Arikara* tracks, so Clyman, scared to death again, slipped by down the North Platte's bank.

Secreted from the *Arikara* in a hollow stump 20 feet from the bull boat the very moment Clyman sidled past, lay panting Hugh Glass. Hugh and three trappers landed their bull boat to find food, but found *Arikara* instead. Now two lay dismembered in the brush, while Hugh's eyes darted about for the missing boy. Hugh felt sure young Brian had been the one captured from the sound o' his screams for mercy.

The Virgin was testin' Hugh. Ever since he'd left new Fort Henry to give that black-hearted Fitzgerald his due, he'd been plagued by torment. This was the third time he'd been attacked by the *Arikara* in a single year. Wherever he tread, they lay in wait to take his life -- if not them, the grizzly.

Bereft of rifle and belongings, Hugh headed northeast for Fort Kiowa on the Missouri, the closest Army post. Fitzgerald might have stopped at Fort Kiowa, even if he gallivanted on to Fort Atkinson as he'd told young Bridger. If Fitzgerald tarried at Fort Kiowa, he might still be there!

Often driven across the prairies at a run by his zeal for revenge, Hugh devoured the 300 miles to Fort Kiowa in two weeks, foraging off the land like a varmint. But there was no John S. Fitzgerald at Fort Kiowa, so Hugh floated south with a party of traders down the Missouri to Fort Atkinson.

Crouched in the bow of the boat, Hugh Glass rejoiced at sight of the huge American Flag whipping in the morning sun over Fort Atkinson. It marked the end of his quest for the traitor Fitzgerald. The trader's boat still drafted three feet of water when Glass floundered ashore, dashing into Sixth Regiment Headquarters.

Bracing the stocky First Sergeant behind the scarred desk, Hugh blurted, "Have a message from Fort Henry for one John S. Fitzgerald who shoulda joined here last winter."

Without a word, the mustached Sergeant stalked from the Orderly Room. Soon a quiet, balding Captain with wire rimmed spectacles eyed Hugh, "I'm obliged to tell you that one Fitzgerald, John S. did join this Regiment December past and shipped out from here the instant April."

"Where'd he go?"

"Not obliged to say," the Captain said resolutely. "Mr. Glass, everybody on this frontier knows you're looking for the men who left you to die. Some even want you to find them. I don't. You've been through enough. Kill a soldier on a military post, and you will be shot by a firing squad. Though bullets will free you from the sentence of your own vengeance, I believe merciful words can do the same. If you look at my insignia, you will see I wear God's crosses, not crossed rifles or sabres. I release you from your mission of death and absolve you of your blood oath. Go home, Mr. Glass. Just go home!"

Hugh Glass stumbled from the stifling office. He settled on the split log bench outside it, put his mangled face into his hands, and wept. It was over.

* * *

Clyman beheld wild horses gliding through the wind, their manes and tails streaming out like wings that would soon let them fly. A bounding white stallion with a black blaze flaming the length of his face whinnied fiercely, halting the heaving horses to steam in the cold air.

Clyman thought if he could graze the stallion's head with a bullet, he could stun it enough to loop the strap of his possibles bag around its lower jaw as a war bridle. He aimed his revered rifle with great care and fired. The stallion's head whipped, and he collapsed with the bullet in his brain. Clyman wanted to mourn this classic beast with its nostrils oozing blood, but he was too swamped with sorrows, so he simply walked on.

Husbanding his bullets, he shot buffalo, then cut out his lead and reshaped it with his teeth for another shot.

Two months later, on plains devoid of buffalo Clyman spied a *Pawnee* village. His mind said not to approach it, but his growling stomach won the argument. Four gleeful *Pawnees* used him for sport, knocking his fragile body about with the shoulders of their ponies until he fell unconscious under their hooves.

When Clyman awoke, he found they'd taken his heirloom rifle, blankets, ammunition, firesteel and flint and haggled for the privilege of taking Clyman's scalp. He hadn't had a haircut since he'd left St. Louis. He'd lost his hat in the first battle with the *Arikara*, so his dark hair'd grown long and wild. He signed to them to take his hair instead of his scalp.

The *Pawnees* took turns hacking off handfuls of Clyman's hair with a dull butcher knife. His agonized thoughts toyed with Shakespeare's Brutus plotting the death of Julius Caesar: *To cut the head off and then hack the limbs ... Let's carve him as a dish fit for the Gods, not hew him as a carcass fit for hounds.* Finally, only patches of hair like pinfeathers on a chicken adorned his head.

The fun-loving *Pawnees* paid him two handfuls of corn for his hair and kicked him repeatedly until he staggered east across the prairie. He was thankful Bright Elk had not witnessed his disintegration as a human. He couldn't believe he'd ever even known her. Not any more. She must have been a dream.

A horse's bleached thigh bone became Clyman's weapon. He bashed the skulls of two brawling badgers, and ate their maggoty carcasses as he wandered eastward along the Platte.

One bright dawn, James Clyman saw the Stars and Stripes being raised above Fort Atkinson. Dry, soundless sobs rasped in his throat. His 600 mile, 80 day odyssey ended when a scouting detail hauled his limp body to Fort Atkinson's Infirmary and left him to die.

But two days later James Clyman sat up on his cot as another detail brought in two pitiful creatures once known to Clyman as Fitzpatrick and Branch. Fitzpatrick could only croak through cracked lips, so he pointed to his possibles bag. Clyman opened it and found a letter addressed to General William Ashley in the fine hand of Jedediah Smith. Realizing, they'd likely all die soon anyway, Clyman opened the letter.

Jedediah's letter was too long to be read aloud by a man near death to other men barely breathing, so Clyman just recited its last eloquent sentence. "*The Upper Green streams are rich in fine quality beaver, and through South Pass, found once more, the gateway to the West lies open so that one day wagonloads of our families and friends may join us here among the snow capped towers of God.*

Your Obedient Servant,

Jedediah Strong Smith"

Clyman's ragged voice dropped to a whisper," I didn't realize what South Pass was till I read this letter. Jedediah sees bigger than most men."

Fitzpatrick gasped, "The man's an explorer."

CHAPTER 19

A HORSE THIEF BY 40 FALL 1824

Brawny James Pierson Beckwourth's first meeting with General Ashley was purely by chance. Jim was working in a lead mine. By coincidence Ashley'd come to the mine campaigning for governor of Missouri and was laboring through his speech when the rains came. A stately young woman dressed in black opened her white-beaded, black parasol and waited for Ashley in her splendid carriage behind a team of stunning, but diminutive gray Arabians.

Rain chased the speech crowd. Jim stood shirtless with his pick, his triangular upper body gleaming like burnished mahogany. Standing six feet, with long black wavy hair and a piercing gaze, Jim observed, "Too few candidates drive carriage horses sired by Napoleon's Marengo."

Ashley gaped, first at Jim's fine elocution, then at what he'd said. "How could you possibly know that, Mister ...?"

"Beckwourth. James Beckwourth, sir. I've admired the horse as man's friend through the ages. As a child I indulged in dream rides on Alexander the Great's Bucephalus. I recognize the blood line of these Egyptian Arabs of Abukir. I read that English General Angerstein bought Marengo after Waterloo, and that he sired several twins. My eye says this is such an exalted pair."

Jim never bothered to tell the candidate he'd read about the horses of Ashley's wealthy fiancee, Eliza Christy, in the *Missouri Intelligencer*.

Ashley turned to the dignified woman in the carriage, "Did you hear what this man concluded about your team, Eliza? Isn't that remarkable!"

Having the newspapers about her fiance's campaign, Eliza had more than an inkling of where the muscular miner had come by his horse information, but she rather enjoyed Bill Ashley's credulity. "Truly remarkable, dear!" Eliza replied, but she couldn't resist a knowing smile at the miner to let him know she hadn't been hoodwinked.

After displaying such a discerning eye for horseflesh, Beckwourth had but to tell the General of his five years of blacksmithing to get hired as horse buyer and wrangler for Ashley's third fur expedition.

This small deception on Marengo's offspring aside, Jim Beckwourth was a horseman to the bone. He rode a horse like it was part of him, and in a way it was. He loved the horse's smell -- the feel of its muscles -- the noble way it stood with neck arched and eyes afire.

Jim's elegant speech was no accident either. Born in Virginia in 1798 of a union between Sir Jennings Beckwith and a Negro slave, his noble father'd had Jim tutored incessantly, while forcing him all the while to shelter in the slave quarters and showing him on plantation books as a slave. Jim's schooling flourished even after his family removed to St. Louis, but withered when his father bound him out at 14 to Casner and Sutton's Smithy. Though Sir Jennings Beckwith officially freed Jim after the fiery parting with Casner and Sutton, Jim styled himself Beck*wourth* to renounce his father's name.

Jim bought the finest horses available at prices that consoled the financially tottering Ashley after his August election loss.

Ashley's expedition departed St. Louis September 24th, far too late in the year to begin an overland journey to the mountains.

Jim Beckwourth got his horse job by devious means, but there was nothing devious about his adoration of the horses. Each time the expedition halted for the night, Jim checked every horse's body. By the tension of the muscles and the look in the eyes, Jim knew exactly how the horse felt.

With General Ashley's backing, Jim demanded that riders rub down their horses and tie loads better to ease the lot of pack animals. He checked their hobbles and staked heavy ropes into a makeshift corral every night. The horses knew Jim and ate the daily handful of grain he gave each soft muzzle with loving pleasure. Having lavished his popularity on the horses, there was none left for Jim amongst the men. They would neither eat nor bed down near him.

Somebody shot a tough old bull buffalo along the trail. After they'd roasted it twice as long as usual, it defied chewing. Moses "Black" Harris sat down beside Jim Beckwourth as they struggled to down the charred meat. Jim didn't acknowledge the company. Moses kept adding salt to his buffalo. Moses said, "We jist as well eat dis ole bull -- argh -- wit de hide still on it!"

"Learned to eat in the slave quarter, didn't you, boy?" Jim asked, curling his lip.

"Why you -- argh -- say dat?"

"The salt. It's the way slaves eat everything. With enough salt, a slave can eat a rope, Mister Moses Harris."

"I ain't -- argh -- neber been no slave, Mista Recruit! You jist keep suckin' on -- argh -- dat bull bone. I sees why nobody neber set wit ya. How'd ya know mah name?"

"Know your name? I know your life story. So does everybody who reads the *Missouri Intelligencer* -- including some overseer who's after your reward. Plenty stupid exposing yourself to a flogging for the fleeting glory of an interview."

"You -- argh -- ain't said jist how you done knows how dey eats in dem slave quarters yo'self, Mista Recruit."

Jim leaped up, hurling his inedible meat into the darkness. "Well, I'm no slave, you can bet the bounty on your head on that!" Jim flexed his muscles to vent his rage.

"Fo you gits it into yo -- argh -- little head to tack ole Mose, I best tell you in de mountains mah life depend on you -- argh -- and yo life depend on me. Dats de way wit all o' us. Time'll come in dese mountains if we does nothin', you die."

Four rifle hammers cocked. A deep voice said, "Mose, you best eat with us. We ain't up to buryin' that wrangler fore we git the first chaw o' this whang leather buffalo down. The meat's bad -- but it ain't *that* bad."

* * *

If there was one thing you could count on an Irishman for, it was endurance. Over Clyman's feverish protests, Tom Fitzpatrick had stumbled from his death bed in the Fort Atkinson Infirmary, got an outfit from Lucien Fontenelle and gone back to Independence Rock to reclaim his fur cache.

As if rising from the dead weren't enough, Fitzpatrick was back at Fort Atkinson by October 26, 1824 culminating his lightning resurrection of the furs he'd been bull boating south for Ashley. Ashley arrived at Fort Atkinson, and the money Fitzpatrick got from Fontenelle for the recovered furs enabled Ashley to buy the rest of the trade goods for his Rendezvous Plan. Ashley admitted it was a miracle. Fitzpatrick said it was the luck of the Irish, and they drank a pint of Ashley's private stock brandy in robust toasts to the success of the upcoming Rendezvous on the Green River.

Ashley'd heard about the way Milton Sublette'd materialized here last year with two bales of plews and financed Drew Henry. Real Mountain Men got the job done.

Drew Henry'd sent word that he was quitting the fur trade. That was depressing, but what if Eliza wouldn't wait for a failed Governor to find himself in the wilderness? Ashley felt her loss was a certainty if his speculative Rendezvous plan flopped.

General Ashley wouldn't have left Eliza's side, but he had to try out his grandiose plan. He'd sent expresses to every trapper and tribe he could reach to sell him their furs and buy supplies at the Rendezvous at Green River and Henry's Fork on July first, 1825. If his plan worked, William H. Ashley would be rich. If it failed, he was bankrupt. Eliza Christy would not marry a man who followed one botched venture with another.

Ashley didn't have to worry about Hugh Glass rampaging among his men. Fort Atkinson's Chaplain assured him Glass had left for Taos two months ago.

Colonel Leavenworth stiffly wished Ashley a "profitable hunt," pompously urging him to stay clear of the *Arikara*. Ashley used all his political skills to suppress his overwhelming desire to tell Leavenworth if he ran afoul of the *Arikara*, Leavenworth was the last chucklehead on earth he'd tell about it.

Benjamin O'Fallon was too sick with liver ague to

receive Ashley, so he wasn't forced to explain to the treacherous Indian Agent why he was outfitting to trap beaver all over when he was only licensed to "*trade with the Snake Indians.*"

In the first week of November, Ashley led a party of 25 men, 50 pack horses and a wagon through the stubble of the harvested grain fields of Fort Atkinson. Beckwourth quit feuding with Moses "Black" Harris long enough to fuss over the horses every night. Somehow Fitzpatrick convinced Clyman to come along when both knew winter was about to crush them like a bull buffalo rolling on a sage hen's nest.

Gradually, Jim Beckwourth realized he needed Moses to learn how to trap the icy streams and skin out his catches. Big enough not to carry a grudge, Moses trained Beckwourth. Finally, Moses and Jim fell in with each other, though they were unalike as any two men could be.

Game eluded Ashley's expedition the way the governorship had. The wagon shattered an axle and had to be abandoned a few days out of Fort Atkinson.

Ashley took the wagon's demise as an omen, muttering to Fitz, "Never should have wasted money on the wagon. Everybody knows a wagon can't tolerate the boulder-strewn mountain country, and none ever will!" Ashley ordered the wagon's trade goods cached, transferring enough to the already overburdened horses to purchase supplies and fresh horses from the Grand *Pawnees*. Beckwourth sulked over the added weight on the horses.

Jim Clyman hoped to find the mangy *Pawnees* who'd stolen his Clyman family rifle and hacked off his hair. If Clyman found them, the buzzards would be eating *Pawnee* come the spring thaw. But all the *Grand Pawnees* left were deserted villages and old tracks filling with snow.

Daily rations for Ashley's men got cut to half pint of flour and water. Now and then a stray goose got wolfed down half raw. Everybody but Beckwourth ate off the first horse that died. Beckwourth vowed to protect the remaining horses, no matter the consequences.

On the Platte, Ashley's men found the *Loup Pawnees* in winter camp and willing to help. Clyman skulked about till he made certain these were not the Indians who'd defiled him.

After meals of banjo-string badger meat and jerked buffalo, Ashley's men skirted the drifted snow up the South Platte River.

After ascending the Continental Divide, they entered Great Divide Basin. A phalanx of 32 Crow horsemen thundered out of the snowstorm, brandishing their feathered lances. Like snow ghosts, they cut all 17 horses out of Beckwourth's "spares" herd and drove them back into the blowing snow.

Beckwourth charged after the Crow cavalry on foot, screaming into white winds that screamed back. The swirling northers turned the snow drifts to jagged ice. Beckwourth fell to his knees and smashed his bare hands through the brittle snow until it was pink with his blood yelling, "Horse thieves! I'll hang every filthy one of you!"

While James Clyman wondered if Bright Elk's cousins had been among the phantom Crow horsemen, Beckwourth wandered back out of the white air, beating his bloody chest. He shouted about his lost horses until Fitzpatrick and Moses Harris calmed him.

Tom Fitzpatrick felt sorry for Beckwourth. The man grieved as though his family'd been kidnapped. Fitzpatrick opened his small Bible exposing a pressed shamrock to the sanding snow pecking the page around it's faded green leaves. "Here Beckwourth. Take me four leaf clover from County Cavan. Never give it up till you're ready to give me luck back. Tis lucky enough to get them 17 horses back -- safe as babes."

The shamrock stuck to Beckwourth's bloody finger till he inserted it between the pages of Aristotle's *History of Animals* in his possibles bag. Beckwourth grated, "Let's go *now* before the snow obliterates their tracks!"

"Who'll be goin' with us?" Fitzpatrick asked, his steamy breath masking his face.

Jim Bridger raised his bare trigger finger through a hole in his otter skin mitten. Clyman volunteered, but Fitzpatrick shook his head. "Could get too complicated if we had to chase them to a certain Crow camp. No man should meet The Reaper for havin' his loyalties divided."

Even without Clyman, Fitz raised eight men, and split them into two parties, Fitzpatrick commanding one and Bridger the other. Fitzpatrick beat his mittens together to stir the blood in his hands, then motioned them to move out.

Having shod many of the stolen horses himself, Beckwourth easily read the trapper horse tracks among the barefooted Indian ponies until the trail ended at an encampment. The confident Crows had merged Beckwourth's friends with a hundred other horses guarded by half a dozen horsemen. Crow sentinels hunched over their horses, snow mounding on them.

Fitzpatrick mustered his trappers behind a snowy hummock. "Simple plans work best. My men will charge the Crows from the off-side, so we won't run the horses away from you. Bridger, take Beckwourth and your men and stampede all them sweet horses down that draw. We'll cover your back, shootin' every Crow fool enough to follow."

Fitzpatrick's simple plan turned into a wild gun battle and a major stampede, but Beckwourth, riding insanely, drove about 60 horses into the draw. Bridger and his group closed behind Beckwourth, herding the horses well clear of the Crow camp. Fitzpatrick's men fired several fusillades, leaving six dead Crow in the bloody trampled snow. In the blizzard the Crows mistook these ferocious fighters for Blackfeet and fell back.

Fitzpatrick thought about posting a rear guard, but seeing no pursuit, galloped his force to catch Bridger and help move the herd. When the horse herd reached the expedition, Ashley's other men were still holed up to escape the storm.

Hearing the thunder of the horses, trappers burst from under their robes. Running men, their arms waving in the snowy twilight, herded the horses into a clearing. The heaving ponies stomped their feet and closed up to keep warm. Several of the older horses wheezed. Many stood shivering in long winter fur.

Beckwourth drifted among the snorting mustangs like some ghostly equine spirit in the dying dusk. Wherever Beckwourth went touching them and whispering, calm followed like he'd put a spell on them. When the horses stood quiet with their heads down, he took a final tally of 57 horses -- 17 that he'd lost and 40 new Crow mounts.

Fitzpatrick and the other rescuers ate snow hare, squirrel and boiled Indian maize until Beckwourth joined them at the fire. Beckwourth appeared dazed and exhausted as if he'd given his last vestiges of life to the horses. Several men pressed morsels of food into his hands and slapped him on the back. Fitzpatrick asked, "How many o' them ever lovin' horses did we bring back?"

Beckwourth gasped, "Fifty-seven."

Fitzpatrick countered, "You think horse thieves should be hung, do you, Beckwourth?"

Beckwourth flopped beside the fire and bit into a cold rabbit thigh. "I surely do."

"Then we'll be gettin' a rope, Mr. Beckwourth! The way I see it, you're a horse thief by 40 right where you sit!" The snow laden forest rang with laughter.

But Beckwourth saw no humor, growling, "Gentlemen, stealing a horse is no laughing matter -- as you shall all come to know one day."

CHAPTER 20

HENRY'S FORK RENDEZVOUS FALL 1824-FALL 1825

When Major Andrew Henry discovered the marmots were already hibernating in August, he knew the fall of 1824 was lying in wait for him with an icicle in its teeth. The wrinkles around his eyes deepened as he squinted at the lofty crags with their eternal snow caps. He tasted the piney wind and heard the breeze etching the air around the pines with its whispers. Andrew Henry'd spent 16 years in the mountains, risking death every day to be free among these sights and tastes and sounds. He muttered, "Waugh! It's time to go home to Potosi."

He ambled back into the Fort Henry trading post, his swoll-up knees full of rheumatism from years of wading ice water on trap lines. Captain Weber's boys'd be in from the Wind River in a day or two. So would Davie Jackson's brigade from up north. His farewell called for a shindig!

Sliding his fiddle case from under his cot, he visualized the legion of mules he'd tied the case on -- and remembered it once shooting the Big Horn River rapids by itself. He popped the old case open.

After he swabbed the spider web off the bridge, the battered fiddle's strings pluck-tuned well enough. The bow was dryer'n last year's corn cob, but its hair held together, squawking over the strings. He didn't practice. His born fiddle sense always took over when his bow bit the strings.

Food for his festival was out in the brush. With the rutting bull moose bugling their mawkish calls, they'd be a mortal cinch to find. He'd watch for grizz cause they'd be stalking moose calves. Trick'd be to shoot a cow or calf with them bulls making all the ruckus.

Andrew Henry'd never forget the Hugh Glass mauling. He wondered to this day why Bridger or Fitzgerald hadn't freed Glass from his misery with a bullet. That's what he'd expected when he left them with the mangled Irishman. Yes, sir. He would look for bear sign!

* * *

One thing Mountain Men weren't bashful about was eating. Major Henry'd bagged a moose cow and both her calves. It was still nip and tuck if all that'd fill his 27 men. They hunkered around the crackling fire and ate, wiping their greasy mouths on their sleeves -- belching like it was a competition. They hollered and chucked moose bones in the fire.

They'd made a prodigious fur harvest! Henry broke out several gallon whiskey jugs. Mountain Men whooped and swigged the rot gut. They howled as he let wild Irish Jigs and Scottish Dirk Dances out of his fiddle to chase the stars. All danced and cavorted except those too drunk to rise.

Red eyes of bewildered creatures glowed from beyond the firelight as the Mountain Men collapsed to lay panting.

Winded, the Major lowered his fiddle for a long pull on the jug, then they all got down to the other thing Mountain Men loved most -- talking to somebody besides themselves. This get together was a joy after wading icy streams alone day after day.

Daniel Potts yelled, "Save a jug for Jim Bridger, Major! He won your bet on where the Bear River goes! Bear flowed a good 50 miles past where it quit on your sorry map. Emptied into a Great Salt Lake big as half o' Missouri! We figgered out why the Bear River showed twice on your map. They ain't two Bear Rivers. They's but one. Flows up to Soda Springs, turns and staggers back down to that big lake."

"Waugh! Bridger's won his jug!" Major Henry cackled.

Potts shook his finger in the flickering light, "Don't forget them dozen fishhooks and that pound o' black powder you owe Jim with the whiskey."

"I'll pay it all -- if you'll tell these boys the tale about them three Bears."

Potts leaned back on his elbows. "Two ole boys seen a bear across the river and shot him. Pulled off their buckskins and swum necked across the river with nothing but a Green River knife to cut some bear steaks. But the bear come to and run 'em back in the water. First one tried to outswim that bear upstream an' the second tried to outfloat him downstream. First feller reached shore by his clothes and fired his pistol, spooking the bear back to where it started. Second feller swum ashore by his scairt friend, and that there's the story of the *three* bears."

Major Andrew Henry played the fool, "I don't git no *three* bears outa that!"

"Why you sure do! You had a hoppin'-mad *bear* on one side of the river and *two scairt bares* on the other!"

After the laughter died, thick-set Captain John Weber hissed tobacco juice into the fire. "How long you been Up the Mountain, Major?"

"Well, bout 1808 me an' them Missouri Fur Company boys run inta John Colter on his way back home a year er two after his trip with Lewis and Clark an' Colter jined up with us."

Milton Sublette lowered the jug, firelight dancing on his grin, and bellered, "You sayin' there really *was* a John Colter?"

Major Henry nodded, "Sure as God made maggots in a fit o' temper! Colter worked for me. John mighta even outrun you, Milt less you had some fumin' husband on your trail!"

Milt Sublette slapped his muscular thigh, "When I was a tadpole, my Grandpa scairt me green with some story bout Colter bein' chased 250 miles in 11 days by Blackfoot!"

"Waugh! Cinch nothin's scairt you green since, Milt, but Colter hisself swore he's chased 150 mile in seven days."

Somebody yelled, "By next week, we'll swear it was 400 mile in two days. Inna mountains, first liar ain't gotta chance!" Laughter overflowed the firelight.

"Indians runnin' you off, Major?" David Jackson asked.

"Mostly old age. Waugh. I'm stove up, Davie. It's a lotta things. Been out here longer'n the grizz. This trapper competition has got my goat. When I first come up river with Missouri Fur, competition for furs was pretty much Jacob Astor's American Fur Company and Hudson's Bay Company. Hudson's Bay people been in fur country longer'n God --

chartered by King Charles in 1670. North West Company was always nosin' around here till it got swallered by Hudson's Bay four years back. Missouri Fur's gone busted, but we got all them new boys. They's a new trappin' outfit behind every bush. Fore long, won't be nothin' left to trap but other trappers."

"Ain't *that* the truth?" chimed in a bleary voice.

"Waugh. Gonna play more fiddle music. When you boys wakes up tomorry with yer heads stomped on, me an' a few old hands will be packin' furs to St. Louie! Then I'm agoin' home to Potosi. Druther birth a porkypine back'ards than say good-bye, but it's over. Boys -- it's been good to know you!" Cheers drowned Major Henry's final words and David Jackson started the sporadic rifle salutes blazing into the inky sky.

The Major's bow, strands splaying like witch's hair in the firelight, jumped on the fiddle strings, shrilling a rousing Hornpipe. Major Henry didn't hear Milt Sublette yell he'd be heading to the settlements with him.

* * *

In the last week of June 1825, Jedediah Smith's party caught Ashley's pack train en route to the site of the Henry's Fork Rendezvous.

Jedediah put William Sublette in charge of making camp while the square shouldered New Yorker met General Ashley in a stand of lodgepole pines. Jedediah was shocked by Ashley's appearance. Ashley'd lost 15 pounds, his face was haggard, and he kept opening and closing a locket. The locket's delicate painting of a woman preoccupied him.

"You won't believe what's happened, General!"

"How bad is it?"

"Not bad at all. Twenty-nine Hudson's Bay deserters joined us with over 700 skins."

Relieved, Ashley sighed, "Tell me about it."

"Last September, we came upon a party of Hudson's Bay *Iroquois* hunters hounded by the *Shoshone*. They offered us 105 beaver skins for safe conduct to their Flathead Post on the Columbia River. We escorted them and wintered there. Ross, their Commandant, regarded us as trespassers though we have as much right in Oregon as the British under the Joint Occupation Agreement."

"Could you get to the meat?" Ashley flipped the locket open and shut, then caught himself and stashed it in his pocket.

"Of course. From December through this April, we trapped with the Flathead Post's new Commandant, Peter Skene Ogden, taking a rich haul of beaver. Ogden says Hudson's Bay Company's constructing Fort Vancouver at the mouth of the Columbia River. He claims it'll be the grandest post ever built, attracting trade from all over the west."

Ashley blurted, "And if the Rendezvous works, we'll cut the furs off at their source every year before they ever reach their grand Fort Vancouver! Where's Drew Henry?"

"We ran into Captain Weber in May. He said to tell you Major Henry quit and packed the furs to St. Louis."

"He said he was going home, but it hurts after all these years. Sorry, Jedediah, go on."

"After Captain Weber left, Johnson Gardner's free trappers crashed our camp. Gardner told Peter Skene Ogden the British were trespassing on American soil and better get off if they didn't want war! When Ogden withdrew, 29 of his trappers deserted to our party with their skins to sell. The humorous point of this is that when the *American* Gardner told the *British* Ogden he was a trespasser, we were all on *Mexican* soil!"

Ashley laughed dryly. "You fathom what we're trying to establish with my new Rendezvous approach?"

"Perhaps I don't, General."

"In the 1790s forest runners like John Jacob Astor ferreted out the Indians and traded for furs. Next, fur companies built trading posts and waited for Indians to bring furs to trade. Some times they came and sometimes they left the posts idle. Then, Manuel Lisa sent trappers out to trade for furs with a little trapping thrown in. Major Henry and I changed that game by sending masses of our men to trap the streams, by-passing the Indians and our competition by going directly to the beaver. All our competitors copy us now. So we're switching the game again. With our new Rendezvous approach we take trade goods to the trappers *and* the Indians to corner *all* the furs and sell *all* the supplies *before* our competitors get a crack at any of them. If Rendezvous works, we're rich. If it doesn't, we're bankrupt. We've sent expresses to the trappers and tribes for a year about meeting to trade at Henry's Fork on July 1, 1825. But we still don't know if anybody but us will be there."

* * *

July first came up hot and brassy. Ashley'd camped a mile from the Rendezvous site. The General summoned Jedediah Smith to his tent. Moments later, Jedediah rode off in a one-horse race. Ashley paced his tent. His men packed up for the last mile of the trip. Everybody sweat in the chill dawn -- and waited. Hoofbeats closing on the dead run brought every head around. Ashley hit *parade rest,* bracing himself for the worst.

Jedediah Smith's erect figure atop his horse cut the horizon and grew larger. With a leg over, Jedediah slid from his pony to stand before the General, dust swirling over them.

"Well?" Ashley grated, hands outstretched.

"By the Lord Jehovah, you won't believe it, General! I make out over a hundred trappers and 800 people from the tribes camped in two locations!"

General Ashley extended his small hand, "Let's hope they're friendlies, *partner*! Welcome to the first Rendezvous of Ashley & *Smith*!"

Jedediah shook the General's hand, "I am truly honored to become your partner, Sir."

Doubtless anxious trappers and tribesmen expected big things from Ashley at this first Rendezvous, but none expected his enormous prices. Ashley handled each transaction at a makeshift table -- a confidential distance from the waiting hordes. Jedediah Smith stood by with his rifle in the crook of his arm. Ashley bought beaver for $2 to $5 the pound, depending on who was selling it. After establishing the price the trapper or Indian had coming for furs, Ashley sold him trade goods, charging purchase goods against his pelt money.

Sugar ranged from $1 to $2 the pound, tobacco up to $3 the pound and scarlet cloth the sky-high price of $6 a yard. Trade blankets cost $9 each and watered whiskey went for $3 a pint! Jedediah felt his salvation slipping with each gasp of disbelief from the trappers, and prayed fervently through most of Ashley's dealings. Jedediah wondered how their new partnership agreement would read, then prayed all the harder.

William Sublette watched trapper after trapper slip away

into the *Shoshone* camp and decided to investigate. Tom Fitzpatrick fell in beside Sublette, matching his long legs stride for stride. "Fitz, you seen Clyman?" Sublette asked.

"No but we both know where the man is as the Crow flies, now don't we?"

Sublette was glad Fitz was goin' to the *Shoshone* camp because the Irishman knew most Indian hand signs. Fitz had a warm way with the Indians none of the other trappers had. Fitz knew the Indians were his friends and wouldn't let 'em forget it.

Three *Shoshone* squaws in pale buckskins with beads and flowers in their long dark hair stood around a bent elder with his upper face died blue. A *Shoshone* woman who put Sublette vaguely in mind of Monique Perrault sat cross-legged on her tan buffalo calf robe.

Sublette thought the comely woman on the robe was blind, because she looked without seein' him. She held a wilted wildflower. She made Sublette's heart thump harder.

Fitz quit signing with the elder to exchange hand signs with one of the standing squaws. Sublette rested his hand on Fitzpatrick's wrist and halted their palaver. "Find out why this woman on the robe won't look at me."

"I'm a bit busy meself, Sublette."

"You ain't that busy, Fitz. Find out."

Fitz snorted, then signed with old Blue Face. Fitz turned to Sublette. "His nibs says she cannot see you because of the hair on your face."

"Hope I don't hafta paint my face blue to git her to see me."

"Blue Face says scalpin' the hair off your face will make her see you."

"Must mean shavin' it off," Sublette argued.

"The sign he's making is *scalpin'* it off."

Sublette knelt in front of the *Shoshone* woman. She wasn't beautiful, but she made him glad he was a man. He pulled his straight razor from his possibles bag. "Tell her to shave the hair off my face."

Interested in how far Sublette would go to impress the woman, Fitz signed with Blue Face, then the woman on the robe. "She be Moondancer. She asked your name. Told her it was Cut Face. Wouldn't surprise me none if she speaks English, the way she watches me mouth when I talk to yourself."

Moondancer splashed water from her gourd on Sublette's sandy beard, then shaved it with a vengeance, cutting his face repeatedly with the straight razor until his beard was gone. Moondancer laughed, grasped his bleeding face and kissed him sensuously on each of the razor cuts, then long and hard on his mouth. Her eyes twinkled as she whispered, "Cut Face."

* * *

Four days after the Fourth of July the Rendezvous ended with most of its revelers sick, sorry and broke. That did not include General Ashley who headed for St. Louis with $47,000 in skins and 50 men on the horses once owned by the Hudson's Bay Company deserters. Jedediah Smith led the horse train, and William Sublette rode drag, not wishin' to explain his healin' razor cuts to the General.

En route to the Big Horn River, Ashley ordered Sublette and 20 other men to accompany him to a cache of 45 beaver packs he'd buried a month before near the bank of the Green River. After raising the cache, they made camp.

While they were breaking camp at dawn 60 Blackfeet rode howling from the darkness. But the Blackfeet couldn't attack between rifle salvos, because this time Sublette made some men reload while others fired like he'd told them to in the first battle with the *Arikaras*.

Puzzled by Sublette's steady-fire tactic, the Blackfeet retreated, driving off all but two of Ashley's horses. Beckwourth refused to get out of the horses' way, so the Blackfeet shot him in the thigh as they left. Moses "Black" Harris dug the bullet out of Beckwourth's leg and gave it to him in a little bag of salt to wear around his neck on a thong. And Beckwourth wore it.

General Ashley'd known a disaster was coming, and he hoped the attack was it. He still had to get his furs down river, or the first Rendezvous would be another fiasco like his political campaign. Knowing he could count on Sublette, he dispatched the big blond fellow back to the main party for new mounts.

Sublette bent low on his black and white pinto, ridin' it at a walk through the trees to cut noise and dust. Stayin' off the ridgelines, he ate jerky and made no fires. He stopped often to listen and smell the wind.

William knew brother Milton woulda kicked this pinto in the flanks and outrun every Blackfoot north o' the Platte, but he wasn't Milton. He double checked the charges and prime on his rifle, both boot pistols and the big bore .71 caliber belt pistol he'd traded from one of the Hudson's Bay *Iroquois* for two pints of whiskey. If he got jumped, there'd be at least four Blackfoot ponies goin' home empty. It dawned on him he should be learnin' to sign from Fitz. It'd be a lot quieter signin' with an Indian than blowin' a hole through him. Sublette pressed on quietly, methodically.

While Ashley waited for mounts, his men fought off a midnight attack by the Crows, using the Sublette tactic of staggered firing. The Crows weren't ready for it either and vanished into the dawn mists. Ashley brooded over his constant feelings of doom. First the Blackfeet -- then the Crows -- what next?

Sublette led the rescuers back with the horses, reuniting Ashley's parties. They reached the Big Horn and began building bull boats. Clyman, who'd materialized from no place after the Crow raid, shot buffalo for hides while others cut the willows.

Ashley liked the solidarity in the Judge's boy, Bill Sublette. Placing Sublette in command, he ordered him to take the remaining horses with half the men, and return to the mountains to trap until the snows came.

Ashley's fur caravan glided into the Missouri River. At the mouth of the Yellowstone Ashley was surprised to find General Atkinson with five keelboats of soldiers, but even more shocked to meet Benjamin O'Fallon with his liver intact. They were negotiating treaties with Ed Rose as interpreter. General Atkinson invited Ashley and Jedediah Smith to load all the beaver aboard the keelboat *Buffalo*.

On the way down the Missouri, Ashley confided to O'Fallon that South Pass provided a safe and easy path through the Rocky Mountains. O'Fallon said he'd put that in a letter to the Secretary of War as soon as he reached Council Bluffs.

Slit-eyed, Ed Rose avoided Jedediah, but asked Ashley where Clyman and Sublette were. Ashley decided Rose was too anxious and gave a useless answer.

Ashley and Smith did not debark at Council Bluffs with Atkinson and O'Fallon, but continued on to St. Louis, reaching their familiar dock on October 4, 1825, three months after the fur trade's first Rendezvous. Newspapers exaggerated the Rendezvous' success, but Ashley did not ask for a retraction.

Instead, sure one good Rendezvous deserved another, Ashley immediately set about outfitting a new expedition of 70 men, 160 mules and horses with $20,000 worth of merchandise. But William H. Ashley decided not to leave for the mountains with Jedediah because he had a wedding to attend on October 25th -- his own.

Ashley planned to hire the ballroom in St. Louis's best hotel for his wedding and reception but Eliza Christy would not hear of it. She urged that her father William's stone mansion had hosted many elegant family weddings. And since he'd given them a 98,000 square foot lot as a wedding present for the building of their home, he'd be crushed if their wedding fled his roof.

Eliza Christy's prominent family invited over 300 French and American elite and provided a white-wigged symphony orchestra with liveried servants for *the* gala event of the St. Louis fall social season. Eliza was secretly vexed at most of the guests for abandoning the General's bid for the governorship. She vowed to get even with them in a most fitting way.

In Ashley's mind Eliza had seemed more of a plain woman to be loved for her intelligence, good breeding and social graces. But that was before he'd seen her in her full length white silk wedding gown with its chic embroidery, ribbons and veils. Eliza was a mannerly goddess with more interesting cleavage than he'd ever seen before. Her silken brown hair was coiled at the back of her head, held by a diamond studded mother-of-pearl comb. Several loose ringlets of hair draped over her silver head-band to dangle interestingly about her face. Eliza's face was powdered to alabaster with rose lip rouge, and she smelled divine. She'd even done something to her eyes, but Ashley wasn't sure what.

Even though the vast Christy home was drafty when the first carriages arrived, it was sultry by the time they closed the doors to keep out the rest of St. Louis. Ashley learned the Christy family had definite ideas about decorum, pomp and circumstance. Everything proceeded according to an elaborate plan. After vows were exchanged, their reception began.

General Ashley sat beside Eliza near the orchestra. She'd taken him for outfitting to Godoine's in St. Charles, the area's fashion leader where her clothes had been created. He'd wanted to wear his Militia uniform, but she said it was tired and styleless. A slight graying Frenchman with a thin mustache had dressed the General more ornately than anything he'd ever imagined for himself. He wore shiny black leather-soled dancing shoes just a bit too snug. His dark blue trousers were also too tight in the thighs "to make him look younger." His slate gray cut-away waistcoat with tails and silver gray buttons was topped by a black cravat over a collar with points like small horns protruding on either side of his chin. For all the discomfort and expense, Ashley rather liked it.

At precisely eight o'clock, the symphony played a short fanfare. Eliza and William Ashley rose, bowed, waved to the crowd and sat down to polite applause.

The orchestra filled the room with the Overture to *The Magic Flute* by Mozart. While the polite music droned on, Ashley whispered to Mrs. Ashley," How could you possibly find such a glorious gown in the three weeks since I came home from the mountains?"

Eliza smiled warmly, "Bill, This gown has been a year in the making. It began with a Pandora Doll, presented just as I am tonight, shipped to us by Godoine's niece Monique, a Parisian fashion designer. From that, Godoine and his other niece, Fifi, spent months creating this gown and acquiring my accessories."

Ashley shamed himself for ever doubting her loyalty. "You must have been pretty sure of this wedding."

"Bill, I never doubted it for a second. I'm your second wife, but you are my first husband. I will stand by you till I die."

He raised her hand, smoothed the lace back and kissed her palm with all his heart and soul.

The symphony bid *adieu* to Mozart, but to the audience's chagrin, they ground out a dry rendition of the First Movement of Haydn's *London Symphony No. 93.* Polite coughs and a few screeching chair legs voiced the crowd's quiet agony. When it seemed the evening was doomed, Eliza whispered, "These plutocrats wouldn't talk about you when you were running for Governor, but they surely will after this!"

Eliza rose and walked lightly to stand well poised at the conductor's back. She raised her arms to the bored legion. Haydn trailed off.

Eliza spoke in silvery tones that rang through the grand room, "You came here tonight expecting to dance the Minuet -- or at the wildest a Cotillion or Quadrille, but the General and I will have none of that! Tonight we will *Waltz* in close embrace in those dizzying swirls that set the spirit free!"

The stuffy crowd's mood catapulted from boredom to audible amazement.

"Not too shocked now, please! They've danced the Waltz in stodgy old London for a decade. No one has died from the immodesty of the Waltz! It's a turning, gliding dance in 3/4 time with six evenly accented steps to a full turn per every two bars of music. You need only repeat that until your joy overcomes your intelligence!" She extended her white gloved arm, "William, may I have the honor of this Waltz?"

As he strode toward her, his heart breaking down the walls of his chest, Ashley heard Eliza command, "Maestro -- the *Radetzky March*!" She took him in her arms and began to twirl to the rousing, explosive Strauss. Only a few elegantly dressed couples ventured out to join the Ashleys until her whirlwind gown and the tilt of her head seduced them all. The guests rushed from their chairs to share the bombastic music's magic with the Ashleys. The melody engulfed the hearts of the dancers -- merging all in a lilting fantasy of swirling gowns and laughter and crystal chandeliers, trembling in jubilant splendor.

CHAPTER 21

MILTON AND ACHILLES   SPRING-FALL 1826

Milton Sublette despised St. Charles. It was a city of death. He threw his buckskinned leg over the top rail and straddled the fence bordering the Protestant Cemetery near their old Sublette tavern. The rail sagged dangerously under his 220 pounds. 1826's early spring breezes tossed Milt's black mane over his eyes and his handsome face. He pulled his hair behind his head and tied a thong around it the way Bill used to wear his when he was plowing. This graveyard with its tilted headstones and frozen snow patches was eating Sublettes one by one. It had just swallered sister Polly, and he could feel its hunger for him.

The mound had sunk to a basin on Papa's 1821 grave. Mama's and Sally's graves from '22 were caved in, but black earth mounded Polly's. Polly Sublette died of TB while living with Mama's sister, Levisa McKinney. Milt paid to have Polly buried. He'd buy her a stone with her name on it before he went Up the Mountain. The graveyard's ghosts put a chill through him, but he stood his ground.

Milt remembered walking Mama home through the blizzard after Papa's funeral. She was sobbing. Tears spilled down his cheeks. Mama'd put up with so much from him. She couldn't really be under that spindly grass and that cheap rock. Their family plot had four empty graves, but it growled for Sophronia and all five boys. He began to run from the growing roar. If it wanted Milton Sublette, it'd have to outrun him!

*   *   *

Ewing Young had a way of staring into a man. The balding 34 year-old locked eyes with Milt Sublette across the back table of the empty Rumrunner. "So you're the one newspapers call the *Thunderbolt of the Rockies*." Young sipped his whiskey. "You all reputation, Mr. Sublette?"

Milton snatched Young's grimy glass and slowly poured the cheap whiskey in the burly man's lap. "Only reason I don't stomp a mudhole in you and push your face in it, is cause I need a trappin' job. You got one or don'tchu?"

Young ignored the whiskey christening. "Maybe, but compared to the men I'm hiring, you're a choir boy."

"Long as the pay's good an' you don't talk too much, I'll take the job," Milton grated.

"Why'd you leave Ashley's outfit?"

"Major Henry quit. Ashley's like workin' fer yer father."

"About four years back, I farmed in Charitan, Missouri. Isn't your brother the St.Charles Constable called *One Punch*?"

Annoyed at always being compared to his brother, Milt grated "Bill held my coat when a bloody ruckus come up."

"Heard a St. Louie blue blood challenged you to duel on Bloody Island last Friday for dallying with his wife."

"That duel kinda bottomed out," Milton muttered.

"Why?"

"I seen the stiletto under the glove he was gonna slap me with, so I shoved it some place real private. He'll be eatin' off the mantle while I trap the Gila River with you."

"Brigade forms end of this week at Fayette, about half way to Independence. You need some fresh geography till the Sheriff forgets how you play mumbletypeg. This'll get your kit together."

Milton plucked the gold piece from the air and shook hands, amazed that Ewing Young's grip was like having a draft horse step on his hand. But then Young was 6'2" and near heavy as Bill. "Where you headed now?"

"One of my St. Louie blue blood friends loans me the classics to read on trips. I'm borrowing Homer's *Iliad.*"

"Let me know how ole Homer's lid turns out, now hear?"

* * *

Doubled over with stomach cramps again, Ewing Young

lay abed in Santa Fe while his 18 trapper brigade worked the beaver rich streams far to the southwest around the Gila River.

Trapping under Thomas L. Smith, Milton liked the man at once, a rare thing for him. Both 25 from large families in Kentucky, they'd cultivated a taste for whiskey, gambling and getting shot at over women. Tom Smith said in the light brogue of an Irish emigrant's son, "We be proof the devil stutters."

By early September 1826, Smith's party was trapping Salt River's beaver-rich headwaters, but Smith grew more uneasy by the hour. He and Milt began setting traps at night and collecting them in the morning. After they harvested their traps, they'd go to ground someplace that gave them a lookout. Next night they'd set their traps and go back into hiding.

"How come yer jumpier'n the groom at a shotgun weddin'?" Milton whispered.

"Hair on me neck tells what me eyes don't dare see."

"I see nothin', Tom."

"That's cause they're *Apaches*. They're not like the blunderin' plains Indians we're used to. I lived with the *Choctaw*, *Chickasaw*, *Sioux* and the *Osage*. Spent time joshin' the *Utes* an' the Snakes. Fought the *Arapaho* and *Comanches*. Never seen nothin' like the *Apache*, and still see nothin' of 'em -- but I know they're there. Too bad Ewing's laid up. That man can see to the Millennium in *Revelation 20*! Ewing makes an eagle feel blind."

"They say Ewing's a fair to middlin' shot," Milt muttered as they slipped into the stream to pull their traps up again.

"Ain't no better," Tom nodded through his devilish grin. "They say Ewing's grandfather shot Major Ferguson from half a mile with his long rifle, Sweet Lips, at the Battle of King's Mountain. Ewing still carries Sweet Lips, and she's only sweet, if Ewing ain't aimin' her at you!"

The words no sooner left Tom's mouth than a bullet from a hidden rifle shattered Milt's left heel. Milt fell, seizing his heel as he stifled the yell that jammed in his throat. He knew he was hit bad, but he didn't really believe it till he couldn't walk.

"Gimme your arm, Milt. We'll light out while that devil's loadin'!" Struggling under the larger man's weight, Smith rested in a stand of cedars. He thrust his shoulder into Milton's belly, hoisted him and hauled him through the brush, ominous yips sounding behind them. "*Coyotero Apaches,*" Smith panted. He whistled to alert his other trappers.

Milt Sublette couldn't mount his horse without help, but he could ride hard as the next man. When his heel bled him weak, he clutched his pommel to keep from flopping to the ground. Finally they reached the Chavez Rancho. Chavez sent a rider at once to fetch Ewing Young from Santa Fe.

Milt knew it'd be a while before Young got there. He bedded down in one of the dark adobe huts and saw only *el cocinero* who brought him greasy food too full of *chiles* to eat. He brooded over spending his money on whisky instead of buying Polly a headstone in St. Charles. His heel wound'd mean the end if he got blood poisoning. In his feverish dreams, the Sublette family plot roared after him like a grizzly.

Tom Smith commandeered a Mexican *médico,* who grudgingly stitched Milt's blue-green heel shut, bone chips and all, like sewing up a torn moccasin with a shattered foot inside it. After Smith and the butcher left, Milt doused *tequila* on his crushed heel, then sucked his booze bottle dry. He was the fastest runner in any outfit he'd ever been in. Would Milton Sublette race the wind again? What if he couldn't walk? Was he gonna eat a charge from his Hawken pistol?

Ewing Young arrived at Chavez Rancho with 16 more trappers, swelling his force to 35 men. After convincing the trappers he'd avenge the wounding of Milt and two others and the loss of all their traps and skins at the hands of the *Apaches,* Young looked in on Milt.

Milt cooked his bare foot on a sunny bench in the doorway. Young eyed Milt's mutilated heel, then flopped on the smelly bed inside. "You see the *Apache* who shot you?"

Milton grunted, "No."

"With the *Coyotero,* you don't. To chase them is to herd the air. To even this score, I'll have to use a timeless ploy like the Trojan Horse."

"Never rode a Trojan Horse -- or a ploy."

"Good thing. It's large, wooden and looks like a gift, but it's full of soldiers. It spawned the warning, *Beware of Greeks bearing gifts.* We're gonna fix the *Apaches* the way the ancient Greeks would. Can you walk on that heel?"

"Prob'ly."

"We can learn more from the Greeks."

"'Bout heels or weird horses?"

"Both. Achilles was the strongest and swiftest warrior in the Trojan war. As a baby Achilles' mother dipped him in the River Styx making him invulnerable in battle, except for the heel she held him by. Shot in that heel by an arrow, Achilles died."

"Rotten thing to tell somebody with a busted-up heel!"

"Guess all of us have an Achilles heel of some kind. With me, it's my stomach. With you, it's your heel. To live, we have to overcome our worst weakness. Can you do it, Sublette?"

Milt eyed his foot, then shrugged his shoulders.

"By tomorrow morning?"

"Sweet Jesus, Ewing! Gittin' shot in the heel killed that Greek o' yers! Now you want me hikin' on mine in the mornin'?"

"All right, Sublette. Make it tomorrow *afternoon*!" Captain Young said bulling out the door.

* * *

Young's men worked Salt River's headwaters for a week before the *Coyotero Apaches* grew bold enough to show themselves 300 yards from the trappers. Enraged by their arrogance, Tom Smith yelled, "Shoot one o' them red devils, Ewing. That shot's child's play fer the likes o' you."

Ewing shaded his gaze at the distant *Apaches*. "Same people that butchered four trappers in Bill Wolfskill's outfit last summer." He led his men to a cedar grove. He ordered them to cut cedars and build a log pen for the livestock that would double as a fort for them. Although limping badly, Milt Sublette wielded his axe along side the others. When they finished the log pen next morning, Young sat several squat sacks of flour and two dark blue trade blankets along the pen's top and waved the *Apaches* in.

Appetites whetted by beaver and traps already seized from these same weak fools, their Chief rode trapper James Ohio Pattie's bay horse. Five heavily armed *defensores* followed on foot.

The Chief, resplendent in his broad brimmed palmetto hat, white cotton shirt with scarlet sleeves and scarlet leggings, dismounted and strutted up to the cut logs. The smell of the fresh cedar cleared the chief's nose. His obsidian eyes sparkled. Several of the horses amounted to fortunes if he took no more. These rabbit hearts would soon die when his *guerreros* in the hills received his attack signal.

Ewing Young folded one of the trade blankets and motioned the Chief to hold it. The Chief strode proudly between his *defensores*. Young began to load the blanket with double handfuls of flour. Each time Young stopped, the Chief nodded for Young to add more flour.

The flour soon mounded high in the blanket. Without a word, Thomas Smith poked his .60 caliber pistol up under the bulging blanket and fired, blowing off the Chief's palmetto hat and much of his head in a great white cloud. Flour was still tumbling all over the Chief's scarlet leggings when a fusillade of shots from the pen killed all five of the thunderstruck *Apache* guards.

While James Ohio Pattie caught Little Grizz, his liberated bay gelding, Young stepped out of the floury air, "Those *Apaches* up there don't seem to want any flour. They're leaving. Maybe now we can trap the Salt and the Gila in peace."

"Them Greeks gotchu dreamin', do they?" Milt asked.

CHAPTER 22

THREE ACES JULY 1826

William Sublette heard men hikin' up the trail to where he sat watchin' the 1826 Cache Valley Rendezvous stagger after runnin' hog wild through the first two weeks of July. He recognized their voices as two of the finest men he'd ever known. But *A-ponee-tah* did not know them and rumbled, raising the ruff on his neck. Sublette quieted the powerful wolf-dog with a pat on his silken head. Sublette gripped his buffalo-tail collar.

"That a wolf?" Jedediah Smith asked in his New York accent, squatting a safe distance from Pony's bared fangs.

"Indian pack dog. *Shoshones* call him *A-ponee-tah*. Answers to Pony. Couple months ago, Pony decided he owned me. Follers me all day -- curls up agin me at night. Tried givin' them *Shoshones* somethin' fer him, but they ain't havin' none of it. Their Shaman said this wolf hated men till his spirit met mine. They're sure spirits cain't be bought fer money er beaver."

"There's something to that," David Jackson smiled, deepening the crack lines around his mouth, as he knelt beside Jedediah. "You may have a little wolf blood yourself, Sublette."

"We breakin' camp?" Sublette asked, pushin' Pony down till the wolf-dog laid across his moccasins and closed its eyes.

Smith and Jackson both settled to the ground and sat cross legged in their buckskins with the sun behind them. "Let's talk first," Jedediah suggested.

Sublette nodded and stroked Pony's head deliberately to

let both men know he wasn't givin' up the dog.

"General Ashley wants to quit the mountains," Jedediah said.

Sublette gasped, "Why? We made you and him a fortune this year! I know 'cause I kept the books fer six Messes. Dave yer people alone harvested near four bales in a short season," Sublette said with enough irritation to raise Pony's head and kindle a fire in his yellow eyes.

Jedediah raised his hand to calm the usually stoic Sublette. "When people make big changes, there are the reasons they give -- and the *real* reasons. General says 30 men deserted him on the way up here. He doesn't blame them, because he's lost somewhere between 27 and 60 killed. Says he can't handle the human responsibilities any more. But the *real* reason's because the man's in love."

"He's what?" Sublette snorted. "Hell, the General's older'n you, Dave an' you gotta be 40! Is she from the tribes?"

"Right after we left St. Louis with the fall supply train, General Ashley married Eliza Christy in what he called *an epic celebration*. He adores her. He can't *stand* being away from her. He's made a killing over the last two fur seasons. Wants to go home to St. Louis, and build her a house befitting her beauty. The General wants to supply trappers instead of being one."

"Where zat leave us?" Sublette inquired.

"Well, for all his obsession with Eliza, General Ashley's worried about where that leaves us -- so am I. He suggested talking to you or David about buying into the trapping business. I felt he was right about both of you!"

Sublette knew he'd gained the respect of these men, but he wasn't sure he was ready for this big a leap. "Whatta you think, David?"

Jackson ferreted three Aces from a greasy deck of cards in his possibles bag and held them up. "We fit together like these three Aces. Jedediah's the explorer to open new beaver country. I've been supervisor of trapping operations for two and a half years and I'm good at it er Ashley wouldn't be building Eliza a castle. Sublette, being Constable down there, you know the settlements, so you can step into Ashley's boots transporting supplies in and furs out to St. Louie."

"Don't have the money to buy in," Sublette admitted sadly, pettin' Pony's black and gray haired back. Pony licked Sublette's hand and perked his ears up.

"I've got my cash up from the current partnership of Ashley & Smith. I'm positive Ashley'll take your names on a note for the rest of what's owed," Smith countered. "I've watched Ashley skin beaver skinners since 1822. Ashley wasn't too hard on me because he was still in the business, but when he's getting out, we better watch out! Sublette, you're the judge's son. If you can work out the Articles so we don't end up on willow hoops like three plews, I'll sign," Jedediah laughed.

"Ashley wants to sell and I think I'm looking at two fine partners," Jackson said emphatically. He handed each man an Ace. "As long as we keep these, each of us holds three Aces. Whoever wants out can toss his Ace into the discards."

Sublette grasped his Green River knife and put his other hand on Pony. "We'll dicker this agreement with a butcher knife on the table an' a wolf under it. If Pony was a grizzly, we might could git a draw with the General."

Jedediah Smith looked at his tattered Ace of Hearts. "It's the first and last card the Lord'll ever let me hold." He slid it into the tunic pocket of his buckskins over his own heart.

* * *

When Sublette told General Ashley the agreement would be ready soon, the older man appeared almost disinterested. "Get together with Jedediah and draw up something he thinks is fair, and I'll sign it. Jedediah will be fair to everyone."

Sublette braced Jedediah with Ashley's masterstroke.

"I knew General Ashley was shrewd, but I had no idea he'd turn my own principles against us to get the best deal he could possibly hope for," Smith lamented.

Sublette shook his head. "Ain't there anythin' we kin do to git around *you*, Jedediah?"

"Maybe. I hired a young Scot named Campbell -- Robert Campbell -- when I left St. Louis last October. Man's far too honest for what we need, but at least he'll be detached about it, because he doesn't know that much about the fur trade."

"Who's this Campbell?" Sublette asked, wanting to know more about the man who might soon grab his future by the throat.

"Campbell's a small, cadaverous Scot about 22 -- born in Ireland -- County Tyrone. He's well educated -- clerked for me on the trip and wrote every detail precisely. His script's legible and straight forward."

"Thought you said he's a Scot."

"Born of Scottish parents living in Ulster Ireland."

"Why'd ya say he's far too honest?"

"If you were trying to get a trapping job, would you start by telling me your doctor said you had to go to the mountains to keep from dying of consumption?"

Sublette guffawed, "Campbell's a real judge o' character. He knew right off he could tell you the truth, an' you'd hire him anyway! I'll git with Campbell an' work out sumpthin' fair to all."

William Sublette discovered Robert Campbell scrubbin' his clothes in a clear stream with his buckskin top off. Campbell's spindly white chest reminded Sublette of the starved trapper's corpse he'd found in a tree near the Green River after the snow melted. "You Robert Campbell?"

"Aye and you're Mr. S," Campbell responded, trilling his R's with a Scottish burr. Campbell's eyes bugged out at this blond man's massive arms and chest with thighs like trees. "Might I ask how loong you've been in the mountains, Mr. S?"

Sublette got the drift of the question. "Few years up here, you'll make me look like a gangly girl, Campbell. Mountains does wonders fer a feller."

"Aye. Mr. Smith said you'd be askin' me to coompose soom Articles. Mr. S you must have been up here longer than all the other trappers to look so healthy."

Sublette nodded, "General's in a sweat to go home. You be ready to start on the agreement in the mornin'?"

"Why no, Mr. S, it's near doon. Just need a few figures, dates and places to poot in it."

"Jedediah didn't tell ya what to say in the agreement, did he?"

"No, sir. Mah brother Hugh in Philadelphia buys and sells businesses, so I thought through soom o' Hugh's transactions. I've kept the books up here for Mr. Smith and helped audit the books of your Messes with the General. What is it you eat mostly, Mr. S?"

"If your papers are sound, I'm personally gonna beef you up like the champeen bull at the Lincoln County Fair!"

In his tent General Ashley read quickly over the Articles drafted by young Robert Campbell with help from Sublette. When he'd finished, the General said, "Campbell, find the new partners and bring them back here." After Campbell left, Ashley studied the brief document carefully. Eliza's future could be resting on how well this first trapper supply agreement worked.

Ashley saw that the Articles established the partnership of Smith, Jackson & Sublette to whom Ashley transferred his $16,000 worth of merchandise in the mountains, with $5,000 of that due Smith under his dissolution with Ashley. The new firm agreed to turn over the beaver they collected to Ashley, until their debt due on July 1, 1827 at the Bear Lake Rendezvous was paid. Ashley would either buy their beaver at the Rendezvous for $3 the pound or take their beaver skins to St. Louis and sell them at the best price, charging $1.12 a pound for transportation with the net proceeds being used to pay off Ashley's debt. Ashley also agreed to supply up to $15,000 in merchandise at the Rendezvous, *but they absolutely had to notify Ashley of their needs by March 1, 1827.* The agreement was already signed by Smith, Jackson and Sublette, witnessed by young Robert Campbell and dated July 18, 1826.

When Campbell returned with Smith, Jackson and Sublette, Ashley emerged from his tent, dragging a small writing table behind him. He nodded to each of them, then nonchalantly signed the Articles.

They were obviously waiting for the General to say something, so he added, "Gentlemen, I'm transferring all my agreements for the services of 42 trappers, including yourselves, to your firm. Actual papers are in St. Louis. There's another 77 not under contract that came out here with the last two pack trains. You may not want all the men. Some will refuse to proceed with you. I think you should be working things out with the men you want to keep. I trust each of you like a son."

Ashley's final remark triggered a reaction none of them expected. Suddenly, the new partners and Ashley were hugging each other and slapping each other's backs. Warm, vigorous handshakes went the rounds of all the men, then Sublette said, "This is either the beginnin' or the end of somethin' wonderful!"

"I'm sure it's both," Ashley observed, shaking Sublette's hand again as he spoke.

Ashley immediately headed his mule train for St. Louis with 125 packs of beaver, 100 skins to the pack, worth $60,000 and a valuable agreement with three Mountain Men whom he deemed to make the Rocky Mountains small by comparison.

* * *

Jedediah Smith kicked his horse in the flanks and charged up the grassy knoll to the cabin site, whooping as he rode. William Sublette buried his axehead in the pine log he was shaping for the winter quarters and stood sweating, the sun gleaming on his massive arms and chest.

Reining in his horse, Jedediah jumped to the ground beside Sublette. "David gave another 50¢ a skin on the trapper's share and 119 men in Cache Valley signed to trap for Smith, Jackson & Sublette! Not a man walked away!"

Sublette offered his sweaty hand, then pulled it back. Jedediah seized the great square hand and shook it, sweat and all. "Let's look at them rosters," Sublette said.

"David's right behind me with them."

David Jackson joined them and together, they laid out their plans. Jedediah would take 17 men and head southwest to open new beaver country. Jackson and Sublette'd take the other 102 trappers and strike north into the Tetons for the fall beaver hunt, then bring the men back to winter at Cache Valley. Pony sat panting with dripping tongue behind Sublette, alertly watching every move the men made and cocking his ears at their voices.

Sublette said, "We need Brigade Leaders and a good man to head up each Mess. I see Brigade Leaders bein' Tom Fitzpatrick, Moses 'Black' Harris, Jim Bridger and Jim Beckwourth."

Jedediah nodded while Jackson said, "We can let the Brigade Leaders pick their Mess Bosses."

Sublette added, "We gotta sign this new man Robert Campbell as Clerk. Ain't much to him, but he's got fire in his lantern. I promised to beef him up some."

"He did a fine job for me -- and more lately for all of us," Jedediah Smith agreed.

Sublette smiled, "Better add Clyman on the list to head a Brigade -- in case you get your ear tore off again, Jedediah. I cain't sew!"

Jackson glanced at Pony. "Put Clyman on fer sure! I'm just hoping that wolf of Bill's doesn't rip me open somewhere south of the belt line."

Sublette stared at Pony and set the husky pack dog's tail to wagging. Pony might not be as valuable as the Sublette family's old American Fox Hound, Seneca, but Milton would think this was a *one of a kind* dog an' Milton would be right.

CHAPTER 23

BEWARE THE FIRST OF MARCH   FALL 1826-MARCH 1827

In his three years Up the Mountain, William Sublette had seen plenty of peaks and lakes -- but these three jagged, snowy Tetons thrusting thousands of feet into the clouds above their amethyst reflection in the crystal lake stole his breath away.

David Jackson, awed by the majestic sight, murmured, "Makes a man understand why the Blackfeet'll kill to keep these Tetons."

"You hear Mountain Men brag around fires bout the *Trois* Tetons an' you think it's jist trapper talk. Dave, I ain't never seen a *woman* purty as this -- an' there ain't *nuthin'* purtier'n a woman."

"Except the old English ballad about a woman -- *Green Sleeves*." David Jackson serenaded the resplendent scene with his pure lyric tenor:

"Alas my love --you do me wrong to cast me off discourteously
And I have loved you oh so long -- delighting in your company
Green Sleeves was all my joy -- Green Sleeves was my delight
Green Sleeves was my heart of gold and who but my lady Green Sleeves."

"You sing like a Angel! I'm givin' yer name to this lake -- *Jackson Lake* -- on the map Ashley tole me to make fer the Army. Fact is, I'm puttin' yer name on this valley -- *Jackson Hole*! Only wish ever'body that ever sees the place could hear yer voice. Mebbee they will -- in a way."

"Tetons are more like *Green Sleeves* than you think!

Ballad's from 13th century England about women who followed soldiers into battle along with army families. Ladies of the evening wore green sleeves so knights could tell them from the wives. But over time history was forgotten, and *Green Sleeves* even became a hymn. Just goes to show you -- beauty and time make strange bedfellows!

Sublette shook his head and walked along the sandy shore with Pony leaving man and wolf tracks in the sand.

* * *

Jackson and Sublette's Brigades had left Cache Valley heavy with trade goods. They'd traded with the Snakes, Crows, *Sioux* and Flatheads. Their pelts were piling up -- but the Blackfeet in the Tetons wanted only to drive the huge parties of trappers from their mountains.

Blackfeet periodically fired rifle bullets through the treetops, snapping off pine branches above men and pack horses. Two years ago, Ed Rose'd told Sublette how Blackfeet hated fish, so Sublette stuck extra trout they'd caught on bushes along their trail to answer bullets from unseen rifles with fishy insults.

Sublette never would have known Pony was eatin' his Blackfoot messages, if the wolf-dog hadn't fetched a fish to Sublette the same way he brought rabbits and squirrels. Sublette chucked the trout into the trees, mystifyin' Pony, then rode on with a grin. Mebbee insultin' Blackfeet wasn't right. Like Dave Jackson said, this was Blackfoot land.

The arctic 1826 Autumn made beaver fur extra thick, so Jackson and Sublette had their hundred hunters laying double trap lines before the "rats" denned against winter. All were to meet in ten days, then move through the Tetons together. Plews were plentiful enough to bale by the time the trappers reached a giant crystal lake sprawling across 20 miles with channels fanning out in several directions. David Jackson joined Sublette on the shore of the icing lake to roast juicy venison and discuss their fall hunt.

"Bill, you still making that map for the Army?"

"It'll be better after Clyman puts a surveyor's hand to it."

"Do me a favor?"

"What's yer pleasure?"

"Name this *Sublette Lake* on your map."

"Lake lays out crazy. Havin' trouble mappin' it."

"Bill, just tell me you'll put your name on it."

"Oughta call it *Pony Lake* cause it looks like him layin' down, but I'll do whatchu say."

Pony stopped gnawing his venison hip to see what his man wanted, then shattered it with his powerful jaws to get the marrow.

"Dave, you ever see anythin' like that hot water and mud explodin' down at the end o' this lake?"

"*Sublette Lake,*" David Jackson corrected. "Truly never have. Daniel Potts -- skinny feller with the eyeglasses -- is over under the trees writing a letter about them to his brother. Just read it to me. Potts has a pleasing way with words, but if I got that letter, I'd never believe it -- and I *know* it's true. Wonder what his brother'll think!"

Sublette wiped his greasy hands on his buckskins. "Heard bout this place as a boy. My Grandpa Whitley tuck me an' Milt an' some apple tarts down to the dungeon under his big ole house in Kentucky. Lit a torch an' told us bout John Colter findin' brimestone bubblin' straight up from Hell. Said the newspapers didn't believe Colter, but Grandpa did. Now we're seein' why. Smart ole man. More I think about it, he's likely why I'm out here in these mountains today."

"Bill, I'm glad you're out here -- and so's Thomas Eddy. I thought Clyman was our only surgeon, but Eddy told me you got a bullet out of his thigh with a spoon handle after the *Bannocks* ambushed us by *Jackson* Lake."

"Them *Bannocks* cain't shoot a lick. Bullet barely busted Eddy's hide. If I'da shook Eddy's leg, bullet woulda fell out."

"Bill Sublette, you're the cagiest Mountain Man I've ever seen! You want everybody to think you're so dumb you'd drown if it started raining while your head's tipped back."

"Tom Eddy ain't all that grateful. He jist quit us an' went off with a party o' free trappers to work the head waters o' the Yellowstone."

"Must've ducked out to beat your bill, Doc!"

"That's what we oughta do -- duck out. Ducks is aflyin' south while we're agoin' north. Let's head fer Cache Valley fore we have to den up with them tree eatin' beavers."

* * *

Their Cache Valley cabins were cozy and tight before the clawing fingers of icy winter gales. Trapping done for the year, Mountain Men gathered at fiery hearths to heal their wounds, bring their equipment up to snuff and talk over their season. Sublette spent time learning Indian hand signs from Tom Fitzpatrick. Groups shifted from cabin to cabin. The same stories were told and retold, often to the same tired ears. Most wouldn't let on till somebody tried to stick the same yarn in their ear for the third or fourth time.

William Sublette's cabin was always crowded, and that was all right long as they left room for his wolf-dog Pony. Sublette waited for Brigade Leader Moses "Black" Harris to come in, then launched his favorite story about the burly Negro. "Me an' ole Mose was beddin' down fer the night up in them Wasatch Mountains when we hears this bull grizz abellerin' in the brush. I look over an' see Mose pullin' on his boots. I says, Mose, it ain't gonna do you no good puttin' them boots on -- you cain't outrun that grizz nohow.' Ole Moses looks at me an' gits that silly grin o' his, then he says, 'I don't gotta -- argh -- outrun no grizzly, Mista Bill. All I gotta outrun is *you*!'"

When the laughter died away, genial Albert Gallatin Boone, a strapping 20 year old two hundred pounder with a face like the Rocky Mountains, cleared his throat loud enough to let everybody know it was his turn to spin a yarn.

"My folks, Jesse and Chloe Boone, moved us to St. Charles, Missouri, on my Granddad Daniel Boone's place. Grandma Boone died, so Granddad had a carpenter to cut up a walnut tree from their yard to make her a right fine coffin. But that tree give so many boards, Granddad Daniel tole the carpenter to fix him a coffin too. But fer all his gruntin', Granddad Daniel couldn't die right away, so he had to figure somethin' to do with his coffin while he was awaitin' fer the Reaper. Drug it onto his front porch and filled it with apples, so's ever' boy fer miles knowed where to git a apple. Finally one day Granddad Daniel says, 'I hope they's worms in them apples.' I asks him why, and he pops back, 'So's I can eat them worms now, cause I know they's sure fire afixin' to eat me, soon's I git in that coffin!'"

"Turn about's fair play," Jim Clyman yelled over the chuckles. "Got a story that isn't all that funny, but if you're American, you likely need to know it."

Settling quiet gave him the go-ahead. "Some of you aren't all that pleased with our President John Quincy Adams after the shenanigan he pulled with Henry Clay to keep Andy Jackson out of the White House. But strange coincidence came to pass with his father John Adams and Thomas Jefferson. Trader left a *Missouri Intelligencer* here saying that on the 4th of July -- while we were frolicking here at the Rendezvous -- former Presidents Adams and Jefferson both *died* exactly 50 years to the day after they signed the Declaration of Independence in 1776."

Some men hinted a grin, waiting for the joke. But when no joke followed, they sat fidgeting until Clyman dived in again. "Told you it wasn't funny, and you can see how right I was. Here's another one that isn't funny, but one of us really needs to know about it. In Shakespeare's *Julius Cæsar*, a Soothsayer warns Cæsar to '*Beware the ides of March*,' which we later learn foretells Cæsar's murder by his friends on the 15th of March. With New Years of 1827 upon us and this blizzard howling out of the north, I must tell someone here that I read some Articles last July that make me say, '*Beware the First of March*!'"

William Sublette kept a poker face, but his gut flinched inside him. Clyman was right. Grizzly maulin's weren't the only thing Clyman could look after. He'd foretold a disaster far worse for the young firm of Smith, Jackson & Sublette than two Presidents dyin' the same day. "That's gonna do it fer me today, gents. Got a pack to make up. Mose I gotta talk to you." Trappers filed out knowing something had gone bad wrong.

Sublette confided, "Under our contract, General Ashley has to supply S,J & S with goods for the July 1, 1827 Rendezvous, *if we put the list of our needs in his hand by March 1, 1827*. I never counted on this blizzard. S, J & S'll fer sure go busted if I cain't make it to St. Louie in 90 days."

Moses Harris grinned, "Mus' be 1200 mile. Take dat 90 days --argh -- on horseback to make it in good weathah."

"Mose, it's yer right to say no, but I'm askin' if yer willin' to try mushin' to St. Louie with me on snowshoes?"

"Is pigs uglier -- argh -- dan us?" He took Pony's pack off its peg in the wall. "Gonna put all I kin -- argh -- on dat pack dog o' yers. We boaf haul all we kin carry -- argh -- we might could git dere in time."

"Gitchur snowshoes an' pack, Mose. I'll strap this on Pony, so he'll have time to git used to it agin."

"Time's what we ain't got -- argh -- none of."

By noon Sublette, Moses and Pony were bucking icy gales east through the mountains. With his heavy pack Pony's huge feet sank deep in the snow. They expected to find buffalo around Ham's Fork, but ate jerky instead, diving for cover from hunting Indians that barely missed Pony with an arrow.

They reached Independence Rock somewhere around the middle of January. While Moses tracked and shot a buffalo, Pony brought a winter hare to Sublette. When Moses came running with a red knife, Sublette gave the rabbit back to Pony and helped Moses dress out the buffalo. They found a niche in Independence Rock and braved the night's blowing snow. In the morning, they packed all the buffalo they could carry and let Pony gnaw on the frozen carcass.

Moses and Sublette took turns breaking trail in the crackling cold. They stumbled onto the frozen North Platte, then staggered through low hills near Ash Hollow. After first trying to dodge *Pawnee* sign they fell into friendly Big Elk's camp. Sublette made the hand sign for *Pawnee* by raising two fingers in a "V." The Indians shared what little they had and sent Moses and Sublette on their way into the eery white dawn the next day.

Just past Cold Camp Creek, they met a small band of Indians, but couldn't tell what tribe. Sublette traded a hunting knife for a buffalo tongue. He tried to give part of the tongue to Pony, but the once mighty animal had fallen weak and listless. Sublette moved the sugar, coffee and dried meat from Pony's pack to his own, hoping Pony'd git his strength back. He wondered if he could carry the supplies, but they were all used up before he could decide. They floundered on without food.

At Grand Island, Sublette shot a raven, but he and Moses were so hungry they wolfed it down raw without knowing how it tasted. Pony ignored his piece of the gaunt bird and weakly licked his raw feet. Fifty miles further, Sublette got too feeble to walk. He and Moses collapsed under three low trees frozen together like crystal folds in a lady's fan. Harris passed out. At dawn Moses knew he'd die if he didn't eat. He shook Sublette awake. "We gotta -- argh -- eat yo dog or die."

"Cain't eat Pony," Sublette whispered through lips split by frost bite.

"We dyin'. We gotta eat," Moses rasped as the wind blew a shawl of frost across the black man's face, turning it white as glistening salt.

Moses was a man among men. Sublette could not let him die. "I'll do it, Mose. He might turn on you." Sublette's huge hands closed around Pony's throat. The wolf-dog's yellow eyes went glassy. Pony coughed, but did not fight for life. A vision of Milton as a boy bounding through a field of spring flowers with Seneca blinded William. "Milton must never know what we done here," Sublette sobbed.

His own tears freezing to his face, Moses lunged to grab the dying dog's throat. "Dis' killin' you, Bill. I'm gonna say I done it." But Moses collapsed, and Sublette squeezed until his beloved Pony lay still in his great square hands.

Sublette roused Moses and motioned for him to eat. Sublette dropped Pony to retch, spitting strings of yellow. Pony lasted Moses three days, but Sublette ate only the leather scabbard of the knife he'd traded for the buffalo tongue.

Moses went lame, staggering on his unraveling snow shoes behind Sublette, who'd long since kicked his snowshoes off. Suddenly, six bony Indians sat their horses in the path.

Sublette fired one of Colonel Whitley's boot pistols in the air to unload it, then bartered it to get Moses a horse. The Indians would not give up a second horse even for the other boot pistol and rode off, doubling back to shadow the reeling trappers. Sublette slapped Moses's Indian horse on the hip, then went back ready to kill as many of the Indians as he could before he died. But the Indians were having none of the huge ghost coming out of the whiteness and fled.

It seemed like many days passed, then a horse pulling a tattered buggy stood before them in the road. Sublette staggered up to it. A preacher with his collar on backwards hunched forward in the buggy seat beside a plain-faced woman who gazed at the lurching, wild haired giant with disgust.

Sublette gasped, "You know the date?"

The bug-eyed preacher answered, "Why it's the 4th day of March in the year of our Lord, 1827."

"You sure?" Sublette grated as Moses rode up on the bony Indian horse.

"Of course I'm sure. I preach my sermons every Sunday and work them out weeks in advance.

Recognizing the low rolling hills where he'd hunted as a boy, Sublette began to sprint toward St. Louis, yelling, "C'mon, Mose, kick that pony in the slats!"

The preacher's wife shook her head and rolled her eyes, "That disgusting man's not even civilized. Can you imagine walking, while your *nigra* rides your horse?"

"He may be having delusions, dear. Looked like he hadn't eaten for a day or two and his lips were cracked bloody."

"All the more reason something should be done about him! Man should be locked up for carrying on like that."

Sublette ran toward the outskirts of St. Louis, his heart smashing at his ribs and his heaving lungs about to explode. He'd never failed before. What in God's name was he gonna tell Jedediah and David?

CHAPTER 24

UNDER ARREST SUMMER 1826-SPRING 1827

Jedediah sat his horse erectly, leading his 17 horsemen out of the 1826 Cache Valley Rendezvous. As a devout Methodist, it was his duty to take stock of himself from time to time, and he did it as he rode south toward the Great Salt Lake.

At age 27, Jedediah was the senior partner of Smith, Jackson and Sublette -- second in size among U. States concerns only to the American Fur Company owned by John Jacob Astor, richest man in the country. Jedediah's mission was to explore and record what he saw, hoping to open rich new beaver streams. His rifle and his Bible were his inseparable companions. He would do right no matter what obstacles Satan put in his path. He knew he'd been called "inflexible," but then what true New Yorker wasn't? And what did he care of how he was perceived -- as long as God's Will was done?

But God had a way of testing even the best of men, and Jedediah's test began almost at once after his expedition descended south of the Great Salt Lake.

The great tree forests withered to clumps of sagebrush, and the rich black soil bleached to reddish, clay-laced sand that spawned lizards and rattlesnakes.

Jedediah seldom found it necessary to talk with his men. He led by example, and they followed, except for *Manuel Eustavan* and the Indian *Nepassang*. These two deserted the minute they entered this Godforsaken country, reducing his party to 15 men.

Without pause, Jedediah pressed right on through the "Country of Starvation." Jedediah would not stray from his path if it led through the front gates of Hell! If temperature was any measure, perhaps it had.

The Black Mountains of Arizona decimated so many horses, Jedediah's entire party was soon afoot in the shimmering heat. His men were starving, and the remaining horses were too weak to ride.

God showed Jedediah no beaver, but miraculously produced hospitable *Mojave* Indians. They generously traded him supplies and fresh horses and told him of the bountiful Missions of California. Their Chief told him to follow the Mojave River, which he took to be the only course his men could travel. He did not tell Jedediah the river would lead him through the fiery oven of the Mojave Desert for nearly a month or that it would disappear underground for miles at a time before reappearing full of alkali.

Near the end of November 1826, Jedediah's floundering legion descended the Mojave Trail into the San Bernardino Valley and entered the cool, sheltered patios of California's Mission San Gabriel. Safe in the arms of God at last in the solicitous care of Father *José Sánchez*, Jedediah wrote to Mexican *Gobernador Echeandía* in San Diego requesting permission to hunt beaver throughout California, but was promptly summoned to San Diego under arrest.

Jedediah felt certain that if he could actually meet *Gobernador José Echeandía*, he would be seen for what he was -- a wandering servant of God and menace to no man. It didn't help that his New York vocabulary contained no Spanish, or that his Excellency had never even *heard* of beaver trapping and described Jedediah Smith in the official records as *pescador* -- fisherman -- which is one reason Jedediah was held under house arrest until January of 1827.

Jedediah discovered that the Mexicans depended upon American ships, as well as others, to bring the amenities not available in California provinces. He sent a plea for help to Captain Cunningham and masters of two other sailing vessels in San Diego Harbor. One afternoon, Captain Cunningham arrived at the head of a delegation of three ship Captains, all in full sea faring regalia.

The slender, blue-eyed Cunningham's New England accent was sweet in Jedediah's ears, even if his words weren't, "Are you insane?"

"Hardly, I'm Captain Jedediah Smith, senior partner of the Smith, Jackson and Sublette Company of St. Louis. I'm here to locate beaver for our enterprise."

"You just wandered into California without a passport. You're an illegal alien, and so are your men. The Mexicans watched Jackson take Florida and but for the Americans, Spain would have retaken the Louisiana Territory upon the collapse of Napoleon. They see you as land-mad opportunists to be distrusted in all things."

"Aren't you three Americans?"

"For certain, we are that," one of the older Sea Captains answered, "But we're Americans who bring Parisian dresses, bubbling champagne and delicate fans -- not beaver bait and bad manners."

"I asked you gentlemen here for help. If I just wanted obtuse insults, the Mexicans were doing quite well at that, even if I had to have them translated."

"He has something there," Cunningham interceded. "Listen, Mr. Smith -- if that's your real name -- if we get you out of here, it will be upon your unrecantable promise to leave California at once, by the way you came. Is that understood, sir?"

"Most assuredly, Captain."

"You understand we're giving our word to the Governor that you're out of here!"

"I understand, perfectly. I'll pack. I'm anxious to get back to my men."

"To lead them straight out of California, right?"

"Right."

Captain Cunningham promptly sailed to San Pedro with Jedediah restricted to his cabin.

By the middle of January, Jedediah's trapping party was resupplied and ready to depart California. Jedediah scrupulously led his men into the San Bernardino Mountains, but swerved back into rich beaver country along California's San Joaquin

River.

By late April, they'd taken 1,500 pounds of prime pelts, but when Smith tried to cross the Sierra Nevada to get his beaver back to the 1827 summer Rendezvous, the snow lay drifted too deep to cross.

The American trappers went into camp on the Stanislaus River, but heard that *Gobernador Echeandía* was at Monterey, furious that the American invaders had not left California as solemnly promised.

Jedediah wrote him a letter of explanation, which so impressed the Governor that he sent troops with orders to bring *pescador* Smith back in chains. However, Jedediah Smith disappeared into the mountains with Robert Evans and Silas Gobel, leaving 11 other men -- and all of his beaver -- behind in the care of the Almighty and the troops of *El Honrado Gobernador José Echeandía*.

CHAPTER 25

PINCKNEY'S SAVIOR   MARCH-JULY 1827

St. Louis waterfront rabble were used to seeing Mountain Men after bare knuckle brawls, but Cutface Bill Sublette still turned heads aplenty jumping pot-holes in the street with his hair flying, his mouth bloody and a corpse-like Negro loping behind him on a skeletal pinto. Sublette grabbed the horse's war bridal and steered him into the livery of the first hotel he found among the welter of brothels and grogshops.

Hoisting Moses "Black" Harris over his shoulder, Sublette lugged his unconscious companion to the gimcrack registration desk. He looked down at the sallow clerk. "Book this man a room and gimme the one beside it. Git crackin'."

"This establishment don't rent rooms to drunks er niggers."

Sublette felt weak as watered whisky, but bein' cast out by this fop after staggerin' through a 1,200 mile blizzard infuriated him. With his free hand Sublette reached over the desk and picked the scrawny clerk off the floor by the front of his vest. "Inna mountains a man's judged by what he does, not what he is. Moses Harris ain't a nigger. He's a *Mountain Man*! You better holler fer yer manager while you still can!"

A heavy, balding man with broad red suspenders and a boozy violet face, yanked the clerk from Sublette's grasp. "Git out and take your nigger with you."

Sublette laid Moses carefully across the desk top. Pulling his boot pistol as he rounded the desk, Sublette jammed the stubby Hawken down inside the fat man's pants. "You wanta hear a loud noise one time?"

The manager shook his head, his jowls flopping like a bloodhound's.

"Then book a room fer Moses Harris an one fer W. L. Sublette. I'm acomin' back in bout a hour. If Harris ain't in his room, happy as a gnat on a bar rag, I'm gonna grab this penny-ante clerk by the ankles an' bust you up with him. Now are you clear on nat?" Leaving both hotel minions nodding, Sublette charged out the door and down the street toward Ashley's office.

General William Ashley had never seen young Bill Sublette in a rage before. "Now calm down. Sit down here. What happened that you missed the first of March? I had to sell your goods to another outfit."

Sublette flopped in the big leather chair, "Me an' Mose walked 1200 mile through a raft o' blizzards to deliver this list. Mose hadda eat my dog an' he's dyin'. Here's our list. You gonna git us more supplies, er should I git 'em from somebody else?"

"This isn't much of an apology, Bill."

"Good as yer gonna git today. I spent mosta the mornin' dyin' an' all afternoon ready to turn dyin' into a epidemic."

Ashley remembered the first time he'd ever seen this remarkably handsome young man who now resembled a derelict trampled by a stampede. "Well Bill, you've swayed me with your eloquence. I'll get the goods on this list financed if I have to pay for them myself, Mr. Sublette." Ashley began to laugh. Sublette lay snoring in the chair. The man was a winner even when he'd lost. Ashley had the feeling Sublette would have a lot of people calling him Mister before he was through.

* * *

By Sublette's second mornin' in St. Louis, most of the ravages of the Cache Valley trip'd worn off. He and Moses'd bought new clothes, and he was wishin' he'd treated General Ashley a whole lot better. The man was his second father.

Sublette ordered two stubby pistols at the Hawken gun shop, then headed for his uncle Solomon Whitley's home in St. Charles to see his family.

According to the white-haired Negro mammy sweeping

Solomon's front porch, his uncle wasn't home, and his brother Pinckney was in school half a mile down the road.

The walk to the tiny school pinpointed all the sore places on William Sublette's battered body. He filled the doorway of the one room school and tried to recognize his brother Pinckney. A thin boy with big gray eyes looked up from his speller and yelled, "Bill!" Pinckney's 50 year old teacher nearly fainted with fright, but she let Pinckney go outdoors "to visit" while all the bright little gawkin' faces made William Sublette feel strangely old and out of place.

William hugged Pinckney's slender body outside near the school well. The boy was bony as a baby bird. "When was the last time you sat a horse, Pinckney?"

"Long time, Bill. We gonna ride?"

"How old're you now?"

"Just turned 15."

"You need some beef on ya. Wanta go Up the Mountain with me in a day er two?"

"I got to, Bill. Everybody keeps dying here. Got to get out of St. Charles."

"Brother Solomon all right?"

"It was Polly, Bill. She died, and I know I'm next."

"An' I say yer not! We'll find uncle Solomon, thank him fer all he's did fer you, offer him some money fer keepin' you an' Andrew an' Solomon, then we're agoin' to a Rocky Mountain Rendezvous!"

"Bill, I can't even spell Rendezvous!"

"Well let me tell you Pinckney, you'll like it jist the same!"

Pinckney tackled his big brother around the middle and filled the brisk spring morning with boyish laughter.

William took Pinckney across the river to St. Louis and outfitted him for the mountains. Together, they went into Hawken's. "Got my stubbies finished yet?" William asked the young gunsmith at the forge.

"Not yet, but I got somebody else's!"

"What?"

"Some Scottish nobleman -- William Drummond Stewart -- ordered these pistols with a *W* inlaid in silver here in the handle. But we can always make him another set, and you need yours right away, Mr. Sublette."

William hefted the inlaid pistols. He liked their balance and smooth actions. They fit his boot holsters. The smell of gun oil always reminded him of when he used to go to Grandpa Whitley's study when he was little. He'd give Grandpa Whitley's remainin' stubby pistol to Pinckney to keep it in the family. William bought Pinckney a used Halfstock Hawken Plains rifle.

They bailed a sleepy Moses Harris out of the cheap waterfront hotel. Pinckney laughed till he choked at the way Moses talked and carried on.

Sublette purchased the Smith, Jackson & Sublette two year trading license and posted the partnership's bond. He liked doin' these things. They made him feel all right agin after he'd failed to keep the contract date with Ashley. Bein' late had taught Sublette somethin'. Don't let yer contract git busted, but if it does, pick up the pieces an' put 'em back together. Man ain't dead till they shovel dirt in his face!

Ashley'd already dispatched their supply pack train on March 15th, so they rode hard to catch it. Pinckney floundered about his horse at first, but quit ridin' "like a empty shirt" after William gave him a few pointers.

William was surprised that the pack train hauled a four pound artillery piece on a two-mule vehicle to impress the tribes. Even with the slow downs the cannon caused at fordin's and steep hills, the supply train made good time along the Platte and Sweetwater, arrivin' at the Bear Lake Rendezvous site on the 27th of June 1827. William Sublette'd failed by three days in gettin' the March 1st notice to Ashley, but he'd delivered the trade goods three days early to Rendezvous at the place specified in the Articles, so the contract was none the worse for wear.

*　　*　　*

Jedediah watched the Mexican troops coming, but the better part of valor was to get resupplied at the Rendezvous and come back fresh. On May 20, 1827 he led Evans and Gobel with seven horses through Ebbetts Pass and back into the scalding desert. After three weeks, their water was gone. Three horses got sacrificed for food. Evans collapsed from thirst.

Jedediah decided there was no use waiting there to die when they could do nothing for Evans, so they struggled onward with Jedediah praying as they went.

They reached Skull Valley Springs, but it was dry. Then like a miracle, the water bubbled up from the ground. Jedediah carried a kettle of water back to Evans and revived him. By July 2nd, they were but a day's ride from Bear Lake.

When Jedediah's small party rode in to Rendezvous, the other trappers, certain Jedediah was dead, began to cheer. Somebody fired the four pound cannon in salute, scaring good sense out of the horses and all the Indians who didn't know thunder could come from a pipe.

Sublette ran to Jedediah, "Where's the rest o' yer men?"

"In California along with the beaver we couldn't get out over the mountains through the drifted snow."

"California? What's that like?"

"It's a land of outrage!"

* * *

After hearin' Jedediah's California adventures, William took crusty old trapper Sam Tulloch aside from the merriment of the Rendezvous and explained how Pinckney needed watchin' and didn't need to go to the Snake Indian village until next Rendezvous.

Tulloch took to Pinckney right off. Pinckney smiled at his older brother. "Guess you're pretty important around here, Bill. Don't worry. I'll make you as proud of me as you are of Milton."

"You don't have to go that far, boy!"

"Bill, I promise you. You'll never regret bringing me Up the Mountain -- not for a second!"

CHAPTER 26

BLACKFEET AT BEAR LAKE   JULY 1827

Pine Leaf became James Beckwourth's Crow wife, after her Canadian trapper husband was buried in a cave-in. A female warrior, Pine Leaf was cantankerous, even brutal, but he loved her dearly. She'd just left a group of Snake Indians digging roots in a meadow to return to the 1827 Rendezvous camp at Bear Lake. Beckwourth stood aghast as a Blackfoot war party charged through the Snake diggers ramming lances in them, then rode their thundering war horses down on Pine Leaf.

Beckwourth bolted from the camp, snatched the defiant Pine Leaf from the path of the Blackfoot charge and carried her kicking and screaming into a sheltering hut, where he cursed her silent in Crow.

The cook sounded the alarm by banging inside his triangle. Thirty Blackfeet stormed the camp, bashing fleeing Snakes and trappers with their war clubs, then galloped out streaking for refuge in the nearby hills.

The old Snake Chief, known only as The Prophet, came to Sublette's tent. "Cut Face, the Blackfeet killed five of my people. We were promised safety to trade with you. What will you do to avenge our dead?"

Without answering, Sublette turned to the throng of trappers aroused by the attack. "I dunno how many people them Blackfeet brained, but I know one thing. They cain't stand to see a Mountain Man have a good time! Them Blackfeet is gonna kill the Rendezvous if they git away with this raid. You wanta Rendezvous next year -- an' the year after that?"

Their roar needed no words to be understood. They snatched up their rifles and swarmed to their horses. Infuriated by their attack on Pine Leaf, Beckwourth leaped astride his horse and rode maniacally after the Blackfeet.

Sublette turned back to The Prophet. "I'll letchu know what we're gonna do to avenge them dead Snakes -- after we done it." He sprinted for his horse, yelling to Fitzpatrick, "Git somebody to shoot that cannon towards them Blackfeet one time!"

William knew he was actin' like Milton, but he charged his cavalry into the waitin' Blackfeet stead o' sneakin' up an' snipin' at 'em the way he should have. The Blackfeet had never seen trappers so ferocious, and many were killed before they could run.

When Sublette finally bellered, "It's over!" and waved his arms to call off the attack, the meadow's grasses were strewn with dead Blackfeet. Seven trappers were shot up and one was dead.

Sublette hollered, "We gotta take them Snakes sumpthin' to even things up. Round up all them Blackfeet war clubs an' lances an' take 'em to the Snakes. They'll come back fer the scalps an' lootin'." He knelt beside a sprawled Blackfoot. The brown scalp on the dead warrior's belt was not Milton's. "Remember sumpthin'," he muttered to the fallen Indian, "Never come between a Mountain Man an' a good time."

* * *

The victory celebration lasted four days. Snake Indians left gifts outside Sublette's tent, and one or two squaws even delivered their gifts inside.

During these "disgusting debaucheries" Jedediah Strong Smith sequestered himself in his tent to write a detailed account of his California journey to General William Clark. Jedediah was honored that God had selected him to be the eyes of a new nation that might one day claim these foreign lands for its people. Now he would be the voice that showed them the way.

Jedediah avoided letting his pride in the journey show, for it would not be Christian. He read critical parts aloud to get the sense of them. *"My situation has enabled me to collect information respecting a country which has been, measurably, veiled in obscurity, and unknown to the citizens of the U. States. I allude to the country South West of the Great Salt Lake, and West of the Rocky Mountains.*" That sounded self effacing and objective.

He discussed the fauna, since any troops or travelers entering the area might have to forage. "*After leaving the little Uta Lake, I found no further sign of Buffalo -- there were, however, a few of the Antelope and Mountain Sheep, and an abundance of Black Tailed Mares.*"

Description of the terrain was vital, particularly if he couldn't complete the maps he'd started. "*Leaving Ashley's River, I passed over a range of Mountains, S.E. and N. W., and struck a river, running S.W., which I named Adams River, in compliment to our President. The water of this river is of a muddy cast, and somewhat brackish. The country is mountainous to the east, and on the west are detached rocky hills and sandy plains.*"

General Clark, himself the famed explorer of Lewis and Clark, would doubtless be interested in the indigenous inhabitants. "*Passing down this river some distance, I fell in with a nation of Indians, calling themselves Pa Utches. These Indians, as well as the Sumpatch, wear robes made of rabbit skins; they raise corn and pumpkins, on which they principally subsist -- except a few hares, very little game of any description is to be found.*"

Unusual land features would be significant to cartographers or geographers. "*About ten days march further down the river turns to the S.E., where, on the S. W. of it, there is a remarkable cave, the entrance to which is about ten or fifteen feet high, and five or six feet in width : after descending about fifteen feet, it opens into a large and spacious room, with the roof, walls and floor of solid rock salt, (a piece of which I send you, with some other articles which will be hereafter described.)*"

His lamp sputtered. It was time to sleep even with Sodom and Gomorrah still raging in the debased world of the Rendezvous. Jedediah knew his written report would run over a thousand words, but he felt good about what he'd written. It would make the Lord feel better about what went on at this fetid temple of sacrilege.

The moment he finished the report so it could be expressed east when the pack train returned to St. Louis, Jedediah assembled his party of 18 men and two squaws to relieve the 11 men he'd left in California.

Riding as regally as ever, and mindful that he risked being thrown in prison again or even murdered by Mexican authorities, Jedediah headed for California.

CHAPTER 27

THE TRAPPERS' FANDANGO SPRING-SUMMER 1827

Early in the 1827 trapping season, Thomas Smith decided to leave Ewing Young's band. Unable to convince his crony, Milt Sublette, to join him, Smith trapped the Virgin River with Dutch George Yount, two Mexicans who went by ever-changing first names and a man called Branch. Smith's trappers soon expended their lead in several battles with the *Mojave* Indians. Starving and without bullets, they couldn't even hunt.

Smith muttered, "Dutch, yesterday you said you found a few bits o' metal in a creek bed."

Square-jawed Dutch George grimaced, "Could be gold, Tom."

"Aye, and it might be copper, but if we starve ourselves to death, you'll be givin' whatever 'tis to whoever finds your body, now won't you? I'll take the metal, Dutch."

Pounding the metal with a stone, Thomas Smith shaped one of the yellow chunks to fit his rifle bore. That night, Smith ambushed a mountain goat. Smith dumped the goat in front of Dutch George. "If you dress 'im out, you'll mine your nugget from his chest. There was niver any doubt in me mind it was gold, but don't be spendin' it yet, cause I may want to mount that settin' in another goat!"

The following day Thomas Smith's party discovered a dead trapper curled around a yucca plant with a full shot pouch and three orange berries too shriveled to eat in his possibles bag.

The same day, they chanced upon a tribe of *Piutes*, but these Indians were so shy they cowered before the tiny trapping party.

"A curse on them red heathens!" Smith growled. "They know where them beaver are, and by the Blessed Virgin, they're goin' to tell us!"

Thomas Smith approached the *Piutes* alone, but they still scattered before him. He spoke a few words in their tongue. He lay beads and buttons near the skinny man he thought was Chief. Soon the Chief talked and signed. They had no food except for a few red berries they handed to him, but the Chief told Smith of many beaver tails slapping the water on a big river to the east and how to get there.

Smith's party soon located the river and searched it for miles till it went dry, finding neither food nor beaver. By that time, the red berries had blanched to orange, and Smith fed them to the winds.

"Them *Piutes* taught us a grand lesson," Smith confided to his starving men.

"What was that?" asked Dutch George.

"The strong Indian smashes your skull with his war club. The brave Indian shoots you with his rifle. The shy Indian kills you with a lie -- or little red berries that turn orange when they dry."

By the time Smith's band reached the *Trujillo* Rancho 12 miles north of Albuquerque, they were living on roots and boiled leather ropes although they had taken and eaten many beaver near the Gila River. *Señor Trujillo* had more bad news.

Trujillo's friend, an *Alcalde menor* in the government of *Don Manuel Armijo*, divulged that James Baird had ruined the beaver business for all other American trappers in New Mexico.

Thomas Smith hooted, "James Baird? I once run a whiskey still with him, an' the only thing that man could ruin was the linin' of your stomach! What's the man done now?"

"Baird has become the Mexican citizen, *Señor*. Baird's letter to *El Comandante* of the El Paso District said the U.S. trappers was looting $100,000 per annum in furs from this territory. *Gobernador Antonio Narbona* was deposed and replaced by *Don Manuel Armijo*. Baird has got *Gobernador Armijo* to enforce the Mexican law that only the Mexican citizens can trap in Mexican territory, so the furs of all foreigners must be confiscated! As we talk, Ewing Young's entire fur catch worth over $20,000 *es en captura*!"

Smith suggested, "Ewing Young is a direct man, *Señor Trujillo*. Young probably sought Governor *Armijo* to talk it over."

"Far from it! Young hid the skins *en la casa de Don Luis Cabeza de Vaca* in *Peñablanca*. *En Junio, el Alcalde* and many *soldados matan* -- killed -- *Don Luis*. They took the 29 packs of wet beaver to the *Guardia* in Santa Fe and put them on the parade ground to dry! *Mi* spy said *mi Rancho* is *el primero lugar* they will look for you and your furs."

* * *

Ewing Young prided himself on diplomacy, but *Armijo* had Mexican law and an American traitor named Baird on his side. Governor *Armijo* ordered James Baird to sell all the furs of Young and the men in his party on behalf of the Mexican Government. Ewing scratched his balding head and eyed the furs drying in the quadrangle of the Santa Fe *Guardia*. It was time for the afternoon siesta when the Mexicans hibernated for an hour or two. It made a man connive.

While Young was thinking about repatriating his furs, Milt Sublette reigned in his Buckskin horse and halted the two pack mules behind it. "Ewing, you know which two of them bales of furs is mine?"

"That one by the Armory door and this one right in front of me are branded with your symbols."

Still hobbled by his heel wound, Milton limped over and grabbed the furthest bale, then hoisted it to his shoulder and tottered to the front mule where he lashed it to one side of the pack saddle.

The small Mexican soldier on guard followed Milton, clucking and shaking his finger at the largest of the Sublettes as if he were a very bad boy. The guard's musket sported a shiny steel bayonet. As Milton walked lamely after his other bale, the guard jabbed at him with the needle-pointed bayonet. Milton ignored the cutlery and snatched up his furs. This second bale was dryer and much lighter than the first. Furious at being ignored, the guard cocked his musket and aimed it at Milton.

"*¿Se habla Inglés, Señor soldado*?" Milton asked the guard.

"*Si, mas o menos*," the irate guard answered, admitting knowledge of a smattering of English as he aimed his musket at Milton's chest.

"Then you know how unreliable them old muskets is. It's gonna misfire. An' when it don't shoot, I'm gonna bust it over yer face. Step aside!"

The Mexican closed his eyes to pull the trigger in desperation. Knowing his bale of wet beaver plews would stop any rifle bullet, let alone a smooth bore musket ball, Milt Sublette held the bale between himself and the grimacing soldier and kept coming. "Pull that trigger and leave a widder. Step aside and spend *siesta en la cantina con su amor*." The soldier dropped the rifle like it was afire and ran into the Armory to get *mas soldados,* praying all the old guns would not fail.

Sublette lashed the second bale on the front mule, grabbed the lead rope of the unladen hind mule then clambered astride his horse.

Ewing Young had to ask. "Why'd you bring two mules if you knew you'd put both fur packs on the first one?"

Milton kicked his horse and bolted for the Armory door that had filled with the sound of rushing boots. "Thought it'd be worth a good mule to see how them *soldados* handle a trappers' *Fandango*!" Milt let go of the empty pack mule's lead rope, sending her charging straight into the crush of soldiers like ten pins in the Armory door.

"What'll I do after you pulled this wicked stunt, Sublette?" Young bellered at the dust cloud behind the trapper.

Milton's voice trailed back, "You'll think o' sumpthin, Ewing. Ask one o' them Greeks."

* * *

Because of flagrant defiance of Mexican authority, *Armijo* jailed Young then mobilized the Santa Fe garrison to ride down the *bandido Soblet* -- but he had vanished!

Ewing "*Joon*" was brought to trial "... *for the part he took in the daring action of his fellow-citizen Soblet in the robbery committed by the latter on a load of beaver skins.*" Only Young's remaining beaver skins were found guilty and sold.

However this conviction never resulted in a jail sentence for "*Ewing Joon*" as it would only have added more glory to "*Soblet's*" legend as *The Thunderbolt of the Rockies.*

* * *

Thomas Smith's party was not about to add their beaver to the long list of skins seized in Santa Fe. They left *Trujillo's* early in the evening, traveling by night to miss all settlements to sell the contraband skins to a bold fellow named Pratte in Taos.

On a windy morning, they came around a bend to find a cabin with an open door. The local *Alcalde* and several rumpled *soldados* blocked their way. The wind revealed beaver skins under the whipping blanket on one of the pack mules. The *Alcalde* produced a writ requiring seizure of the beaver skins.

Thomas Smith asked for a private pow wow with the *Alcalde.* Speaking broken Spanish, Smith advised the Mexican that there was no confiscation law when he left to trap the beaver. The *Alcalde* shook his head and held his palms up.

Before the *Alcalde* could summon his men, Thomas Smith said it was his wish to make a gift of $30 to the brave men of Mexico who worked in the wilds where no one even knew what they were doing. The *Alcalde* turned his back in anger and was about to yell for his men, when his wife came forth from the cabin. A smile warmed Smith's face. He recognized the *Alcalde's* wife as an enchanting woman he'd once given a silk shawl and a bit of "companionship."

She argued to her husband that he was paid ignobly for a noble job and that providence wished to remedy this injustice. Smith sweetened the $30 bribe with five pounds of gunpowder and three new butcher knives, lowering all official barriers to the passage of the beaver. Smith quickly herded his party up the hill beyond the cabin, but stopped at the top to wave.

Several days later, Smith's band smuggled the beaver into Taos and sold them to Sylvester Pratte. Thomas Smith's return called for a celebration, during which the jovial rogue was regaled with the tale of Milton Sublette's "beaver robbery," followed by a night long dance and *tequila* parade that aroused all the people of the village.

Thomas L. Smith, waving a long haired scalp on a pole, was lugged in a chair at the head of the procession of the entire torch toting population of Taos. The last thing Smith remembered was rising as best he could to toast Milton Sublette with a bottle of *mescal*, "Wherever you are *amigo*, you're my kind of rotten, beaver thievin' son of Kentucky!"

CHAPTER 28

CALIFORNIA CALABOZO SUMMER 1827-SPRING 1828

Jedediah Smith's 1826 stay with the *Mojave* Indians had been pleasant and peaceful. The *Mojaves* of the Virgin River area insisted they were as friendly as those he'd visited on the Grand River a year ago, but Jedediah sensed hidden hostility.

Tolanda, the oldest of the two Indian women with Jedediah's current party of 20, spoke some *Mojave*. He asked her to mingle with the *Mojaves* and learn their true feelings about the trappers.

The following morning *Tolanda* rushed to Jedediah at the river's edge. "Captain, *Mojave* people attacked by whites under Chiefs Ewing Joon and Smith, the killer of 12 *Mojaves*. Say you are killer Smith or brother and want kill you."

"I've only cherished the *Mojaves* as brothers, and Smith is the name of many whites. I will explain to them at my religious service in the morning."

"Your scars say you scalped long time back, but *Mojaves* do it again quick. *Mojaves* wait for good time to kill all. We go now."

Jedediah formed his troop and left abruptly, with scouts at the rear of his party. All was peaceful by the time they reached the Grand River, which the *Mojave* called the *Colorado*. Apparently the *Mojave* had not followed. Jedediah wondered if *Tolanda* had misapprehended their words.

Deciding it would be safer to camp on the west side of the river, Jedediah loaded seven men and part of his goods onto several old rafts they found on the east bank. While 11 men, the horses and the two women waited their turn, Jedediah ordered his men to float the rafts across the broad river.

The *Mojaves* had circled Jedediah's party and reached the *Colorado* ahead of them, attacking on horses at the dead run while the rafts were still midstream.

Jedediah watched in shock as the shrieking *Mojaves* fell upon those who waited behind, slashing, shooting and braining Henry Boatswain Brown, William Campbell, David Cunningham, Francois Deromme, Silas Gobel, the mulatto Polette Labross, the Spaniard Gregory Ortago, Canadians John Ratelle and John Relle and the half breed Robiseau. Thomas Virgin was clubbed bloody but jumped in the water and swam to the last raft.

At first Jedediah thought *Tolanda* and the other squaw'd been killed, but spied them being tied over a couple of his horses. Jedediah beached the rafts, discovering they had only five rifles. They headed for a grove of trees beside the river and forted up to make a stand.

When a dozen *Mojaves* approached, Jedediah took two of the rifles and walked toward them. He stopped in the clearing beyond the trees in plain sight of the *Mojaves*, barely controlling his fury as he spoke, "You are carrion eating coyotes -- liars, thieves and butchers. We came as friends and you attacked us. But you cannot kill me because God will not let you." He spread his arms and invited them to shoot, pointing to his chest.

The Indians muttered among themselves. Finally two wearing only wet breech cloths and head feathers approached. "We kill no more if you put guns on ground and go. . ."

"You deceived me once, but not again," Jedediah yelled, aiming his rifle and shooting the speaker's head just beneath the feather in his hair. As the remaining Indian gaped, Jedediah shot him over the eye with the other rifle. "Never mistake Christian charity for weakness," Jedediah growled from the black powder smoke.

He reloaded both rifles, but the other ten *Mojaves* fled to the river, leaving their dead behind. Jedediah would not depart until he gave Christian burials in shallow graves to the two he'd slain. Jedediah's only prayer was, "Lord, please forgive these

Mojave Indians. They knew not what they did."

* * *

When Jedediah's expedition reached the San Bernardino Valley, he bought supplies at a *rancho*. Isaac Galbraith loved the country. Jedediah allowed Isaac to remain to watch over Thomas Virgin till his wounds healed. Jedediah led his remaining six men to the camp of the 11 men he'd left last year on the Stanislaus, trapping beaver on the way and arriving September 18, 1827.

Directing his men to trap, Jedediah headed for the coast. Sure Christians would help their own faith, Jedediah sought refuge at Mission San José. Father *Duran*, dressed in a brown robe with a crucifix dangling from his waist, was curt, but gave the Americans gruel and placed Jedediah alone in a *padre* cubicle for the night.

Jedediah awoke with three bayonets in his face. The soldiers yanked him to his feet, made him dress and trussed his hands behind his back with a leather *reata*. When Father *Duran* came to translate for the *Sargento del Guardia,* Jedediah impaled him with his piercing blue eyes.

Father *Duran* said, "The Sergeant says you are charged with fraudulently claiming for the Americans all the Mexican land you have passed through."

"The charge itself is fraudulent as you are as a Christian. I have claimed no land for anybody!" Jedediah rasped angrily.

"Do not add blasphemy to your other vile crimes, infidel. You are going to prison in Monterey!" Father *Duran* snapped, telling the soldiers, "¡*Al calabozo inmediatamente*!"

The *calabozo* was a pathetic mud hut with rusted square bars on the windows and nothing in each cell but a dirty pitcher of water and a fly infested board someone had used for a plate. A guard in a foul uniform entered and dumped an armful of straw on the floor. Jedediah waved the flying dust and straw fragments from his face. The guard left, bolting the cell's decrepit wooden door. A three inch scorpion, its poison-fanged tail over its back, struggled from the straw, waddled boldly to the door and slipped underneath to freedom. It was the only time Jedediah could remember envying such an evil beasty.

One of the jail's Mexican officials could read and write

English, though he could not speak it. He left a note that Governor *Echeandia* demanded that Jedediah pay for his transportation to Mexico City to stand trial. Jedediah simply wrote, "No." on the bottom.

The Governor's next note ordered Jedediah to write his men and tell them to come to Monterey. Jedediah fashioned a note to Harrison Rogers to be carried by Joseph LaPointe. "*After you have taken the pretty plews to my Auntie Bode Gabay, see me in Monterey for a striped sun burn.*"

Jedediah was content Rogers could decode the note, take the beaver plews to Bodega Bay and avoid a sun burn through the bars in Monterey. He also felt LaPointe would see the smaller note and ask ship captains at Monterey Bay to heave ashore.

LaPointe reached William Hartnell, an English trader. Hartnell convinced the Governor that where there was no consul, four ship captains should appoint an agent to act as consul. Former Bostonian Captain John Cooper was appointed. He came to the jail in the third day of Jedediah's incarceration.

Cooper was a proper man with a hatchet face, crisply starched shirt and a crisper New England accent. He refused to enter the cell because of the fleas that made Jedediah scratch constantly. "The Governor says you came last year and left, promisin' not to return."

"And I would have, but the snow in the mountains prevented me from getting my men and furs out through drifts 15 feet high. I was forced to come back for them," Jedediah responded.

"Poppycock! It appears that the men who make history never learn from it -- not even their own. You've made all the same blunders you did last year. If we extricate you this time, by the binnacle we'll not be back for thirds!"

"Do whatever you must do to get me out of here. I'll leave California at once, never to return."

"Not sure what it'll take. There's talk of standin' you in front of a wall with muskets to see you don't come back. That's Father *Duran's* idea. Shouldn't've told him you're a methodist!"

By the next night, Captain Cooper appeared with a $30,000 Bond for Jedediah to sign. "Don't even think of askin' to change it. Just sign that you will pay the Governor $30,000 if he catches you in California again after you've had the chance to leave."

"What about my beaver plews?"

"Captain John Bradshaw has agreed to buy your beaver for $2.50 the pound. Rogers said you wanted to buy horses to trade later for merchandise. The Governor is issuin' you a passport for yourself and your men and 250 horses and mules. Bradshaw will take you to Bodega Bay to pick up the beaver, but only if you swim out to his ship."

"Why should I swim to his ship?"

"Bradshaw doesn't want a new strain of fleas aboard his vessel. And one other thing."

"What?"

"Beside the $30,000 bond, if the Governor catches you in California again, he's goin' to have you castrated."

"That's no laughing matter, sir!"

"That's what *he* said."

*   *   *

Jedediah was allowed to veer to San José to buy horses. As if by divine coincidence he met Isaac Galbraith and Thomas Virgin and shared Christmas prayers and dinner with them. All avoided the Mission at San José and the vengeful Father *Duran*.

Just before New Years of 1828 Jedediah left San José with 20 men and 315 horses but only 47 beaver traps. He planned to sell the horses across the mountains to recoup his losses. It wouldn't do for the senior partner of Smith, Jackson & Sublette to show up empty handed at another Rendezvous. Jedediah didn't want to make humiliation a habit.

The Chico area was prime beaver country, and the Indians were peaceful basket makers who said the grizzly bears roamed in packs. Having never heard such an outlandish grizzly story, Jedediah took it as folk lore.

The following day, Harrison Rogers began to scream as he was mauled in a draw by a yearling sow. Jedediah and Joseph LaPointe rode to Harrison's rescue, only to meet two more snarling bears loping down the wash to join in on the kill.

Waiting till the charging bears were nearly upon them, Jedediah stepped off his horse and shot it behind the shoulder.

The fallen horse's screams were irresistible to the grizzlies. The sow dropped Harrison Rogers to feast upon the downed horse's neck as the other two ripped bloody flesh from its hind quarters.

As the men slipped away, Harrison Rogers staunched the bleeding in his lacerated arm with the strap from his possibles bag. LaPointe muttered, "Never have I seen such a fearless man, with such presence of mind, Captain!"

"My horse would be quick to disagree if he could, gentlemen," Jedediah pronounced calmly, though his heart convulsed and his hands trembled wildly in remembrance of his own cataclysmic mauling. Though four years ago, it seemed only that many seconds since the bull grizzly'd nearly bitten his head in half. The stench and deafening roars still invaded his sleep whenever he got too tired to bar them from the fortress of his mind.

Fighting to maintain his counterfeit composure, Jedediah swung north by northwest, aiming to reach the Pacific above the Klamath River by late spring. Even with their scant traps, their plews piled higher. The terrain was toilsome for the horses, laming a few, but the herd remained largely healthy and intact.

On May 19, 1828 Jedediah Smith's expedition reached the Pacific Ocean. Standing amid the horses milling about in the sand, Jedediah raised his eyes and arms to a heaven gone crimson at sunset. "God is good," Jedediah whispered, then added in a growl, "And so am I!"

CHAPTER 29

PEG-LEG SMITH   SUMMER-WINTER 1827

Milton Sublette never thought he'd get tired of the Taos *cantinas* and the fiery *señoritas,* but he had. The summer of 1827 vanished along with Milt's money into a haze of *tequila*. Pain chewed his left heel like a rat was in there. Bone chips bulged the heel's hide, then got butcher-knifed out by some drunk as the *cantina's* main attraction of the evening.

Milt and his drinking crony Thomas Smith whooped and howled through nights that all ran together, but by summer's end Smith too was broke. Bleary-eyed, he pulled Milt's ear to his slobbery lips, "Milt, I've had meself a talk with Sylvester Pratte about trappin' the mountains north o' here."

"Whatchur sayin' is that Sylvester's belly cain't take no more rot gut neither."

"Ain't that what I said?"

"I'm in, but I gotta git a kit together."

"Sylvester'll stake us, but he's leavin at dawn."

"At dawn? Sylvester drunk as we are?"

"I wouldn't be knowin' that."

"Why donchu ask the man, Tom?"

"Can't."

"Why not?"

"He's passed out."

"Well wake 'im up."

"Can't."

"Why?"

"We're sittin' on 'im, Milt."

* * *

Well provisioned by Pratte's largesse, Milton Sublette and Thomas Smith rode out with the French and American trappers. Whenever they could, they trapped the icy streams together, adding to the expedition's haul of over 300 plews.

It was almost like old times in Taos till Sylvester Pratte upped and died at Park Kyack on September First. Pratte's best rifle was missing. Milt and Tom stood beside Sylvester's grave.

"Tom, our kind ain't meant fer town buryin'."

Smith nodded and crossed himself. "Seein' Sylvester at the bottom o' the grave like this could break a man o' drinkin'."

"Only if Sylvester gits up an' tells us we gotta quit."

* * *

Trapping continued under Ceran St.Vrain who agreed to square accounts for the dead Sylvester Pratte.

After the first heavy frost, Thomas Smith was trapping the headwaters of the Platte. He'd just waded to a mud bank when he saw a puff of smoke from a distant bush. The heavy bullet broke his left leg above the ankle. As Smith stepped for his nearby rifle, both of his leg bones pierced his flesh and stuck in the mud. Smith got off a shot at the bush as he fell, then lashed a thong above the wound to dam the blood.

The Crows tried to reach their downed warrior in the bush for an hour, but Smith kept them at bay with sharp shooting until rescuing trappers killed nine Crows and chased the rest. Pratte's missing rifle lay across the Crow Smith killed in the bush. Trappers gathered.

Smith groaned, "Somebody's got to cut me foot off."

"Sublette's the one with guts enough to do it. Ain't seen him since we spooked the Crows," somebody muttered.

Smith shook seeping blackness from his head. "Snatch the cook's knife and I'll hack the leg off meself."

Trappers turned away as Smith sliced through torn muscles and sinews with blood flying everywhere. Milt Sublette arrived panting. Only the Achilles tendon held Smith's bloody foot on. Smith sawed it, but couldn't sever it.

Sublette seized the knife and slashed the tendon.

Smith shrieked as his calf muscle snapped up behind his

knee, knocking him unconscious.

"Heat a iron so's I can sear his wound," Sublette yelled.

But Smith came to. "Cover the stump with one o' me dirty shirts and bind me leg with leather thongs."

Milton bound the gory leg as he asked.

"Milt, be off with you. I cannot move."

"Tom -- jist shut up. Nobody's leavin' here till you can." Milton opened his buffalo coat showing four pistols in his belt that he'd picked up on the battlefield. Milt Sublette asked, "Ain't that right, boys?" then he and another trapper lugged Smith to camp.

Milt and a powerful Negro, who spoke only French, carried Smith for two days in a litter. Finally Smith's litter was tied across the backs of two mules in tandem. Milton gave a fine pistol to the Negro who pointed to himself grinning, "*François.*"

Reaching the Green River in November 1827, a month after Smith's leg amputation, they prepared to winter there. An old hand at yanking bone splinters out with his bullet mold, Milt pulled a pair from Smith's leg stump. "Here, they make good toothpicks, Tom."

Forty lodges of *Utes* joined the trappers for the winter. A large, fierce Chief named *Walkara*, who'd earned a reputation as a horse thief, bulled into Thomas Smith's tent. "Old Friend -- *Tevvy-oats-at-an-tuggy-bon*e -- do you remember *Walkara*?"

"Who's he?" Milt asked as he cut into the oak leg he was carving for Smith -- while secretly hoping he'd never have one like it.

"*Walkara*!" Smith leered. "One time down on the San Juan River, *Walkara* stole several o' me mules. Bein' toad-frog green, I charged into the *Ute* camp and demanded me mules back. *Walkara* come near laughin' hisself to death at a fuzzy cheeked trapper bein' ready to die for three mules. *Walkara's* been a fine friend since! Says I have the Great Grizzly's spirit."

"He's right bout you havin' the spirit o' the grizzly, and fore long you'll have the great leg 'o wood," Milt laughed, shaking *Walkara's* huge callused hand and pouring him a cup of rot gut.

Smith grinned, "It's *Walkara* that's got the bull grizz in him! His horse thievery in Mexico's a legend. One day *Walkara's* pushin' a band o' fresh-stole horses toward the Colorado River with 50 Spaniards hot on his trail. When them hot horses balks at goin' in that cold river, *Walkara* cuts out the four finest, and drives them into the teeth of the Spaniards. Says he's led a revolt against *Walkara* and kept their best horses from crossin' the river at great risk to himself, extractin' a reward for the four horses. While the Spaniards be herdin' their four horses home, *Walkara* returns to the river and drives the cooled down 40 horses across."

"That yarn buys the world's brassiest horse thief another snort!" Milt shouts, filling *Walkara's* tin cup again.

The *Utes* shouldered Smith and placed him by the fire ring in the center of their lodges to give his lost leg a wake. The ritual began with chanting, wailing and incantations. Squaws chewing roots gathered around Smith and spit on the proud flesh of his stump. The wake outlasted Milton's whiskey.

The ceremony ended when *Walkara* jammed his feathered lance into the ground where Smith's left foot would have been and chanted, "No longer shall you be known to us as *Tevvy-oats-at-an-tuggy-bon*e -- big friend. Now your *Ute* name is *Wa-ke-to-co* -- man of one foot."

Milton rose unsteadily to present Smith his oak leg, but the whiskey made Milton use the sleek leg to support himself, muttering, "You once was Thomas L. Smith. Now yer Mountain Man name is Peg-Leg Smith. This here wooden leg's holler an' will hold a pint o' whiskey -- that will age right nice in this oak."

CHAPTER 30

SAFE IN ST. LOUIE   SUMMER 1827

For the first time, William Sublette took a room in St. Louie's respectable *City Hotel*. Wasn't jist that the summer of 1827 got unbearable humid on the levee. It was cause he could.

Still in fancy Crow buckskins, Clyman leaned over the hotel lunch table, "Bill, I'm trying to keep from wolfing my food like an animal, and you're dressed up like Astor's plush horse!"

"First new suit o' clothes I ever owned," Sublette mused. He put his elegant brown *Beau Brummel* top hat with its dove gray band and molded brim on the table between them. "Trapper wades ice water, bettin' his own ha'r agin a beaver's to make that hat. Battles Blackfeet, grizzlies, bad whiskey an' other trappers fer this. It ain't worth dyin' over -- but it smells good an' if you're a trapper you won't live long enough to wear it out." He set the hat over his long, wavy blond hair and gave it a pat on top.

Clyman added,"Best avoid the levee in that frock coat. Crooks'll traipse after you like the Pied Piper of Hamelin."

"My sister Sophronia's married to Grove Cook. I'm havin' them to the hotel fer dinner tonight, so my brother-in-law kin see how well I done. After dinner we're agoin' by carriage up to that mansion Ashley built fer Eliza. What you gonna do?"

"Going to buy a farm in Illinois with my beaver money."

"Jim, I wasn't ready fer that. Figured if you's to settle down, you'd go back to Bright Elk an' the Crows."

"Can't," Clyman said wistfully.

"Cain't live with a squaw?"

"Can't live with the Crows."

"Why?"

"Remember when Jedediah and Ed Rose were about to kill one another in the spring of '25?"

"Yep."

"You sided with Jedediah and left Rose that note about killing him if he came back to camp before you left."

"Note was nicer'n a pistol ball."

"Not much. Rose stuck your note to a tree and butcher-knifed it to bits. Thought that ended it, but Ed Rose don't get over a fury till somebody's dead."

"I liked Ed. We was a lot alike. Never seed him takin' that note so hard."

"If you see Ed coming, don't stop to apologize."

"Ed Rose after me?"

"Has been. Remember the Crows attacking Ashley's fur caravan after the '25 Rendezvous?"

"Blackfeet hit us, an' I got sent after horses from the main party, but heard the Crows tacked Ashley's men in the dead o' night."

"Bill, I was in that Crow war party. Rose was after you! I was ready to shoot him, but somehow, during the battle Rose found out you'd left, so he called it off. Then Rose said he knew I'd plotted against him with you, and that if he laid eyes on me again, he'd skin me like an otter. I left the Crows and shot buffalo for Ashley's bull boats. Rose even tried to kill your brother Milt to even the score."

"Did he get 'im?" Sublette blurted in alarm.

"Came close -- got men with Milt."

"Where is Milt?"

"Where's the wind?"

"Rose is one strange halfbreed," Sublette mused.

"The man's a maniac," Clyman growled.

"Only part o' the time. Ashley told me he met General Atkinson and Major O'Fallon at the Yellowstone River on the way back from the '25 Rendezvous. They was negotiatin' peace with the Crow nation. Crows went on the rampage agin the whites and Rose went to swingin' his rifle like a crazy man. Busted up eight Crows "

Clyman muttered, "Rose just felt like busting heads that day. Rose lives with the Crows and still has a death sentence on me. If he didn't, I'd get Bright Elk and our little girl, Mountains of Sand, and take them to Illinois."

Sublette stood and extended his hand, "Jim, you been a dear friend. Hope you'll write now an' agin. Gitcher plew money direct from Hunt. I gotta meet David in the bar."

Clyman rose and bowed, "*Now cracks a noble heart. Good night sweet prince; And flights of angels sing thee to thy rest.*"

Sublette's eyes misted, but he didn't look back. He wondered why Clyman waited so long to tip him off bout Ed Rose. He'd warn Milt -- if he ever saw Milt agin.

David Jackson lowered his newspaper and squinted through the smoke from his cigar. He smiled, deepening the cracks in his face, as Sublette sat down at his table. "What do our numbers look like, Bill?"

Sublette pulled a folded paper from the inside pocket of his frock coat where he kept his wallet. "Ashley give us a fur credit of $22,690. Supplies cost us $22,447.14 agin our fur credit, so that's pert near a wash. But we made enough off supply mark-up to pay Ashley's $7,821 note. An' we'll still be able to pay fer raisin' a little Cain fore we pick up our supplies at Lexington with the $20,000 Ashley's loanin' us an' go back Up the Mountain."

Jackson bit his cigar angrily. "If this newspaper's right, Ashley'll get $4.37 a pound for our beaver. He'll make three times what we do, and we're the ones looking down the gun."

"Look at it this away, Dave. We got no beaver from Jedediah this year an' he's sure to do better. We made money. We're learnin'. I'm follerin' Ashley's moves like a Crow cuttin' culls from the keepers in a horse herd by readin' tracks. If things works out at Ashley's house tonight, your brother George'll be a *judge* before the snow flies."

"Thanks aplenty, Bill. I'm going straight to George's place and tell him you think he's one step from the bench."

* * *

Sublette had to rent a carriage for the trip to Ashley's tonight, but he wanted to inspect it in daylight. He left the plush hotel and headed for a reputable livery. St. Louie was a town of a thousand smells -- most o' them bad -- but he liked its safety.

A man could walk down the street and watch fer puddles instead o' Blackfeet or grizz. He wondered how much brown gold was sittin' in those fur warehouses along the levee. St. Louie had the fur trade by the throat. Men went upriver to trap beaver. The men didn't always come back, but the furs did, one way or another.

Sublette remembered Clyman recruiting "Falstaff's brigade" from the grogshops with him to get trappers for Ashley & Henry -- he was gonna miss Clyman like a man'd miss his thumb. Them rum dens was fulla hard muscled men who come to drink an' fight. William wondered when St. Louie'd take that last step to civilization an' git a police force.

A dark young man wearing a gold ring in his ear and expensive clothes jumped out and confronted Sublette with an antique pistol. Before Sublette could lunge or pull one of his own pistols, the man fired, then sprinted between the buildings.

Sublette waved the gun smoke from his face. His Beau Brummel hat was gone. He saw it on the street and snatched it from the dirt. A small crowd gathered. Sublette put his little finger through the hole in his hat, then brushed the dirt off the crown and brim. "These St. Louie crooks need a heap o' trainin'. Robbers gotta talk er they git nuthin'. Murderers gotta shoot center." A man brushed Sublette off, although he wasn't dirty. The crowd broke up and Sublette walked to the livery cursin' himself under his breath for not gettin' a shot off. Surely, Ed Rose couldn't reach all the way into the heart o' St. Louie.

Ready to pay the $35 the livery wanted to rent their best carriage and a team of matched blacks, Sublette reached for his wallet, then patted all the pockets of his new clothes. He eyed the livery hand. "I guess these St. Louie crooks don't need quite as much trainin' as I thought right there at first."

"Look Mister, if $35's too much, you can pick out a cheaper rig."

"That ain't zactly what I was talkin' about. Hold onto that rig and them fine blacks. I'll be right back if the bank ain't closed."

CHAPTER 31

THE NORTH EDGE OF FOREVER SUMMER 1828-SPRING 1829

Fog shrouded the northern California coastline. Surly waves ripped the billowing mists to rumble up and sprawl on the beach. Seated on a rock jutting from the sodden sand, Jedediah Smith penned notes for his June 1, 1828 journal entry, "*Reed and Pombert deserted, leaving 18 men to herd 297 horses. We make our way northward with incredible difficulty -- often some distance inland -- sometimes taking to the ocean to avoid rock barriers. This unforgiving country is so like -- but unlike -- the land of my boyhood. The Indians we've just left neither understand sign nor speak beyond a grunt. They delve the sand for shell fish -- but they do not attack us nor steal our horses.*"

Jedediah led his men and horses ever northward, passing the Rogue River's reunion with the sea near the end of June.

The day before July 4th, they saw something so barbaric, the most placid of Jedediah's men was moved to fury. Nine Indians gathered about a fire to roast a young boy trussed to a pole. The child was lowered screaming into the flames, then raised to the laughter of his tormentors. Thomas Virgin seized his rifle and tomahawk, and bellered, "I'll not watch another second o' them heathens burnin' that boy alive!"

Jedediah grabbed the sleeve of Virgin's buckskins, "Thomas, you cannot fight all those Indians by yourself. Wait till I detail men to tend the horses."

"Captain, you of all people know it's our Christian duty to save the boy NOW -- horses or no horses!" Virgin raged, his usually angelic face florid.

"Thomas, we'll rescue the boy *with* a horse. "His captors would rather have a fleshy horse than that bony boy."

As Jedediah's men advanced, the Indians abandoned roasting the boy to grab crude cudgels and wooden spears burned to a point. They crouched, their dirt-smeared faces twitching and clubs jerking in a grunting battle ritual.

Jedediah halted a few feet from them and pointed to the boy then to his nearest horse and back to the boy. The Indians stopped and eyed each other.

"It isn't worth a horse to avoid combat with these primitive devils. Thomas, fire your rifle in the air," Jedediah ordered without turning.

"Captain, why don't I blast their hide bucket by the fire?"

"Thomas, be my guest."

BLAM! Blood exploded from the flattened bucket. The Indians fell to the ground with their hands over their heads.

"If all that blood come from the boy, he's sure to die," Thomas Virgin gasped.

"Not Marion blood," squealed the boy lashed to the pole.

"Cut that boy loose, Thomas and tell the men to start moving the horses."

Virgin freed the boy. The stench from Marion's singed black hair made Virgin gasp for breath. The boy's blue left eye strayed as his brown right eye looked straight ahead. His buckskin pants were scorched, and his arms branded with watery blisters. He looked to be nine or ten. They ran to the horses together. "You speak English. Who are you?" Thomas panted.

"Marion of Willamette Valley. Father Jeremy and mother *Oseewah* there."

"Where's the Willamette Valley, Marion?"

"Father calls it the north edge of forever," he sobbed.

As Jedediah arrived, Virgin wrapped the frightened boy in a soft blanket, then patted his head. "I'll take you to the north edge of forever, boy. That's a solemn promise -- or I'm no Virgin."

"You saved the boy, Thomas. He's your charge till we return him to that place."

* * *

By mid July Jedediah's party reached the Umpqua River. They bartered trade goods with the *Kelawatset* women for beaver and sea otter pelts. The eldest squaw told them of the Willamette Valley four hills away to the east. Jedediah felt she lied but wasn't sure why.

Jedediah didn't want the frail boy riding miles to the wrong place with his open burn sores. Taking Harrison Rogers aside, he ordered, "Keep a close watch on the horses. I'm taking Turner and Leland to look for this Willamette Valley. Do not let the *Kelawatsets* back into this camp till we return."

Hoof beats of Jedediah's search party still played among the trees when 37 *Kelawatsets* crowded the camp. At first the oldest squaw signed that they'd been cheated in the trading and must have five guns, 25 pounds of powder and three bars of lead. When Harrison Rogers shook his head "No," two braves seized him from behind, and the white-haired squaw slashed his throat with her butcher knife.

In moments the *Kelawatsets* massacred eight trappers and all four horse wranglers. Thomas Virgin seized Marion and raced through the trees, breaking off low branches and scattering butterflies. Arthur Black sprinted the opposite direction.

At sundown Jedediah, Leland and Turner drew nigh their camp site where orange shafts filtered between the stately pines. Jedediah's horse shied from something on the ground.

Thomas Virgin's eyes were leathery in the orange sunlight. His slit throat gaped like a huge mouth, and his back was arched over another small body. Even in death Virgin's pudgy fist held the lifeless little hand of his newest friend.

Jedediah's face blanched. "Thomas Virgin has taken the boy to the north edge of forever as he promised. He has also warned us that our camp has been looted."

A rifle bullet sheared off the branch beside Jedediah's head. Shots cascaded through the forest. Jedediah's horse screamed, tumbling as Jedediah jumped clear. Leland's horse was gutshot and a greenish liquid sprayed from its side. Turner toppled backward with a ball through his hand as his horse bolted.

Jedediah crouched and blew away most of a charging *Kelawatset's* face with his pistol. He ripped open the belly of another with his knife as the brave tried to tomahawk Leland, whose leg was trapped under his horse.

"Give me your pistol," Jedediah commanded Leland. As the gun reached his hand Jedediah splattered the head of another *Kelawatset*. The woods went silent. Jedediah and Turner freed Leland's leg as Jedediah whispered, "Too many hostiles to fight. Take what you can carry. We'll head for the Columbia. They're too glutted with spoils to follow us far."

* * *

On August 10, 1828 three haggard derelicts staggered from the trees within rifle shot of majestic Fort Vancouver flying the flags of Great Britain and the Hudson's Bay Company.

Jedediah motioned Leland and Turner to their knees. "We must thank God for letting us find this haven in the wilderness." But the others stumbled on, entranced by the fort's grand appearance. Jedediah thanked God, then caught up.

Leland gaped at the fort. "Have you ever seen the likes of this in the mountains? Must be 600 feet long and a couple hundred wide -- sharpened logs 15 feet high -- it's a log castle!"

A giant in a dark broadcloth suit with gray-white hair flowing from under a beaver stovepipe hat towered in Fort Vancouver's main entrance. Hands outward, the huge man stood as the Mountain Men reeled toward him. "Welcome to Fort Vancouver," he boomed in a jovial but dignified tone. "You must be Jedediah Smith, Mr. Turner and Mr. Leland. I'm Chief Factor Dr. John McLoughlin."

The bedraggled men paused to stare in awe at the huge man then drifted by him into the fort wondering how in God's world he knew their names.

* * *

Having been fed a hasty meal and provided with warm bathing water, Jedediah's curiosity bested his exhaustion. He eyed the fort's interior then crossed the parade ground from the Bachelor's Quarters to the Chief Factor's lavish residence, counting 15 buildings and a well inside the fort's walls. It was a self sufficient city ringed by a stockade fence.

Jedediah asked to see Chief Factor McLoughlin and was ushered into the splendid dining room that bisected the big house. A long table under a single white cloth was being set for

30 people with ornate China, fine goblets and crystal wine decanters. Jedediah hefted one of the several forks at a place setting. It's weight declared it solid silver. Lighted candles flickering behind crystal shields adorned the walls between vast oil paintings in gilt frames from Europe. The silence shouted the enormous cost of its luxurious chairs and rich blue carpets.

Aromas of roast duck, puddings, pies and fruit wafted from the pantry, though the cool air said they'd been cooked in another place.

"We request the pleasure of your company at dinner, Mr. Smith!"

"Thank you, but I just ate, Doctor."

"That was sustenance. This is dinner. It's an honor to host a partner of Smith, Jackson & Sublette."

Jedediah smiled. "I take it we were not the only survivors of the massacre."

"Quite astute, sir. Arthur Black preceded you here by two days. We'd have sent out search parties, but Mr. Black's hope for you was nil even though you and your two men were scouting when the *Kelawatsets* attacked. Of course we've known of your explorations and other deeds for years. Peter Skene Ogden is a respected member of our field force."

Jedediah's conscience bit him as he recalled Johnson Gardner's threat of war on Ogden if he didn't leave American soil -- and the 29 Hudson's Bay deserters with 700 pelts Jedediah had welcomed to Ashley & Henry's force in '25 just before the first Rendezvous at Henry's Fork. "I assure you, Doctor that Johnson Gardner was an independent trapper when he became embroiled with Mr. Ogden."

"Let us retire to my office and chat until the table is set."

Jedediah followed the man with flowing white hair, who stood a full head taller than his own six feet, to an elegant office furnished in cherry wood with maps on every wall and quill pens in ornate inkwells at every turn. "How tall are you, Dr. McLoughlin?" he asked as they took seats in the office.

"About 6'7" without my stovepipe hat," Dr. McLoughlin smiled, stretching half way across the room dwarfed by his mass. "Before you fret more, sir, let me hasten to say I know competition between firms can get out of hand. Ten years ago when I was with the North West Company, I was tried in Court for murder because some of our trappers killed Hudson's Bay people when I was not present. I was acquitted, as I'm acquitting you." The Doctor dipped his chin so his eyes bore into Jedediah from beneath huge frosty brows. "What we must prosecute now -- is dinner and that small bell says it awaits."

Seating was strictly by seniority. The men at Jedediah's senior end of the table did all of the talking. The junior clerks at the far end said nothing unless directly addressed, and there were no women. Turner, Black and Leland were absent, having been fed in the Bachelor Quarters.

Jedediah Strong Smith had never even envisioned such a feast. Each time another course came, he waited to see which fork or spoon the Doctor selected before he commenced. Dinner conversation was droll, accompanying thick soup, chopped cold duck, steamed rice, stewed tomatoes, breaded trout, broiled salmon and poached sturgeon, roast beef, clove-spiced ham, fresh garden vegetables, a separate course of bread and butter, culminating in a welter of pies and rice pudding with a brown sugar sauce. Jedediah recalled that yesterday, he'd eaten an owl's leg raw. The contrast was simply beyond his comprehension.

Their dinner digesting, the men retired to the game room where several round tables draped in green felt cloths awaited them with cards, clay pipes, and stone jars filled with aromatic tobaccos to be smoked around a genuine metal stove.

Jedediah did not want to start the conversation, but he had to. "How much territory do you administer from here?"

Doctor McLoughlin lighted his clay pipe and blew his words out with the smoke, "About 670,000 square miles -- an area about seven times the size of Great Britain. We deal with the Russians and Mexicans in California, the Americans to the south and the French Canadians in the east. We try to get along with all of them, including the Indians."

Jedediah mused, "I've seen your superbly orchestrated grounds and out buildings, but you have no garrison for soldiers. How do you keep the Indians from taking all this?"

Dr. McLoughlin responded, "Looks -- as they say -- are deceiving. Our clerks, trappers, mechanics and storekeepers are expert marksman -- as is our American blacksmith, William

Cannon. The fort is easily defended once its three gates are closed and the bastion manned. But we have scant problems with the local Indians. They trade with us. We allow them to keep their customs. There is harmony when you do not try to change them -- or let them be perverted by our customs. Our paramount concern is protecting them from our diseases after the epidemics of 1824 and 25 when so many perished."

"We did not try to change the Indians who massacred my men and stole our horses last month," Jedediah countered.

"There are necessary exceptions. When rules are broken, punishment must be swift and sure. We have hanged Indians on rare occasions. Hudson's Bay Company cannot let the massacre of your men and the seizure of your property at the Umpqua River pass without punishment. Alexander McLeod's force leaves tomorrow to confront the *Kelawatsets* and recover your goods."

"I wish to go with them," Jedediah said quietly.

"And so you shall, sir. But tonight we talk. I understand you are a learned man and perhaps the most eminent explorer of our contemporary world. I have interests in land exploration, botany, cosmogony, religion, the United States, and the treatment of wilderness ailments. Surely, we have much to learn from each other, Mr. Smith"

Jedediah could see that Dr. McLoughlin was about to devour another mighty dinner.

* * *

The *Kelawatset* punitive expedition struck Jedediah as a morality play given for his benefit. The *Kelawatsets* were easily found. Surprisingly, they surrendered most of Jedediah's beaver and a few of his horses. But when it came to locating the murderers of a dozen men and a boy, the farcical play floundered. In less than three months, the punitive expedition returned to Fort Vancouver without avenging Smith's dead.

Sir George Simpson presided upon their return. To Jedediah's amazement, Sir George, a talkative dumpling of a man, offered to buy Jedediah's recovered beaver at $3 per pound and his horses at a fair price, amounting in all to $2,369.60. Jedediah gratefully accepted their draft, though he wondered what the 60¢ was for. By then a fierce winter had frozen Fort

Vancouver's world in place. Jedediah remained until the onset of the spring thaw.

Dr. McLoughlin strolled the fort grounds with Jedediah one chilly evening. "Your country's new President, Andrew Jackson will soon be inaugurated on March 4, 1829, ending the tranquil and prosperous term of John Quincy Adams."

"My partner William Sublette will be delighted. He's a vigorous Jackson man. Even resembles him. Myself, I would have preferred someone less volatile."

"As would we, sir. As would we. Jackson is an explosion seeking a place to occur. I'll bid you goodnight. I know you're planning to leave any day. I've enjoyed our mind explorations, Mr. Smith."

On March 12, 1829 Jedediah and Arthur Black bade farewell to Dr. McLoughlin. Jedediah bowed. "The Bible says, *There are giants in the land*, and surely you are such a giant. Your great physical dimensions are dwarfed only by the vastness of your intellect."

Dr. McLoughlin merely stood smiling at the Fort Vancouver gate and waved as he had when they'd come as destitute beggars so long ago.

CHAPTER 32

BLACKFOOT COUNTRY SUMMER 1828

The 70 Mountain Men with 300 Flatheads and *Shoshones* gathered at the south end of Bear Lake for the July 1828 Rendezvous were glum. Jackson and Sublette brought their supply train out in November of 1827 and by the following March everybody had bought their supplies. All their whiskey was gone. The Rendezvous was awash in boredom.

Hope flared when Joshua Pilcher rode in with his small supply train, but soon waned when it turned out that the newcomers' supplies were water-logged.

Joshua Pilcher left his partners in charge of trying to sell their water soaked goods and located William Sublette's crude cabin where Sublette and Jackson were discussing business. Pilcher pulled back the flap. "Some Rendezvous, Gentlemen! As a former medical student, I must say I've seen more enthusiasm at an autopsy!"

Sublette grinned. Pilcher reminded him of the perfectly sketched model they used to sell clothes in St. Louie newspaper ads, but he looked a lot older than Sublette remembered. "Well Joshua, mebbee yer goods'll liven the place up."

"Not likely. Crows stole all our horses near South Pass last fall, so we had to cache our supplies for winter. Seepage got 'em. If we had whiskey, we might sell soggy trade goods, but nobody's going to buy 'em sober."

Jackson laughed, "Don't be so sure. People daft enough to sit around Blackfoot country waiting to be attacked will buy anything."

"I see nothing funny about the Blackfeet. They bankrupted my Missouri Fur Company in May of '23 when they killed Jones and Immel and stole all our furs. They're a deadly peril to us one and all."

The fun went out of jovial David Jackson's face. "Nobody thinks the Blackfeet are funny, Joshua, but you gotta remember, we're on their land. If you were back on the farm and a bunch of strangers took over the north 40 and started killing your cattle, wouldn't you attack them?"

"Obviously, but that analogy doesn't begin to address the Blackfoot menace."

"Why doesn't it?"

"Dave, I've studied the Blackfeet. Included in this tribe are four distinct bands, the Blackfeet or *Siksikau*, the Piegan or *Pikuni*, the Bloods calling themselves *Kainah* and the Gros Ventres or *Atsina* in their tongue. They're nomadic. Blackfoot land is where they happen to be standing, and they start killing the minute they get there. Not just whites. They've slaughtered other tribes for centuries. Their perpetual state is war."

"Hudson's Bay Company trades with them, and I'm about to try. They control the richest beaver country I've ever seen."

"HBC's had minor success trading with Piegans. Nobody'll ever dream how many Mountain Men and tribesman have succumbed to Blackfeet wrath. You have children, Dave?"

"Four and a wife that actually knows them."

"Sublette, unless want your partner's scalp dangling from a Blackfoot lance, you'll talk him out of trading with them. They killed two of my partners."

Sublette uncorked his only bottle of brandy. "How about a calm-down, Joshua?"

"I could use one. Blackfeet bankrupted Missouri Fur for us, now the Crows've likely sunk Pilcher & Company."

Sublette poured them each a stiff brandy. "Thought this Rendezvous was plain dismal till Hugh Glass come into camp. Hugh's tellin' the free trappers to revolt agin the Rendezvous cause o' poor prices we pay fer beaver an' high prices we git fer goods. Hugh's been bear-mauled, bit, burnt, shot, kicked an' cut. Man's gotta face like a chicken house choppin' block. Now he's broke on top of it. Talkin' to Hugh'd make a man on the gallows kick up his heels fer joy on the way down."

"Sublette, I guess you're telling me I don't know when I'm well off."

"None of us do, Joshua. But ole Drew Henry said it best. *Grand success in the mountains is not acquirin' a extry hole in yer head -- today.*"

Sounds of distant gunfire wafted on the wind. Sublette leaped up. "Hot toddies! Blackfeet's back! Here's yer chance to work off them brandies!"

"I'm in," Pilcher chimed.

"I'll keep an eye on the homestead. Don't wanta shoot a customer," David Jackson replied.

Sublette tossed his trapper's saddle on his prancing pinto while Pilcher grabbed somebody else's horse. They rode into the whirling dirt cloud of trappers, Flatheads and *Shoshones* already taken to horse. Whooping and hollering, they headed their ponies toward the popping of the rifles and pistols.

Robert Campbell and a Spanish trapper, galloping their lathered horses toward the Bear Lake Rendezvous for help, pulled up as the thundering band of horsemen bore down on them. Campbell yelled, "We've got dead and wounded. The Blackfeet...."

But like the Mongol hordes of Genghis Khan, the trapper-Indian horsemen slowed not. Campbell waved the dust from his face and blinked through the murky air at the Spaniard. "Seems our boys is spoilin' for a fight!"

The 200 Blackfeet that had Campbell's trappers and Flatheads pinned down had expected trouble when the two whites escaped on their horses, but nothing like this thunder in the ground with its dirt cloud blocking the sun. The Blackfeet scrambled for their horses and lit out amid a horizontal hail storm of rifle bullets. Eight Blackfeet and several horses died instantly while their kin rode off bleeding.

Pursuing trappers and Indians realized quickly that their spent mounts, having run nearly six miles from the Rendezvous, were not going to catch fresh Blackfeet horses. They swerved toward the Campbell party to help with the dead and wounded.

Only the cook, Louis Bolduc, and a young Flathead girl

were dead. Many Flatheads were wounded, but none seriously. Sublette asked where Pierre Tevanitagon, leader of the former Hudson's Bay *Iroquois* hunters, was. A handsome squaw said Blackfeet killed Pierre near Cache Valley two moons back.

Samuel Tulloch motioned William Sublette to the edge of the encampment. The exhilaration of battle had worn off. Sublette's sweat made rivulets in the grit caked on his face. He wiped the dirt from around his eyes with a rag from his possibles bag, but Tulloch didn't say anything.

"What's this about, Sam?"

"Mr. Sublette, your brother's dead!"

Sublette sank down on a rock and held the rag to his face. "Milton or Pinckney?"

"The boy."

"Oh, sweet Jesus," Sublette groaned, remembering Pinckney's bright young face as he promised William would never regret bringin' him to the mountains. "What happened?"

"We split into trappin' parties fer the fall hunt, headin' northwest from the Sweet Lake Rendezvous along the mountain divide. Settled in fer the winter near the mouth of the Blackfoot River. The follerin' March -- this spring -- we trapped our way to the Portneuf River. Pinckney was slow at first, but by this here time, he was mindin' his traps good as any. One dawn was fulla Blackfeet -- must been a hunnert of 'em. Kilt Pinckney and two other men outright."

"You sure they kilt him?" Sublette asked.

"Seen a hatchet buried to the haft in his head," Tulloch answered quietly, then continued, "Chased the rest of us fer a week and kilt one more. Went back to look fer their bodies, but you know them Blackfeet -- they leave nothin' cause they know how that eats on us."

Sublette shook Tulloch's hand, "I know you done yer best, Sam. Thanks fer tellin' it straight. I don't hold you fer what them Blackfeet done to Pinckney. I jist wish I knowed about it earlier. I'd a rid my horse dead to git the rest o' them today."

"Don't worry, Captain. They's plenty Blackfeet left fer tomorry -- an' a hunnert tomorries after that. Them Blackfeet'll be up here long after we all bin forgot."

Young trapper Jacob Hawken, still wet with the sweat of

the chase bailed off his horse beside Sublette. "I'm the one that sold you them inlaid boot pistols last year in St. Louis, Mr. Sublette! I jist shot my first Blackfoot!"

"I'll bet both them boot pistols agin a beaver plew, it ain't gonna be your last!" Sublette growled.

* * *

David Jackson readied a trapping party to head north into Flathead Country as Sublette prepared to take the year's product to St. Louis. Sublette asked, "David, you gonna trade with them Blackfeet after they kilt Pinckney?"

"If I was, I wouldn't tell you, Bill."

"You know where Jedediah is now or if he's got beaver for St. Louie?"

"No. Heard rumors Jedediah's herding horses up through California. He's to meet us at the Pierre's Hole Rendezvous next summer. Best head for St. Louis, Bill. What's our year look like so far?"

"Word is we'll git $5 the pound fer beaver. Based on nat, I'm figgerin' our 7,710 pounds of beaver, 27 pounds of castoreum, 49 otter skins and 73 muskrat hides oughta bring us about $35,800. After we pay Smith, Jackson & Sublette's debt to Ashley, we oughta clear about $16,000 an' more if Jedediah has peltry."

"I hope you're right."

"I'm right, an' there ain't no hope to it, David. It's jist cold, hard cipherin'."

"Didn't mean it that way, Bill. Meant I hope you get it all to St. Louis. You taking Pilcher's wet skins too?"

"I told Pilcher his boys could foller us back with their shirttail of plews if they wanted. Small band alone's like to draw Blackfeet like flies to new plews."

"You heard they were breaking up their company, didn't you, Bill?"

"No."

"Fontenelle, Drips and Bent will probably be going along with 17 packs of beaver."

"Well if they're prime and dry, that's only about $8,500 for a season," Sublette calculated."

"Compared to that, I'd say we're a success, Bill."

"Success? I dunno, David. All our costs ain't on our books. We pay a staggerin' price fer skins we take outa these mountains. My brother's dead with his blond ha'r ahangin' in some Blackfoot's lodge up on the Portneuf. Startin' with them *Arikaras* in '23, I know o' 60 Mountain Men kilt by Indians and 20 more that's missin' -- a staggerin' price, Dave. Why do we keep doin' this? Why don't we go home afore they butcher us all?"

Jackson put his arm around Sublette's burly shoulder, "Because we can't, Bill. It isn't in us to walk Down the Mountain."

CHAPTER 33

BROTHERS AGAIN SUMMER-WINTER 1828

Smith, Jackson & Sublette's mule train of 75 mounted men hauling furs from the 1828 Rendezvous to St. Louis moved cautiously along the bank of the Sweetwater River. The back of William Sublette's neck was never wrong. It said they were bein' stalked. He thrust his hand up and halted the train near Independence Rock.

Sublette was about to speak, but the sight of the big rock brought back his nightmare trip with Moses when he had to choke his wolf-dog Pony. He grimaced the painful vision from his head and yelled, "We're bein' trailed by hostiles. Check yer weapons fer prime an' full charge. Double the point and drag. We git hit, pull off the beaver packs fer breastworks. They'll stop anythin' Indians got but a naggin' squaw. Number off now. Odds'll shoot while evens load and vice-versey. Don't shoot yer mules lessen you have to. I ain't eager to pack this beaver on my back to St. Louie!"

A few tight laughs followed. All checked loads and primes, and extra men moved out to front and rear of the pack train. Sublette hoped his inlaid Hawken boot pistols shot as heavy as they were loaded. He didn't have long to wait.

The Blackfoot charge met Sublette's pack train half way out of the North Platte River. Their shrieking attack was startling and effective, killing Olney and Batten, wounding Hiram Scott and driving off two mules with several hundred skins.

Sublette's double loaded pistol blasted a huge hole in the chest of a painted brave who fell dead, and he broke the shoulder of another who rode off. One of the point men headshot a Blackfoot who clung dead to his horse for a quarter of a mile before flopping to the prairie.

Twilight turned them pink by the time one large grave was dug. Sublette said, "Bury 'em four abreast in the hole -- trapper an' Blackfoot -- so they kin do in death what they cain't do in life -- git along together. Take no scalps. Pile on the rock an' keep them coyotes skinny."

"Ain't you gonna say any words over 'em, Cap'n?"

"Let somebody that feels like talkin'. Two o' you bind Hiram Scott's chest. Float 'im to the great bluff in a bull boat. Don't let Hiram smile. Indians see his gold tooth, they'll tack fer sure. We'll jine up there. Rest o' you mount up an' ride till we find cover. Blackfeet're big on comin' back fer seconds after they got stove-in the first time."

* * *

"Meredith L. Marmaduke" sounded like a sissy name when the little Colonel first told Milton Sublette who he was, but the small whang-leather man was feisty as a bulldog. He wanted to buy 1,200 horses in New Mexico and bring them back to Missouri. The Colonel mentioned Milt's newspaper name, *Thunderbolt of the Rockies,* and Milt's daring exploits in their St. Louie talk before Milt agreed in the spring of 1828 to head Marmaduke's expedition.

Milton remembered how excited Papa Phillip always got when the Sublettes started a long trip. Milt felt the same way. Seemed like their 20 man expedition was leadin' a charmed life till they reached the Arkansas River. Suddenly 200 *Comanches* in bright feathers with bloody handprints all over their ponies charged them on the open prairie.

"No place to run," Colonel Marmaduke yelled to Milton.

"Good, cause runnin's what them *Comanch* expect us to do. They'd ride us down in a heartbeat. Ole Peg-leg Smith taught me how to handle *Comanch.*" Milton swung his horse toward the oncoming Indians and kicked it in the flanks. "Wave them rifles like ya love this and foller me! *Yeeeoooow*!"

The *Comanche* charge faltered, then stalled, the ponies

whinnying and switching their tails to clear the dust.

Milton yelled, "Pull up! Every man draw a bead with yer rifle. Don't shoot unless they tack me." He sauntered his pony toward the shifting *Comanches*, filling each hand with a big-bore horse pistol from the holsters on his pommel. Then he eased the pistols part way into their holsters and made hand signs.

He signed that his tribe's women died of sickness of the whites and that *Comanches* should not come close unless they wanted their squaws to die. Milt added his men raged because they now did woman's work instead of enjoying the backs of their horses and the hunt. They wanted somebody to kill as the *Comanche* could see from the way they held their rifles. His men would soon bring bullets and sickness to the *Comanche*.

The *Comanches* retreated from Milton as he signed. Several raised their lances. Milton loosened his horse pistols in their holsters then signed that as they could see from his hair, he was half *Comanche* and wanted to save his brothers of the prairie from washing cooking pots and chewing deer skins. The *Comanches* wheeled and rode swiftly away.

"What in God's name did you tell 'em?" Colonel Marmaduke gasped.

"Why Colonel, I told 'em you was the *Thunderbolt of the Rockies* and if they didn't hightail it, you was personally gonna kick the chief's butt right in front o' all his warriors."

* * *

William Sublette halted his fur train below the great bluff so men tending Ashley's clerk, Hiram Scott, could catch up. When they did, one trapper told Sublette their bull boat capsized below the Laramie Fork and Hiram Scott died in the water.

"Ashley's gonna be beside hisself that ole friend Hiram wasn't even buried. Oughta make you boys tell 'im, but I won't. We gotta be at the Aull Brothers in Lexington before the heavy snows, so git to gittin'."

Sublette scanned the prairie around the Platte with his glass. He'd be in St. Louie by January -- and by God he was gonna winter there. How many more o' his people was gonna die so men in the cities o' the world could wear a beaver hat?

* * *

Milton bought 1,200 sound horses for Colonel

Marmaduke for about half what they was worth. Horses was twice as hard to herd as cattle, but by the end of August 1828 Marmaduke's dust-tornado reached the Arkansas River. Trail hands, gleeful at sight of water to cut their dust, drove half the horses across to the north bank.

Coming out of the sun, several hundred *Comanches* stormed along the river bank, expertly herding off the 600 wet horses, leaving a lance stuck through the bloody white chest of a trail rider who'd taken his shirt off.

Marmaduke signaled to his wranglers on the south bank and yelled, "After them!"

Milton raised his own thick arm to cancel the command. "Colonel, that's what the *Comanch* wants! You leave these 600 here unguarded to chase their first grab, them other *Comanch* waitin' over there herds these off too. You lose 'em all. Let them first 600 go an' you'll sell these here in St. Louie."

"Sublette, I pay you to keep this kinda thing from happening!"

"No, Colonel, you pay me fer keepin' yer ha'r off a *Comanche* war shield. Considerin' what I bought them prime horses fer, you still ain't out nothin' but hurt feelin's."

* * *

William Sublette liked doin' his business away from the wharf in St. Louie's Green Tree Tavern on Church Street. It had a swingin' sign in front an' a big wagon yard in back, puttin' him in mind o' the old Sublette family tavern at the Crab Orchard in Kentucky. All the news that was news come through the place. Owner Benjamin Ayres was like Papa Phillip. He could laugh off a fight between the drovers and the trappers and keep a evenin' goin'.

General Ashley'd grown used to better fare and seemed uncomfortable as he spoke with Sublette. "There's growing interest in Oregon on a state and national level. My former opponent for Governor, John Miller, said in his second inaugural address that the annual value of the fur trade to Missouri alone was $300,000 -- and that this figure might be increased to a million if it weren't for robberies by the Indians and interference by British traders. Money talk like that moves the electorate."

"I guess you know the Blackfeet killed my little brother

Pinckney."

"I didn't. My condolences, William. I'm truly sorry. You know where Milton is?"

"Nobody every knows where Milton is."

"That means Milton's all right. St. Louis newspapers have turned Milton into a folk hero of the Rockies. William, you'll be pleased to hear that Governor Miller mentioned Smith, Jackson & Sublette several times in his recent campaign. Papers quoted him as saying you boys are *Heralds of Manifest Destiny,* blazing trails over which generations of pioneers will travel to the Pacific slope.

"Sounds good," Sublette smiled, wishin' his Grandpa Whitley could hear this.

"It's excellent! *Manifest Destiny* is the darling of Senator Thomas Hart Benton. He believes it's the Manifest Destiny of the United States to extend from the Atlantic to the Pacific, and that all Americans should strive to insure that destiny. Benton's kind of a lone voice in the wilderness, but he's attracting a following on this."

"How's Eliza?"

Ashley's face drained. "She's sinking. Really terrifies me. You know I lost Mary in the fall of '21. I can't stand to lose Eliza. Can't even think about it. I've got to go, Bill. We'll get together soon. Eliza thinks you're the most solid man she's ever met." Ashley got up and left.

Sublette muttered to his drink, "She wouldn't think so, if she seen me after they kilt Pinckney. God, I hope Milt takes care o' hisself -- there's a joke."

"You bookin' trappers, Mister?" asked the huge man bending over William's table. "I'm lookin' fer a position -- not a job -- a position."

William exploded from his chair, "Milt!"

Milton grabbed his brother in a bear hug. "You're gittin' fat, Bill!"

"Fat's better'n dead, Milt." He slapped Milton's broad back, then returned the hug.

CHAPTER 34

TIME TO TRY WAGONS MARCH 1829-FEBRUARY 1830

William signed Milton as a Brigade Leader for Smith, Jackson & Sublette and the Sublette brothers did the drudgery for the March 1829 expedition to the summer Rendezvous. They tried to get along, but their same old tensions plagued them. Things weren't smooth, just tolerable like Milton's limp.

William wouldn't turn 30 for another seven months, but the mountains put hard years on a man. William eyed the small group who'd come fer trapper jobs at his table in the Green Tree Tavern. They minded him o' Pinckney Sublette, who hadn't lived a year after goin' Up the Mountain. He wanted to tell them to run, but they deserved their chance. "How old're you?" he asked, pointing at the reedy boy on his far right.

"I'm 19, Mr. Sublette."

"Yer face's familiar. What's yer name?"

"Joseph L. Meek."

Sublette laughed, "Yer brother Stephen's down at the wharf daubin' rum on our stored plews to keep the moths off. If yer jist interested in the rum, that job's took!"

"No sir, I wanta be a trapper. "

"Whatta you bin doin'?"

"Workin' at my other brother Hiram's saw mill in Lexington, makin' $2.50 a week fer stackin' lumber ever day but Sunday."

"Top pay fer saw mill work. I see why you wanta go Up the Mountain, but our work ain't no easier'n the mill. Got no

Blackfeet er grizzlies in a saw mill."

"Mr. Sublette, I ain't lookin' fer easier work. I know yer wage's near double what I'm makin', plus a share of my catch. Besides, it's dang near as hard fer brothers to work fer one another as havin' Indians and bears on your butt."

"Ain't *that* the truth! Yer hired, Joseph. I'll make sure you don't work in yer brother Stephen's Mess. Who're you?"

"Robert Newell."

"You look older'n 19."

"Turned 22 this month."

"Hands look callused. Whatta you do when you ain't lookin' to go mountaineerin'?"

"Saddle maker, Mr. Sublette."

"Got enough sand in yer craw to go up agin a grizzly?"

"Long as I don't have to put a saddle on him!"

Sublette nodded, "We'll sign you, Robert. Since my friend Clyman's gone to farmin', we need somebody who kin sew a feller's ear back on after a maulin' like ole Jim Clyman done fer my partner Jedediah."

In turn, Sublette hired young George Ebberts of Bracken County Kentucky, John Gaither and John Hannah, leaving only Jesse Applegate. "You fellers go see my brother Milton fer yer kit. I'm gonna talk to Jesse." Sublette shook the hand of each new man as they left the Green Tree.

"Jesse, you ain't a day over 16."

"I'm 17."

"Jesse, at least two o' them boys I jist hired is walkin' outa here dead. I took my brother Pinckney up the mountain in the spring o' '27 -- Blackfeet tomahawked him in the head. Jesse, you may be old enough to learn about livin' -- but you ain't old enough to die. That'll hafta wait a while."

* * *

On March 17, 1829 William Sublette headed the Smith, Jackson & Sublette mule train with 55 men toward the summer Rendezvous. Only the creaking of pack saddles and ring of a mule shoe striking an occasional rock marked much of the journey's first leg.

Sublette promised Ashley he'd find Hiram Scott's body and bury it. For some men, such a promise would be easy made and easier forgot, but William Sublette knew he was not such a man. When the pack train neared the great bluff, he rode ahead alone and scoured the land.

He was elbowin' sweat from his eyes when he saw a long thigh bone under a sage brush. Wolves had cracked it for the marrow, but it was likely Hiram's cause he was tall as Milton. Sublette located three ribs half-buried in dirt. Close by, he found a skull with a gold tooth in front -- Hiram's fer sure. It rested on several back bones by an upper arm bone. Sublette buried the skull and bones on a ledge of the great bluff, then heaped stones on the grave.

Milton rode up on his mule, "Think that's Scott's grave?"

"Know it is, 'cause I jist put 'im in it."

"Well, it were jist bones warn't it?"

"Yeah. Bones an' a skull with a gold tooth in front."

"Whatta ya gonna do about this, Bill? Maybe Hiram got left like them other fellers left Hugh Glass."

"I'm gonna name this place Scott's Bluff, then git back on my mule an' ride west. Nobody'll ever know fer sure what kilt him. Hiram here -- he ain't gonna tell us.

* * *

On July 1st, William Sublette opened for trading on the Popo Agie River -- which the Indians called the Po-po-shia. It was quiet in the grassy valley bordered by mountain ranges and red sandstone bluffs that glowed in the morning sun.

Robert Campbell rode up to the table. The young Scot had gained 25 pounds of muscle since the first time William saw him when Ashley got bought out. "Bobbie, yer lookin' husky enough to go bear huntin' with a broom straw! Whatchu doin'?"

"You'd never believe it, Mr. S," Campbell answered, trilling his Rs.

"Why?"

"Would you be rememberin' that me an' Jim Beckwourth went trappin' in Crow country along the Pooder River after the '28 Rendezvous?"

Sublette nodded, wonderin' if Edward Rose tacked their party, "So what happened?"

"Jim went wi' his Crow wife Pine Leaf. She taught him the tongue. Jim meets another Crow woman. Calls her Little

Wife. So there's Beckwourth wi' two Crow wives -- and that's where he stayed! I went to the Pooder River wi' a trapper and he changed to an Indian. Isn't that the most peculiar thing you've heard since Lot's wife turned to a pillar o' salt? The man's not coomin' back, Mr. S."

"Man loves horses like Jim, it's only natural he'd fall in with the world's greatest horse thieves, Bobbie."

* * *

David Jackson's trappers reached the edge of Pierre's Hole, a splendid valley split by the Teton River and watered by many streams. David played his glass over the two mile wide valley floor. No sign of Jedediah or his herd of horses, but the river basin had abundant pasture for them. Ranging north to south for about 20 miles, Pierre's Hole was an emerald meadow spiced by waving bouquets of red, yellow, blue and purple wildflowers. To the east rose the mist-shrouded Three Tetons towering over 13,000 feet to take a man's breath away. Across the valley to the west, rolling hills billowed into prairie. The magical sight made David feel like singing, but he didn't because he didn't want the men to scoff.

Jackson wanted to see Jedediah after two years. He didn't know if Jedediah'd be at the Rendezvous, but he knew Sublette would. Sublette kept better time than a store-bought watch.

"Looking for me?" Jedediah asked at Jackson's elbow. Jackson grabbed Jedediah by the arm and started whooping as he batted him on the back with his free hand. Already geared to Rendezvous, the other trappers, nearly a hundred strong, began hollering and cavorting in the flowers until somebody's pack mule spooked and had to be chased down.

"Where's your horses, Jedediah?" Jackson asked when he caught his breath.

"Since the *Kelawatsets* make their living with canoes and fish nets, my guess is they've probably eaten our horses by now."

"Does make 'em tough to ride! Let's try to beat Sublette to Rendezvous. You can tell us both of your travails in the west," Jackson said as he motioned his column to move out.

William Sublette's 50 man party coming west raced the Smith and Jackson groups heading south to Rendezvous, packs flapping on the mules, horses galloping and trappers sprinting through the tall grass with their rifles over their heads, wheezing war hoops to the winds. Sublette panted, "I'm pickin' the spot fer the Rendezvous, so what're we runnin' fer -- we're here!"

Sublette shouted, "Halt," but had to fire his boot pistol to stop his men. "Pull up, we're here!" The mules showed him he'd been lucky enough to stop by a clear stream to furnish water for the camp -- and he'd won the race to Rendezvous! He stepped off his mule, threw himself on his belly and sucked up the tasty ice water flowing down from the Teton glaciers.

"Like discardin' four an' drawin' to a full house findin' a stream here, Bill," Milton said belly flopping into the frigid water with a booming splash, scattering wide-eyed, bucking mules.

William watched his brother's laughin' face pop out of the water like an otter full o' mischief. His mouth was ready to harangue Milt for runnin' off the mules, but he just shut it and walked away. Milton Sublette was never gonna be over ten years old if he lived to be a *hunnert*.

* * *

Joe Meek had watched the Rendezvous blossom from 160 yowling trappers in the first week of August to a sprawling mix of tipis and tents. He was surprised by the wild savagery of the horse races, foot races, arm wrestling and drinking.

It amazed young Joe that most trappers purchased goods to the full amount of their year's wages and that the free trappers squandered their earnings at hundreds of dollars a day. Joe Meek wrote in his journal: "... *clear summer heavens flecked with white clouds throwing soft shadows; the lodges of the Booshways [Smith, Jackson & Sublette], around which cluster the camp in motley garb and brilliant coloring; gay laughter, and the murmur of soft Indian voices, all made up a most spirited and enchanting picture in which the eye of an artist could not fail to delight.*"

* * *

At Rendezvous' end, William put Milton in charge of a 40 man brigade to trap the Big Horn River, then headed for the valley of the Wind River to winter there with his partners, David and Jedediah, and a large force of trappers.

At their second camp, an early morning Crow war party

deftly made off with 26 horses, leaving a lone lance stuck in the meadow where the stolen horses had milled about moments before. Moses Harris removed the small bag dangling on a thong from the lance. It held salt and a crushed rifle bullet.

Thomas Fitzpatrick vaulted from his horse. "What'd the Crows leave us?"

"I cut dis Blackfoot bullet -- argh -- outa Jim Beckwourth's leg and gib it to him in dis bag o' salt afta de furst Rendezvous. I gonna melt dis bullet down -- argh -- and remold it. If I evah lays eyes on Jim Beckwourth agin -- argh -- I gonna gib him back dis bullet."

Fitzpatrick shook his head and smiled bitterly. "I give me own precious shamrock to the man to bring 'im luck. When you shoot him, Mose, see if he has me shamrock!" Fitz rubbed his chin. "Remember, I called Beckwourth a horse thief after we come home with 40 extry horses rescued from the Crows and he told me horse thievin' was no laughin' matter."

"He was more right -- argh -- about dat dan he knew!"

* * *

Smith, Jackson and Sublette huddled in their Wind River hut. Its only room was frosty. One log lay beside the smoldering coals on the dirt hearth. Jedediah Smith was finishing his lament on his last California trip and his days at Fort Vancouver.

"I've taken 33 men to California and 26 are dead. I know the men call me *Disciple of Death* behind my back. I have nothing to show for both trips but seven otter skins and this Hudson's Bay draft to us for $2,369.60 for salvaged beaver and horses." He pulled the battered Ace of Hearts from his pocket and laid it carefully on the stool between them. "Leave the card there if I'm no longer welcome as a partner."

Sublette stuffed the Ace back in Jedediah's shirt pocket. He eyed them, then said, "I been over our books. Our total losses in horses, furs, traps and supplies since S, J & S started July 18, 1826 is $43,500. With what we took in before this Rendezvous, we've about busted even. I figger the load Campbell's takin' to St. Louie will bring about $23,000 an' we'll net bout half o' that. We add Jedediah's $2,400 an' split it all three ways -- each partner has $4,633 an' three Aces. That's more'n most workin' men make in a lifetime. I say let's try it fer another year."

Jackson and Smith nodded, but Sublette added, "It's time to try the supply train with wagons."

Jedediah exclaimed, "Plain insane, Bill. Everybody knows that can't be done."

"I woulda said a man cain't ride 16,000 miles through Indian country an' keep his ha'r, but you done it! Remember we rolled the cannon out and back to St. Louie fer the '27 Rendezvous."

Jackson countered, "Bill, a pipsqueak four-pound cannon weighing same's a mule isn't a caravan of two ton wagons."

"Mebbee so, but I made more St. Louie trips than either o' you. You know I ain't a risk taker, but if them wagons don't work, you two kin take my share of everthin'."

Jackson and Smith's eyes met with their answer. Jackson voiced it, "Bill, toss that last log on the fire so Jedediah and I aren't found frozen when you bring back those supply wagons next spring!"

William Sublette and Moses Harris left the frozen Wind River valley right after Christmas with snow shoes and a ten dog team pulling a sled to deliver their list to Ashley before March first in St. Louis. They cleared the first hill with ease. "Don't be spectin me to -- argh -- eat all ten o' dese dogs befoe we gits to St. Louis, now Mista Bill."

This time, they flew over the snow, reaching St. Louis February 11, 1830.

* * *

Sublette spent every dime of their $28,000 and barely got Ashley to advance $2,000 more for the spring supply train. Ashley scratched his balding head. "How're you going to haul $30,000 worth of goods to Rendezvous, Bill?"

"Freight wagons."

"Freight wagons! The War Department and the Senate have intense interest in Wagons West, but they say it's impossible. So do I -- but if there's a man alive who can do it -- I'm talking to him!"

Ashley made the rounds of his political cronies trying to drum up financing for the wagons. Failing dismally, and angered by the derision, Ashley thought he might get investment money from the businesses who'd profit most if it worked. More scoffing. Ashley enlisted the newspapers to rally public support. The papers printing the stories hinted money was needed, but the public plan backfired.

The townspeople soon treated William Sublette like a lunatic. Jokes circulated about the fur trade firm of Broken, Down & Lost. Sublette controlled his fury. He wasn't used to bein' laughed at. His last hope for financin' in St. Louie was to get the wagons built on credit.

Sublette padded quietly into Irish Joe Murphy's dark wagon works after the workers were gone on a Friday night.

"I need ten sturdy wagons built by April 15th."

"Meanin' no disrespect, Mr. Sublette, I'll need a third down, and I gotta be paid in full before they leave me shop."

"No credit?"

"No credit."

"Don't know how I'll git the money, Murphy, but I'll be back."

"There's always the little people, Mr. Sublette."

"The *who*?"

"Leprechauns, Mr. Sublette. They must reveal their treasure if you catch them," Murphy chortled.

CHAPTER 35

OPENING THE WAY WEST   FEBRUARY-OCTOBER 1830

General Ashley sat across the table from William Sublette in the Green Tree Tavern. "Bill, this idea of taking wagons to the Rocky Mountains is a torch tossed into a political powder keg. Many in congress and the press are violently opposed to the very western expansion a multitude of others cry out for."

"General, I ain't got time fer politics. I got $30,000 sunk into supplies that's gotta go to the 1830 Rendezvous in wagons. Ain't no other way to haul that big o' load without goin' broke hirin' men an' buyin' mules. Sure, I dreamt o' breakin' new ground fer this country ever since my Grandpa Whitley told me bout Lewis & Clark when I's eight. But everythin' I own's on the line here! This ain't politics! This's real life!"

"Bill, in Missouri, politics *is* real life! Why do you think my money sources are afraid to fund this? Nobody knows how the scales will tip. But they know one thing -- there'll be big -- big winners or big -- big losers."

"Which way you goin' on it, General?"

Ashley dropped his gaze. "I tried helping you with the newspapers, and that blew up in our faces. I'll soon be running for Congress. I've got to line up with the winners, Bill. Besides, with the money I've already committed to you and what you'll need when you come back to tide you over till your skins sell, I'm milked dry."

"Give my best to Eliza. Hope she's better real soon."

"Thanks, Bill -- Eliza's *very* sick. Remember her in your

prayers."

* * *

The tall sinewy young man in front of William Sublette was not John Gaither or John Hannah who'd signed up last year at this very table only to git killed by Crows on the Green River. This was Andrew Whitley Sublette with Papa Phillip's raven hair and Mama Isabella's gentle smile.

"Drew, you know I tuck Pinckney Up the Mountain an' he's dead. I ain't got it in me to kill another Sublette."

"Uncle Solomon told me to remind you that you and Milton are still alive and that two outa three's not bad odds." Andrew finished with the warm smile that nobody could resist.

"Uncle Solomon's biggest risk is gittin' the gout."

"Bill, I've been at his knee for years. Solomon's made more at cards than he ever did at real estate or manufacturing. He knows the odds."

"Good, I'll git him into a game with Chief Little Soldier an' he kin see what an inside straight is like when it means four inches o' steel stuck in his belly."

Andrew grinned. "You think of me as some little kid jumping off a tree limb into the swimming hole at the Crab Orchard. I'm 22 years old. What if I could outshoot you, Bill?"

"Rifle er pistol?"

Andrew forefingered his chin. "Either one."

William plucked his Ace of Spades from his buckskin tunic pocket, then pulled his inlaid Hawken boot pistols and laid them on the table. "I'm takin' you to the wagon yard."

Convinced a challenge to a duel had been accepted, the Green Tree Tavern emptied into the wagon lot. William pinned the Ace on a corral post, then stepped off 20 paces.

"We supposed to hit that card from here?"

"The big spade in the center, Drew."

While William checked his pistol, Andrew fired. William raised his weapon, but the card'd vanished. Together they strode to the fence post, the crowd behind them. Andrew picked the center-shot Ace out of the dirt and peered at his big brother through the bullet hole. William put the plugged Ace in his pocket and eased his pistol back into his boot holster. "When my pistol's cleaned and reloaded, yer hired Drew!"

* * *

General Ashley tipped his hat as he and William Sublette met an influential banker and his wife entering Ashley's church.

"I ain't goin' in, General. Jist come to ask how Eliza is."

"Bill, she's sicker than ever."

"Tell her all the Sublettes is prayin' fer her to git well."

"Andrew signed with you now?"

Sublette nodded.

"Heard about him outshooting you for the job."

"Best I coulda got was a tie, so I give in. You could say I got my Ace knocked off."

"But you aren't going to concede on the wagons?"

"That ain't a concession. That's a disaster, General."

"Well, it's not over. Three Missouri papers are backing your wagon effort. Eastern papers are derisive. A London paper likened your venture to building a line of sentry boxes from Montreal to the North Pole."

"You kin tell the London paper what to do with the North Pole, General."

"The North Pole piece did it for the Aull Brothers. They're financing you for 40 mules."

"Hot damn!" William blurted.

"Bill, this's my church's vestibule. I'm a deacon going in to pray for my dying wife."

"My apologies, General. I'm comin' with you. That's one -- very fine woman. Let's pray her right outa that bed!

* * *

Andrew thumped William's door upstairs at the Green Tree Tavern. William's head pounded from the quart of rum the Sublettes sent to its grave at dawn. He opened the door, his hair a haystack, "What is it, Drew?"

"Barkeep gave me this note downstairs."

William held it up to the light and mumbled it aloud, "*Mr. Sublette -- Murphy's Wagon Works has commenced manufacture of ten of the finest heavy duty wagons ever built. You can pick them up 4/8/30 with my letter explaining the business arrangements. That letter is not to be read until you are out of Missouri.*"

"Drew, there ain't no signature. It's a woman's writin', but

Uncle Solomon has to be behind this. Is it because I signed you like he wanted?"

Andrew put his hand on his disheveled brother's arm. "Look at me, Bill. I know nothing about this. Day bar man found it in the front door. It's a mystery, but so is life. Accept it and let's ride to Rendezvous in style!"

"Bein' a business man's ruint my sense o' fun. Somebody's abailin' me outa jail, an' all I kin think about is how much interest it's gonna cost! Lemme git my pants on an' I'll buy yer breakfast!"

"You may not want to eat when you hear what's happened."

"Huh?"

"Drunk from American Fur Company let it slip last night. Fontenelle, Drips and Rubyducks -- or somebody -- left St. Louis a few days ago with a pack train to sell all the trappers and tribesman before you get to Rendezvous."

"Lucien, Andrew an' Joe makes up in guts what they ain't got in smarts. Gittin' the jump on me's a good idea, but leavin' in February's way too early. Blizzards'll freeze 'em blue. We kin beat 'em by leavin' in mid April."

"I thought you'd be furious, Bill"

"Them boys is jist tryin' to outdo us to make a livin' -- but they're up agin the wrong fellers."

* * *

At dawn on April 10, 1830, 81 recruits, ten supply laden wagons drawn by five mules, two mule drawn Dearborn coaches, 12 beef cattle and a jersey milch cow stood in the mist on St. Charles Street near Franklin Avenue in St. Louis. Since riding a wagon still made William Sublette sick to his stomach, he gave his command from the back of a mule, "Move out!"

They followed the Santa Fe Trail 40 miles, then put wagon tracks in the tall grass along the Blue River through Indian country northwest to the Platte. After forting up for the night, Sublette opened the letter he'd gotten with the new wagons at Murphy's. Its small delicate script read:

"Dear Mr. Sublette --

My William told me of your predicament in getting money to make this first ever, epic journey to the Rocky

Mountains in wagons -- an endeavor so vital to our country's future.

Although my family is quite well off, I have only limited means myself, so I sold my twin carriage horses sired by Napoleon's stallion, Marengo, to buy your freight wagons.

If your venture fails, you owe nothing. If it succeeds, please pay Murphy's charges for the wagons to General William H. Ashley, as Executor of the Estate of Eliza Ashley. Thank you for letting me be part of this grand adventure, for it is surely the most important thing I have ever done except to marry William. I regret I shall not see you again, Mr. Sublette.

Affectionately,
Eliza Ashley"

Sublette kissed the letter, folded it and put it in his buckskin tunic pocket.

"Who sent the letter, Bill?" Andrew asked.

"An angel."

* * *

At the Platte, Sublette kept to the rarely used south bank markin' a new trail along the river to avoid swampin' his wagons in the spring run-off.

Sublette figured he had to reach the Rendezvous at the Popo Agie and Wind Rivers by July 30th or the American Fur Company mule train'd turn his wagon trip into a disaster even if he made it. He pushed the wagons hard along familiar paths, averagin' 15 to 25 miles per day. Grass was plentiful and Sublette's men found large herds of buffalo grazing in the early going.

Since each wagon weighed 1,800 pounds, they stood helpless at fords and embankments. Often they were lowered by block and tackle -- sometimes by raw brute strength with William Sublette grappling the ropes till his hands bled. Once he knew what to do, he sent men ahead to dig ramps in steep banks and lay plank bridges over little cricks.

One man was buried in an earth slide. Sublette planted a cross atop the cave-in and read the 23rd Psalm over the man's makeshift grave. He finished by observing, "What God buried, let no man er beast dig up. And may all o' us be buried this deep to keep the coyotes from crackin' our bones."

* * *

"Drew, you're lookin' at the head of the Wind River where it issues from the mountains. We'll be at Rendezvous by July 16th! I know Milt'll be glad to see you! You got the best parts o' both of us without the worst."

On July 16th, the wagon train rolling into Rendezvous created such a sensation among the 200 trappers and hordes of Indians, they abandoned their squaws, alcohol, card games, wrestling matches and roasting buffalo humps to surround the wagons and gape.

William stepped off his mule. "American Fur Company pack train here yet?" Someone answered, "No," then David Jackson and Jedediah Smith were pounding Sublette's back.

"How'd you do it?" Jedediah asked.

"On the arm of a angel," Sublette replied. "We gotta talk. Let's find your hut."

Once inside, Sublette said, "Jedediah, I found out the mornin' we left that your mother passed away."

Jackson put his arm around Jedediah, but Jedediah shed it and left the hut.

Sublette grunted, "Let's meet here after we eat. Got sumpthin' important to talk over with you and Jedediah."

When Jedediah returned red-eyed to the hut, Sublette said, "We bin Up the Mountain seven er eight years -- twice as long as most Mountain Men live. We got a big haul o' furs out there now. Competition's acomin' -- American Fur Company, Hudson's Bay an' plenny others. So's the silk hat. Beavers'll jist go back to bein' big rats stead o' hats. If we kin git somebody to buy us out, we kin live high in the settlements fer a long time on what we'll make here. Got $30,000 worth o' supplies in them wagons. I'm settin' up to trade. Wanta talk now or think on it fer a few days while I work the tradin' table."

Jackson put his Ace on the stool. Smith added his asking, "What happened to that?" when Sublette laid his Ace down with the middle shot out.

"Never play cards with strangers, even if yer related to 'em," Sublette grumbled.

* * *

On August 4, 1830 Smith, Jackson & Sublette sold their

fur interests to Tom Fitzpatrick, Jim Bridger, Milton Sublette, Henry Fraeb and Jean Babtiste Gervais as the Rocky Mountain Fur Company for $15,532.23 with an overall sum of "$16,000 and upwards" to be paid on or before June 15, 1831.

William tried to teach Milt bout keepin' books, but Milt growled, "Bill, I done forgot more bout runnin' a fur business than you ever knew. Guess you fergot who come Up the Mountain first."

Saying his good-byes around the Rendezvous, William looked for friend Moses Harris. They shook hands and slapped each other's backs. Moses grinned, "I has jist seed de last an' greatest mountain miracle -- argh -- a trapper leavin' de mountains wit *more* dan de shirt on his back!"

Smith, Jackson and William Sublette left for the settlements on August the 4th with 70 men, a herd of pack horses and mules, a few cattle, two Dearborns and ten freight wagons laden with pelts. They were barely five miles out of camp when Andrew Sublette, riding a lathered Indian pony, caught up with William aboard his mule on the trail.

"Bill, these trappers are lunatics," Andrew panted.

"They ain't like this year round, Drew. Rest o' the year they're broke an' act like ordinary folks."

"Doesn't take a wizard to see why they all die broke. Mind if I stick with you, Bill?"

"Might go fer it, if you tell me howya learned to shoot like at."

"Uncle Solomon said if I was anything like Milton, I'd be dueling displaced husbands on Bloody Island all the time -- made me shoot every day, Bill! Now how about it?"

"C'mon, Drew, let's give her a whirl!" William bellered, then whacked Andrew's pony with his reins and showed Andrew how a fresh mule could outrun a flashy pony that was plumb tuckered.

Chill fall winds chewed the wagons as they rolled back to the United States along primitive wagon roads Sublette had made on the way to Rendezvous. Most nights, Jedediah, David and William got together around their own fire to discuss what should be done before they got to the settlements.

William worked up the financial report after reviewing

figures and property on hand. "Looks like were're gonna gross about $85,000, our biggest haul ever. We owe Aull Brothers for 40 mules, but we're gonna pay for 45 on account o' how they stuck their necks out fer us. We owe fer 10 wagons, and I hope to pay a certain lady for those, whatever they cost."

Jedediah replied, "You've done a capital job with our finances, Bill. You've been honest, able and undaunted when we told you wagons couldn't work. I'll say good-bye now in private."

"Been real edicatin' knowin' you too, Jedediah. But I gotta say, I not only ain't dead yet, I got no plans fer dyin', so yer good-bye's jist plumb early."

David Jackson added, "Bill, you've done the job like a hard-headed business man without acting like one. I'll remember you fellers when I start my spring plowing down by my brother George's place. Gotta introduce myself to five people who couldn't pick me out of a crowd."

"Yer wife an' kids, Dave?" Sublette asked.

"Exactly!"

Sublette said, "General Ashley wants us to write a letter to the Secretary o' War Eaton bout this trip an' conditions out here inna mountains."

"Letter like that takes time and forethought," Jedediah mused.

"Seen your letter to General Clark inna *Missouri Republican* in '27, Jedediah. You're the one oughta write it."

"An honor," Jedediah answered. "It's something we can compile on the way to the settlements -- give me your thoughts as we go."

Over the next few weeks, Jedediah assembled their notes for the letter to Secretary of War Eaton. Near the Blue River Fork of the Kansas River, Jedediah said it was important to cover their fatalities, adding "My records show that during the six previous years, including two years of Ashley's regime, this fur company employed between 80 and 180 men each year. Some 94 were killed by Indians -- 26 during my California explorations."

"What about men like Ed Rose an' Jim Beckwourth who come out here as trappers and become Crow Indians?" Sublette asked.

"Jedediah mused. "There are probably many we think of as dead or missing that have assumed new identities -- or lost old ones."

"And the men we carry as missin'?" Sublette queried.

"We need to go beyond statistics in this letter. A compelling epistle will bring people choking on city smoke out here where they can breathe and raise strong children. We need to get Congress and some of the border states to repeal their laws barring expansion into these new lands."

David Jackson scratched his head. "What about Indians who've raised their children out here since before there was a Congress or any border states?"

"The letter should help our country. It should describe the powerful British establishments on the Columbia and the unequal operation of the 1818 convention -- which ought to be extinguished. I want to urge Americans who will cross this continent on trails we've blazed to occupy the Columbia River region. Bill should include details of his outbound wagon trip as I'm recording them on our way back. People must know that wagons *have* crossed the Great American Desert -- in spite of the oceans of scientific and political gibberish to the contrary!"

"We gotta tell 'em *how* to make the trip. If they jist come out here an' founder, they'll die!" Sublette argued.

"So they will understand our letter's scope, I'm making maps to right the early maps done by guess work. When we get home, I want your help with them, so we can send them to the House of Representatives."

"I'll help," David answered.

But William just looked into the fire where he saw a little boy with a cut chin leanin' over the Lewis & Clark map with a fierce eyed man who'd built explorer's dreams in his head. Sophronia was still keepin' that Lewis & Clark map for him.

"William, will you help with the maps?" Jedediah asked.

William leaned back and looked at the stars, "Been waitin' all my life to do them maps. Got a fine old man up there wants to see 'em."

* * *

Andrew Sublette rode his pony along side William's mule

as a Methodist mission hove into view about a mile west of the Missouri border. "We're really doing something with this caravan, aren't we, Bill?"

William nodded toward the mission, "They're really doin' sumpthin' right there. Who we are ain't important. Sublettes'll be forgot in a week. What we done -- that's important. We opened the door to the west fer families an' we made enough money to keep us fer quite a spell."

"Think we'll be famous, Bill?"

"If you gotta choose between fame an' money Drew, take the money. Fame's gone in a fingersnap but money ain't if you got the good sense of a squirrel."

"Life's got to mean more to you than squirreling your money away, Bill. You're still a young bull. What're you going to do?"

"After listenin' to Milt, I bin thinkin' bout gittin' into the fur business down Santa Fe way. You be interested in nat?"

Looking just like Milton, Andrew grinned, "Soft nights and sweet *señoritas*!"

"I's thinkin' more along the lines o' business!"

"Sure you were, Bill!"

The caravan rolled through small settlements where people turned out to cheer and wave. "How they know who we are, Bill?" Andrew asked.

"Has to be them nosey newspapers. Always got to be goin' on bout sumpthin'. Guess fer now it's us."

"What are we going to do in all these waving crowds?"

"Wave back an keep yer eye on where you're goin'."

At Columbia, Missouri, the entire town turned out to wave and shout. A little blonde girl dancing about in white cotton threw flowers on the startled lead team of mules. Her flowers triggered a trend along the road.

On Sunday morning October 10, 1830, the southwest wind wafted gentle rain across the shiny buildings of St. Louis. As the sky cleared, sun sparkled the air. The caravan's wheels cut deep tracks through the dampened dirt streets where 5,000 people swarmed, waving and yelling what happy crowds yell.

William remembered Grandpa Whitley's description of Lewis & Clark's return to cheering crowds in this town. He wondered if Colonel -- no *Grandpa* -- Whitley was watchin' from up there -- or maybe from along the streets with Mama and Papa Sublette. William searched the crowd for their faces.

Instead of his family, William saw Irish Joe Murphy from the wagon works cheerin' and wavin' his hat. He reminded himself that one day he should drop by and knock Murphy on his butt for that crack about the leprechauns -- but more'n likely the way he could never hold a grudge -- he'd buy Murphy a drink.

William saw General Ashley and reined up his mule. He jumped down. "How's Eliza, General?"

Ashley's eyes filled with tears. "She passed away June first -- right after you left for Rendezvous, Bill."

William turned away in dismay, his eyes shut. "She believed. I wanted her to see this more'n anybody."

"She saw it before she died, Bill. She told me exactly what it would look like when your wagon train returned to St. Louis -- and it's awe inspiring just the way she said it would be. Eliza's not really gone, Bill. I see her every day in her wedding gown swirling among the clouds."

THE BEGINNING

EPILOGUE

When William Sublette commanded, "Move Out" on the morning of April 10, 1830 in St. Louis, Missouri, to the wagon caravan that opened the Oregon Trail, he set the stage for the greatest mass migration in the history of the United States. Between 1843 and the beginning of the Civil War in 1861, over 500,000 emigrants left Independence Missouri for Oregon or California over the "impossible" wagon trail blazed to the Rockies by William Lewis Sublette.

The five page letter dated October 30, 1830 described in Chapter 35 was sent to Secretary of War, John H. Eaton, by Smith, Jackson & Sublette. The letter was reprinted by newspapers throughout the country and was used by the champions of Manifest Destiny to further their cause of westward expansion of the United States. This letter was published in *Senate Executive Document 39, 21st Congress, 2nd Session.* The letter also mandated our writing of *BEHOLD THE SHINING MOUNTAINS,* Book Two of our Talking History Series, which you can order using the form on the last page of this book.

In the June 1832 *Illinois Magazine* an article read in part: ". . . *convinced as [Jedediah] Smith was, of the inaccuracy of all the maps of that country, and of the little value they would be to hunters and travellers, he has, with the assistance of his partners, Sublitt [sic] and Jackson, and of Mr. S. Parkman, made a new, large and beautiful map; in which are embodied all that is correct of preceding maps, the known tracts of former travellers, his own extensive travels, the situation and number of various Indian tribes, and much other valuable information. This map is now probably the best extant, of the Rocky Mountains, and the country on both sides from the States to the Pacific* . . . ."

Smith's map shows a "Sublette Lake" for what is now known as "Yellowstone Lake" in Yellowstone National Park. It also shows "Jackson Lake" in Grand Teton National Park and "Jackson's Hole" for an area of western Wyoming, both still proudly using the names given them by William L. Sublette in honor of his partner, David E. Jackson.

In 1839 the Geographer of the United States House of Representatives, David H. Burr, published a map of the United States of North America embodying all of the features of the map of Smith, Jackson and Sublette, thus completing the boyhood dream of William Sublette inspired by his celebrated grandfather, Colonel William Whitley of Lincoln County, Kentucky.

BIBLIOGRAPHY FOR *PONDER THE PATH* [159 VOLUMES]
by Gary H. Wiles and Delores M. Brown

Alter, J. Cecil. *James Bridger, Trapper, Frontiersman, Scout and Guide.* Shepard Book Co.Salt Lake City 1925

Axelrod, Alan. *Art of the Golden West, An Illustrated History.* Cross River Press, Ltd. New York 1990

Bancroft, Hubert Howe. *History of Arizona and New Mexico 1530 - 1888.* Horn & Wallace. Albuquerque 1962

Bancroft, Hubert Howe. *History of Oregon.* [Volumes 1 & 2] The History Co. San Francisco 1886

Beckwourth, James P. *The Life Adventures of James P. Beckwourth* as told to Thomas D. Bonner. University of Nebraska Press 1972

Bryan, William Smith and Rose, Robert. *A History of the Pioneer Families of Missouri.* Genealogical Publishing Co. Baltimore 1977

Bureau Developments, Inc. *U.S. History on CD - ROM.* IBM Version [using 85 of 102 Volumes] 1991

Campbell, Robert. *The Rocky Mountain Letters of Robert Campbell.* Printed for Frederick W. Beinecke. New York 1923

Chittenden, Hiram M. *The American Fur Trade of the Far West.* [Vol. 1 & 2] University of Nebraska Press. Lincoln, NE 1986

Clokey, Richard M. *William H. Ashley - Enterprise and Politics in the Trans-Mississippi West.* University of Oklahoma Press 1980

Clyman, James. *Journal of a Mountain Man.* Edited by Linda Hasselstrom. Mountain Press Publishing Co. Missoula, Montana 1984

Coman, Katharine. *Economic Beginnings of Far West: How We Won the Land Beyond the Mississippi.* [Vol. 1 & 2.] Kelley. New York 1969

Coutant, C.G. *The History of Wyoming from the Earliest Known Discoveries.* Chapin, Spafford & Mathison. Laramie 1899

Dossenbach, Monique & Hans. *The Noble Horse.* Portland House. New York 1987

Franzwa, Gregory M. *The Oregon Trail Revisited.* 4th Edition. The Patrice Press. Tucson, Arizona 1988

Gilbert, Bil. *The Trailblazers.* Time-Life Books. New York 1973

Goetzmann, William H. *New Lands, New Men - America And The Second Great Age of Discovery.* Viking. New York 1986

Gowans, Fred R. *Mountain Man & Grizzly.* Mountain Grizzly Publications. Orem, Utah 1992

Gowans, Fred R. *Rocky Mountain Rendezvous: A History of the Fur Trade 1825 -1840.* Peregrin Smith Books. Layton, Utah 1985

Hafen, Leroy R. *Broken Hand: The Life of Thomas Fitzpatrick: Mountain Man.* Old West Publishing Co. Denver, CO 1973

Hafen, Leroy R. *The Journal of Captain John R. Bell for the Stephen H. Long Expedition to the Rocky Mountains, 1820.* Edited by Harlin M. Fuller. Arthur Clark Co. Glendale 1957

Hafen, Leroy R. Editor: *The Mountain Men and the Fur Trade of the Far West.* [Vol. I thru X.] Arthur H. Clark Co. Glendale, CA 1965-72
Holy Bible.
King James Version.
Horn, Huston. *The Old West -- The Pioneers.*
Time-Life Books. Alexandria, Virginia 1974
Irving, Washington. *The Western Journals of Washington Irving.* Edited by John F. McDermott. University of Oklahoma Press 1944
Lloyd, Trevor Owen. *The British Empire 1558-1983.*
Oxford University Press. New York 1984
Maughan, Ralph W. *Anatomy of the Snake River Plain.*
Idaho State University Press. Pocatello, Idaho 1992
Morgan, Dale L. *Jedediah Smith and the Opening of the West.*
Bobbs, Merrill Co. Inc. Indianapolis 1953
Morris, Ralph C. *The Notion of a Great American Desert East of the Rockies.* Mississippi Valley Historical Review [Vol. XIII]1926
Pugnetti, Gino. *Guide to Dogs.* Edited by Elizabeth Meriwether Schuler. Simon & Schuster. New York, London 1980.
Rawling, Gerald. *The Pathfinder - The History of America's First Westerners.* Macmillan Company. New York, London 1964
Riley, Glenda, *Women and Indians on the Frontier 1825 - 1915.*
University of New Mexico Press. Albuquerque, NM 1984
Rollins, Philip Ashton. *The Discovery of the Oregon Trail.* Robert Stuart's Narrative. Eberstadt & sons New York 1935
Russell, Osborne. *Journal of a Trapper.* Edited by Aubrey L. Haines. Bison Books - University of Nebraska Press. Lincoln 1955
Schlesinger, Arthur M. Jr. *The Age of Jackson.*
Little, Brown & Company. Boston 1953
Secoy, Frank R. *Changing Military Patterns of the Great Plains Indians.*
University of Nebraska Press. Lincoln, NE 1953
Sullivan, Maurice S. *The Travels of Jedediah Smith Including Journal.*
Fine Arts Press. Santa Ana, California 1934
Sunder, John E. *Bill Sublette: Mountain Man.*
University of Oklahoma Press. Norman, Oklahoma 1959
The Software Toolworks. *Illustrated Encyclopedia IBM Version 2.0.*
[21 Volumes] on CD- ROM. Grolier, Inc. Danbury, CT 1991
Triplett, Frank. *Conquering the Wilderness.*
N.D. Thompson & Co. New York & St. Louis 1895
Unruh, Jr., John D. *The Plains Across -The overland Emigrants and Trans- Mississippi West.* University of Illinois Press. Chicago 1979
Victor, Frances Fuller. *River of the West: Adventures of Joe Meek.* Winfred Blevins, Editor. Mountain Press Pub. Co. Missoula, MT 1983
Wilson, Elinor. *Jim Beckwourth, Black Man and War Chief of the Crows.*
University of Oklahoma Press. Norman, Oklahoma 1972

INDEX [With Identifying Data] For 173 Real People, 29 Tribes and 13 Business Firms or Organizations

References are to page numbers.

Adams, President John 192

Adams, President John Quincy 192, 207, 236

American Fur Company [AFC - Astor's Outfit] 98, 165, 196, 261

Angerstein, General [Bought Napoleon's Arabian Stud Marengo] 155

Apache Indians 177 - 179

Arapaho Indians 150, 177

Arikara [Ree] Indians 97, 101 - 123, 132, 136, 139, 151, 153, 158, 170, 242

Armijo, Governor Don Manuel [Governor of New Mexico Replacing Narbona in 1827] 210 - 212

Artemis [Slave Freed by Sublettes] 6 - 8, 12, 28, 30, 38, 45 - 52, 54 - 56, 65, 67, 68, 83, 130, 133

Ashley & Henry [Fur Partnership] 69, 78, 80 - 82, 97, 119, 121, 233

Ashley & Smith [Fur Partnership Succeeding Ashley & Henry] 168, 172, 183

Ashley, General William H. [Politician & Fur Trader] 76 - 79, 83, 84, 94, 96 - 106, 108 - 111, 113, 115, 117 - 121, 148, 154 - 159, 166 - 168, 170 - 174, 176, 181 - 186, 201, 203, 226, 227, 241, 245 - 249, 254 - 256, 259, 266

Ashley, Mary [Daughter of Ezekiel Able & Deceased First Wife of General Ashley] 105

Assiniboine Indians 101

Astor, John Jacob [Head of American Fur Co & Richest Man in U.S.] 167, 196

Atkinson, General Henry [U.S. Army Commander of Western Dept] 112, 171, 172, 226

Aull Brothers [Lexington, Missouri Outfitters for Wm. Sublette] 245, 258, 262

Avery [Newspaper Man in Kentucky] 46 - 52

Ayres, Benjamin [Proprietor of Green Tree Tavern] 246

Baird, James [American Trapper Becoming Mexican Citizen] 210, 211

Bannock Indians 190

Barron, Commodore [Captain of the Chesapeake Court-Martialed in War of 1812] 40

Batten [Mountain Man with Smith, Jackson & Sublette Killed by Blackfeet] 243

Beckwith, Sir Jennings [Father of James Beckwourth] 156

Beckwourth, James Pierson [Mountain Man & Crow Chief] 155 - 162, 170, 186, 205, 206, 250, 253, 263

Benjamin [Servant of the Whitleys] 15, 24, 26, 27, 37, 38

Bent [Mountain Man with Fontenelle's Outfit] 241

Benton, Thomas Hart [U. S. Senator from Missouri] 247

Big Elk [Pawnee Chief Helping Wm Sublette & Moses Harris] 193

Black, Arthur [Mountain Man with Jedediah Smith's 1827 Expedition] 231, 233, 234, 236

Blackfeet Indians [Includes Siksikau, Bloods or Kainah, Gros Ventres or Atsina & Piegan or Pikuni,] 33 - 35, 101, 103, 111, 161, 170, 171, 189, 205, 206, 226, 228, 237 - 241, 242 - 244, 246, 249, 253

Bonaparte, Emperor Napoleon 21, 40, 50, 59, 155, 198

Boone, Albert Gallatin [Mountain Man Grandson of Daniel Boone] 191

Bradshaw, Captain John [American Ship Captain in California] 219

Branch [Mountain Man] 154, 209

Bridger, Jim [Mountain Man & Partner in Rocky Mountain Fur Co] 121, 125, 135, 136, 140 - 143, 151, 160, 161, 164, 186, 261

Bright Elk [Crow Consort of James Clyman] 144 - 149, 153, 225, 227

Brown, Henry Boatswain [Mountain Man Killed by Mojave Indians] 220

Buford, Colonel Abraham [Andrew Jackson's Commanding Officer in Revolutionary War] 48
Burr, Aaron [Guest in Andrew Jackson's Home Later Tried for Treason] 51
Calhoun, Congressman John C. 36
Campbell, Congressman from Tennessee [Shot Congressman Gardinier in Duel Over War of 1812] 41
Campbell, Robert [Mountain Man] 183 - 187, 239, 250, 253
Campbell, Hugh [Robert's Brother Living In Philadelphia] 184
Campbell, William [Mountain Man Killed by Mojave Indians] 220
Cannon, William [American Blacksmith for Hudson's Bay Co at Fort Vancouver] 234
Chambers, Colonel [Arrested 2 American Fur Company Agents on Indian Agent O'Fallon's Orders] 98
Charbonneau, Toussaint [Voyageur Husband of Shoshone Woman Sacagawea] 137
Cherokee Indians 5
Cheyenne Indians 150
Chickasaw Indians 177
Chippewa Indians 42
Choctaw Indians 49, 177
Christy/ Ashley, Eliza [2nd Wife of Wm Ashley] 155, 156, 158, 172 - 174, 182, 185, 225, 247, 256, 259, 262, 266
Clark, General William [of Lewis & Clark - Indian Agent & Missouri Governor] 22, 33, 96, 206, 263
Clay, Congressman Henry 36, 51, 65, 192
Clyman, Jim [Surveyor & Mountain Man] 76 - 84, 99, 104 - 106, 108 - 110, 114, 116, 117, 121, 128, 130 - 134, 144, 145, 147 - 153, 158 - 160, 169, 171, 187, 189 - 192, 225, 226, 228
Coffee, Brigadier General John [Hero of the War of 1812 and Close Friend of Andrew Jackson] 45 - 52, 64
Colter, John [Mountain Man Who Discovered Yellowstone] 32 - 35, 165, 190
Comanche Indians 177, 244 - 246
Cook, Grove [Married Sophronia Sublette] 225
Coon Dog [Mountain Man] 127, 128, 130
Cooper, Captain John [American Ship Captain in California] 218, 219
Corps of Discovery [Lewis & Clark Expedition] 22, 32
Creek Indians 48
Crow [Absaroka] Indians 103, 112, 132, 133, 144 - 146, 160, 161, 171, 189, 222, 225 - 227, 237, 253, 257, 263
Cunningham, Captain [American Ship Captain in California] 197, 198
Cunningham, David [Mountain Man Killed by Mojave Indians] 220
Dawn's Wing [Pawnee Wife of Hugh Glass] 82
Delaware Indians 42
Deromme, Francois [Mountain Man Killed by Mojave Indians] 220
Dickson, Robert [Fur Trader Arrested by Indian Agent O'Fallon] 98
Drips, Andrew [Mountain Man Associated with Lucien Fontenelle] 241, 259
Duran, Father [Catholic Priest at Mission San Jose] 217 - 219
Eaton, Secretary of War John H. [Addressee of Letter from Smith, Jackson & Sublette] 263, 267
Ebberts, George [Mountain Man] 249
Echeandia, Governor Jose [Mexican Governor of California in 1826 & 1827] 197 - 199, 218, 219
Eddy, Thomas [Mountain Man] 121, 127, 128, 130, 133, 190
Erskine, Minister [Diplomat Negotiating for Britain During War of 1812] 41
Evans, Robert [Mountain Man in Jedediah Smith's Caravan] 199, 203, 204
Fitzgerald, John S. [Mountain Man Left with Hugh Glass After Mauling] 121, 125, 135, 136, 151, 152, 164
Fitzpatrick, Thomas [Mountain Man & Partner in Rocky Mountain Fur Co.] 82, 104, 121, 130, 132 - 134, 148 -150, 154, 158 - 162, 169, 170 - 171, 186, 191, 253, 261

Flathead [Saalish] Indians 189, 237, 239, 241
Fontenelle, Lucien [Mountain Man & Fur Trader] 158, 241, 259
Fraeb, Henry [Mountain Man & Rocky Mountain Fur Co Partner] 261
Gaither, John [Mountain Man Killed By Crow Indians] 249, 257
Galbraith, Isaac [Mountain Man with Jedediah Smith's Caravan] 217, 219
Gardinier, Congressman from New York [Shot in Duel with Congressman Campbell Over War of 1812] 41
Gardner, Johnson [Mountain Man] 121, 167, 233
Gervais, Jean [Mountain Man & Partner of Rocky Mountain Fur Co.] 261
Gibson, Reed [Mountain Man Killed by Arikaras] 106, 108
Glass, Hugh [Mountain Man] 81, 82, 94, 104 - 108, 121, 123 - 126, 135 - 140, 151, 152, 158, 164, 238, 239
Gobel, Silas [Mountain Man Killed by Mojave Indians] 199, 203, 216, 220
Godoine [Owner of St. Charles Haberdashery & Half-brother of Pierre Perrault] 59, 69
Hamilton, Colonel [James Clyman's Commanding Officer in Illinois During War of 1812] 78
Hannah, John [Mountain Man Killed By Crow Indians] 249, 257
Harris, Moses "Black"[Mountain Man] 94 - 96, 104, 107 - 110, 157, 159, 160, 170, 186, 191 - 195, 200, 201, 203, 253, 254, 262
Harrison, General William Henry [Future President Who Fought Indian Campaigns in War of 1812] 42, 43
Hawkins, John aka Hawken, Jacob [Mountain Man & Nephew of Gunsmith Samuel Hawken] 240, 241
Henry, Major Andrew [Ashley & Henry Partner] 69, 78, 93, 97 - 104, 109, 112 - 115 - 125, 136, 141, 142, 146, 158, 163 - 167, 176, 239
Hidatsa Indians 113, 137
Hudson's Bay Company [Crown Chartered British Company] 165, 166, 170, 171, 232 - 235, 238, 240, 261
Immel, Mike [Missouri Fur Co Man Killed by Blackfeet] 111, 238
Iroquois Indians 166, 171, 240
Jackson, President [and General] Andrew 47 - 52, 64, 79, 192, 198, 236
Jackson, David E. [Mountain Man & Partner in Smith, Jackson & Sublette] 112, 113, 121, 122, 163, 165, 181, 182, 186 - 190, 227, 237 - 239, 241, 242, 251 - 254, 261 - 264
Jackson, George [Brother of David] 113, 115, 122, 227
Jackson, Rachel [Undaunted Wife of Andrew Jackson] 49
Jefferson, President Thomas 3, 16, 21, 22, 40, 51, 192
Johnson, Colonel Richard [Commandant of Colonel Wm Whitley in the War of 1812] 43
Jones, Robert [Missouri Fur Co Man Killed by Blackfeet] 111, 238
Kelawatset Indians 231 - 233, 235, 251
Knott, Osborn [St. Charles Constable Appointing Wm Sublette Deputy] 65, 66
Labross, Polette [Mountain Man Killed by Mojave Indians] 220
LaFitte, John [Pirate Kidnapping Hugh Glass from British Ship] 82
LaPointe, Joseph [Mountain Man with Jedediah Smith's Expedition] 218 - 220
Larrison, Jack [Mountain Man in June 2, 1823 Battle with Arikaras] 108
Leavenworth, Colonel Henry [Commandant of Fort Atkinson] 96 - 99, 109, 111 - 119, 158
Leland [Mountain Man with Jedediah Smith's 1828 Expedition] 231, 232, 234
Lewis & Clark [Explorers of Northwest] 21, 23, 32 - 34, 43, 44, 165, 256, 264, 265
Lewis, Meriwether [of Lewis & Clark] 22
Lisa, Manuel [Fur Expedition Leader] 33, 35, 102, 147, 167
Little Soldier [Arikara Chief Negotiating Treaty After August 1823 Battle] 117, 257
Little Wife [Additional Crow Wife of James Beckwourth] 251
Lucas, Judge J.B.C. [Vocal Opponent of Ashley & Henry Entering Indian Country] 97, 98

Ludlow, Captain [Commander of American Frigate President in War of 1812] 41
Lyncoya [Red Stick Creek Indian Infant Adopted by Andrew Jackson in 1813] 49
Madison, President James 36, 41
Mandan Indians 22, 33, 123, 125, 137 - 139
Marion [Boy Rescued from Primitive Indians] 230, 231
Marmaduke, Colonel Meredith L. [Horse Buyer] 244 - 246
McKinney, Levisa [Wife of James & Married Sister of Isabella Sublette] 68, 175
McLeod, Alexander [Leader of Hudson's Bay Co Punitive Expedition Against Kelawatsets] 235
McLoughlin, Dr. John [Hudson's Bay Co's Chief Factor at Fort Vancouver] 232 - 236
Meek, Joseph L. [Mountain Man] 248, 249, 252
Meek, Stephen [Mountain Man & Brother of Joe Meek] 248, 249
Miami Indians 42
Miller, Governor John [Missouri] 246, 247
Minnetaree Indians 102, 131
Missouri Fur Company [Fur Co. with Numerous Owners] 96 - 98, 104, 110, 111, 115, 165, 166, 238
Missouri Legion [Force of Army, Trappers and Sioux Combined to Fight the Arikaras] 115
Mojave Indians 197, 209, 215 - 217
Moondancer [Shoshone Woman at 1825 Rendezvous] 169
Moore, Daniel S.D. [Mountain Man] 121
Morris, Lieutenant Kenneth [Artillery Officer in August 1823 Battle with Arikaras] 116, 117
Murphy, Joseph [St. Louis Wagon Maker] 255, 259, 266
Narbona, Governor Antonio [Replaced as New Mexico Governor by Armijo in 1827] 210
Newell, Robert [Mountain Man] 249
Nonatuo [Mandan Aiding Hugh Glass] 137, 138
North West Company [Competing Fur Company Acquired by Hudson's Bay Co] 166, 234
O'Fallon, Major Benjamin [Indian Agent at Fort Atkinson] 96 - 98, 109 - 112, 118, 158, 159, 171, 172, 226
Ogden, Peter Skene [Hudson's Bay Field Official] 167, 233
Olney [Mountain Man with Smith, Jackson & Sublette Killed by Blackfeet] 243
Ortago, Gregory [Mountain Man Killed by Mojave Indians] 220
Osage Indians 177
Otoe Indians 110
Pakenham, Major General Sir Edward [British Commandant Killed in Battle of New Orleans] 51
Parsons, Lieutenant [U.S. Army Officer at Fort Leavenworth] 122
Pattie, James Ohio [Mountain Man Trapping in Southwest] 179, 180
Pawnee Indians 82, 110, 151 - 153, 159, 193
Perrault, Annette [Daughter of Pierre & Sister of Monique] 60, 63, 64
Perrault, Fifi [Daughter of Pierre & Employee of Godoine's Haberdashery] 60, 69, 70
Perrault, Monique [Daughter of Pierre] 60 - 64, 70, 83, 169
Perrault, Pierre [Father of Monique, Annette & Fifi & St. Charles Landlord of Sublettes] 59, 62, 63, 69, 70
Pilcher & Co [Fur Co Bankrupted by Crow Attacks] 238, 241
Pilcher, Joshua [Mountain Man & Partner in Several Fur Companies] 110 - 118, 237 - 239, 241
Pinckney, William [Diplomat Negotiating for U.S. During War of 1812] 41, 43
Pine, Tommy [Shipmate of Hugh Glass Killed by Pawnees] 81, 82
Pine Leaf [Crow Wife of James Beckwourth] 205, 206, 250
Piute Indians 210, 211
Potts, Daniel [Mountain Man] 141, 142, 164, 165, 190

Potts, John [Trapping Partner of John Colter Killed By Blackfeet] 33

Pratte, Sylvester [Mountain Man & Fur Trader] 213, 221, 222

Ratelle, John [Mountain Man Killed by Mojave Indians] 220

Red Eagle [Chief of Red Stick Creeks During Ft. Mims Massacre in 1813] 48

Relle, John [Mountain Man Killed by Mojave Indians] 220

Robiseau [Mountain Man Killed by Mojave Indians] 220

Rocky Mountain Fur Co. [Partnership of Bridger, Fitzpatrick, Fraeb, Gervais & M. Sublette] 261

Rogers, Harrison [Mountain Man with Jedediah Smith's Expedition] 218 - 220, 231

Rose, Ed [Mountain Man & Crow Chief] 102 - 105, 109, 110, 114 - 117, 121, 128 - 132, 144 - 146, 148, 171, 189, 226, 227, 263

Sacagawea [Shoshone Woman with Louis & Clark] 22, 137

Sanchez, Jose [Catholic Priest at Mission San Gabriel] 197

St. Vrain, Ceran [Fur Trader Taking Over After Sylvester Pratte's Death] 222

Scott, Hiram [Mountain Man for Whom Wm Sublette Named Scott's Bluff] 243 - 245, 249, 250

Seminole Indians 64

Shawnee Indians 5, 6, 22, 42

Shoshone [Snake] Indians 22, 137, 149, 150, 159, 166, 169, 177, 189, 205, 206, 237, 239

Simpson, Sir George [Hudson's Bay Co Official] 235

Sioux Indians 101, 103 - 116, 126, 128, 130 - 132, 177, 189

Smith, Jackson & Sublette [Fur Partnership Succeeding Ashley & Henry in 1826] 185, 186, 192, 196, 198, 203, 219, 233, 241, 243, 247 - 249

Smith, Jedediah [Mountain Man & Partner in Smith, Jackson & Sublette] 100 - 104, 106, 109, 112, 115, 117, 119 - 121, 127 - 134, 146 - 151, 154, 166 - 168, 171, 181 - 187, 196 - 199, 203, 204, 206 - 208, 215 - 220, 226, 229 - 236, 241, 251 - 254, 261 - 264

Smith, Thomas "Pegleg" [Ribald Mountain Man] 177 - 180, 209 - 215, 221 - 224, 244

Snelling, W.J. [Writer Perpetuating the Notion of the Impenetrable Great American Desert] 64

Stewart, Captain William Drummond [Scottish Nobleman] 202

Sublette, Andrew Whitley [Mountain Man & Brother of Wm.] 2, 5, 7, 8, 10, 11, 28, 30, 43, 54, 56, 68, 202, 257, 258, 260 - 262, 265

Sublette, Mama Isabella [Mother of Sublette Mountain Men] 2 -5, 7, 10 - 12, 15, 17, 18, 21, 23 - 26, 28 - 32, 37, 38, 43, 53 - 60, 65, 66, 68, 175, 209

Sublette, Milton Green [Mountain Man & Brother of Wm.] 3 - 8, 10 - 13, 15, 23, 26, 28 - 35, 38, 39, 44 - 48, 51, 52, 54 - 56, 58 - 60, 64 - 70, 78, 93, 112, 113 - 115, 121 - 123, 158, 165, 166, 171, 175 - 179, 211 - 213, 221 - 224, 226, 245 - 248, 252, 262, 265

Sublette, Phillip [Father of All Sublette Mountain Men] 2 - 8, 10 - 12, 16, 17, 24 -31, 36, 38, 47, 53 - 56, 58 - 60, 62, 64 - 67, 70, 78, 100

Sublette, Pinckney [Younger Brother of Wm. Killed by Blackfeet] 54, 68, 202 - 204 , 240, 242, 246, 248, 257

Sublette, Polly [Infant Sister of Wm.] 6, 28 - 30, 54, 68, 175, 178, 202

Sublette, Sally [Infant Sister of Wm.] 56, 57, 67, 68

Sublette, Solomon [Younger Brother of Wm.] 54 56, 68, 202

Sublette, Sophronia [Sister of Wm.] 6, 28 - 31, 54, 67, 68, 175, 225, 264

Sublette, William Lewis [Mountain Man & Partner in Smith, Jackson & Sublette] 3 - 35, 38, 43, 44, 47, 48, 51 - 57, 60 - 70, 78 - 84, 93 - 95, 99, 103 - 109, 113 - 118, 121, 122, 128 - 130, 133, 134, 146 - 149, 166, 168 - 171, 176, 181 - 195, 200 - 206, 225 - 228, 236 - 266

Swope, Morgan [Backer of Phillip Sublette in St. Charles Tavern] 64, 67, 68

Tarleton, Lt. Colonel Banastre [Ruthless British Cavalry Commander in Revolutionary War] 48

Tecumseh [Shawnee Chief Uniting Tribes Against Americans in the War of 1812] 42
Tenskwatawa [The Evil Prophet and Twin of Tecumseh in War of 1812] 42
Tevantigon, Pierre [Iroquois Trapper & Namesake of Pierre's Hole] 240
Tolanda [Indian Woman with Smith's California Expedition] 215, 216
Tomayo [Mandan Shaman Who Chanted Over Hugh Glass] 138, 139
Trujillo, Señor [New Mexico Rancher Sheltering American Trappers] 210 - 213
Tulloch, Sam [Mountain Man Entrusted with Pinckney Sublette] 204, 240
Turner [Mountain Man with Jedediah Smith's 1827 Expedition] 231, 232, 234
Ute Indians 177
Virgin, Thomas [Mountain Man with Jedediah Smith's 1827 Expedition] 217, 219, 229 - 231
Walkara [Ute Indian Chief & Famous Horse Thief] 223, 224
Washington, President George 5, 6, 67, 130
Weber, John H. [Ex-Sea Captain Mountain Man] 141, 142, 163, 165, 167
Wilkinson, General James [Treacherous American Leader in War of 1812] 51, 52
Whitley, Andrew [Brother of Isabella Sublette] 56
Whitley, Esther [Wife of Colonel & Grandma of Wm Sublette] 12 - 15, 24 - 26, 30, 31, 37, 38, 65
Whitley, Solomon [Brother of Isabella Sublette] 56 - 60, 62, 65, 68, 104, 201, 202, 257, 259, 262
Whitley, Colonel William [Grandfather of Wm. Sublette] 4 - 7, 13 - 44, 47, 53, 57, 129, 165, 190, 194, 247, 256, 265
Wolfskill, Bill [Mountain Man Losing Trappers to the Apache] 179
Wyandot Indians 42
X [Fugitive From a Hangman's Noose in Terra Haute Hiding in the Mountains] 85 - 92, 133
Young, Ewing aka Joon [Mountain Man & Fur Trader] 176 - 180, 209 - 213, 215
Yount, Dutch George [Mountain Man] 209, 210

We set these 2 convenient pages aside for your Notes! [If you liked this book and want to know what happens next, use the easy order form on page 279 or the listed telephone number to order the sequel, *BEHOLD THE SHINING MOUNTAINS,* on your Visa or Mastercard!]

Gary H. Wiles and Delores M. Brown

NOTES

PHOTOSENSITIVE™
DEPT. PTP
P.O. BOX 7408
LAGUNA NIGUEL, CA 92607
☎ OR FAX (714) 495-8897

BOOK ORDER FORM

Sold To: ______________________________
____
____
____

Telephone ______________

LIBRARIES, MUSEUMS, BOOK STORES & DEALERS CALL FOR VOLUME DISCOUNTS.

Disregard Sales Tax Unless You Are Ordering From California!

BOOK & ½ SHIPPING COSTS	NO.	PRICE EACH	SALES TAX CA ONLY	TOTAL
PONDER THE PATH by Gary Wiles & Delores Brown	_____	$12.95	$ .99	$______
BEHOLD THE SHINING MOUNTAINS by Gary Wiles & Delores Brown	_____	$14.95	$1.16	$______
HOW TO STOP SMOKING WHILE SMOKING* by Gary Wiles [who quit this way over 20 years ago]	_____	$ 9.95	$ .77	$______
You pay ½ shipping @ $1 per book		$ 1.00 Shipping		$______
		GRAND	**TOTAL**	**$**______

* Money-Back Guarantee If You Do What Our Book Says and Don't Stop Smoking!

___Check ___Money Order Payable to PHOTOSENSITIVE™,

___ Visa ___ Mastercard No. ______________________ Expires ______

Signature of Ordering Party______________________________

INSTRUCTIONS FOR SHIPPING, AUTOGRAPHING AND FREE AUTHOR PHOTOS:

____

____

____

TEAR OUT AND MAIL TO ADDRESS AT TOP OF THIS PAGE